Don't Ask Me Again

REBEKAH JOHNSON

Paperback ISBN: 979-8-2957-2264-6
Library of Congress Control Number: 2025919778

Cover art elements commercially licensed from Veris Studio, cover designed by WSIB.

hello@rebekahjohnsonbooks.com

This one is for my old friends in the operating rooms who once made me carry a BKA to pathology.

Every story starts somewhere.

Content Note

Don't Ask Me Again is a historical romance and includes open-door romantic scenes between consenting adults. The story is set in France in 1917, in a hospital in a war zone. Sensitive, non-graphic content includes amputation, pregnancy termination (not a main character), shell shock, and descriptions of surgical procedures.

Military and medical sources are noted in the Afterword.

La Croix-Rouge (The Red Cross) is a new series that includes side characters from The Truxtons and takes place nine years after that series concludes.

Chapter One

By October 1917, Victoria Harper had assisted with four hundred and thirty-six amputations without a moment's faintness or nausea, a record among the nurses at Red Cross Hospital No. 43. She was only bested by a few of the older physicians, battle-hardened officers who met the maimed soldiers from the trenches with good cheer that didn't quite disguise their weariness with the war and their work. After forty years serving Britain from South Africa to the Balkans, nothing rattled Dr. Malcolm Bowden's nerves, but when he saw his steadiest, staunchest nurse clutch her stomach as two men approached with a stretcher, he pulled her aside.

"Who is he?"

Victoria could only stare.

The courtyard of their schoolhouse-turned-hospital on the outskirts of Amiens, France, bustled with movement from the ambulances recently arrived from the front, but she stood rooted to her spot outside the doors to the surgical building. No sound emerged when she tried to answer the doctor's question. She turned back to the dark-haired man on the stretcher and her mouth went dry.

Abrasions covered his left cheek, his jaw was swollen and bruised, and a stained white dressing hid a wound to his forehead. Out of habit, she reached for his identification tags to add his name to her notebook with the other wounded soldiers, but when she brushed her fingers over the embossed metal, she read the letters like Braille and looked only at his closed eyes.

"Where are you taking him?"

"Up to Carraker in triage, Nurse Harper," Dickie Lampett called back to her, out of breath as he and another ambulance driver maneuvered the stretcher up the stairs. "Back in a jiffy." He bobbed his head in a sideways salute and disappeared.

"Look at me, Harp." Bowden squinted like he'd fit her for spectacles. "Who is that?"

"No one."

He released her. "Is he an old school friend? Not a friend's husband, I hope. Go see him. I'll have Nurse Scott assist on my next case."

"He's barely conscious. I doubt he saw me."

Victoria bit her tongue before she could admit she doubted the wounded soldier really wanted to see her. He had once been closer to her than anyone in the world, and after the way they parted, she couldn't imagine a less romantic reunion. She clenched her hand in her skirt pocket, grinding the fabric with her fingernails.

Bowden watched her, gray brows lifted, with an inquisitive, paternal look she knew well. He was an academic who liked answers, and she had no desire to confess that she and the man on the stretcher had loved and lost and broken one another's hearts.

"Damned bad luck anyway, Harp." He cleared his throat and looked away. "You must go see him. Go on."

"Dickie just said he's taking him to Dr. Carraker, sir, and I doubt he needs my help. We have cases scheduled, so let's get on with it."

Let's get on with it was a frequent refrain. Brusque and resigned, it was a shove forward into action when words about the devastation around them wouldn't come. It was palatable, with a sheen of bravery.

Bowden gave a curt nod of agreement. Surrounded by medical staff who donned their stiff khaki uniforms only when called to service for the war, his military bearing made him seem taller than he was. He made no great show of his rank and was happy to fling his service coat onto whatever surface was convenient when he put on a surgical gown, but his authority as the hospital's commanding officer sat on his shoulders like a mantel.

Victoria shot a quick glance at the other nurses watching, glad she had raised her voice enough for them to hear her call him 'sir,' most properly, even if he did just call her 'Harp' as he only did in the operating rooms. Every doctor had his team of assistants he preferred to work with, but she was mindful of the head nurse's constant exhortation that she and the other senior nurses set a good example for the ever-changing roster of volunteers. Favoritism could look like the colonel preferred her company—or worse, her looks—instead of her skills.

"We'll check on your mystery friend after lunch." Bowden nudged her toward the door. "If they had enough morphine or ether on hand, the clearing station might have given him a bit for the ambulance ride."

A rutted road connected Amiens to the edge of German-occupied France. The Western front had shifted dozens of times since they arrived, but no matter which new patch of mud marked their territory, the wounded soldiers picked up an upset stomach and a headache on the way to their hospital.

She had met more ambulances in the schoolyard than she ever met gentlemen at a dance or in a drawing room. Her debutante days were a dusty, distant memory since she left North Carolina and joined the British Red Cross at the start of the war, but one glance at the third stretcher off Dickie Lampett's ambulance twirled her right back into Matthew Berger's arms.

The classroom that served as Bowden's favorite operating suite had pale blue walls decorated with a cheerful painted border of balloons and letters for the school's youngest students—kindergarten, *l'école maternelle*—and lent a soft edge to the clinical white sheets and grim black irrigation tubes coiled like a nest of vipers.

"You'll have to tell me about him sooner rather than later, you know," Bowden said as they walked in. "He *is* from home, isn't he? Perhaps Carraker will stop pestering you to speed the American army along with a personal call to your president."

She allowed a small smile. "I don't think he knows how to greet me any other way," she said. The bluff, genial lieutenant colonel was Dr. Bowden's second-in-command. For two years, he led every encounter with Victoria with a broad smile and a complaint that her army was taking too long.

She hung her Red Cross apron by the door and slipped into a clean surgical gown as her thoughts whipped into a whirlwind.

When she sailed from New York to London in late 1914, Victoria had hoped to pass the war without seeing a soul from home, especially Matthew. Base hospitals were the third point in the evacuation chain and the last stop before a wounded man was sent home. Emergencies were stabilized by the aid stations at the front lines or the field hospitals behind them, and many men recovered well enough to rejoin their units from there. Normally, a soldier only came to a base hospital if he had a debilitating illness, a lengthy, complex recovery ahead of him, or was so badly wounded he would not fight again—and Matthew was there.

He should not be there.

He should be safe and home and happy without her, not so injured or ill that he couldn't get well. Not so close that a moment of tenderness might catch her unawares and set her stumbling. He'd held her heart for years, proposed to her three times, and, in his typical infuriating fashion, managed to get the last word even when she declined him.

But that last word was no longer the last. He was in Amiens, in her surgical ward, and her chest tightened at the thought of the blankets over his stretcher hiding whatever painful reason sent him there.

"What do we have today?" Bowden called from the sink as he scrubbed his hands.

"Two left arms off, a right leg either might come off or might be you can set it with a plate." The new surgeon, a medical college graduate so new the starch hadn't worn off his uniform, scanned a clipboard and mumbled a bit.

"Read it again, Dr. Denys."

Victoria calmed herself by counting ampoules of iodine and sterile solution into neat rows on her tray, outwardly serene as Denys snapped to attention and read the list again, this time including the details the colonel preferred. Two left arm amputations, both below the elbow, one of them a repair of an attempt yesterday that hadn't gone well for the patient or the doctor who took a stray bullet while doing it. One right leg with a broken tibia required either a wound debridement or an amputation but might be saved if Bowden could re-situate the bone with a steel plate.

It would be a long day with difficult surgeries and a new doctor at the table who neither she nor Bowden knew well yet, and Matthew would have to wait. He'd waited for years already.

Victoria helped position the first patient on the operating table and didn't flinch when the wounded soldier groaned. Tying the black rubber tourniquet tight around his upper arm, she watched his eyes as Denys adjusted the gas settings on the anesthetometer.

"Easy there," she whispered when his good arm jerked. "Look right here at me. My name is Victoria. What's yours?"

His lips moved soundlessly but she remembered the name from the schedule.

"Hi there, Harvey. Where are you from?"

His mouth moved again, slower, and from the corner of her eye Victoria saw Bowden beckon Denys to his side. He drew a quick line on the patient's left forearm above the bandaged gash from the previous day's botched surgery in a field hospital.

"Did you say Toronto, Harvey? Gosh, that's a long ways

away." She glanced at the gauges on the oxygen and nitrous oxide tanks and drawled a little slower as the patient's eyelids fluttered. "I'm from way down in North Carolina. Do you have a wife or sweetheart back in Toronto? We'll get you fixed right up and you'll see her soon."

When Harvey didn't respond, she pressed her stethoscope to his chest for a moment and counted. With a quick inflation of his blood pressure cuff, the mercury fell in the meter and she noted the valve settings on the anesthesia machine. She moved woodenly, a nurse made of prosthetic limbs, handing off instruments and supplies as she fought a vision of Matthew years before, droll and dreamy-eyed.

Bowden rambled on as they worked and showed Denys where they would cut and stitch to allow the patient to retain full use of his elbow. Victoria passed him the bone saw and readied herself for the sickening squeak that sent others running for a basin. With one hand on the patient's wrist for his pulse, she shifted supplies to ready her trays. She looked up as the young doctor grimaced behind his surgical mask. Harvey wasn't the only one who needed to relax.

"Dr. Denys, what was your favorite type of surgery in medical school, beyond battlefield mending?" she asked. "I imagine being fresh out of your training you know all the latest practices."

He swallowed heavily. "I enjoyed maxillofacial surgery."

"What a timely specialty, sir." She caught Bowden smiling behind his mask and kept up the fake brightness in her voice. "Many soldiers come to us with terrible facial injuries from gas and explosives, and they will be grateful to you forever. Goodness, all those tiny little bones. I imagine amputations seem barbaric to you."

"I think there is an art to all reconstruction, even when—"

The saw squeaked and he jolted.

"There's a basin behind you, Dr. Denys, if you like," Victoria said. "I always put out an extra when we have a new face at the table."

"That's my girl." Bowden didn't look up from his work. "Hold this, Denys, just so. Nurse Harper could probably do this on her own, so her time is in demand. I'm the goddamn commanding officer and even I have to ask nicely for my preferred schedule. The head nurse thinks the ladies need domestic rotations for their sanity. Knitting and rolling bandages help the fragile female constitution recover from all the blood. Horse shit."

"Don't mind him, Dr. Denys. He forgets that I haven't been on knitting duty for years. You can ask for any of us if you have a preference in assistants."

Bowden snorted. "'Don't mind him,' the nurse says of the colonel. It's a laugh here, Denys. Whose hospital is this? The British Army can't command the Red Cross, and the Red Cross can't make His Majesty's army act like gentlemen."

As they worked, he spouted the latest facts and figures from studies back home, from hospitals back in Britain where therapists and prosthetic manufacturers doubled amputees' quality of life compared to the archaic support they had before. "If either of you care to play with investments, get in now with the artificial limb-makers," he said after the injured limb was set aside. He held out his hand and Victoria passed him the Rongeur forceps. "What am I doing with these?" he asked.

Denys looked at her.

"He means you," she whispered.

"Ah. Right. Well, we need to tidy the ends of the bones before we close up." He pointed at the end of the radius. "Can't have those rough edges on it."

"Why do you suppose I like the Rongeur for this work?"

"The scooped blade allows small, clean cuts for a gentler healing process." He cleared his throat. "I believe some of your friends in England wrote as much in a recent paper about how to speed healing and reduce scar tissue in amputations."

"Excellent. Show us how it's done." He handed him the forceps. "This damn war is only good for one thing, and that's advancing medicine. The cost is sickening, so we'd better do some good with it." He pointed over his head to the painted mural over the classroom window.

Nous aimons apprendre!
We love to learn!

"And so, since we shouldn't let the years of war sour us on learning," he said, "Harp, do you want to learn how to suture a flap? That's the right kind of needlework for you. To hell with knitting. Mama will be proud."

"I think you speak in jest, but she will be. She taught me fine needlework and always despaired of how I never enjoyed it as she does."

"Well, we'll get you some practice and you can bring in the camera someday to send her a photograph of your latest sampler." He chuckled under his breath.

"She's always supported my work. I think she'll love it."

Bowden squinted at the end of the radius. "Fine job on this, Denys. That's damn near polished. Now both of you, look here." He gestured with a needle driver from the tray Victoria prepared with the suturing supplies. "We're going to leave the flap a little bit open, just so. That allows us to debride the wound and continue to flush it with sterile solution for a day. This way, we get out any leftover dirt before we close it up for good. We use a fine disinfectant developed by a British doctor last year," he said. "Toxic if you don't mix it right, though, and then you've done more harm than good."

With one hand, Victoria checked the patient's pulse. With the other, she pointed at the glass beaker full of Dakin's solution, a clear fluid she'd mixed while then men worked through the muscle and bone.

"What's toxic about it?" Denys asked.

She positioned a sponge for the blood vessel he'd just nicked with his needle. "Bleach."

Chapter Two

Dearest Victoria,

Pause in your hectic day to remember your old friend and enjoy a laugh at my expense.

I found myself yesterday at a volunteer group with your sister Edith and several other ladies in her circle. You know them. They are not my kind of ladies but I am always recruiting for my causes, and so there I was, knitting away like a good patriot. Edith was praising you and I waited my turn to brag on your life-saving adventures. When she paused for a breath, I jumped in with the story you shared in your last letter: about your patient who named his bayonet something rather crude and didn't think of the meaning of jabbing it into the enemy until another man made a vulgar joke.

My darling, I said the word. I cannot even write it. I said the word aloud, that very un-ladylike word for parts ladies do not have, and I said it in company with your sister's friends. Oh, and while doing it, I waved my arms about and speared some poor girl with my knitting needle.

In sum, Edith's friends will not be joining my chapter of the Raleigh Women's Club.

I miss you always. Keep writing to me of your patients and your new girl friends and all the funny things everyone says in English and French, *s'il vous-plaît*. I read your letters aloud to distract Cooper when he's in a foul mood. He's often in a foul mood these days and talks every evening about quitting politics entirely. Emmeline punched a boy at school this week for calling her father a coward for not enlisting. I told her we can't expect a child to know that sitting legislators are not allowed to enlist, but I gave her extra sweets anyway.

It is hard to believe they are already raising the age for the Selective Service. They have a million men training now but will call up men as old as forty-five in the new year. How many men do they think we will need? Georgia is now worried for Leo, of course, since this makes him eligible, as are many of our friends. Edith fretted a bit about whether William might have the choice to join up with his brother's unit, supposedly still somewhere in France where they were in the summer. The censors are hard at work on our soldiers' letters, so that's all they seem to know about his location.

But enough with that! The children and I had a delightful five minutes choosing your candy treats (Calvin spit a peppermint at the cigarette stand and Mr. Redding suggested we head home quickly) and the enclosed tins are from Georgia. She's learning to mix botanicals to make the most lovely salves and ointments, and when I told her you complained of your dry hands from too much washing, she insisted I send you some. Cooper, Leo, Angeline, and all the old gang send their love. Your mother says Edgar still asks for you every day. He is most determined, isn't he?

As always, dearest, I pray daily for your safety and nightly for your happiness and your health. Write me soon.

Maudie Truxton

Victoria stared at the last page of the letter as she worked the healing salve into her chapped hands. The package had arrived two days before with a shadowed mention of Matthew. 'His brother' could refer to any one of the men Victoria could claim as in-laws since her sister Edith married William Berger in 1907, but there was only one who Maudie wouldn't mention by name. She'd only tiptoed around the subject once before, when she wrote that 'William's brother' was going overseas.

Somewhere in France.

Maudie would get a laugh out of her unintentional prescience when she wrote back, and the thought of it brightened her smile and strengthened her resolve to lift her chin and do her duty as a nurse to care for a good man who deserved the best her hospital could give. She had seen and touched and smelled things that would send her mother into a heart-clutching fit, so she could certainly set aside pride and muster a quick hello for Corporal Matthew James Berger and see that he was well-tended. Then, she would do what she'd always done—she'd leave him and go back to work.

Her dash home had given her an excuse to avoid seeing Matthew until the end of her shift, but it shortened her already-short lunch break. She picked up her pace and grappled with her skirts in the breeze. She should have grabbed food instead of cuticle treatments, a sandwich instead of a pocketful of peppermint candies to see her through the afternoon surgeries.

The warm floral fragrance of the homemade salve followed Victoria on a quick jog from the boarding house where she was quartered and back to the antiseptic burn of the schoolhouse. Her hands had been chapped and even raw in places since influenza swept through the wards three months before. Bowden monitored the sinks with an eagle eye and gave the nurses permission to reprimand any of his men, any rank, for not following his cleanliness protocols.

She lifted her hands, clouding herself in the rosebud scent again before the smells of salt and damp cotton hit her. Her hands smelled like summer, not the bitter snap of autumn leaves in Amiens, and nearly distracted her from the clock.

She bolted up the stairs and grabbed the doorframe to keep from throwing herself into room eight when she saw the surgeons had started their rounds early. Bowden caught her eye and didn't stop his recitation of symptoms and surgical plans to the physicians, only pointed to the rear of the group and nodded for her to take her place.

Her friend Nora Scott squeezed her hand in greeting. "A Red Cross nurse is never late," she teased in a whisper. "I thought we were meant to be the role models for the new girls."

"A Red Cross nurse is of even temper and calm demeanor," Victoria said as she tucked a loose wave of blonde hair under the crisp white veil pinned over her neat chignon, "and this moment, I am neither." She squirmed and peered around the doctors huddled at a patient's bedside.

"What's wrong?"

"Oho!" Bowden's voice rang above the murmurs. "What did they try on you, soldier?"

"Doc said he could cut my risk of trench foot in half, and boy, did he."

Victoria's heart leapt into her throat when she heard the patient's voice: American, and unmistakably Southern.

Bowden wheezed a laugh. "So he did, young man. So he did. How long's it been?"

"Five days."

"And how is your pain today?"

"It was hell on the ambulance until I passed out. One of your girls gave me a shot when I got here, so I'll do for now."

"Look here," Bowden said, and the group shifted closer to the bed. "Denys, why do we call this a guillotine amputation?"

"Because they took it off clean across."

"Very good. Hawkins, justify the doctor's decision for removing the foot this way instead of sending this man to the hospital with his limb intact."

"Transport timing may have been a factor. Likely there was either an indication of gangrene or the wound to the foot was so severe infection was inevitable and would compromise any of the limb that might be saved."

"Excellent. And Wentworth, tell Corporal Berger why, despite this fresh stump looking properly pink around the edges, he should allow us to perform another surgery so his limb terminates just below his knee."

Dr. Wentworth was an arrogant young captain with an

aristocratic lineage, a steady hand, and a bedside manner that brooked no nonsense. In the year he'd been at the hospital, half of the nurses swooned for his handsome face and the other half made up ridiculous titles for him, like the Duke of Fiddlesticks or Lord Smitty-Witherington-Bore. His snide dismissal of nurses' contributions in the operating room won him Victoria's constant ire and creative nicknames.

Nora peeked past another doctor to see him and Victoria yanked her back.

Wentworth scanned the group to ensure everyone was looking at him. "The muscle at the surgical site will retract from the distal edge of the bone as it heals, leaving a protrusion that is likely to necrose over the—"

"I asked you to tell the patient, not us," Bowden said. "In plain English, please."

"Reducing the length of the leg up to the knee will allow us to create a better situation for you with a prosthesis, sir," Wentworth said. "Our latest studies show there are more comfortable options in your future if we re-shape the stump and tidy up the bones and nerves involved."

Nora shook Victoria's fingers out of hers. "You're crushing me, honey. Are you well?"

As the men in front of her shifted to watch Bowden point and prod, Victoria pretended to scratch her nose to hide her twitching lips. She bit down hard on her tongue as nausea brushed over her, then passed.

"What do you say to that, soldier?" Bowden asked.

"There's no sense in healing up from this now and doing it all again later," the patient said. "I'll be glad of those 'more comfortable options' you speak of."

"When did you make it over?" Dr. Carraker interjected. "I

thought we weren't supposed to see the American army until the New Year."

"I'm with the reserves, sir, and we began mobilization immediately after Wilson made up his mind in April. A few communications units like mine came over in August to meet up with your fellows and help wherever we could."

"Then for your sake, I suppose I'll stop heckling our dear American nurse about her absent army. Nurse Harper, do you hear that?"

The patient's faintly-flushed cheeks went pale.

Carraker scanned the group as Victoria tried to duck behind the doctors, but Dr. Wentworth turned aside and left her rooted to her spot, unable to hide. Her eyes met Matthew's and her lips parted to whisper his name.

He'd been a boy who wanted to be a soldier at a time when his country was at peace. When Europe went to war, he had jumped at the chance to join the reserves and prepare for the moment he'd be called to do something great. She wondered, as she watched the emotions chase over his face, if he felt proud or foolish. The look that finally settled in his eyes was not happiness to see her, but a calm mask over uncharacteristic panic.

Bowden watched with a wry smile. "There you are, Harp. You know he's in the best hands. Mine and yours anyway, maybe the rest of these buffoons. You're excused to catch up with your friend now. Back to *l'école maternelle* in thirty minutes." He slapped Carraker's shoulder and nodded for the group to follow him to the next patient.

"Well, sir, he's not—"

"Aren't I?" Matthew asked as the group retreated. Nora

watched over her shoulder, wide-eyed and stumbling backward, as Victoria approached the bed in silence.

"Victoria? Are we not even friends anymore?"

"We weren't very friendly the last time I saw you."

"It's been years. Time should have mellowed us by now."

"I suppose it should have."

"Has it?"

She bristled. "You tell me. You're the one who was so bitter."

"You know quite well that if I was bitter, it's because you were—"

"Please don't. We needn't pick over the past." She looked down, fidgeting with her apron. "I can be sure other nurses are assigned to your care. It will be easier on both of us. But I'd be happy to write a letter to your family for you, since it might be of some comfort."

"My hands aren't hurt. I'll write my own letter." He waited for her to look up, and his gray eyes held hers. "Since it sounds like you do not wish to see me."

She paused and tried not to glance at the stump of his left leg as she took a step closer to his bed. "I do not want to see you here, like this."

"You didn't want to see me at home, either."

"I meant I never wished you ill. I never wished you hurt. I'm so sorry."

"I've dealt with greater heartbreak, so I am well-prepared."

She fought to keep from glaring. "I'm flattered to be compared with the loss of a limb that will make your life harder every day."

"Who said it was you?"

"You always had such a wit."

"It's been four years. I'm surprised you remember me."

"It's been almost four years." She crossed her arms and refused to admit she remembered the exact date. "And I haven't been lonely."

His words teased but his eyes were tired, and when his voice softened he gave up the pretense of not caring. "You're a terrible liar, Vi. But I've had lonely dreams the last few nights. When I sleep, I wonder if I'm still alive, and if I'm not, whether I'm in heaven or hell. When my leg hurts, I'm either alive or in hell. When it doesn't, maybe I've died and gone to heaven. What do you make of that?"

"It is just like you to try and reason with yourself in your own dream."

"And now my leg hurts and I am certainly alive, and I see a living hell before me."

Cheeks burning, Victoria leaned on the metal rail at the foot of the bed. "Hardly an old friend, I see. I'll fetch you some paper and get on with my day."

"Don't do that." His voice lightened, trying to joke even as the corners of his mouth pinched in pain. "Maudie says you're popular for amputations. Let's savor the irony for a moment."

Victoria froze. "When did you speak with her?"

"Before I left, there was a little party to see me off."

Color flamed in her cheeks. She bit her lip and said nothing.

He shifted in his bed, wincing. "If we are to be friends, you cannot carry on with this jealousy. I thought we put this to bed years ago."

"Friends? You just called me a living hell."

"A living hell is seeing you so close and not being able to touch you, Vi. And now I can't run after you when you walk away. It hurts already."

His tender tone disarmed her and she nearly reached for his hand like she did every soldier who needed a comforting touch. She gripped the folds of her skirt instead. Matthew's flirtations had often been dry and double-edged, playful and infuriating until the moment of sincerity that made her heart skip.

"I am not jealous of Maudie. She is one of my dearest friends. Perhaps you have amnesia from that knock on your head."

"That's not very nice," he said. "I saw a recruiting poster at home that said angelic Red Cross nurses will carry soldiers out of sickness."

"How lucky for both of us you are not ill."

"Your sister told my brother you have a stellar reputation here. I'm sure I'll be in capable hands if you are part of the team doing whatever they plan to do to me." He paused and looked down. "Have you done it before?"

"Four hundred and thirty-eight times," she said after a quick tally of the morning's cases. "But Dr. Bowden will probably do the surgery and one of the other men will assist him. I just keep the room tidy and so on."

"You're modest. Maudie shares bits of your letters, you know. Your tales are even more captivating than they were in your training at the hospital back home."

"She what?"

"All good things, I promise. She admires you so."

She gripped the bed rail to keep from shrinking into herself and turning back into the mousy girl she was when she met him: a handsome college boy with captivating eyes and a laconic smile. He was droll and clever, and she was as intimidated by him as much as she was infatuated with him. That younger Victoria never knew what to say to hold his attention. She never knew how to turn his eye from vivacious, headstrong Maudie, who held him rapt for so long and who never thought of him as more than a friend.

"When will it be?" he asked, tapping his left knee.

"Probably tomorrow or the day after. It depends on what the ambulances bring in."

"Do you have chloroform?"

"We have everything for anesthesia. All the latest."

He closed his eyes. "I had a jab of morphine and a whiff of ether on a cloth out there, and it wasn't nearly enough."

"The field hospitals do their best, but I—oh, that must have been torture."

"They strap you to a board so you don't flop around and make it harder for the doctor. I had to wait my turn for the board, if you can believe that." He looked up. "Well. I guess you can believe that."

"I can."

"Then you bite down on an old boot or whatever you can get so you don't tear into your lip or tongue and make it all worse. After that, the shock kind of takes you."

"Are you in pain now? Or hungry? Or cold? I could get you something." She stepped closer, moving to the side of the bed, hands twitching to check his pulse and feel his forehead. "Matt, you're shaking a little."

"I wouldn't mind another blanket if you can spare one."

"I'll be right back."

She steadied herself walking to the supply closet, grateful

her stomach no longer churned and whatever momentary heat gripped her chest had passed. She returned to his bedside with a blanket in her arms just as he yawned.

His nose scrunched and his cheeks went taut, freckled from the sun on the gutted French farmlands. The wound at his hairline was unbandaged and black with crusted blood, and the abrasions and bruises peeking through the dark stubble on his jaw shortened her breath when the yawn made him wince.

She unfolded the blanket and draped it loosely over his shoulders and chest, keeping her distance.

"I have to go back to surgery now."

"I knew you were a busy girl."

"Our volunteers will be here if you need anything," Victoria said quickly, stepping back. "They'll get that gash on your head cleaned up and check your dressings. It wouldn't do to have you pick up an infection."

"And I suppose I'll see you and the good doctor tomorrow or the next day."

"I could come this evening." She bit her lip as soon as the words fell out.

He stared at his left leg. "I don't want to fight with you."

"We weren't really fighting, were we? Already?"

"Well, I'm already brooding and nostalgic and you're already defensive."

"I am not."

"I am."

She reached under the blanket and put her hand in his. "I'm sure the Red Cross also promised I'd boost your morale with my sweet, feminine demeanor. Is that better?"

She'd held men's hands as they wept, held men's hands as

they died, held more intimate parts to keep them out of the way of the doctors' work removing shrapnel that threatened femoral arteries. She should be steel-willed and leather-skinned so Matthew, the only man she ever let crumble her heart, should not be able to revive her nerves with a touch.

His fingers intertwined with hers and stroked her skin with calluses he'd gathered since the last time he touched her. She slid her thumb over his knuckles, condensing years into days, days into hours, and a weight settled on her heart with the pain of those last minutes.

"Yeah, Vi. It's a little better."

Chapter Three

The old half-timbered house Victoria shared with three English nurses sat crowded cheek-by-jowl with others on a quiet residential avenue. The canals of the River Somme wove between the streets of Amiens and rose and fell with the seasons, bordering street-side markets and surrounding the city's famous floating gardens. A green bridge led their avenue to the bustling shopping district in the Rue de Trois-Cailloux, and a blue one crossed another canal toward the hospital.

Victoria leaned forward on the dining table and rested on her elbows, yawning as she considered the white lump of baked fish and the green beans on her plate. A click of the tongue announced she was being watched, and she sat up, acknowledged by a gracious nod from the silver-haired Frenchwoman in the doorway with a steaming dish of sliced potatoes in her dishcloth-wrapped hands.

Blanche Barbier, their hostess, signed up to board Red Cross nurses so she could be someone's *Maman* again and not lose herself in grief after her husband and son were killed in

Flanders. Her home was considered a prize lodging for the nurses who arrived in Amiens before the Red Cross built quarters closer to the hospital. She used everyone's ration cards to grocery shop and prepare their meals family-style so the girls didn't have to cook, a finer arrangement than any of their friends in other town quarters had.

Three weeks earlier, amid talk of more staff needed at the hospital, Blanche cleaned out an attic room and offered to board two volunteers. The new girls had arrived with the Voluntary Aid Detachment's transport that day and lingered in the doorway, hands clasped while the senior nurses wrangled their seats. Nora Scott wriggled past them on her way to the table.

"I have been looking for you all afternoon," she said, tucking her skirt under her to slide onto the bench at Victoria's side. "Tell me about that man." She tapped her knife on her plate and didn't touch her food. "Who is he? How do you know him? Why was he looking at you like that?"

"Like what?"

"Like he could eat you with a spoon."

"Heavens, Nora. He's family. It's not like that."

The tapping stopped. "He's what?"

"Well, he's sort of—my sister married his brother. That's how we met."

"Oh, that's not family." She narrowed her eyes. "But you really know him, don't you? I could tell. Was he your sweetheart?"

Victoria bit into a slice of her fish and chewed slowly. "It was a long time ago. Years and years."

"It can't have been that long ago. You're hardly older than I am."

"I'm twenty-nine. I was nineteen when we met, and then it carried on until about four years ago."

"Then you were with him for six years?"

"Oh no, not the whole time. It's just that—"

"With whom for six years?" Bridget Walker scooted into a seat across the table. "That man in room eight? I peeked in. He's so handsome. How awful about his injury."

Victoria narrowed her eyes. "How do you know about him?"

"Marlene and Polly both told me. Frances told them. Six years and you didn't marry him?"

"I told Betty and Frida, too," Frances Kendall announced as she entered the dining room behind Blanche and placed a basket of sliced baguettes on the wide oak table. She pushed her bobbed blonde hair off her cheeks and gave Victoria a wicked wink. "I couldn't help it. He's just dreamy, isn't he? And obviously sweet on you."

"When did you see him?"

"I was on rounds with you, goose. But of course you didn't see me." Frances laughed. "You practically swooned for him."

"I certainly did not."

"Tell us all about him, please," Bridget whined. "We will be so happy for you."

"A lot of things went wrong between us." Victoria folded her hands in her lap primly. "Some things just can't be resolved and you have to walk away with your head high."

Bridget pouted and cut into her fish. "You are no fun. Why do any of us bother setting a good example for the new girls? They'll just think we're dullards."

"Speak for yourself," Frances said. She tucked a loose strand of hair behind her ear. "But if she doesn't spill by tomorrow evening, I'm bobbing your hair because I'm so bored."

"I'll do Victoria's." Bridget snipped her fingers together like scissors. "Let's see if that gorgeous man of hers likes his women modern."

Victoria stuck out her tongue. "He loves my hair long and loose, and he makes a tangled mess of it."

Frances and Bridget exchanged a glance and giggled.

One of the new girls slid closer, holding her friend's hand. Her eyes were bright and her cheeks plump and pink like Victoria's were when she arrived in France. Many of the VAD general service girls came from England with little more than a basic first aid course, years younger and often in awe of the formally trained nurses who accompanied the doctors in surgery and examinations. They were the enlisted ranks and the staff nurses were their officers in the faux-military of the Red Cross, all under the watchful eye of their general, the indomitable Nurse Perry.

"How do you know you should walk away, even if he's very nice?" the girl asked, fidgeting with her auburn braids. "Did you want to marry him and then decide against it?"

Victoria's fingers twitched on her fork, tingling again from Matthew's hand clasped around hers. The new girl couldn't be more than nineteen. How long ago nineteen was, when she first danced with him and placed a gloved hand in his for a quadrille. He was so dashing in his formal suit, and she twirled in her lace-tiered blue evening gown in the romantic glow of her sister's wedding to his brother. It felt to her girlish heart that no one in the world had ever been so handsome or witty. When he drew away with a quick bow at the end of the dance, her hand went cold.

"I wanted to marry him once," she said slowly. "And he wanted to marry me. We just couldn't make it work."

"Oh no. That's just heartbreaking."

"It was at the time."

"Did he ask you to marry him?" Bridget asked.

"He did."

"It must have been very hard to say no."

"It wasn't hard at all. The first time, anyway, which was just awful. The last time was—" She rested her forehead in her hands. "Please forget I said anything. Never mind."

The new girl squeaked with excitement and pulled up a chair. "He proposed more than once?"

Nora set down her knife and fork and threw her arm around Victoria's shoulders. "Enough of all that. She was with him once, and now she's not. That's all any of you nosy Nellies need to know." She glared first at Frances and Bridget, then at the new girl. "I don't even know your name. You're awfully bold to be demanding a woman's romantic history."

"Sorry." She blushed and pulled her friend close like a shield. "I'm Ingrid Russell, and this is Marie Howard."

"Well, I'm Nora Scott and this is Victoria Harper. If you know what's good for you around here, you won't pester her."

"Nora, please." Victoria squirmed away. "You're correct. I don't want to talk about him anymore. Ingrid and Marie, we're glad to have you here. You're our sisters now, and sisters are a little protective sometimes. Please let us know if we can help you settle in."

"I really didn't mean to be nosy, Victoria."

"All is well." She poked her fish and resolved to be grateful. "Do you have a special someone in your life, Ingrid? Perhaps we can tell you what to do with him."

"I'm sorry I was so touchy at supper." Nora curled into a ball on her bed in the room she and Victoria shared. Freshly rinsed black stockings and lace-trimmed cotton drawers draped on the radiator fluttered in a breeze from the window propped open by a one-franc coin. "I don't know what's the matter with me lately, but goodness. Bridget and Frances are just being silly, and I have been so sour to everyone. The last time we had new VAD girls, I lined them up in the courtyard in their new uniforms and posed them for photographs to send to their parents. Now I want to ship them right back home so they can stay happy and sweet and we won't ruin them here. It's awful."

"And?" Victoria prompted.

She glanced at her camera on the bedside table, her cherished Kodak Autograph No. 1, and sighed. "I'll apologize tomorrow, and I'll offer to take photographs. Poor Ingrid. When did I become so nasty?"

"Is Viscount Tiddlywinks talking down to you? You've had a million cases with him lately, and he treats the nurses like servants and the patients like fools. It would certainly grate on my nerves."

"Dr. Wentworth's not so bad."

"Charitable of you, darling."

"He's under a lot of strain, as we all are. Dr. Bowden reprimanded him for his attitude the other day."

"Good." Victoria squeezed her damp blonde hair into a towel and combed her fingers through the waves. A hot bath almost steamed away the ache of being called a living hell.

"Perhaps you could get away for a bit. Take a quick weekend at least."

"I used up my leave on that trip to Rouen, which was not restorative in the least," she said wistfully, tossing a small lace pillow at her. "How I wish it had worked out for you to come along."

Victoria grimaced and looked at her left ankle, the one she'd badly twisted before the trip in question. "So do I, but you'd have had to carry me everywhere."

"I'd have managed." Nora grinned. "A Red Cross nurse is strong and true."

"And a Red Cross nurse should be a good example to the younger girls." Victoria plopped onto Nora's bed and groaned. "Not a wobbly, sentimental romantic like I was today."

"You are strong and true for everyone else," Nora said. She sat up. "It's all right to wobble a little. Let your friends hold you up."

"Matthew used to talk about being strong for me and taking care of me. Why does it sound so much prettier from a friend than it does from a man?"

She pulled a brush through Victoria's long hair, working through the tangles. "From a woman, it shows an understanding of our common struggles. From him, it sounds condescending and implies you cannot take care of yourself. It's very old-fashioned, coming from a man."

"And yet no one is old-fashioned anymore," Victoria said. "Look at everyone falling in love and getting married to people they met on two-week leaves. Did you know Iris Banks only knew that patient for nine days before he proposed? I've lost all sense of time here. Nine days, and off they went."

"Iris was never the same after Ronald died. I think she just wanted an excuse to feel alive again. At least Charlie was a good-looking excuse."

"Are you defending romance? You?"

Nora stopped brushing mid-stroke. "I just think I understand Iris's choice a little better these days. So much has changed, in work and out of it."

"Too right it has. The world has gone mad, and we will never have those innocent days back. We were hardly allowed to touch male patients back home, and now we have seen testicles. Unmarried women are not supposed to see testicles."

Nora nearly dropped the brush. "Even married women are supposed to keep to a certain pair. Oh, what wartime does to a girl."

"A Red Cross nurse is bold and unflinching when she holds a man's parts out of the way during a groin injury repair." Victoria laughed. "Let's add that to the manual. I'd hold a hedgehog if they needed me to."

"Did your man—did Matthew not want you to work? Before, I mean."

"It didn't matter what he wanted. I'd have been cut from my training program in a blink if I married him."

"That's always the rub, isn't it? For Iris and everyone else."

Victoria nodded. "He's a traditional man with a name that's important in a small town. He was raised to think a certain way, so in the end, it was always supposed to be him, me, and a houseful of babies. I was often doubtful about how supportive he'd be if I really had the choice to marry him and keep working. In looking back, it pains me to admit that much of that was my own childish insecurity."

"About what? Your name is obviously good enough since his brother chose your sister."

The name Matthew would have preferred was Maudie's —Maudie Hamilton then, before Cooper Truxton fell head-over-heels for her and she for him. Despite Victoria eagerly awaiting her turn, Matthew didn't see her and didn't take the news well when Cooper, his friend since they were boys, dodged ahead of him and proposed.

That was the day he noticed her.

She was always second place to Maudie, but hers was a shadow she never minded before. Maudie's friendship and energy buoyed everyone around her. Under her tutelage Victoria grew confident and curious and shed her girlish fears of being wrong or disliked. There was no truer friend.

"My name wasn't a problem, of course." Victoria pulled her hair over her shoulder and began a braid. "But Matthew never paid me any mind when I was more of a traditional girl, knitting and fussing over dresses and dances. I've told you about my friend Maudie."

"Of course."

"Maudie is one of the finest women I know, and to be compared to her is an honor from anyone but him. But all the things he liked about her, he later said he liked about me. If any other man had said I was as bold or clever as she is, I'd have been flattered. By the time Matthew got around to it, I was tired of being ignored and decided I didn't like him anymore."

Nora sighed. "What rotten timing."

"It was so confusing. Shouldn't I want to be with a man

who loves that I'm independent and smart?" Victoria toyed with a ribbon to tie in her hair. "And he's such a good man, really. I've never thought otherwise. But we had layers of obstacles."

"He proposed to you. More than once."

She watched herself in the mirror. Her foolishness still hurt to admit, but running from it had not helped before and it wouldn't ever again. "The first time was at Maudie's wedding. It was humiliating."

Nora's eyes narrowed. "Did he interrupt the preacher or something?"

"No. We were dancing, bickering about something political. He's a lawyer and he just loves to wind me up with conversations like that. At the end when I stepped back to curtsy, he pulled me against him and held me tight and whispered, 'Marry me.'" Victoria covered her face with her hands. "At least he had the decency to whisper. I said 'What is the matter with you?' quite loudly, just as the music ended."

"What did he say to that?"

"I don't know. I ran out of the room like a frightened girl and didn't talk to him for a year."

"I don't understand." Nora bobbled the hairbrush from hand to hand. "You cared about him and he obviously cared about you. He wouldn't have asked you to marry him if he didn't. Why not work it out?"

"I don't know what came over me but a moment of pique. I thought I was just the next best girl since Maudie was gone." She rose and paced in front of her bed, gliding her fingers over the flower-patterned coverlet. "I am not proud of how I behaved, but you must understand, I had given up looking for a husband and chose to focus on myself. My nursing certificate program was through a local women's college, and I threw myself into schoolwork and activities with my girl friends. Matthew and I were in the same social circles and quite friendly, but we were always around other people. It's not as though we were whispering in corners."

"So he never courted you or acted romantic in any way?"

"Never. But I humiliated myself that night and I could not face him. I didn't even have a pumpkin carriage waiting when I ran away."

"But you worked things out later, somehow. You said he proposed more than once."

Amiens was a hundred miles from the ocean, but the breeze from the window suddenly carried a tang of saltwater and a searing memory of a starlit beach on the other side of the world.

"I fell in love with him," she said. "He fell in love with me. We didn't get married, and that's the end of it."

"That *was* the end of it, but here he is. Have you missed him?"

Picking at her fingernails, Victoria didn't respond.

Nora tried again. "Well, did you part on good terms?"

"It ended very poorly."

"He never married anyone else, though. Neither did you."

"I haven't tried, for obvious reasons."

"Do you wonder whether he hasn't tried, either?" Nora slid under her covers and squirmed to find a comfortable place on her pillow with a head full of rag curls. "I'm sorry I teased you before. It's only that when you saw him, you seemed to go to a different place and he went there with you. I said goodbye as we left the room and you didn't even hear me."

"You did?"

"You didn't take your eyes off each other."

"We were arguing. Again. He packed his hurt feelings along in his haversack and apparently I still keep mine in my pockets."

"You were holding hands and looking cow-eyed at each other."

"And arguing. I even offered to come see him this evening and he didn't want me to come because he thought we'd just fight some more. Maybe he's right. Maybe nothing good can come of this."

"Oh, Victoria."

"I know." She rubbed her eyes. "He asked me if I'd assist in his surgery. He heard from Maudie and my sister that I'm the best in this sad business."

"Dr. Bowden would excuse you."

"I cannot imagine going through that injury so far from home and all alone. Matthew asked me to be there, so I will." She closed the window and left the coin on the sill to prop it up in the morning. "I like to think I've grown up enough to keep my wits about me. I've comforted dying German soldiers, so I can comfort him and not lose my head in the process."

"But you'll have to watch when they cut him. I don't think I could do that with someone I loved."

Victoria flopped onto her bed and pulled the chain on her bedside light. "As long as I'm not going anywhere near his testicles, I'll be fine."

Chapter Four

A night tossing and turning through uneasy dreams about being Matthew's living hell showed on Victoria's face in the morning when she inspected the pale violet circles under her eyes. It was bad enough that she had to see him in her prissy uniform that might as well be a nun's habit, but she had to look exhausted and careworn to boot. A daub of her rosebud salve willed some life into her skin and the snap of the morning air pinkened her cheeks with a healthy flush when she arrived at the hospital a little early for her shift. She hoped he was asleep.

The sun rose later every day as October advanced. Predawn light glowed like silent artillery fire and warmed the windows of the east-facing rooms as Victoria tiptoed past two sleeping soldiers and stood at the end of Matthew's bed.

The wound on his forehead was clean and uneven stubble on his jawline prickled through the greening bruises. Whoever tended to him the day before had helped him into a plain cotton hospital tunic and sent his uniform for washing, and under the thin fabric the muscles of his arms curved in contrast to the sallow hunger in his cheeks.

She picked up a corner of his blanket and tucked it over his hand without letting herself linger and touch him. Tangling her fingers with his yesterday kept her awake half the night thumbing through memories like photographs until her fists clenched and she wasn't sure who to be angry with.

"Good morning, Vi," he murmured. "This isn't how I like to say good morning to you."

"I didn't mean to wake you."

"You didn't." He opened his eyes. "I was awake and wondering why you didn't come see me yesterday evening."

"You didn't want me to."

"I said I didn't want to fight with you."

Her eyes narrowed. "Yes, but you said that when I offered to come in the evening, so it certainly sounded like you didn't want me here."

"That's not how I intended it."

She sighed. "Say what you mean. Don't give me your legal double-speak and ask for interpretations. Just say it plainly."

"I'm happy to see you whenever you can spare the time."

"Was that so hard?"

He yawned. "Your turn."

"To what?"

"To say something you mean."

Only one thing was certain enough to call absolute truth. "I'm glad you're alive."

"And I'm glad that if I must be alive in this sorry state, it's here with the finest nurse in France." He held out his hand. "Even if she's just out of my reach."

Her fingers twitched as she fought the urge to touch him. "Don't tease me."

"I'm not."

"I don't want to flirt with you. I don't care about your morale or your heroics or anything I ought to care about, only—" She caught herself. "I'm exhausted."

"Were you up late thinking about me?"

She didn't move.

"Victoria, have I already offended you so much?"

The truth tumbled out before she could stop herself. "I don't know how to talk to you now. I don't know if you're teasing. I don't know what to say."

"But here you are, up early to visit me." He pursed his lips and grimaced as he shifted his weight. "Why?"

"Don't fish for compliments."

"I'm not."

"I wanted to see you last night," she admitted. "I felt awful that you didn't want me when I'm probably the only person you've seen from home and I know you're still so angry with me—"

"Stop. Sit down, Vi. Sit with me. My morale is shit and I'm glad to see you, since it is your Red Cross duty to cheer me whether you like it or not." He took her hand when she sat gingerly on the edge of his bed.

"My Red Cross duty is to cheer everyone, so don't get big in the head." She looked at his left leg. "What happened?"

"Ordnance. The battlefields are salted with dud shells and grenades just waiting for one wrong step to set them off. We were up north and it was a walk to scout a hundred yards to see if we could throw down a cable. The man I was walking with went right on it. He's gone and if I'd been much closer I might be, too."

A quick terror swamped her. Even if he no longer belonged to her, Matthew, with all his smarts and dry wit and deep love for his family and friends, belonged in the world. At the thought of him leaving it, she wanted to fling herself onto him, to cover him and protect him, and all she could manage was to hide her trembling hands and whisper: "No."

"They got me back to the aid station and tried to wash out all the dirt and the mess in it. My foot was... well, it was bad."

"My good reputation here is partly due to my strong stomach. You can tell me if you wish."

"There wasn't a lot to save, and they said they should take it off right away or I'd risk blood poisoning setting in pretty fast because of how mucked up it was." He dragged his thumb over his bruised jawline. "The rest of this is from the fall. I dislocated my shoulder, but they popped that right in so fast I didn't feel it."

The vision of him in the field hospital pale and bleeding burned her eyes and she let her hand go limp in his. "I'm sorry."

"I'm not angry with you, Vi. I haven't been for a long, long time. Everyone tells me how happy you've been in your work, and I am happy for you."

"Everyone? Who?"

"Maudie, of course. Edith and William. Trux and Rigby. Everyone we know, really."

"I didn't know they talked about me. To you, I mean. They don't talk about you to me." She forced a laugh to stop stumbling on her words. "Dare I ask what devilry you've been up to, since I didn't ask any of them?"

"I'm sure you knew I signed up with the reserves just before you left to come here. I still had some boyhood soldiering dreams in me, and drilling broke the monotony on just the right cadence. At the office, it was cases and more cases, a bit of legislation for Trux to take to the General Assembly here and there. The occasional good trial."

"Will you go back?"

"I hope so." He tapped his left thigh. "I can do my work on one foot. I thank God over and over it wasn't one of my arms."

"Your morale sounds fine." She mustered a wry smile.

"Victoria, they talked to me about you because I asked them to." He gripped her tighter, pulling her down the bed closer to him. "I always asked about you. I knew you were here and there was fighting close by for a long time. I needed to know you were safe and—darling, I just needed to know you were safe."

Goosebumps prickled her arms. He didn't let go and she didn't pull away. "It was difficult for a little while, but this is a base hospital. It's not as frantic or close to the fighting as a field hospital. Unless there's action nearby, we work fairly regular schedules and some patients recover here for weeks before we send them home. It's safe."

"I thought of you when I was hurt, and how ironic it would be to worry about you all this time and end up being one of the reasons you're here."

"I'm safe here. And you're safe now, too."

"Am I?"

She tucked his blanket closer. "You are. We're not in any danger here. And you're shivering again. Let me get you another cover."

"You know how I hate it when you walk away from me."

"I'll have to go soon, though."

The mask crept over the panic in his eyes, as it had the day before. "The procedure your doctor talked about. What will you do?"

"Shall I show you?" She already knew the answer. Matthew was a lawyer; he liked precedent and order. Details always made him feel better.

"Please."

She stood and drew her finger over the blanket covering his left leg. "Instead of taking off the same amount all around like before, the doctor will leave a length of skin and muscle and cut the bones closer to the knee. Then we fold that part over, rather like a flap on an envelope, and stitch it up around three sides. The muscle will protect the ends of the bones and since the scar tissue will form on the sides of your leg and not the end, it will be easier to wear a prosthesis one day." She paused. "Does that help?"

"It does. I always wanted to see you at work."

"I suggest you reconsider your means to an end."

He grinned. "It's a bit late now. Gosh, Maudie is going to give me some hell for this when I get home, isn't she? She'll say I planned it so I could add to her stories bragging on how proud she is of you."

"I hope you don't bother her."

"I hope I don't, either. She's been busy with—"

"I know what she's busy with. She writes to me."

He swallowed thickly. "Don't do this."

"Why can't you say *you're* proud of me? Why did you make compliments to me all about her?"

Matthew pulled at her hand. "Did you expect me to stop talking to an old friend, a dear friend of yours, who is still very present in both our lives?"

"I wanted you to stop talking about her. To stop comparing everything I did to her."

"Victoria, I did not do that."

The pig-headed, insecure girl in her heart unfolded and whined louder than any sensible words. "You did. All the time. It's a miracle Cooper let you in the house to drool over his wife."

The warmth in his eyes faded, "I thought we were past this. You're acting like a child."

She shook off his hand and stepped away. "I see some things never change."

"Everything has changed. Sit down. I want to—"

The door creaked open and a girl came in with an armful of clean linen and another followed, pushing a cart. Murmurs in the hall rose from the physicians preparing for their morning rounds.

"You're here and I'm here," he continued, lowering his voice. "Did you think maybe that's no accident?" he asked. "What are the odds?"

"You don't believe in fate," she retorted. "You're too logical for that."

"And so we are back to the idea that I shot my foot off on purpose so I could see you. That's one logical way to make my way here where you're stuck with me, isn't it?"

"How funny you make light of it." Her words trembled even in disdain. "And ironic, considering how you wished me to be 'stuck' with you before."

"That is not what happened." His neck corded with strain.

"That is not—that is not what I ever intended. I thought that if you loved me as much as you said you did, things would have turned out differently."

Orderlies and volunteers turned their heads and listened, and what little resolve Victoria had left snapped.

"Matthew, I loved you so much, long before you loved me, and you never noticed. Maybe we—"

"What are you talking about?"

She shoved her clenching hands in her apron pockets. "Perhaps we were doomed from the beginning. Terrible timing. It wasn't until Maudie got engaged that you decided to pay attention to me."

"Christ, this again. Is a man not allowed to change his mind?"

She turned away, tongue between her teeth to stop any more bitter, heartbroken words from spilling.

"Victoria, get back here!" He pushed himself up from his pillows and the room went silent. "I can't come after you anymore. Is this how you get the last word?"

"No," she whispered.

"Then come back here now."

Had Matthew died, part of her heart would have died with him and her regrets might have lived forever. But he lived, and the piece of her soul that still belonged to him flooded her body with hurt and fear.

Bowden's voice in the hall stiffened her spine and excuses gathered on her lips. She had her shift. She had patients who needed her and a schedule to keep—excuses Matthew had heard a thousand times before, but she could not look back and say them. The look on his face that she knew would follow might tear her in two, for he *was* the patient now, on the schedule with a span of time she could devote to no one else, and for the most devastating reason.

Denys approached and held out his clipboard. Victoria straightened her veil, brushed down her apron, and called back to Matthew's bed without looking at him: "I'll see you this afternoon at two."

Chapter Five

Halfway through the morning's first surgery, Dr. Bowden held out a hand for a probe and didn't look up.

"Drop in on Harry after we're done here, Harp. Tell him to be good and sick by one o'clock. His father's delegation is checking in."

Dr. Wentworth laughed. "You're sending a nurse to parlay with the diplomats over the Kaiser's precious boy?" He spun a forceps by the ring handle on his finger and winked when he pointed it at Victoria like a pistol. "An officer should do it. I'll do it. I've got a matter to discuss with our German princeling, and I only need one shot."

Bowden glared at him. "Do I owe you an explanation of some kind, Captain Wentworth?"

"No, sir. Of course not."

Dr. Bowden never addressed his men by rank unless he wanted to remind them of his.

"I'm pleased they sent a little more notice this time, sir," she said, since she was expected to respond to the order. "I'm supposed to do rounds after this case, but Nurse Walker has an early lunch, so I'll have her relay the message to Harry."

Victoria shoved the thought of Matthew away for the hundredth time, along with the tray of soiled instruments she replaced with a new one on her supply table. Harry was not the distraction she needed.

Oberleutnant Heinrich Kurz was the son of a high-ranking friend of the Kaiser's and the hospital's unofficial prisoner since he no longer needed medical care. Bowden called Harry their security blanket, for as long as he was under their roof his father might avert the German field marshal's eyes from the railroad that passed through Amiens and over the river. The town's brief moment of importance in the fighting left thousands dead, and the endless bloody days of the French offensive on the Somme were still too close for comfort. Any shield was better than no shield at all.

Victoria usually enjoyed a quick chat with their former patient, but on a day when her head was already spinning with Matthew's pained words and her own foolish ones, she didn't need to dizzy herself chasing Harry's endless racing thoughts and demands to listen to his latest poorly translated German joke.

Bowden didn't give her the choice.

"No, you switch and have Nurse Walker do rounds," he said. "Get Harry sorted and make sure whoever they send is satisfied with their report. I need you back right after the visit because we have your fellow at two o'clock."

Her stomach tensed. "Of course, sir."

"Apparently you are the only person I can count on to do a damn thing around here," Bowden continued. "I'll take that retractor just there."

Wentworth eyed her, then him. “What happened, sir?”

“That hawk of a head nurse barked at me like a dog because one of the new VAD girls didn’t like meeting a German prisoner when she delivered the mail. Leaving out the color of his coat, Harry’s an all right fellow. Harp, you get on with him. Don’t the other girls?”

“Some of them. Who did you send?”

“Russell, maybe? Rudder? She accompanied Miss MacDougal. Wentworth, pull this back, just so.”

Victoria’s shoulders slumped. “Miss Russell’s father is up north, sir. You know how Harry likes to joke and it doesn’t always translate right. Perhaps she misunderstood something he said.”

“Or perhaps she thinks our cheerful Hun is happy to stay here so he can send information to his people,” Wentworth said, tensing as he moved the retractor to Bowden’s specifications. “Is it really safe to send the nurses to look after him alone?”

“Are you scared of him?” Bowden lowered his brows. “A lone German without a weapon has you soiling your britches now?”

“Not at all, sir.”

“What the hell is that boy going to report from here to the Central Powers? ‘We had fish three days this week, Uncle Willie. Perhaps the French have captured the sea.’”

Victoria snickered. The Earl of Skullduggery was on thin ice.

“He’s pleasant enough and never disrespects the ladies, which is more than I can say for some of the men we see, including you.” Bowden pointed a clamp at him. “I do not see the Swiss contingent anymore because my presence places an enemy combatant under the control of the British Army. Nurse Harper's presence makes him a guest of the International Red Cross. Do you see the difference?"

Wentworth poked around the tray of probes at his side and selected one. He didn't look up. "The Red Cross has no enemy."

"So you have learned a few things here after all," Bowden said. "Now, Harp. A mistranslated joke? Miss Russell should grow a thicker skin."

She nodded. "Of course, sir, but most of the VAD girls are very young and being around so many men is a shock of its own, never mind everything else they see here."

"She was tasked with delivering mail, not buttoning his trousers." He waved a hand and grumbled. "Shield your fellow women then, and the German princeling is all yours. I don't want to hear from Nurse Perry about her fragile darlings again. Please keep the boy happy enough to stay, and keep him sick. You know what I mean."

Harry had been gaunt with pleurisy and in constant pain from a botched surgery on a broken shoulder when he arrived in August. He'd been stable enough to travel to a prisoners' camp for two months, but he insisted he was a traitor to his homeland and would like to stay on with his new allies.

Bowden had dismissed the idea at first, but in a panic during the first unannounced visit of a diplomatic delegation, Harry flung himself down a flight of stairs, knocked himself unconscious, and nearly separated the shoulder he didn't maim in the fighting. The delegation agreed he should stay a while longer, and he wrote pitiful letters to his father every week embellishing the delays in his healing.

"Is he playing sick this time?" Victoria asked, passing

Wentworth a knife with her right hand while accepting another one back from Bowden with her left. "I suppose we don't want to revisit the last episode and really hurt him."

"If he's actually sick or injured, someone has to tend to him again," Bowden said. "He's fine on his own and we don't have any other Germans to stick him with if he did take an inconvenient fall. I'd have to bring him back up on the ward." He chuckled. "I'll put him right next to your fellow Berger. He's got a sense of humor."

"He's not my—"

"You know how I hate when someone hints that an old man can't see in front of his nose." He squinted at the blood vessel in his clamp. "Hate it."

"Why must you explain yourself to this party of diplomats?" Victoria asked as she shuffled folded blankets onto a shelf in the storage room that doubled as Harry's private quarters. It wasn't quite a cell, since he had Dr. Bowden's blessing to walk the grounds and collect his own meals from the kitchen, but he rarely did much else. "Certainly your father would rather you stay here than go wherever they're sending healthy prisoners."

Harry bounced on his toes and jumped, one arm outstretched to touch the ceiling. "I don't know if he can send his Swiss friends to those places to check on my comfort. Here, I am safe and treated well by the Red Cross." He jumped again, swapping languages with every hop. "*Der Oberst* Bowden says *la Croix-Rouge* knows no enemy."

"What are you doing?"

"Trying to break a sweat for my fever, of course." He ran a hand over his short blond hair and frowned when it came up dry. "Am I red yet? I should be red."

"Your father should be happy you are safe here, not send men to review you for transfer to a prison camp."

"Perhaps he wants me healthy to trade me, but I don't wish to be traded. I tell you what, Nurse Harper. You punch me."

"I think you might have the wrong word. I'm not going to hit you."

He made a fist and pretended to hit his stomach. "No, I have it right. If you punch me hard, I'll be green and sweaty when they arrive. I might even have a good vomit."

"I'll bring you a warm cloth if you need to sweat, silly boy. I am not punching you."

Harry laughed. "This is why I like when you visit me. Many of your friends are very kind and have good sense." His German accent clipped the corners of every word. "But you are funny when you lecture me. I can be more myself with you."

Victoria thumbed through a stack of towels and sorted them onto another shelf. "You are not supposed to be yourself today. Hold your forehead and groan, then complain of feeling weak. Cough a few times. I'll make them all wear masks and tell them they mustn't come past the doorway. Then I'll tell them you have a fever and we fear an outbreak of influenza."

"But you could punch me anyway, if you like." He flopped onto his bed and crossed his arms. "Men are fighters because they are tense and the fighting lets it go. You work in this place. I am sure you are tense."

The tension from fighting with Matthew lingered in her neck and throat, whipped again to a fever pitch after so many years dormant. Every time she stepped away rather than confront a problem with him, he knew just the right moment to grab her shoulder and spin her back into his arms. He knew. He always knew she would fall into him and whisper her apologies while he whispered his, murmurs through kisses.

She twitched her head and pushed the thought away. Matthew was on the schedule and would have to wait a little while longer.

"I am not punching you, Harry, and that is final."

He held his forehead and groaned like a whale sat on his chest, then looked for her approval.

She pushed last towels onto the shelf. "I am not convinced."

"*Vater*, I am near death and only my dear Nurse Harper can save me." He paused. "You don't like my theater?"

"My soldiers wouldn't whine like children. Try to sound like you are stoic and suffering bravely through the pain."

His smile disappeared. "You think of me as a child?"

"I think you sound like a spoiled boy, not a sick soldier."

"If you say this is not good, I will try again."

She whirled to face him and finally gave in to a smile. "Who knew a girl had to go halfway around the world to find a man with such good sense?"

"And here I am." He grinned. "I am good company as well, aren't I?"

"Usually, you are. But what did you do to frighten Miss Russell yesterday? She brought your mail and her squawking made its way up to Dr. Bowden."

"Squawking?"

"She complained of something you said to her."

"My joke, maybe?" He chewed his lip and thought. "*Der Oberst* is not upset with me, I hope. I say things wrong. Your English friends make no grace for a man in translation. Americans are better. The English say you have already butchered their language, so I think we shall butcher it together. I would prefer to go to America from here."

"You really won't go back to Germany?"

"To some lonely castle in a Bavarian forest, if there is a Bavaria to return to? No, I am a traitor. I have changed my allegiance and will hitch my horse to the winning cart."

She sat on the chair at his bedside. "You will hitch your cart to the winning horse, you mean."

"As you say. This war is for kings and cousins." He propped his feet on the end of his bed. "It has ruined Germany already and will not end well for them."

His cadence and confidence were oddly soothing. "You talk like my grandmother," she said. "She pretended she could tell fortunes and see the future."

"This trick would be useful in war, yes? My own grandmother said *das Fingerspitzengefühl.* My books say it translates as finger-tips feeling." He drummed his fingers quickly over the top of her hand. "But that does not seem right."

A chill chased up her spine, but she thought better of trying to explain to Harry why prickly skin was named for geese.

"Perhaps it's like what we call a gut feeling," she said instead. "It's a sense or an instinct about something and it makes your stomach sensitive. No punching."

He made a fist and knocked on his stomach. "As you say.

Gut feeling. When it is over, Germany will be humbled, and I will go to America."

"So will I. I cannot wait to go home."

"You told me you chose to come here. Could you choose to go home?"

"I could," she said slowly. "I have no commission or contract, but I came here to help, and I will help as long as I am needed. I could not sleep at night if I left simply because I missed the comforts of my own bed and my mother's cooking."

"Now that the Americans are coming, will you have friends out there fighting mine? Family? A special man?"

Her heart skipped. The man who wasn't 'out there' any longer had made her more homesick in two days than she'd been in two years.

"My friends and family are back home for now," she said carefully.

"Ah."

"What do you hear from your family?"

"Like all brave men, *mein Vater* is still nowhere near danger. He shines his medals and rides in parades. My friends, though. Eastern front, Western front, all the fronts. Too many fronts to count anymore."

Victoria looked at Harry's eyes and turned quickly away. Perhaps he hadn't fired whatever ordnance exploded and nearly killed Matthew, but he was the face of the men who did.

"I'm sure the ladies of Bavaria would welcome you home if you were traded," she said, forcing the brighter tone she used with convalescents and nervous new physicians. "They must be missing attention from you and your friends."

"Did I ever tell you I was married?"

She shook her head and stole a glance at his bare left hand.

"Too young, still in university, but Father insisted on the match before the fighting began in earnest. Her family, my family, castles and money. You know how it is, yes? We were strangers and lived as strangers until she died of consumption a few months after the wedding."

She covered her mouth. "Harry, that's so awful. I'm sorry."

"I am sorry for her, really. I was already gone to war and she was alone with only my mother," he said, idly kicking the wall at his bedside. "Karolina was a pawn of her parents as I was. I think we tried as well as a set of mismatched young people can try. I will miss the Germany I once knew, but I do not mean to go back to what it has become. Industrial mud. Blind allegiance."

"That makes a little more sense."

"And I am twenty-four years old. Not a whining child."

"As you say."

He popped up from the bed and grinned. "I only know the America of French schoolbooks in these cupboards and what newspapers I saw at home, so you must tell me where to go when your friends defeat mine. I want to see cowboys and train robbers and a baseball game. What a delightful country to swear allegiance to."

"America is a big place," she said. "Would you like me to find a map?"

"Please. I need something new to pass my days."

"Well, I need my lunch and I'll see you when I bring your guests at one o'clock. And Harry?"

"Yes?"

"What was the joke Miss Russell didn't like?"

He patted his chest. "I am a German businessman on my way to Paris. I am stopped at a checkpoint to see my papers. The man asks 'Name?' and I say 'Heinrich Kurz.' The man asks 'Occupation?' and I say 'Not this time, just a quick visit.'"

She covered her mouth and laughed. "Oh, that is one of your better ones. The wordplay is well done, Harry. It truly is."

"But why did it offend her?"

"Because your army has been trying to occupy Paris for more than three years, you dunce."

He jumped for the ceiling again. "You must bring her back then, and I will apologize in two languages to be sure I am clear. I'll save that joke for the friends I will make in America after they win this war."

Chapter Six

Victoria managed an apple and a sandwich for lunch and took extra care with her appearance during her break, straightening her uniform collar and cuffs, tucking every loose hair into her veil, and switching to a new apron even though the one she wore that morning was still clean.

The last time the delegation from Switzerland visited, they had turned up their noses at the hospital's disarray. The diplomats had arrived with no warning in the middle of a bilateral lower leg amputation and demanded to see Dr. Bowden, who was elbow-deep in blood. He sent Victoria instead to fetch Harry, who promptly flung himself down the stairs and broke his arm.

The Red Cross emblem stitched on the front of her apron glittered with starch, but her stomach was uncharacteristically unsettled when the visitors arrived half an hour late under their neutral Swiss flag. Her silent, frantic prayers alternated between making the visit fly by so she could be with Matthew in surgery as he wished, and letting the visit drag on all day so she could hide from his beautiful eyes and would have an easy excuse for her absence.

They greeted her in German and French and she responded in English for the translator. “We must all be very careful near our patient,” she said as she handed surgical masks to the three men. “We lost many people to influenza only a short while before the *Oberleutnant* arrived. It was terrible, you see. I hope I do not catch it.”

The men muttered amongst themselves and two of them, including the translator, elected to wait by their car. “How long is the fever?” the other man asked in German-accented English.

“Only since yesterday, but I have been very attentive.” She led him down a hall that avoided the patient wards so no one would overhear. “That poor man has had a run of bad luck. I wonder if he was always in such ill health.”

“I do not know, Nurse. I get my news from the ambassadors.” He paused. “He is very young for an *Oberleutnant*, is he not? He did not earn that. His father has a great deal of influence.”

“The Germans have a well-organized military,” she said. “*Oberleutnant* Kurz seems like a fine young man. I cannot imagine they would give command to a fool.”

“You think highly of your enemy.”

“The Red Cross has no enemy.” She stopped outside the door to the little storage room. “Harry,” she called. “Your guest is here. The others chose to wait outside since you are not feeling well.”

Harry’s hair was damp from the washcloth tucked under his pillow and his cheeks were red from pinching them. “Thank you, Nurse Harper. *Guten tag, Herr...?*”

"Fritzholm, sir. I bring greetings from your father, *Oberleutnant.*"

"Herr Fritzholm. I am sorry I cannot rise to greet you. My nurse says I must rest." He coughed.

"*Dein Vater wünscht—*"

"English, please. I do not wish they think I am—" Harry coughed again and held his head. "*Ach*, this hurts. They are good to me here and I do not wish to be suspect."

"Your father wishes you good health. I believe he will negotiate a trade of prisoners." Fritzholm turned to Victoria. "You are American. We see more Americans these days. Perhaps we return countrymen of yours, Nurse."

She stepped back from his line of sight before she rolled her eyes. No American prisoner would be released before hundreds of thousands of British, Canadian, and French soldiers ahead of him.

"I am no worth to Germany in this state," Harry said. He hit his fist against his chest and coughed with force. "Sick, and my shoulder not fully well. I cannot fight again."

"You can go home."

"Then I am a useless trade."

"Your mother would like to see you safe."

"Safe in wartime is a coward." He pressed his hand to his forehead. "An exchange for me when so many rot in camps is shameful. You must hurt my pride as well as my head, Herr Fritzholm? I am offended."

The man started and stopped speaking, grasping for words. "*Deutsch, bitte.*"

"*Nein.* We speak English here."

"A translator, then."

"You did not bring one?" Harry shot a glance at Victoria. "Or it is someone who waited in the car?"

She nodded.

Harry lay back on his pillow and closed his eyes. "I am so tired from speaking, Fritzholm. You must have misunderstood my father's concern. He and Uncle Willie would never do Germany dishonor. Send them my respect and say if I am offered a coward's trade I will die of shame before I take it, as surely they would wish." He coughed again. "If this wretched influenza does not take me first."

Fritzholm stepped back and handed Victoria his mask. "I will give him your exact words, *Oberleutnant*."

"Give him any words of mine or my nurse. There are no coded messages here. I am in a Red Cross hospital and *Der Oberst* in charge says the Red Cross knows no enemy."

"As you wish, sir."

After escorting Fritzholm to the waiting car, Victoria bolted up the stairs and darted into the operating room at three minutes past two o'clock. The delegates' visit was already a shadow in her memory and the humor in Harry's charade melted away when she saw Matthew's dark hair at the edge of the bed.

"I'm sorry, Dr. Bowden." She struggled into a gown and dislodged her veil. "The Swiss delegation arrived late and they just left. Everything went well."

"Catch your breath." He inclined his head at Matthew and raised his eyebrows.

"I'm ready, sir. I set everything out before they got here."

Her cheeks burned as she tied on her mask. The resolve she had bottled up when she squared her shoulders and turned away from him that morning slipped further away with every breath.

Matthew couldn't chase after her anymore, and if she thought any further about what that meant, she'd cry—and she couldn't cry. It had gripped her throat all day. Matthew couldn't run and she couldn't cry. Not into her pillow, not on a friend's shoulder, and never, ever in the operating room.

Bowden pointed to the head of the bed and cleared his throat. "We gave your fellow a little morphine, so he's groggy already. Let's get on with it."

Denys handed her the nasal tubing and adjusted the valves on the anesthesia machine. A tiny hiss of the gas whistled.

She bobbled the tubing between her hands, searching for words as she watched Matthew's eyes. *L'école maternelle* was bright with afternoon sun giving his fair skin an ethereal paleness, vulnerable and soft. *I'm sorry* lingered on her tongue, and if she said it, her welling tears would overflow.

"Are you cold?" she asked finally.

He shook his head. "If I say I am, you'll leave again."

"The blankets are just over there. I won't leave the room."

"No. Stay with me."

"I will. I'm here. Right here with you."

"Will it hurt? It hurt so much before."

Her usual calming words escaped her. There was no point trying to distract him like she would any other man. She knew his name and where he was from. She knew he didn't have a wife or sweetheart at home. And she knew very well the color of his eyes, his deep and visceral pragmatism, his need to understand every nuance of every little thing, and the hurricane of his panic when he was truly afraid.

"It won't hurt this time." She bent closer. "This is an anesthetometer. We can mix oxygen, ether, and nitrous oxide very precisely based on your blood pressure and breathing. The gas is delivered through this tubing. It will go a short way up your nose, and all you have to do is breathe."

"I thought—I thought it was a mask sort of thing. Those damn gas masks."

"This is much safer because we can adjust it any time. You're safe here. Entirely safe."

"Keep me breathing, Vi."

"Oh. I don't really do anything with this, only—"

"Do you remember what you said to me the first night at the beach? The last time, I mean."

Her stomach clenched. "Please don't."

"It's so funny now, darling."

The morphine might make things funny that simply weren't. She squeezed his hand to distract him. "Breathe in for me through your nose. A deep breath."

His smile was dreamy and wry. "How funny that you told me you couldn't breathe around my love sometimes. I always wondered if you meant that in more than one way."

"Shh."

"But now here you are breathing around my love, and my every breath is still in your care. Remember?"

"I remember." She tapped his nose as Denys watched them, distracted, and accidentally swiped a broad stripe of orange iodine onto the white blanket.

"We had some very fine days, my love." Matthew closed

his eyes when she lowered a stethoscope to his chest. "And that was one of the finest."

"Don't say that like it's goodbye."

He drew in a deep breath and smiled. "Don't let me get the last word."

"Nurse Harper, have you always been able to do this?" Denys asked as he wrapped the basins of used instruments. Matthew, still groggy, had been taken to the convalescent ward, and Bowden and Wentworth disappeared to see another patient.

Victoria put her surgical gown in the linen basket and tied on her regular apron. "Do what? Dr. Bowden taught me most of what I know about surgery."

"But you stay so calm. I understand that from the old man because he's seen so much, but that patient was someone special to you, and you just—you separated yourself from that and got on with it somehow. Most women would have been bawling."

She whirled around. "How old are you, Dr. Denys?"

"Twenty-four."

The lecture about women's fortitude died on her tongue. He hadn't known manhood without his country at war. Brave, but shaking in his boots, Denys reminded her of the new VAD girls. Their hands were allowed to shake, though. His couldn't. It was lucky he hardly needed to shave because he might nick his throat with the razor.

"This is why Dr. Bowden is so fond of telling us to put our feelings aside and get on with our work. We have little choice, so we do what we must," she said. "And I'm sure that when you go to a field hospital or aid station, you'll fall back on your training and you'll trust your hands when you need to."

"I don't believe that." He looked down. "I don't know if I can."

"Yes, you can. This is why you work at a base hospital first. We're usually not rushing around so much, and you will build faith in yourself and your skills."

"That man loves you, and you just—" He paused. "He was telling you he loved you and you held yourself in like you didn't even hear him, then you turned around and handed me a saw to cut off part of his leg."

"It's not as though it was easy," she snapped. "I heard him. But we cannot let our feelings run roughshod over our good sense. This is our job."

"I couldn't operate on someone I loved."

"Well, I hope your loved ones always have another doctor handy in case you decide your feelings are more important than their health. He asked me to be here, so here I am."

Denys scowled. "That's no help. Never mind."

She crumpled the last drape and tossed it into the basket. "I put my feelings and fears in tiny boxes in my brain and label them to be opened later. Is that what you want? A magic trick? A line of little boxes you can open and shut when you like?"

He looked down and spun a forceps from hand to hand, clicking and unclicking the lock.

"You will encounter more feelings in these rooms than you will blood and bone," Victoria said. "You'll hear deathbed confessions and dreams from people who think you're someone else. You'll hear everything they regret not saying to someone at home. Organize your boxes, Dr. Denys.

Leave your feelings out of your work, and you'll keep a clearer head."

"He was talking to you, not someone at home."

"When you have to take care of someone you know, you know what they need. I know him well. Boring facts and tedious details are a lullaby to that man. He told me to keep him breathing." She grabbed the instrument basin and turned to the door. "And I did."

Chapter Seven

In the hospital courtyard, walking paths sliced through the browning grass from corner to corner, and when Victoria peeked outside after her last surgical case, an orderly with a ladder and lighting pole was making his way among the old-fashioned gas lamps along the paths in the early evening light.

She lingered in the doorway of room five, a converted classroom on the ground floor, and watched Matthew while she caught her breath. He was reclined on his bed, eyes closed but not asleep. His lips moved in a silent conversation with himself, a scene so familiar to Victoria that the hospital faded for a blink and she saw him as he used to be: pacing and working out an argument under his breath, always pacing when he needed time with his thoughts.

Lawyers didn't need both feet, but in a moment's panic Victoria wondered how he would work if he couldn't tread the threadbare path he'd worn in his office carpet while thinking in mutters and grumbles. He was never theatrical in court, but the senior partner back in Raleigh loved to recount the day a judge asked him to vary his course a bit because his dogged pacing in front of the jury box during his opening statement made one of the men seasick.

She made her way to his bedside and scanned the convalescents, several sleeping and six gathered around a small table with a deck of cards and assorted coins. Many of the men in the little ward had been in her operating room in recent weeks; all of them left that room with lighter bodies and heavier hearts. Young Private McKeever, a hefty soldier who always asked for second helpings, had pestered Victoria for two days to see if his removed leg was still in their pathology room, and if so, could she please see it weighed so he could tell his mother how many kilos he'd lost so far. He'd let her be pleased for a few weeks, he explained, and then he would tell her why.

Matthew stirred and opened his eyes. On seeing Victoria, every muscle relaxed infinitesimally and he smiled.

"How are you feeling?" she asked.

"Back and forth between bruised and numb. Better than the last time, though. A little hungry for something more than broth, if you can rustle it up."

She stroked his hair back from his forehead. "Not until tomorrow. Would you like me to go so you can rest? I'll come back in the morning, I promise."

"Stay."

His bed faced a window to the courtyard, and Victoria pulled the closed curtain aside. Light from the pathway lamps spilled into his corner of the room.

"I asked the orderlies to give you a bed with a view, which isn't saying much. But I figured you wouldn't mind being the hospital busybody. Several of your roommates are real chatterboxes, and you can see everyone's comings and goings from here."

He yawned and gave her a sleepy smile. "My family's reputation as incorrigible gossips followed me across the ocean, I see."

"These wards are a fine place to get everyone's news and little dramatics. I've seen so many men come in from different units, even different armies, and they play the 'do you know' game until they connect the dots. Suddenly a stranger is family because they have someone in common. They sing and cheer and teach each other the marching songs from their units." She cleared her throat. "Some of which are unfit for a lady's ears. I have picked up some disgraceful French in addition to all the verses of 'La Marseillaise.'"

"You sound like home, Vi. Keep talking. I've been hunkered down with New Englanders for months and they sound awful. Tell me what I'm looking at out there. Tell me everything."

"To begin with, you are the honored guest of British Red Cross base hospital number forty-three, the smallest of the Red Cross hospitals in and around Amiens, and one of the oldest."

"How very exclusive."

"This building is a primary school and it houses all the surgical patients and operating suites." She pointed out the window. "Any time the weather is good, Dr. Swann will have patients in the courtyard working on their exercises. That's where you'll practice on crutches. The men with arms or hands gone practice throwing a ball. Others race on their crutches or in wheeled chairs. They make a contest out of everything and have some fun with it."

"That sounds all right."

"Hopscotch is legal but jump rope is not." She poked his chest. "Dr. Bowden has threatened an international court-martial on anyone who tries that again."

He saluted. "Yes ma'am."

"Across the way is the secondary school, and that's been made over into the sick ward and the holding pen."

"Livestock?"

"Soldiers waiting for transport either back to their unit or back home. When they don't need much medical care anymore, they have a barracks-like setup and we only check on them for meals. I'm always on the surgery side unless there's some catastrophe. I'll be close by."

He squeezed her hand. "I was probably ridiculous in there talking about how I needed you to stay. I'm sorry if I embarrassed you."

"We've all heard far more dramatic monologues thanks to the pain medicines. You weren't ridiculous at all."

"You do sound like home, Vi. You smell like home."

He breathed in deeply when she waved her hand under his nose. "Rosebud salve from Georgia Rigby's garden. She takes care of my tired hands." She inspected the cuts and scrapes among the calluses on his fingers and fished the tin from the pocket of her apron. "Let's try this on you."

"Home crossed an ocean. God, I have missed home."

She worked the salve into his palms, massaging with her thumbs to loosen his dry skin. "Have you seen anyone else you know?"

"Not outside my unit. Do you remember Jacob Feeney?"

"I remember his name, but I'm not sure we met. A college friend?" She stroked his fingers one by one, stretching and flexing and relaxing them until they curled around hers and she had to peel him off to do the next hand.

"Jake was walking next to me when the—" He pointed at his left leg. "When it happened."

"Oh no. I'm so sorry."

"He didn't feel a thing." He rolled onto his hip to take weight off his left side. "I sure do. My left leg feels heavier than my right and there's a lot less of it. Am I allowed any more morphine yet?"

"Not unless you want to start blithering again about how I must stay within arm's reach."

"Then I'll manage without it." He twisted his fingers around hers, slippery with rosebud salve, and he took his chance to return the favor and rub her hands. "I would rather you choose to sit with me than feel you must."

Her chest tightened. "I like the sound of home, too. I haven't heard anyone say 'Raleigh, North Carolina' just right for years."

"Maybe you need a fellow from Raleigh, North Carolina to help with that." He drew out the words a little. *Nawth Careline-a*, with the last syllable an almost inaudible breath.

She hardly allowed herself to think of home. Her mother, her sister. Her father—gone two years ago when she couldn't get back for a final goodbye.

Her voice cracked. "Maybe I do."

"But you also need to have some supper and rest, I'm sure. Where do you live? One of these other buildings?"

Victoria pointed to the pale stone buildings at the shorter ends of the courtyard. "That little one is mostly offices. The other is the laundry, kitchens, supplies, and cleaning. Behind the laundry building are the temporary buildings that house the doctors and the volunteers. The permanent nursing staff and a handful of VAD girls are billeted around the community wherever they can fit us in. I'm a short walk away in a house with five other girls and a sweet mother hen who cares for us." She sat straighter. "Goodness, I almost forgot. Have you written to anyone? Does your family know what happened?"

His cheeks flushed. "I wrote a letter before I got here and it's with my field kit, wherever that ended up."

"I'll find it. Personal things come on the ambulances and they check it all in. Someone will bring your uniform back from the laundry soon."

He tugged the neckline of the linen hospital gown that didn't quite cover the dark curls on his chest. "The hero soldier in a nightdress. Is there a bandage for my pride?"

"It's not as though I haven't—"

"Victoria."

Her eyes darted to the patients playing cards and she ducked her head. "I'm sorry."

"Don't be." He smiled, still groggy. "It's funny, though, how your work breaks all the rules about what a young lady from a good family ought to see, but they require a dress fit more for a nunnery than an operating room."

"It has to be modest enough to dissuade lecherous soldiers and satisfy any nosy gossips who think a woman's mere presence is a flirtation."

He stroked the crisp white cuff at her wrist. "I am neither dissuaded nor satisfied."

"Are you unconvinced of my modesty?"

"Quite the opposite. There is far too much of it."

"Matthew."

"I was thinking of the beach, and I blame the morphine for that. What's your excuse?"

Her lips twitched. "I have none."

Amiens was still dry from summer and overdue for steady rain to rinse the streetcars and clean the dusty cobbled streets. The rushing water in her ears was the ocean along North Carolina's barrier islands.

She stroked her thumb over his and watched their fingers in another slow, familiar dance. Even when he masked his expressions and guarded his words, his touch gave him away.

Years ago, when he took her in his arms to dance at Maudie and Cooper's wedding, his hands had filled her with flame. His gray eyes had been hungry, bright with excitement and a warmth she'd never seen for anyone but Maudie, and it was finally for her—wasn't it?

The doubt crept in like it always did. At the end of the dance, when he pulled her close and asked her to marry him, he didn't have a ring. He hadn't asked her father. He hadn't even courted her properly, just proposed marriage at the end of the dance like it suddenly occurred to him it might be a good idea. Since Maudie was gone, she was the next best thing.

"Your eyes are far away, Vi."

Her cheeks burned. "Raleigh, North Carolina."

"I didn't think I'd be so homesick. Are you?"

"I try so hard not to think about it, but sometimes when I hear from my mother I feel like I've abandoned her. Of course, she'd never say that outright. I miss her so much."

He tried to sit straighter and clutched her hand. "Oh, God. I'm shamefully late in saying this, but my condolences on the loss of your father. I went... well, I imagine someone told you I went."

Gerald Harper's death from liver disease was not unexpected, and when Victoria left for the war he said he'd lingered so long already that he was sure he'd linger at least until she got home. In those days, everyone thought the war wouldn't last a year. The war continued, and Victoria's father passed on.

"Thank you," she said softly. "Mama didn't mention it, but after the funeral she took to ignoring her sorrows and only giving me news of Edgar to cheer us both up. He's been such a blessing for her, and quite persistent, asking after me every day when I only knew him for about six months."

"Edgar?"

"Didn't Cooper tell you about Edgar? He must have."

Matthew tightened his lips. "He did not."

"Cooper went to Florida a while back to meet with some other legislators about railroad things and came back with him, pleased as punch. He thought Maudie and I would take to him immediately, but he was only half right. I adored him at once."

"What? Why?"

"Well, he's very handsome, obviously, and so very sweet. And he can do some interesting tricks. We never see anyone so exotic in boring little Raleigh, you know."

"He what?"

She watched the tension cord his neck and fought a laugh. "And he's got quite the pecker."

"Jesus Christ, Victoria!"

"He's a parrot, Matthew. I have a pet parrot because

Maudie couldn't stand him and the darn thing learned to say my name."

He groaned and slouched on his pillows. "And is he really called Edgar, or was that part of you making me jealous of a bird who seeks your affection?"

"If I were inventing a suitor to make you jealous, I'd give him a better name than that." She tapped her chin and faked an English accent. "Wilberforce Whistledown Hitherto-Smythe the Fourteenth, heir to the Earldom of Porridge."

He snorted. "Are you cavorting with eligible aristocrats now?"

"We have an insufferable lordship of a surgeon here and we give him silly names. I'm not cavorting with anybody." Victoria averted her eyes and fidgeted, trying to pull back her hand. "The reason I thought you'd know about Edgar is because Cooper accidentally taught him to say something in the two weeks they had him. I was sure he'd brag about it."

He didn't let go. "Tell me."

"The children drove Maudie to distraction trying to play with the bird and make him talk, so she made Cooper keep him in his study. Of course, he practices all of his speeches and his witty remarks that he keeps stashed away to look clever later."

"Trux is such a card."

"So the bird learned how to say 'And furthermore.'"

"Oh, no." Tears filled his eyes and nearly spilled when he laughed so hard the bed frame squeaked. "God, this hurts. I can just hear him. And now I hear him in a bird voice. You're not supposed to make me laugh in this condition."

"It's the best medicine, though."

"Quoth the parrot, furthermore."

"I thought Edgar Allen Poe would appreciate a parrot's mimicry of a raven."

"Your Edgar sounds delightful."

"I'll bring you a picture of him. He has a blue chest and belly and black and white wings, and he keeps my mother company." She paused and arched a brow at him, fighting a giggle. "He really does peck a lot."

Dearest Maudie,

~~You will never believe~~

~~I am devastated to tell you~~

Matthew is here. His left foot was amputated in a field hospital and today Dr. B took off the rest of his leg below the knee. He says Matthew will be more comfortable in coming years since we did this. He is well and resting and sends his love. Please do not tell his family. He is writing to them separately.

~~In lighter news, I should tell you about how Harry~~

He wanted me in the room and so I was in the room. I handed them the saw to cut into his bones. I couldn't look but I had to listen. I had to listen to him tell me he loves me and then I had to listen to that and I watched him breathe and I could hardly keep breathing, but I got on with it because I had to. I had to be there because he wanted me to be there and I kept my chin up and I stayed, and when I saw him later he smiled at me and all I could think of was what I heard in that room.

He laughed so much when I told him about Edgar and still all I can hear is the operating room.

~~Sometimes I think~~

~~I might have been wrong about the way~~

"Go to sleep," Nora groaned when Victoria crumpled the paper. "It's past eleven. You'll think more clearly in the morning."

She smoothed the paper, re-read her scribbles, and crumpled it again before trying a fresh sheet.

Dearest Maudie,

Matthew is here. He is well and resting and sends his love. Please do not tell his family. He is writing to them separately.

He said something to me today about the beach and I nearly went to pieces.

She tore the letter into strips and the strips into squares and let them flutter into the wastebasket like snow.

Chapter Eight

"It is literal shit, gentlemen." Dr. Bowden jabbed a finger at a young physician's nose. "They might send you to Italy or Africa or Turkey after we're done with you, but in France and Belgium, our men plowed under fertilized fields to make those trenches. We blasted the hell out of the land with artillery and we tore up thousands of kilos of rotting manure in the process. So what do we find when we dig the shrapnel out of our boys today?"

Brows lifted, the French soldier looked at the doctor, at his bandaged and splinted right arm, and back to the crowd around his bed.

Dr. Hawkins cleared his throat. "Bacteria associated with feces, sir. *Clostridium* pathogens."

"Good. Bryson. Why is this shit bacteria of particular interest in battlefield wounds?"

"Tetanus, but particularly gas gangrene, sir," Dr. Bryson said. "Shrapnel bearing particles of *Clostridium* from animal feces on the battlefield can lodge bacteria deep in a man's body. Superficial wound cleansing might not reach them.

The bacteria proliferate and produce toxins in the muscle tissue when the wound is closed."

The patient went pale and held his stomach. "*Le merde?*"

"It's all right, old boy." Bowden patted the injured soldier's unbandaged left arm. "Your aid station did the best they could under shitty circumstances. There's more we can do for you here. Tell you what. We'll clean out the rest of the shrapnel and you can keep your arm."

The soldier's voice shook. "I will take that trade, *docteur*."

"It's funny how quickly you can tell whose pride will hurt them more than any blast," Victoria said, tying her surgical gown. The morning sun energized her, and the sight of Matthew sleeping peacefully was balm on her heart after a restless night. She never sorted her cluttered thoughts enough to write a letter to Maudie and scrubbed the ink smears from her hands that morning until she needed a dollop of salve to soothe them.

"Did you see Lord Tuppence Snizzleworth on rounds?" she continued. "Nose in the air like the shit speech offended him. His pride will get the best of him."

Nora tucked her hair into her veil. "He's heard it a hundred times."

"We all have, but I'll take a little laugh where I can get it."

"I suppose."

"Are you all right?" Victoria set down the instrument basin she'd just lifted. "Darling. You don't look well."

"Maybe it was the shit speech."

"Sit down. I'll finish setup."

"I'm all right." Nora swayed.

"Sit down immediately, or I will tell Dr. Bowden to come make you sit down."

"Victoria, don't. He asked for me to assist today. I want him to ask for me."

"Fainting in his operating room will ensure you are never asked back. I'll reassign you someplace and he can blame me."

"I'm not sick," Nora insisted, straightening her shoulders. "It's a cold. My nose tickles a little so I sneezed myself dizzy after breakfast, but it's wearing off. Did you see Matthew this morning?"

"Oh, there's a fine turn of phrase."

"Well, I'm interested."

"I'll indulge you. He was sleeping when I tiptoed by earlier. I'll try again at lunch. Help me with this drape."

They lifted a cotton sheet over the rolling cart that would hold the anesthesia supplies. "How lucky for him to have you right here," Nora said. "Wives back home don't understand what the war does to a man."

"I'm not his wife."

"Wives. Sweethearts. You know what I meant. They don't really understand until he comes home. They get a letter with news of his injury and it's an awful shock. My friend Hannah is at one of the hospitals in London and says a letter doesn't really prepare families for seeing their men like that. When it's finally real to them, it hurts the men all over again. Matthew has someone by his side who's not a stranger." She shot Victoria a look. "Whatever else you call yourselves, friends or anything. You're from his home."

"Thank you for the reminder." Victoria tied the corner of

the drape and reached for another basin. "I promised to hunt down his field kit and send his letter home, if it even made it here. Five francs says Dickie dumped everything from the ambulance in a box in the offices and didn't sort a thing."

"I don't want to lose five francs, thank you. Good luck."

"Maudie sent me some eucalyptus salve. You should try some. It's swell for head colds."

Nora lifted her chin. "I will try it later. But first, as Dr. Bowden says, we must get on with it."

Leaving Nora to finish cleanup after the first case, Victoria gathered her skirts to her knees and jogged across the courtyard to the laundry rooms. Steam escaping through the vents smelled of starch and soap and hissed through the chilly air into the trees. She waved at two patients enjoying a patch of sun and darted down the stairs.

"Ingrid?" she called out. She caught a young woman by the shoulder. "I'm looking for Ingrid Russell, please."

"She's with the driers today." The girl pointed over her shoulder. "But she just got back from her break, and she can't take another until lunch unless the matron says."

"Perfect. That's perfect, actually."

She found Ingrid loading damp sheets from a wringer into a wheeled basket. Sweat clung to her brow and flushed cheeks and one of her auburn braids escaped her veil.

"Ingrid, dear. Would you like some help?"

The girl jerked upright. "I'm stronger than I—oh. Hello, Victoria."

"I came to see if you needed an extra set of hands today."

"You're a surgery nurse. You came to see if I needed help in the laundry?"

"You do, don't you? Come with me."

"But I can't just leave."

"Bring your basket. It's time to hang these, isn't it?" Victoria grabbed an armful of sheets from the pile at the end of the wringer.

Ingrid's eyes darted around the crowded laundry room. "Don't you have to be with the doctors?" she whispered.

"Dr. Bowden is the colonel in charge of the hospital and he approved this little experiment." Victoria grabbed the basket handle and pushed it toward the door to the courtyard. "He knows the head nurse and I are very protective of the girls here, especially when they are new, and I was so sad to hear you were upset the other day."

"Oh no. Victoria, I didn't mean to complain. He heard about that?" Ingrid clapped her hands to her face. "Oh, I will die of shame if they send me home. Please don't let them send me home. I won't complain again."

She shoved the basket into a corner near the door to the courtyard. "No one will send you home." She took Ingrid's hand and pulled her back to the surgical building and the convalescent ward. "It's important that we trust our superiors to run the hospital with order and discipline, isn't it?"

"I suppose so." Ingrid tried to match her strides. "What's this to do with—?"

Victoria rapped on a door. "Harry," she called. "Get up. You're going to work."

"Nurse Harper?" The voice inside was groggy. "I am what? I am not dressed. One moment."

Ingrid yanked her arm back. "No. I don't want to see that

horrible man ever again. He's—he's horrible and he's a spy and—and he's horrible. No."

"He's not horrible, and he wants to apologize to you."

"Well, he can send me flowers." She crossed her arms. "I don't collaborate with the enemy."

"Try not to think of him like that."

"How can I not? He's German."

"Keep your voice down. He's a human being. Dr. Bowden trusts him, and so do I."

Ingrid's cheeks flushed bright pink. "He's a prisoner. My parents didn't send me to work in a prison camp."

"Whatever you think of his allegiances, you work for the Red Cross here. England sent you, but you work for the Red Cross. If we received an ambulance full of German soldiers, we would do our duty and tend to them. Parts of Amiens were destroyed by shells two years ago, but the hospital was untouched. That flag protects us. That cross on your apron protects us."

Ingrid's lip quivered.

The door opened. Harry took one look at them and fell to his knees.

"Miss Russell. I have offended you. I begged Nurse Harper to bring you back so I may apologize."

She didn't speak.

"I am learning English and telling jokes poorly," Harry said. "All sense went from my brain. In English, different things are funny. I was careless and offended you. I beg your forgiveness."

Victoria nudged the door open wider so Ingrid could see into the storage closet better. "Harry is not allowed to leave the grounds and often doesn't leave his room, so he doesn't get much practice in English. He is tall and will be useful to you in hanging the laundry."

"But you don't mean—"

"He is at your command, Miss Russell. You've been promoted."

"I can't."

Harry jumped up. "This is splendid, Nurse Harper. The sun is out today."

Ingrid grabbed her sleeve. "Please don't."

"I am *Oberleutnant*, Miss Russell," Harry said. "So you must be *Hauptmann*. Captain Russell."

"But you are—what am I doing?"

"Hanging the laundry." Victoria took her hand and nodded for Harry to follow them. "Harry will help you as long as you need him. When you choose, you will relieve him of his duties for the day. You can relieve him right now, if you wish."

Ingrid looked him up and down, glanced at the laden laundry basket, and bit her lip.

"I am at your service, Captain Russell." Harry swung open the door to the courtyard. "Oh, this is fun. Nurse Harper, why did you and *der Oberst* doctor not assign me a job long ago? I will earn my keep with my allies."

"We didn't realize you were so offensive and needed to be redeemed."

"Ah! This reminds me. Captain Russell, I was up very late thinking, and I have a better joke you will like."

Ingrid froze. "I don't enjoy jokes much, sir. Ober— um, Harry."

"*Nein*, no, this is perfect." He patted his chest. "I am a

German student and I go to the English library. I tell the librarian I want to check out a book about war."

Victoria winced.

"And the librarian waves me away," he continued. "So I say to her again, 'I want a book about war.' She looks at me and says, 'War? You are German. You would only lose it.'"

Chapter Nine

After work, Victoria pulled a chair next to Matthew's bed and took his hand. "I came by this morning, but you looked so peaceful I didn't want to wake you. How are you feeling?"

A sleepy smile curled across Matthew's lips. "Like that train I heard last night ran me over."

"It's often like that for a few days after surgery."

"I already feel better with you here." He nodded at the window to the courtyard. "I got to watch you for a little while this morning."

"What do you mean?"

"You were out there with another nurse and one of the orderlies for a bit. It looked like you ladies had fun ordering the fellow around."

She stifled a laugh. Few people knew all the details of Harry's extended stay, and few people needed to. Matthew might see the humor in the endless imagined illnesses that were his excuse to stay out of a prison camp.

"Harry's not an orderly," she said. "He's our prisoner, in a way. We saved his life a few months ago and he's well enough to do a little work now. We keep him here instead of sending him to a prison camp because it might keep his father's best friend in line. Harry embellishes the poor state of his health so he doesn't have to leave, and Dr. Bowden allows it."

"His father's best friend?"

"Dear Uncle Willie."

"You must be joking."

Victoria shrugged. "One might think that, but his mail comes and goes through Switzerland so it reaches the right diplomatic channels. Our friend *der Oberleutnant* is a well-connected fellow."

"You call a German officer your friend?" Matthew narrowed his eyes and looked to the courtyard as if expecting to see Harry there again.

"He came here as a patient, and we care for all patients no matter what uniform they wear."

"It's only that he looked quite taken with you."

"Excuse me?"

"It seems like you get along well with him."

She fought the urge to yank her hand from his. For Matthew, of all people, a snipe about jealousy was a turned table indeed.

"I get along fine with everyone."

"He acted quite familiar—"

"Did you meet Dr. Swann this morning?" Victoria pulled her hand away and reached for the folder at the end of the bed. "I'm sure he's already after you to get up and about."

"Victoria."

"Would you be so snippy if he were just an orderly I chatted with? A British or French man?"

"Do not make this about jealousy."

She kept her voice low and watched the other patients for signs anyone might be listening. "Perhaps Dr. Bowden reads his mail. Perhaps he's engaged in a classified mission to use Harry as a spy to send back to Germany. I do not know and I do not care. The colonel makes those decisions."

Matthew held his breath a moment, then squared his shoulders and forced a smile that pushed past the heavy silence. He took the folder from her. "And it is Dr. Swann's decision to start me on a training regimen for my lungs as well as my leg, I see. Look at this. Breathing exercises?"

Her pulse slowed, back in safe territory. "After anesthesia, the lungs can feel weakened or clogged. Your body is more susceptible to illness." She tapped his chest. "Strong men have strong lungs. What else?"

"Trunk rotations and back stretches. Thigh and hip flexors, but I guess I'll only have to do half of those."

"No, you'll do both sides, and that includes your knees."

"My left hip and knee don't have much to do anymore."

A well-aimed pencil struck Matthew's bed with a metallic clank. "And that's the point, boy," said the man in the bed several feet to his right, separated by a small table. Major Benedict Cartwright yawned, rubbed sleep out of his eyes, and pretended to aim another pencil. "Dr. Swann says we strengthen our good side to get us around." He slapped his left hip. "And we strengthen the bad side so it don't shrivel up and become dead weight."

"No shriveling, gentlemen!" shouted another patient, rousing a cheer. "That's an order from the field marshal himself!"

"One of these days," Cartwright continued, "there'll be a whole shop of nothing but bits to make a man whole again, and I won't have a dicky left hip stop me from getting the finest new leg a man can buy. You've got to be fit to haul around a new one. Not shriveled. Can you imagine a catalog of legs? A store full of 'em?"

The young man on Cartwright's other side pointed at the bandage below his elbow. "My wife thinks this'll go over better with the children if I get a pirate's hook," he said. "Think I could rustle up a silversmith to do some pretty engraving on it? Maybe pop in a few pearls. I could be a real dandy."

"You'll look like a right swashbuckler." Cartwright snorted and turned back to Matthew. "Welcome to room five, Berger. We race on Tuesdays. I'll add you to the list."

"What day is it?" Matthew asked, barely moving his lips.

"Thursday," Victoria whispered back.

"Racing?"

She rapped her knuckles on the wooden crutches leaning against the bedside table.

"Tuesday it is," Matthew announced, loud enough to turn heads. "A race for the lady's favor."

A hot flush crept up Victoria's neck as Cartwright laughed. "You're a bold one, aren't you?" he demanded. "Get up on those crutches and hop to the back of the line of the heroic wounded seeking affection from our angels. I've already called dibs on Nurse Dotson."

"Not so bold, really," Matthew said. "Nurse Harper and I have been acquainted for many years."

Cartwright popped his head up and winked at Victoria. "Was he seeking any affection?"

"I haven't the fortitude to explain, Major. He's welcome to try later."

"My schedule is wide open." Cartwright scooted up in his bed and wrangled his crutches under his arms. "But until then..." He jerked his head at the opposite end of the room where Emily Dotson sat at the card table unpacking a dressing kit.

"He's been here for two weeks," Victoria said as they watched Cartwright deftly swing himself across the room and dodge a meal cart half full of trays. "Dr. Swann thinks convalescent hospitals let too many men lie about and get bed sores. He will want you up and moving soon because sitting in bed doesn't help bring your circulation back to normal."

He smiled and looked around the room at the other patients. "So I am back in basic training, I see."

"In a new unit, with men who are coping with the same changes."

Matthew looked down at his hand still clasped around hers. "But perhaps not everything has changed. I did want to ask you something."

Victoria's throat went dry.

"Perhaps it was foolish of me to ask for you to be in my surgery," he said. "But now that I'm not quite so addled by shock, is it all right to hold your hand when you have a moment? I know you won't skimp on your work on my behalf, but I don't want to cause trouble when you do make time to see me."

"Holding my hand is fine."

"Thank heavens, because I might die if I couldn't."

She pushed back her veil like she was tossing her hair. "If I had a franc for every time I heard that, I'd have the finest house in Amiens. Any wounded soldier is allowed to hold a nurse's hand if she is inclined to let him."

"Do you hold many men's hands?"

"Many, many men."

He lowered his voice. "Cartwright?"

"Ask him."

"Damn."

"Patients only, though. Dr. Bowden is strict about the officers keeping separate from the Red Cross nurses." She clicked her tongue. "The rumors here get quite racy with all the covert hand-holding going on."

Matthew grinned, then winced and held his ribs when he stifled a laugh. "Give me the rumors. I miss that about home. I miss knowing everyone everywhere, going familiar places where you'd always see a friend. Trials were a damned inconvenience because I always knew someone in the jury pool to disqualify. I was spoiled by it, Victoria. Home is in my blood. The sight of you is a balm on that particular wound."

Her heart skipped. Their memories intersected at street corners and tangled in blades of grass: maple cookies from the little bakery in Hillside, Raleigh's oak trees ablaze with color in the fall, the crunch of white gravel paths, the whirr of the electric streetcar. A little pang reminded her Matthew was only a meter away from never going home.

"I had a letter from Maudie just before you arrived," she blurted. "I could tell you a little of what's going on at home."

"You're an angel."

She slapped his arm. "Don't you dare go seeing angels."

"Tell me the most salacious hospital gossip, then tell me about home."

"Do you remember the posh doctor I told you about?"

"The Baron of Flannelcloth Humbug?"

Victoria sputtered a laugh. "Yes. Yes, that's him. Well, he has a wife at home on the Humbug estate and I think he has a wandering eye. He's been awfully chipper here and there, where he was a reliably snobby grump before. We haven't quite figured out if he has a lady hidden among us or out in town."

Matthew perked up. "A scandal, indeed."

"Dr. Swann's protégé Dr. Lambert fancies my roommate Nora, but she is so touchy about that sort of thing and won't give him the time of day."

"And yet he pursues her?"

"He moons after her. She is polite and leaves it at that."

"Poor fellow." He turned his gaze to their hands and slid his thumb over her knuckles. "Even a doctor has no cure for certain ailments."

Heat rose in her cheeks and when he looked up, she looked away. "On the home front, Maudie says Calvin was naughty and was asked to leave Mr. Redding's drugstore and little Emmeline punched a boy at school."

His jaw dropped. "Delinquent Truxton children? We must get back there immediately. The place is falling into disarray without us."

"You'll have to take charge. You'll be home before I am."

He paused and lowered his voice. "Vi, can I ask you a favor to do with that?"

"Yes?"

His eyes were earnest, searching hers. "I upset you yesterday morning, and seeing you walk away nearly shattered the little glass sliver of happiness I found here when I saw you. This moment now is perfect. If we find ourselves veering toward certain topics, could we stop the conversation and stop each of us trying to get the last word? Could we do that?"

The last word, until the last time, always came before a kiss. He had the last word in 1913 and no kiss had followed.

Her words lodged in her throat. "I upset you as well. You said I was defensive and acting like a child, and you were right. I'm sorry."

"God willing, we will both be back in Raleigh one day. We love the same people and we miss the same places." His eyes held a faraway sadness as they lingered on hers. "We have a niece and nephew in common now, and likely more if Edith and William keep up their pace. This foolishness of us avoiding one another cannot go on."

"I agree. We must move on from that."

"I know I cannot ask for exclusive access to your hands, but perhaps in the meantime, and for old times' sake, I wonder if your lips are a possibility."

She caught her breath.

"To talk, of course," he continued with a wink, "like we are now. And perhaps for other things, if, as you say, the nurse is inclined to let me."

"I'm afraid those other things are not allowed when I'm at work."

"I expected as much. Those little courtyard benches look like a fine place to sit some evening after your shift. Since I have to get in racing shape quickly, maybe I'll be able to meet you there soon." He squeezed her fingers. "My love for your conversation remains unchanged."

She breathed easier. "I would like that very much."

Across the room, Cartwright raised his voice to get their

attention. "I tell you, Nurse Dotson, this new American fellow told me he'd race me for your favor, and I told him he'll have to settle for the lovely Nurse Harper, because your heart is already claimed."

"Indeed it is, Major, but not by you." Emily Dotson winked at Victoria as she snapped her suture forceps in the air. "My fiancé will thank you for your gentlemanly defense of my affections."

He clutched his heart. "I am wounded."

"That you are, sir."

"All right, then. Berger," he called, "if I win the race, you must tell us all about your history with Nurse Harper."

Victoria snickered. "Be careful what you wish for, Major. The story has lengthy periods of little action, and Corporal Berger is an attorney and very skilled at talking for hours about nothing."

"And what if I win?" Matthew asked.

"Then we'll all cheer you on as you fix whatever you've obviously cocked up with her."

Matthew's cheeks flushed as he tried to look offended. "You're a madman, Cartwright. I'll beat you on one leg."

"I think the one you've got left is full of bullshit, so I wouldn't bet the farm on it."

"And the one you've got left is about as tough as a Yorkshire pudding."

"Just a moment," Victoria said, slicing her hands through the air. "I was just as responsible for the cock-up as he was, if not more so."

The older man laughed. "Well, then. If he wins on Tuesday, you'll have a ward of broken men cheering you both through the cock-ups. And if he loses, Nurse Harper, perhaps he isn't worth the trouble."

Dearest Maudie,

I will write this plainly because it is hard to say. Matthew is here. His left foot was amputated in a field hospital a week ago after an explosion. The man he was with did not survive. I assisted in his surgery to revise the amputation so he can use a prosthesis comfortably in the near future. He has some scrapes but is otherwise uninjured and is resting well. He is writing to his family separately. You may tell Cooper this part only, but no one else.

(Cooper, I mean it. Go away. This is private.)

Maudie, darling, do not ask me how I stayed upright during his surgery. I can hardly describe it except to say he asked for me to be there, so I had to do it and I did.

And now to the obvious questions. Yes, we've already annoyed each other and bickered. Our first conversation was a wretched mess of hurt feelings and snipes all gone moldy with age. I reacted poorly when he mentioned you. I feel like such a child with this imagination of mine. Of course, he already called me childish, which I deserved, and I stomped off like a bratty little girl. A few hours later, I had to help put him to sleep with the gas and sort instruments covered with his blood. That sort of gruesomeness never bothers me, but the horrible thought in the pit of my stomach was that he might not be here at all. He was one meter from death.

And so, the adult woman has reasoned with her foolish younger self, and I am glad beyond belief to see him here and safe. I haven't said a single cross word to him since, but now a glimmer of hope claws away at my reason every time he smiles. Hope for what, though, I cannot say.

He likely will remain here for at least a month, and he brought along a wave of homesickness that I haven't felt in years. We talked today about Raleigh, and I struggle now to separate the feelings of longing for home and longing for him. My nostalgia may make a fool of me with visions of love and romance when my cravings might be more easily placated with a maple snickerdoodle from Miss Cinnamon's Bakery.

It was sweet today when we laughed and talked about home and he kissed my hand. He is optimistic now, but a day will come soon when he feels unmanned by this injury. It's normal. I've seen it a hundred times. I have reckoned with my girlish pique, but what will come of his boyish resentment with this new space opened between us? All it will take is one stumble or fall where he cannot get up on his own. I saw a glimmer of it today when he snipped a little about seeing me talking with Harry. It was an innocent circumstance that he had no reason to be jealous about except that Harry is on two feet and Matthew isn't.

And of course, even if by some miracle his leg just grew back on its own, and even if we can let go of past struggles, the other difficulty still lurks over us like a storm cloud.

As ever, I welcome the wisdom and experience you bring to the puzzle that is myself and Matthew Berger. Also, I was mad at you for three minutes when I learned he was asking about me all these years and you never told me. You shielded me as I asked you to, so consider yourself forgiven, darling. You are the sweetest and truest friend a girl could wish for.

This ends my private complaint. I'll write again soon with a letter you can share: gossip from the girls and another joke from Harry, and have I ever shared Dr. B's lecture on battlefield manure? Cooper will love it. And in the meantime, thank you for your patience with your old friend and your sympathy for the muddled mess of her heart.

With all manner of confusion and affection,

Victoria

Chapter Ten

Before the war, Amiens rang with the activity of busy families. The cobbled street one kilometer from the hospital was lined with half-timbered houses and peppered with corner shops and cafés under bright awnings. The Germans took the city in 1914. The French won it back only weeks later, but the men of Amiens were inflamed by the slight and joined the army in droves. While the commercial areas of town bustled with railroad activity and soldiers on leave, residential avenues like Rue de Renard remained hushed and tense, waiting for husbands and fathers to return.

Blanche Barbier lost her husband and her son in the first month of the German invasion, and when the Red Cross arrived in Amiens to establish its hospitals, she was first to sign up to board nurses in her home. They brought laughter and music and perfume and pretty things—laces and silks in a home made for the comforts of the Barbier men. Blanche embraced the ruckus of young women who descended on her quiet neighborhood and left her little time to mourn or feel sorry for herself. She had the wobbly piano tuned for Nora to play and invited them all to put their family photos around the house to make it more homey for everyone.

"I can help you, Madame," Ingrid said when Blanche leaned over her shoulder to collect her plate after supper. "Marie and I will wash up."

Finished with her letter-writing, Victoria paused coming down the stairs and hid a grin as Blanche delivered her little lecture. She'd gotten it herself when she first arrived, as had Nora, Bridget, and Frances, all finishing supper and hiding smiles of their own.

Blanche pinched Ingrid's cheek. "You girls work all day. Let *Maman* keep house."

"Oh, but surely I can—"

"Little one, *Maman* takes great pride in two things. One is éclair, which you will have when I find vanilla beans for the crème pâtissière not selling for bricks of gold. The other is hearing around town that all the other girls are jealous of your fine lodgings and sweet house mother."

Marie gulped a bite of soup. "We are very grateful, *Maman*."

"Yes, very," Ingrid agreed. "And we—Victoria, what are you wearing?"

Victoria padded down the rest of the stairs in her felt slippers, loose hair flung over her shoulders, and twirled to Ingrid's seat. "I am wearing an embrace from home. My dear friend Georgia is a whiz of a designer and loves French fashion. She took a design Paul Poiret made for his wife for a costume party and turned it into this."

Her dark green silk harem pants tied loosely at the ankles and waist. The matching bias-cut tunic fell halfway to her knees and was trimmed in cream-colored silk bands dotted with embroidered roses. "Mr. Poiret did his design with beads and velvet like an evening gown, but Georgia thought that would be very impractical to keep clean."

"It's so lovely. You look like a wood nymph, Victoria," Marie said. "Especially with your hair loose. All you need are wings."

"Dear Marie. Isn't it soft?" She held out her sleeve. "Tomorrow is my day off and I am going to relax tonight." Victoria twirled again and skipped to the sitting room where Frances had her nose in a magazine. She plopped next to her on the sofa and flipped around so her feet went over the back of the sofa and her head nearly rested on the floor.

"What are you doing?" Ingrid asked.

"She's fixing her ears," the three older girls replied in unison.

"And my spine," Victoria added. "Would you like to be the first one who believes me, Ingrid? None of them do."

"Believes what?"

"A doctor I met during my nursing training taught that we have bones and water in little rooms inside our ears. They help our hearing and balance." She tucked the end of her silk tunic into her pants so it didn't shift. "It turns out that how these bones are positioned can create or reduce feelings of dizziness and blocked ears. Turning upside down moves it all around."

"Bones in rooms inside your ears?"

"Come on. Flip up here and try it."

"Do it," Frances said without looking up from her magazine. "It just makes my nose stuffy. She'll pester you until you try, though."

Ingrid scooted onto her hip and tried to lift her legs without falling backward, flailing until Marie came to tuck her skirts around her as she raised her feet over the back of the sofa. "This is very—oh. Oh, it is funny to breathe like this."

Victoria grinned. "Wiggle your neck a little bit, see? We spend all day on our feet and our spines get compressed. When you turn like this and let your head dangle a bit, you reverse that pressure. And with all the up and down of working in someplace like the laundry, I'll bet your ears get a little out of sorts and you don't even know it. Ooh." She grappled for Ingrid's hand. "How did it go with Harry today? Did you like having a helper?"

Frances set down her magazine and called into the dining room. "Bridget, come in here. We have news of the great experiment."

Ingrid's cheeks, already flushed from being upside-down, darkened to crimson as Bridget and Blanche appeared in the doorway.

"It's all right if you don't like Harry," Bridget said. "He's not sick any more and the front is a hundred miles away now. I say we ship him off."

"Send him away," Blanche agreed. She took off one of Victoria's slippers and tapped her foot with it. "You are too kind. French prisons are civil. He should go."

Victoria twisted her neck again. The front lines were far enough for a moment's comfort, but the fighting had been locked in the Ypres Salient for months. No one had forgotten that Amiens went from French territory to German occupation and back again in a matter of weeks at the start of the war, and if Dr. Bowden was still worried, so was she.

"You all know perfectly well that Dr. Bowden makes that decision," she said. "As long as Harry's here, we have a little extra security. What harm can he do hanging the washing? If it was terrible, Ingrid, you have my sincerest apologies and I will never bring him around again. Please be honest."

Ingrid bit her lip and tried to survey the room from her upside-down view. "I could tell he was anxious to earn my approval. It was very strange, but I survived."

Nora looked up from a stack of piano books. "That's perfect. That's your diary entry for every day here, isn't it? Dear diary. Today Dr. Bowden's lecture about infections from feces nearly made me lose my breakfast. It was very strange, but I survived."

"My turn," Frances said. "Dear diary. Today I had to dose a man with ipecac for drinking alcohol disinfectant and he cried when Dr. Carraker lectured him. It was very strange, but I survived." She nudged Marie, seated on the floor.

"Me?" she squeaked. "Dear diary. Today I found a mouse in a canteen in the storage room and I screamed and dropped it and made a whole shelf fall over. It was very strange, but I survived."

"Dear diary," Bridget said, "Today I listened to the men in room four conduct a three-language survey of options for a word preferable to 'stump.' It was very strange, but I survived."

"Did they come up with anything nicer?" Blanche appeared back in the doorway with a stack of plates. "It is such a harsh word."

"We got to *une souche*, which works for a tree stump, and that was all right. The conversation turned vulgar and I excused myself." Bridget rolled her eyes. "War proves men will make dirty jokes and innuendo until the very end. Which reminds me." She pulled a lock of Victoria's hair. "How is your handsome soldier?"

Still upside-down, she smiled.

"Look at you blushing."

"Gravity, dearest. Oh, my ears do feel better."

Frances and Bridget exchanged a look and jumped on her, pressing her shoulders to the couch. "We're going to keep you here until you tell us about him."

"He's recovering well from his surgery."

Bridget poked her ribs. "You were all dreamy-eyed talking to him. I saw you."

"We reminisced a bit. We've known each other a long time and have many friends in common, so there was a lot to talk about." She paused. "And we decided together to leave some of our more difficult memories behind us. They're not important now."

"That's a good girl," Blanche said, settling next to Nora on the piano bench. "Past gripes can stay in the past. Life with the ones you love is too short for clinging to little hurts that make no difference when that person is gone."

"I have been so foolish, *Maman*. Matthew almost died while I was in a little snit about my hurt feelings from ages ago. He is a good man and I am still very fond of him. I am grateful he's still fond of me."

"We'll all be your bridesmaids," Marie sighed.

Nora threw up her hands. "Dear child. How do you get there from here?"

"I don't think I can marry him, girls."

Ingrid tried to sit up. "What?"

"It's good to put the hurt feelings aside and appreciate his friendship," Victoria said, "but the same problem exists today that existed then. And it's the same one you'll all face, too. Married nurses don't do what we do. Most married women don't work at all."

Nora tapped out a staccato scale on the piano, treble down to bass, one note per name. "Maggie. Catherine. Aurelia. Eliza. May. Iris. Annabelle. Jane. And that's just from our little hospital in the last year. You get married, you go home. Red Cross policy."

"And there's no work for married nurses at home, either," Frances said. "The Queen's Nursing Corps is taking married women for the duration, but that won't last in peacetime. Back in London, even with a war on, they won't hire a married woman in the hospitals."

"Which is a waste of resources experienced in handling testicles, if you ask me," Nora said. "I heard from Jane Major just the other day, you know. They wouldn't take her on at the convalescent hospital, even just to carry medicines and wrap bandages, and do you know why?"

Wide-eyed, Ingrid shook her head. "Because she's married?"

"Because she's married, which means poor darling might be in the family way, and we mustn't strain her nerves." She smashed her hand onto the piano keys and jolted the room with the discordant notes. "Jane's strong as a horse. She worked in a field hospital before she came here. If you think we see a mess, Jane's seen worse and soldiered on as well as any infantryman. Nurse Perry cried when she left."

"She up and left in the middle of the war to marry?"

Victoria took her hand. "Her sweetheart was badly wounded, and not long before that, his mother passed away.

He had no one to look after him and would have lived on his unkind sister-in-law's charity while his brother was still fighting. It was a wretched situation. Jane did what she thought was right."

"She did more for her country in two years than most women do in a lifetime," Frances said. "But listen, Ingrid, Marie... you're not doomed to a life in the kitchen if you marry. You can deliver babies and make house calls on the infirm, and an educated, experienced nurse can make a difference to many people that way." She glanced between the younger girls. "It is just a shame the world is not very accommodating to married women with brains. If we are widowed, our minds are miraculously restored, we are cured of our hysterics, and we are useful again."

Blanche rolled her eyes. "Bother the war. This is the real international problem. I lost my job teaching when I married. If we are useful before and after marriage but not during, perhaps it is the men making this problem."

"They make all the problems," Nora said. "But truly, *Maman*, you loved André. And I am selfishly glad you did not return to the classroom after your loss. You are so dear to us."

"Twenty-two years of housework for two men trained me for six girls," she said, hugging Nora's shoulders. "After André and Henri died, I needed joy in my life, not bickering schoolchildren. I work for *la Croix-Rouge* by my choice."

"But for Victoria now, that's it?" Ingrid asked. "Here is Matthew after all this time, like fate. Can it really never be?"

Victoria turned and met her gaze, brown eyes to blue in bright pink, upside-down faces. "It has only been a few days. I enjoy his company, but I must be realistic. The world has changed, but if the needs of war and half a million wounded men don't make a married nurse acceptable, then I don't know if it's changed enough."

"But maybe?"

She giggled. "Maybe." She rolled to her side, flipped herself upright, and cranked her head side-to-side in a cloud of blonde hair. "Oh, that feels fantastic. Come on, Ingrid, just roll over and—there you are. How do you feel?"

"I feel all right. My neck feels funny in a good way."

"Very strange, but you survived, right?"

"Hello." Frances tugged her hair. "Wood nymph. What's your diary entry?"

Victoria tilted her head back and stared at the beamed ceiling. "Dear diary. Today I promoted Ingrid to a captain's rank and I was allowed to demonstrate needlework on an amputated arm."

"What?" Nora swayed a little and Marie clutched her stomach.

"Dr. Bowden and I have talked a few times about how important it is to reduce scar tissue in amputations. He asked if I could demonstrate a few stitches that might be a little tidier on curves and corners."

"And you used a—"

"Well, the soldier wasn't using it anymore. I showed Dr. Bowden and then he let me stitch up part of the flap. It sure is different using a needle driver, let me tell you. Who says surgery isn't women's work?"

"How exciting," Ingrid said, eyes shining. "I want to be a trained nurse."

Victoria smiled. "Then I held my old sweetheart's hand for half an hour and blushed like a schoolgirl a few times. It was very strange, but I survived."

Chapter Eleven

The Cathédrale Notre-Dame d'Amiens was twice as large as its counterpart in Paris, and perched on a lofty outcropping high above the rest of the Picardy region to flaunt itself at the enemy. Since the start of the war, clergy and congregation and citizens stacked pyramids of sandbags, the same ones that protected the trenches, against the inner and outer walls. Its medieval stained glass windows and priceless art had been stripped away and sent to safety, but under the soaring thirteenth-century nave, services continued in a sanctuary narrowed by towers of sand.

From the high, Gothic towers, the bells tolled a long, dolorous carillon as Victoria and Nora walked to the hospital, edging their way through an unusual morning crowd of foot traffic on the cobbled walkways headed toward the church.

"Where is everyone going at this hour?" Victoria asked.

"The funeral." Nora looked over her shoulder at the crowd. "Father Arnaud passed away Monday. Didn't you know?"

"I didn't. How awful."

Her cheeks burned with shame at having missed such important news, likely because she was engulfed in hopeless romantic daydreams. She looked down at her dress, a stylish new drop-waist design Georgia Rigby sent her that summer. It was out of season, but it was the prettiest thing she owned and flattered her complexion like nothing else in her small wardrobe. The peach cotton silk and ivory lace bloomed like a flower next to Nora's sedate work uniform, and her rolled-brim hat sported an ivory plaid ribbon over her long blonde braid twisted into a chignon.

"Should I go?" Victoria asked. "Would it be entirely disrespectful to go in this?"

"It's all right. You promised Matthew you'd see him today."

"I didn't tell him what time I would come. I'm off all day, so I could go to the service and come by after."

Nora took her hand. "Wear your pretty dress and visit a handsome soldier. It's your day off. Father Arnaud did the same on his days off, didn't he?"

"His vestments were prettier than a lot of my dresses." Victoria smiled. The elderly priest who visited the hospital was a favorite among the staff for his good humor and gentle encouragement. "What a terrible loss for us all. He had such a calming presence. The military chaplains are all lovely, but they are military. He allowed the men to separate themselves from ranks and battles a bit more."

"Anything to separate yourself from ranks and battles seems like a fine idea to me," Nora said. "Now even the sweetest, gentlest priest has given up and gone home to God. How much longer can this go on?"

"Maudie says they've mobilized over a million American men already and are drafting even more."

"Yes, first it's your dear Matthew and then it will be your friends and neighbors as it has been mine. England will run out of men. They'll have all the unmarried nurses they want at the end of this."

"Nora, you have been so blue lately. What can I do for you, dearest? You are not acting like yourself."

"Perhaps I am ill. I don't know. Every night I feel I could sleep for a week, and in the morning I am never rested. Some days I feel achy, but the next day it's gone and I have no fever." She straightened her shoulders. "But since today is your day off, I am on the schedule as first assistant for Dr. Bowden and I am feeling my best. Dr. Wentworth is Bridget's problem today."

They parted at the archway to the courtyard and Victoria climbed the stairs to the administrative offices. The heavy wooden door was open and a red-headed young woman greeted her while biting her nails.

"Oh Victoria, how pretty you look today!" she chirped, rising from her seat at a tidy desk. "Can I help you with something?"

"Thank you, Rosemarie. I'm looking for a soldier's belongings, please."

"Which soldier?"

"Corporal Matthew Berger. It'll be an American army kit. He arrived on Tuesday with Dickie Lampett, if that helps."

"Ooh, I'll have a look."

Rosemarie MacDougal was a curly-haired, energetic VAD worker pathologically unable to keep her fingernails out of her mouth. The nurses and doctors had tried every concoction from soap to quinine under her nails until Dr. Bowden, who had little patience for any unsanitary habit, lost his temper when he saw her nibble a nail before picking up a bandage roll. He said the matron needed to give her an office job and keep her out of the kitchen, the sterilizing rooms, the laundry, and away from anyone with open wounds. Nurse Perry, who made an exception to the uniform rules to allow her kind-hearted volunteer to wear nail varnish to motivate her, put her in charge of mail and the lost and found. Bowden settled for it, even if she did distribute the mail herself. No one ate, slept on, or dressed their wounds with the mail.

Rosemarie pulled file after file from a neat stack, and her frown deepened with every one she opened. "He came with Dickie? Oh dear. Why do I have Thursday's and Wednesday's inventory, but not Tuesday's?"

Victoria shuffled her feet. "Can I help you look?"

"Sure can." Rosemarie led her to a tiered shelf of boxes marked with dates. "Try that box over there. I should have four boxes from Tuesday. What's an American kit look like, anyway?" she asked, peeking into a crate.

"I guess about the same as all the others, come to think of it, unless there's insignia. I don't see anything like that in here."

Rosemarie cast a longing glance back at the folders. "I really must ask Nurse Perry for another volunteer to learn the system and not just whoever she has free to help each day." She extracted a loose canteen from one crate and peered at the tattered canvas cover. "Oh, rats."

"I'm sure it's here someplace, dear."

"Second thought, probably mice." She closed the crate and poked a fingernail between her teeth. "The rats are mainly by the river, aren't they? There's better eating up there, what with all the restaurants."

Victoria stared. "I suppose if I were a rat, that's where I would like to be."

Rosemarie beamed and pulled a loose paper from the mess in another crate. "Well, finally. Someone just shoved the paperwork in here for some reason. And of course Dickie's records are always a mess. Can you read this scribble?"

"It looks like 'Cpl M J Berger USA' to me." Victoria spotted the haversack pinned with the inventory number and lifted it from the box.

"How'd you make sense of that?"

"It's just messy. Try translating scribbles in another language."

"Ooh, that explains it." She slapped her forehead. "Dickie's Welsh."

Victoria tried to slow her steps and keep from running to room five, but she stopped short in the doorway when she saw Matthew sitting up and back in uniform, watching her with a broad grin.

"We look fine and fancy today, don't we, Miss Harper?"

His olive green shirt had been sweaty and streaked with dirt when he arrived Tuesday. Now it was crisp and starched over his clean wool breeches, tied up below the left knee. His laundered and pressed uniform coat lay folded over the end of the bed.

"You look awfully handsome, soldier," she drawled, swinging his khaki haversack from hand to hand.

"And you look mighty pretty, darling. Have you got something there for me?"

She giggled and held out her hand. "Have you got something for me?"

"Anything you want," he whispered. He kissed her fingers and breathed in rosebuds. "You are a vision, Victoria. I want to take a photograph of you right here and now in your pretty peach dress. I haven't seen your beautiful hair all week since you must keep it covered."

She unpinned her thick blonde braid and pulled it over her shoulder as she sat on the edge of his bed. "It's still here."

"Will you untie it for me?"

"It's so long now. It will be a terrible mess without a hairbrush."

He pouted. "Please. It's for my morale."

"Bother your morale. I'm so happy to see you out of that hospital garb, though. You look more like yourself." She stroked his sleeve. "They didn't give you a pair of pajamas, though?"

"They offered." He nodded at Cartwright in his striped flannel garb. "I am already tired of looking like a broken man. Since the breeches have a lace-up bottom anyway, Swann can check my leg and I can feel a little more like myself."

"Whatever suits you, Matthew."

"Your little friend Miss Russell found my things in the laundry and brought them up this morning. I had her send me an orderly to help me dress since I don't think I can ask you for that. Or can I?"

She tapped his shoulder. "I'll wave my loose hair in your face before I'm allowed to help you dress, silly. If you have any other clothes in this pack, leave them out and we'll get those laundered, too."

"Are we still going for my first stroll in the courtyard?"

"You are not strolling. I am strolling and pushing a wheeled chair for you."

"I have to learn to use these." He pointed at the crutches next to his bed. "I have to beat Cartwright on Tuesday. Dr. Swann said that in addition to my exercises, I should get up on my crutches as much as I can manage, starting today."

"Believe me, you'll only want to go a little ways at a time on those at first. I'll find an orderly to help, because I cannot catch you if you stumble." She squeezed his hand. "And there will be stumbles at first. Lots of them. You might not like me to see that, and I understand."

"I imagine you do understand." He looked over her shoulder to the courtyard where two convalescents pitched a beanbag between them. "Probably better than most people."

"I just meant that I won't be offended if you don't want me present for—"

"I want you there. Please. The surgeon in the field hospital said if I let him remove my pride along with my foot, healing would come easier. Humility seems practical." He reached for the bag before she could protest. "Let's see what's left in here."

"No rations, I assure you. The administrative offices have mice."

"They can have that disgusting biscuit. You could break your teeth on it."

She tried to look in the bag. "Do you have that letter for me to mail?"

"What letter?"

"You said you wrote home already but hadn't posted it."

He rummaged through the pack and didn't look up. "I decided to re-write it. I wasn't in the best state and feared I wasn't going to make it, so it was perhaps a little too honest. One of the girls brought paper and pencils around the ward yesterday evening." He pointed to a sealed envelope on his bedside table, addressed to his parents.

Victoria nodded. "I wrote to Maudie and posted it this morning. I told her she can tell Cooper but no one else until they hear anything from your family. I hope that's all right."

"Of course it's all right. You saved me a letter and I have many of them to write now. Look at this." He pulled out a small Bible and shook out a family photograph. "My next round of correspondence. It is awfully good that I still have my hands."

The photograph was dated 1899, and seven smiling children posed on the steps of a beach house in sailor suits and dresses. Victoria tapped the youngest boy's face, surrounded by the four girls. "This explains a great deal about your spoiled baby brother. I don't think I put everyone's birth order together before. Everyone was grown or close to it when I met you."

"William, me, Angeline, Estella, Catherine, Lillian, Anthony." He tapped their faces. "A lot of letters to write." He glanced back in the bag and grimaced. "I'll get the rest of that later. Canteen, ammunition, and other souvenirs. Filthy laundry."

"I can get those washed up," she said, reaching for the bag just as he pulled it back.

"Not now," he said. "Let's go outside."

"Let's. But first, I promised you this." She dug in her

pocket and handed him a photograph. "I had an autochrome done because you just can't tell how handsome Edgar is without color. Isn't he lovely?"

"You had an autochrome made of your parrot?" He stifled a laugh and traced the blue feathers with his fingertip. "Of course you did. And he is very handsome indeed. What else does he say, besides your name and 'furthermore?'"

"He can ask for a cookie or an apple. Those are his favorite treats. He usually sits in a big cage by my mother's front window but she lets him out to flap around. When he says 'window' it means he wants another view."

"Clever little fellow." He tapped the bird's beak and set the photograph aside. "Are you ready?"

She kissed his forehead. "I'll find you a chair."

"Are you allowed to do that?"

"Of course I am. They're for the patients."

"No." He tapped his forehead. "That."

"What?"

"You just kissed me."

"I did not."

"Oh, but you did."

"Did I?"

"You did, and it was very sweet."

"I didn't mean to do that. I shouldn't do that." Her cheeks flushed. It was an old habit, sneaking kisses with him. It felt as normal and natural as breathing, but with a tiny quiver when she wondered if it really was just habit, just homesickness, or something else pulling her lips ever closer to his.

"Holding hands in uniform is acceptable, but a sweet little kiss like that on your day off isn't?" He shook his head. "The Red Cross will get a sternly-worded letter from an American attorney shortly, lodging an official complaint about its inconsistent, insipid, and damned inconvenient rules."

She giggled and the knot in her stomach loosened. "You do write a blistering complaint. My hero will always win the war of words."

"Then perhaps the sacrifice was worth it."

Chapter Twelve

"Nurse Harper!" Dickie Lampett bent forward, hands on his knees to catch his breath while Victoria untangled a wheeled chair from a room full of stretchers and machinery. "Nurse Harper, oh thank goodness. Dr. Bowden needs you right away."

"I'm off today, Dickie." She kicked the edge of a rolling table and dislodged it from the spoked wheel. There wasn't an orderly to be found and she couldn't help Matthew onto his crutches on her own, but he was determined to get out of doors. "You'll have to grab someone else."

"There is no one else," he panted, brushing back his red hair with a dirty hand. His face was damp with perspiration and mud streaked his coat. "Mine was the first ambulance but there's two or three more coming. He said to get everyone, but there's hardly anyone to get. Dr. Swann's upstairs now and two of the young docs, but there's only four nurses on surgery now."

"What happened?" She looked past his red-rimmed eyes

and up the stairs toward the clatter of steel trays and instruments in the operating rooms.

"Some boys was playing in the old trenches and tunnels down the river out of town. Something blew up, and it all caved in and set off another explosion. They're digging people out and the beams was all split up. We've got wood shrapnel and muck, and it might've been grenades because there was a bunch of steel shards, too. One of 'em got my arm bad while I was digging. I had three people in my truck, and more's coming. A bunch of 'em's kids."

Victoria took the stairs two at a time in her high-heeled boots. She grabbed a surgical gown and cap from the first cart she saw and yanked them on as she opened the door to Dr. Bowden's operating suite.

"Where do you need me?"

He jerked his head toward a tray filled with bits of bloody metal and didn't look up from his patient's abdomen. "It's Swiss cheese in here. I can't close this up for another twenty minutes at least. Get us going, Harp. Wentworth is already setting up for whoever's yowling out there and I just sent Swann and McClellan to get another room started. From the sound of it, I'd like five rooms either going or ready until we have a better grasp of the situation. Cancel whatever else was scheduled." He squinted at his forceps. "Nurse Scott, give Hawkins the smaller retractor, please. Hawkins, on my left, just there."

"Dickie said he's been running all over and we don't have enough help," Victoria said. "We don't have enough staff for five rooms."

Bowden sighed. "Shit. The funeral."

"We planned a light schedule for the morning only, sir,"

Nora said. "Everyone agreed to work late to make up for it. We'll have a full staff at one o'clock."

The clock read ten-fifteen.

"Dr. Bowden, do any of your men have experience in pediatrics?" Victoria asked. "Dickie said there were children in this accident."

"Trowbridge and Carraker." He cursed under his breath. "And if I'm here, Carraker might be at the funeral. Shit. Trowbridge might be in quarters since he worked last night. Jennings. Maybe Fitzpatrick."

"Do I have your permission to pull nurses and physicians from the medical ward and call in staff off-shift, sir?"

"Yes. Go on."

She grabbed Dickie's hand in the hallway. "Go to the physicians' quarters first. Tell them Dr. Bowden wants doctors Trowbridge, Jennings, and Fitzpatrick especially, Dr. Carraker if he's there, and really anyone who's free. Tell them we have children coming and we need any specialists. If you find another orderly or one of the VAD girls on your way, send them to the medical ward or the nurses' quarters for anyone they can spare until we know how bad it is. I want everyone with good French since these boys will be local. Get them yourself if you can't find anyone else to send, but you get the doctors first." She eyed his bloody coat. "Then get back here so we can have a look at your arm."

He bobbed his head and disappeared down the hall.

Victoria looked to her left. "Frances. Go to the schoolyard and meet the next ambulances. Fill rooms seven and eight and we'll start surgeries as rooms open. You tell Marlene and her girls to get to work washing out those wounds, but do not stitch any of them up unless they are gushing blood. Tetanus antiserum for everyone, no exceptions. When extra nurses come, send them where you see fit."

Victoria spotted a nervous young nurse squeezing against the wall behind a stretcher with a groaning young man on it. "Betty. We need supplies. You've done a basic operating room setup before, haven't you?"

"Yes, Nurse Harper."

"Get three carts ready for cases. Instrument trays, drapes, iodine and antiseptics. Emily and Agnes down in the sterilizing room will tell you just what we need. Then we want irrigation setups ready for the doctors. Those wounds will be filthy."

"Is that you, Harper?" Dr. Wentworth's voice rose in the hallway. "Get in here!"

The faces and noises around her blurred as Victoria called out instructions and dodged the groaning patient, but her mouth fell open when she entered room twelve. Bridget cowered in a corner among scattered instruments from a tipped-over tray, trembling as Wentworth and two orderlies, all splattered in blood and dirt, held a thrashing man to the table.

"Knock him out." He jerked his head at the gas tanks and kept his left hand planted firmly on the man's inner thigh. "I don't know how much morphine this bloody bastard's had, but it's not enough."

"Dr. Wentworth, I am not trained to operate the new Connell machine." Victoria's heart thudded when she looked at Bridget, the muddy cuts across her hands, and the dirt on the patient's fingers.

"You've seen enough of the old ones. You know how—

dammit!" The patient flailed and hit his back. "You know how. Do it."

"But surely you could—"

"Oh, surely I could, Harp, and surely you can just shove your pretty little hand in here and hold the fellow's femoral artery away from this goddamn chunk of lumber lodged in his leg. Do it."

She bit back a sarcastic reprimand for calling her Harp, but turned her gaze to the Connell machine and all her ire fell away. The old anesthetometers had gauges in different places, different valves. The newer machine could be twice as accurate but required more settings and more training. She traced the paths of the ether, nitrous oxide, and oxygen through tubes and the flowmeter with her eyes.

"Do it," Wentworth demanded. "That's an order."

She spun to face him. "The army does not order the Red Cross to do anything."

"Do you want to pull one of the other doctors away from helping a child? This man will die if I cannot have him calm enough to fix this. I can't say it any more plainly."

Victoria approached the head of the bed and spoke in her best guidebook French.

"What's your name?" *Comment t'appelles?*

"He's Philippe Bouton," one of the orderlies said, wincing as he tried to hold the man's leg still.

"Philippe, *Je m'appelle* Victoria. Is it your son?" *Ton fils?*

The man's clenched jaw loosened.

"What's his name, Philippe? We will get news of him."

"Fran—Fran—"

Victoria nodded at Bridget. "Nurse Walker, please get us a

new supply cart, then go out front and find what news you can of Francois Bouton."

The man blinked rapidly, his neck corded with strain. "*Merci.*"

"Shhh." She held his gaze. "Breathe slowly now while I place this over your nose. Look at me. We'll take care of Francois and bring you news."

The patient was a large man and thick around the neck, eyes bulging with desperation. She pumped the blood pressure cuff and tried to pray as the mercury level dropped.

Please-please beat in time with the *thump-thump* of Philippe Bouton's heart.

One of Bowden's friends had sent the new anesthesia machine from America only weeks before. She listened when he taught but hadn't so much as turned a dial on her own. It was always operated by a physician, and the only physician in the room was occupied.

One-hundred and thirty kilos to be on the safe side, she thought, assessing the patient's size, and he had some unknown amount of morphine already in his blood. Not enough to help, or perhaps it hadn't set in. An ether drop would be more risky.

"Harp, for God's sake, hurry up," Wentworth barked.

She adjusted the dials and opened the valve.

Four hours later, she leaned her forehead on the cool glass of the classroom window and looked over the empty courtyard. She'd looked out once before, after they finished with Bouton, and saw Matthew in a wheeled chair laughing while

Major Cartwright demonstrated his technique on crutches. When he pushed up on the arms of the chair, ready to stand, her eyes burned. The next case came, and the next. Even Dickie had been dosed with tetanus antiserum and was now curled in a corner with irrigation hooked up to a gouge in his arm from digging among the metal shards in the mud. The ambulance driver was twenty but looked only twelve, like one of the boys in the tunnel, and was fast asleep.

Wentworth approached behind her. "Everyone's back to work, Harp. Want to have a smoke?"

She looked at his smug grin and tempered her disdain. "No, Giles, I don't."

"All right then, Nurse Harper. Want a smoke?"

"No thank you, Dr. Wentworth."

She turned back to the window, away from the piles of linens and trays of instruments crammed haphazardly along the wall. Everything was muddy, bloody, or both.

The old trenches and tunnels were several kilometers from the city, but the sound of an explosion had pricked Dickie's ears as he stood in front of the cathedral before Father Arnaud's service that morning. It wasn't a battlefield noise to anyone else—only a rumble that could have been thunder, since the battles had moved beyond earshot. But the cathedral sat on the highest point in the region, and Dickie looked east just in time to see a puff of debris rise and fall over the artillery-shredded field. Another followed close by.

In a mad dash that would earn him *La Croix de Guerre* from the French army, Dickie ran for his ambulance and dragged a friend along just in case the sinking feeling in his stomach was right. The battlefields were littered with unexploded ordnance, the same kind that nearly killed Matthew, and the French government had named it a crime for any civilian to go within their dangerous boundaries. Without one observant ambulance driver following a hunch, those trapped in the tunnel might have died there unless the two wounded boys on the surface could cross the fields and summon help.

The day's blasts cost one boy a leg and one an eye and caved in the tunnel over their friends, causing crush injuries, hammering them with wooden splinters from shattered beams, and nearly suffocating them.

"You were bloody fantastic today," Wentworth said. "Just unflappable."

"Hm."

"Come on. How about a smile? Most nurses would be happy to hear something like that."

"Most nurses didn't miss something very important today." She cleared her throat. "But of course that is not your fault, sir. If you have enough help for the rest of the patients, I have someone to see."

"We're fine here."

"Good day, Dr. Wentworth."

"Harp—Nurse Harper, wait."

"What?"

"May I count on your discretion?"

She shook her hair out of her surgical cap and raised a brow. "You would like me to not tell the colonel that you ordered me to anesthetize a man with no training and attempted to pull rank on the Red Cross?"

"Do you think he'll care that you did it? You did a cracking job, but if there's any blame, I'll take it. I'll tell them I called out the settings and you just moved the dials. I know it takes a hell of a lot more attention to manage an airway on a fellow that size, and you did it." He blew out a deep breath. "But that's not what I meant."

"What, then?"

Dickie flailed a little with the splint on his arm and let out a snore as if on cue. Wentworth shot him a glance, then ignored him.

"You are obviously very well-read in our field and you don't play coy. I imagine nurses know this subject matter more intimately than most physicians anyway. How long from the time a woman misses her courses should she definitely know she is with child?"

She froze. "Most women know in a month or two. That's fairly common knowledge, sir."

"I meant, at what point do we say she *must* know? Women start showing at different times in their pregnancies. Babies are born bigger or smaller all the time and it's not... well, people are easily fooled because people are taught to be foolish."

Britain went to war three years after Giles Wentworth finished his medical training. By necessity, his expertise was in battlefield injuries and contagious diseases. Whatever he learned about reproduction might be gathering dust with his textbooks back in Flannelcloth Humbug or whatever Matthew called it. Victoria looked at the violet circles under his eyes and thought of his wife.

"You are trying to work out if a child might or might not be yours."

"That is correct. Please spare me your blushes. We are both professionals."

A little warmth crept into her chest at the uncharacteristic acknowledgement. "A pregnancy is made when a man and woman are intimate about two weeks before the first course she misses. Sometimes, that makes it very simple. But not all ladies are regular. Do you know if she is?"

"I don't."

"There's about a week in each woman's monthly cycle when she is most likely to become pregnant. About two weeks after that, if she has conceived, she may start to miss her courses." Victoria ticked off symptoms on her fingers. "She might also feel sick in the morning with nausea, vomiting, and the like. Tenderness in the breasts, sometimes in the belly. Her appetite may change."

"But not definitely."

"No. That makes it tricky. Not all women have all symptoms. Some have none. Some have irregular bleeding throughout. Unless the woman is very regular to begin with and she recalls days when she and her husband were intimate, it is difficult to put a precise date on a pregnancy until the child quickens." She watched his face crease with worry, lines making deep shadows in the waning light from the window. "Of course, there are so many complications to a woman's cycle. I am sure your wife is quite worried for you, and nerves and anxious feelings can affect her."

"I was last with her ten weeks ago, so this should have been clear three or four weeks ago, should it not?"

She fidgeted. "I wish I could give you a simple truth, but without knowing the lady's circumstance, I cannot answer that."

Exhaling deeply, he slouched against the wall and scrubbed his hands over his face. "God, what a fix. This war is hell, and women—well, the women back home don't know what it does to a man, and I don't know how to explain it. The last time I was home, Gloria said I'm not the man she married. Who the hell is the same person they were before this bloody war? I'd like to know."

"You did well today, too, Dr. Wentworth." Her throat scratched. "I wasn't going to tell on you for anything, you know. We did the best we could with what we had. That's all we can ever do."

He gestured at the mess in the room. "How the hell am I supposed to go home after all this and save men whose fate is their own stupid fault? Soldiers are one thing. Does it feel different to you when it's an adult man who led children into danger?" he asked. "That bastard Bouton. I spotted some thick scars on his knee and guess the French army wouldn't have him. He went to the trenches anyway, and those boys could have died while he played war and made artillery noises. It sickens me."

"You didn't flinch when he was on the table, though. It didn't occur to you to resent him then. You saved his life."

"I suppose I did. We did."

Dickie snored again. Victoria folded the last clean sheet in the room into a tight bundle and placed it under his head.

"If that's all, Dr. Wentworth, I would like to go."

"Go see your fellow. And thank you."

Chapter Thirteen

Victoria trudged across room five with aching ankles and knees. Her dress had been protected by her surgical gown, but her good boots, pretty brown and cream leather with high heels, were dotted with dirt and blood. Her hat hung limply in her hand, its jaunty bow crumpled.

"I'm sorry," she whispered, pulling her chair to Matthew's side. "I'm so, so sorry I disappeared like that."

"Shh." He took her hands. "You were doing your job. It had to be done."

"I was supposed to take you outside today."

"I got out. It's all right."

"I missed helping you get up, didn't I?"

"I was only up for a moment. You were right about the crutches. The chair was fine. I doubt I'll be in racing shape on Tuesday, though."

She scrunched her eyes shut to fight the tears again. "I missed it."

"Vi, it's okay. Look, right after you left, one of the girls came down and told me she'd seen you go running. Marie Howard. She said before you ran into an operating room, you called out and told her to tell me. I didn't sit here pouting or anything."

"I don't even remember seeing her up there. My head was just spinning. Marie is one of my housemates. She's a very sweet girl."

"She and Miss Russell adore you, you know."

Her cheeks burned. "I try to set a good example for the younger girls. I'm glad they cannot see me like this. Matthew, it was as awful as it could be today without someone dying."

He stroked her hand, massaging the tension in her palm. "What happened?"

"A troop of boys were playing in an old trench and a tunnel with their fathers on the other side of the river. There was an explosion and the tunnel caved in. Crushed ribs, inhaled dirt, and that was the easy part."

He closed his eyes. "Bastards."

"Whether you mean the Germans or these particular fathers, I agree. One of the boys lost an eye to a splintered beam. The one who stepped on the explosives lost his left foot."

"How old is he?"

"Twelve."

Matthew glanced at his leg and across the room at the other patients. "You could put him down here with me and Cartwright, you know. He might not know how lucky he is to have all the important parts still attached."

She smiled. "It is just like you to have a sense of humor about these things. What a wretched little club you have here. Dr. Bowden put that little exploring party in room seven together. The boys are so scared and their mothers are half furious, half terrified. Our poor ambulance driver is the hero of the day, and now he's asleep on the floor because he wouldn't take a bed in case we needed it."

"All of you do a job I cannot fathom. The military must be here, but you and the other girls choose this calling and thousands of men should be grateful for it." He pulled her messy braid over her shoulder and stroked it. "How beautiful you look right now."

"You flatter me. I am exhausted, and I look it."

"But that peach color suits you so well, and you're here with me when I know you are longing for a hot bath and your bed. I cannot imagine a prettier picture of your sweetness and devotion, and not just to me. To doing the things you do that others cannot."

The words should have thrilled her, but her voice shook. "I feel like my lungs aren't pulling enough air. I ran the anesthesia machine today. I'm not supposed to do that. I had to do it though, so I did, for an entire case until the next doctor got there."

"Will you get in trouble, if there was no one else to do it?"

She leaned forward and squeezed her eyes shut a moment too late and two tears leaked out. "I don't know. I never want to do that again, Matt. Never. Do not make me out to be a hero. I felt so stupid and helpless and just guessing about what I remembered while his life was in my hands. I could have set a dial wrong and put him so far down he couldn't wake up."

He pulled her close to his shoulder and she rested her cheek on him. "I'm sure that patient appreciated what you did."

"He took children to play in a field so dangerous the government has made it a crime to go there. I missed your first steps on crutches because of it. I don't care what he appreciates. He's a horrible father and he has a fat neck."

Matthew choked on a laugh. "What's a fat neck have to do with it?"

"Your muscles relax under anesthesia, but when there is a lot of fat in the neck, it puts pressure on those muscles and the airway can close. Dr. Bowden always tells us we are spoiled by military men being fairly fit to begin with. You have fewer complications when you're healthy before you get hurt."

"How's my neck?"

She trailed her fingers along his jawline and over his ear while his heart pounded against her cheek. Down to his collar, then back over his head, she fought the urge to tangle her hands in his black hair and instead traced a light path with her fingernails until he shivered.

"Your neck is military-grade. Top quality. How's mine?"

He cupped her head in his palm. Sliding his hand down her neck, he twisted his fingers in her hair and pulled loose strands as he stroked her skin, forward along her ear and over her throat.

"Delectable. Highly kissable, if the nurse is so inclined."

She sat up. "Oh, goodness. No. Not here. I shouldn't have been cozying up to you like that."

"You had a horrible day, Vi, and you're not in uniform. You won't get in trouble."

"Who knows what I'll get in trouble for today?" She pressed her hand to her head. "My God. I ran the Connell machine. On a civilian. A non-conflict civilian casualty. Oh no. I'm sure there are rules about that. The Red Cross has a book of rules the size of Belgium."

"The Red Cross says a boost to my morale can cancel out another infraction."

A smile quirked a corner of her mouth. "I could be inclined toward a little kiss, maybe."

"A little kiss? After all this time, darling, if I'm in for the penny, I'm in for the pound."

He scooted up on his pillows and kissed her, burying his hands in her tangled hair as he held her close. Her lips softened on his as he drew her in with familiar tenderness and a warmth that wrapped her entire body, and she reached for him. In her haze there was no homesickness, only a memory, only a man, and a kiss untarnished by the years.

Chapter Fourteen

Seven Years Ago: 1910

A grand hotel opened in Nag's Head, North Carolina in the summer of 1910, filled with ballrooms and fine dining and luxurious suites. Its gables and shingled walls took their inspiration from the older homes on the waterfront called the Cottage Row, the legacy of quieter days in the island town that grew a little more crowded every summer since the Wright Brothers' flight at nearby Kitty Hawk caught the country's imagination a few years before.

For a year after ducking Matthew's proposal at Cooper and Maudie Truxton's wedding, Victoria had managed to avoid him. Her sister Edith excused her from family events if Matthew planned to attend. Maudie, deeply uncomfortable with her passive role in the entire mess, kept up a similar plan and shot fierce glares at her new husband every time Cooper threw up his hands and exclaimed that their friends were obviously in love and just needed to talk about it.

"She must hear him out," Cooper complained every time

his wife tried to manipulate a guest list. "He'll explain. It all makes perfect sense to me, you know. And furthermore, I'm sick of his grumbling."

"And furthermore," Maudie mocked.

Maudie's family and Matthew's had homes next to each other on the Cottage Row and had made the journey from Raleigh to the seaside every year as long as they could remember. The seven Berger children and the two Hamilton children spent months in and out of each other's homes, taking sandy walks and wading, swapping spaces on trundle beds and bunks so Maudie could giggle with Angeline and Estella Berger and Matthew could stay up arguing politics with Jeremiah Hamilton.

What city clothes they brought were rarely unpacked—towering floral hats gave way to straw boaters, high-necked blouses to summery cotton dresses, wool suits to linen and comfortable breeches, ties loosened or abandoned. Parents lingered on deep porches to read, gossip, and make sure no one drowned. Trips to town netted saltwater taffy and fresh seafood, and driftwood fires filled the air with green and purple flames at night.

"Get away for a month," Maudie wheedled that summer. "It's your last chance before the hardest part of your training begins and you won't have any free time for another year. Didn't you say you'll be practically living at the hospital? And all the way down in Durham?" She threw her arms wide. "The salt air will invigorate you. Nine out of ten doctors agree. I saw it in a magazine."

"Are you mad?" Victoria asked, so aghast she nearly dropped Maudie's newborn daughter. "You had a baby six days ago, and you want to go to the beach next month?"

"Of course I do. We always go to the shore in July, and won't it be fine to recuperate somewhere so peaceful?" Maudie blew her little girl a kiss. "My dear Cecelia agreed to come as nanny, but perhaps she can enjoy a vacation as well since you and my mother won't let Emmeline out of your hands for a minute."

Maudie and Cooper's baby daughter was an object of wonder to Victoria. She'd seen a thousand babies, even helped deliver a few, but none of them mesmerized her like little Emmeline Truxton. In one light, she was entirely her mother in looks and sweet temperament. In another light, she was fully her father's daughter and as bright and excited to be alive as he. No biology textbook or lesson on genetics prepared her to understand this tiny person who despite her robust little frame seemed not yet fully formed, a shape-shifter in no hurry to choose who she would be.

A few weeks to snuggle the baby before disappearing into a year of hospital training was a tempting prospect, if only...

Victoria fidgeted, picking at her cuticles. "Will Matthew be there?"

"He won't. He's in Washington, D.C. this summer for a clerkship and it's all through June and July."

"Are you sure?"

"It's what Angeline says."

"But are you sure?"

"She should know. He's her brother."

"I'd rather hide out in the hospital for a year than face him."

"Victoria, please." Maudie squeezed her hands. "Please come. Everything is changing so fast, and the beach is where it all stands still for a little while. I was married only a year ago and now I'm a mother... and it's all a delight, but you're going somewhere different now. Stop time with me. Let's have a summer."

Stop time with me. Such words from Maudie's lips oozed seductive sweetness. She had a magnetism, a gravitational pull as powerful to her friends as it once was to her many suitors, and Victoria loved to be in her orbit. Their paths would diverge soon. Hospital nursing excited and invigorated her, but it would pull her away from her friends and family.

It was one word, one choice, one month at a beautiful oceanfront home with her dear friend, but she tiptoed toward it like something lurked beneath the whitecaps and beckoned her into dark water.

"Imagine." Maudie closed her eyes. "Imagine blustery days and sun hats that go flying. Imagine white linen dresses and bathing costumes and saltwater taffy. Imagine blue, blue skies over the bluest, bluest ocean with gentle waves and—"

"Yes."

Maudie opened her eyes and clapped. "You can't take it back. And if Matthew shows up, we'll put him on a boat and tell Cooper he's his problem."

Despite the casual schedule and dress at the shore, the 'cottages' on the Cottage Row were Victorian luxury like most of their occupants' city homes, only disguised by shingled walls, nautical knick-knacks, and hurricane shutters that creaked when the winds kicked up. The Bergers' and the Hamiltons' homes boasted six bedrooms apiece, with hammocks for night owls and quarters for servants. Two weeks into July, the houses bustled with activity and stray sand. Evenings were starry and breezy on porch swings with books or blankets on the sand with wine and laughter. Victoria stole time with baby Emmeline, gossiped and shopped with Maudie and Angeline, and pestered her sister about every milestone of her pregnancy.

"I want to know how it feels," she said, loading a bowl with shrimp and potatoes from a deep stockpot of tidewater boil. Dinner was at the Bergers', a casual affair as always, where everyone made a dish and found a seat where it suited them.

"Fat," Edith said. "I feel fat already, even though I hardly look it."

"I mean your insides. In the diagrams, it shows how uterus tilts and—"

"Victoria, do not say uterus in company," Edith hissed. "For goodness' sake."

"We're not in company. We're dishing our own dinner into mismatched bowls on vacation."

"You may not say the names of body parts or organs around my husband's family."

Victoria bit her lip. "All right. Does it feel funny inside? Do you feel like your—like the rest of your insides have moved around?"

"Am I supposed to?"

"Of course. It all has to go somewhere." She poked a shrimp into her mouth and chewed quickly. "Maybe it just hasn't moved around yet. It's early days, of course, and my textbook said—"

"Matty!"

Anthony Berger ran through the front room and

launched himself at his older brother, nearly shoving him out the front door when he tried to come in.

Victoria's face went white and Edith caught her bowl just in time to save the rug.

"What are you doing here early?" Anthony demanded, clapping Matthew on the shoulder. "Mother thought you were gone another week or two."

"Did she? I finished up last week." Matthew hugged his little brother and slid his suitcase across the hardwood floor to rest behind a side table, as if the place was waiting for him. He surveyed the room with a proprietorial smile as Victoria ducked behind Edith.

"I'm not complaining." Anthony grinned. "Now it's really summer."

Matthew made his rounds and called greetings to his brothers and sisters as he zig-zagged through the room. Victoria hustled Edith aside.

"Please make my excuses," she said. "I'm going back to the other house. Maudie just went over to nurse the baby a minute ago."

Edith bent her head to whisper. "Has it ever occurred to your nosy little brain to get your own baby if you want so much to know what it's like?"

"Come on, Matthew." His father's voice boomed from the other end of the room. "Beg your mother's forgiveness. She's on the back porch and she'll be furious when she sees you, so best get it over with."

Edith slid the bowl onto a table and did a quick side-step to turn Victoria's back to him as he walked by. "Pull yourself together," she said under her breath. "You are acting like a frightened child."

"Excuse me," Matthew whispered behind her.

He passed his hand over the small of her back, so close in the crowded room that no one but Victoria noticed how he spread his fingers over her waist and trailed his hand along the curve of her spine, almost too low. He curled his fingertips as he walked on, as if to beckon her to follow.

"Why won't she be thrilled that I'm here?" he asked his father. His voice rose over Victoria's head as though he hadn't just seared her with his touch.

"Because she'll have to count beds again. Lillian and Anthony both have friends here this week."

"Oh dear."

"Bunk with us," Maudie's brother Jeremiah called. "We've got room at our house."

Matthew nodded. "Excellent. Mother will be pleased to see me after all."

Victoria looked frantically for Maudie. How long could it take to nurse an infant?

"Truxton and I took the boat out last week," Jeremiah continued. "Let's go again. Trux?"

"Anchors aweigh," Cooper replied drily, taking Victoria's arm. He steered her into the empty living room as Matthew's bold touch still simmered on her back.

"My dear friend," he said, as if he'd prepared an address, "I have a great deal of respect and admiration for you, so forgive me, but my wife has been coddling you and this has to stop."

Victoria stiffened. "It's not really your business."

"It is my business. I know you liked Berger before, and I know you grew out of it right around the time he grew into it. Maudie and I have been friends with him for more than twenty years. That friendship lets bygones be bygones. You have dignity and grace and smarts, Victoria, so why aren't you using them?"

"Are you insulting me or complimenting me?"

He shrugged. "And furthermore, you should consider that if you really think it is impossible for him to let go of his one-time affection for Maudie, that means it is also impossible for you to let go of your one-time affection for him. If Berger's stuck on her forever because he thought that way once, you have to be stuck on him forever."

"That's silly."

"Well, it's your own logic." He rocked up on his toes and back on his heels with a smug smile. "You know, for months, he tried to win your favor."

"He certainly did not. What he said at your wedding came out of the blue like a passing whim, which is frankly a little insulting because he is never unprepared for anything he actually means to say."

"No, he was prepared. He just overshot the target."

She furrowed her brows. "Pardon?"

"He knew what he meant to do and he went a bit too far." Cooper leaned closer. "Tell me, if he'd ended that dance by saying something like 'You are a delightful woman and I enjoy your company, Victoria. I would like to court you properly,' would that have been all right?"

"I suppose so, yes. That would have been very nice, actually."

"Then would you please just give the man a chance to say it?"

She stared.

"Well, there you are." He grinned. "Matthew wants to talk

to you. Please talk to him. Excuse me now while I confess my meddling to my wife and await her wrath."

"Cooper, wait."

He turned around.

"I'm sorry this has affected you. I've been childish."

"I did not mean to insult you."

"You didn't." Victoria kept her voice steady and was pleased to notice her hands had stopped shaking. "We are friends, and you were honest. I think I shall go take a long look in the mirror and examine my thoughts. I'll address things tomorrow with a fresh outlook."

He perked up. "Please don't tell Maudie?"

"I won't. She is very sweet and protective, but you make some very good points."

"Oh, then by all means, do tell her."

She escaped to the front porch and the hush of the waves. A deep breath of cool salt air calmed her as she leaned on the railing, holding out an open hand to catch the breeze. Stars speckled the darkness on the eastern horizon and faded above her where the sunlight still peeked over the house in a wash of magenta and orange.

She pondered the water, dark and inviting beyond the porch lights, and wondered what she was truly afraid of. She had loved him once, before he paid her any mind, but the plans she had committed to since then left no room for romance. Whatever he wanted, the answer would have to be no.

"Hello, Victoria."

The porch swing creaked and she closed her eyes. "Hello, Matthew."

"How are you?"

"I'm well, and you?"

"Exhausted." The aged wood protested when he leaned back in the swing. "The clerkship was a fantastic experience but after six weeks of that, I am in dire need of a rest."

She could picture him patting the seat beside him but she didn't turn around. "I didn't expect to see you here. Angeline said you'd be gone all month."

"A miscommunication."

"A purposeful one?"

"Who's to say?"

She stared at the waves. "I'm glad you had a nice time."

"How is training?"

"Also very busy. The coming year won't leave much time for socializing."

"Indeed. Much the same for me."

"You'll be a real lawyer this time next year."

"You'll be a real nurse."

"I'm a real nurse now. I have my certificate. This is a hospital training program."

"My sister tells me those programs are very selective. It does not surprise me to hear you earned a place." He stood and held out his hand. "Will you walk with me?"

Her heart thudded and drowned out the ocean as she put her hand in his. His eyes in the waning sunlight were still tender and the brush of his lips over her hand was light as a breath.

Courtship had rules, and rules made everyone's intentions clear. Those months before the proposal when Cooper said he was trying to win her favor had passed with long looks and quick touches and words she trained herself to ignore. That was no courtship, only the shade of a friendship and a few pleasant conversations when they saw one another at parties. She didn't want him anymore because he never wanted her until Maudie was gone. When he proposed without ever courting or kissing her, the words rang hollow like he never intended to speak them.

He overshot the target, Cooper said, but he *had* a target.

When they walked off the steps, his nearness warmed her and nudged awake the feelings she tucked away. The tiered skirt of her red seersucker dress lifted in the breeze, but she didn't let go of his hand. His shirt collar was unbuttoned and his tie loosened, and she leaned on his shoulder so she didn't have to look up and be brave at the same time.

"Matthew, I should apologize for how I reacted when we last spoke."

"No, I should apologize for presuming on—well, I don't think I—you see, it's really that—" He kicked the sand. "I only had a year to practice this. Give me a moment."

His flustering unnerved her and she squeezed his hand without thinking. "Please don't apologize. To ask a woman to marry you is a high compliment, and I behaved so rudely."

"I should have thought things out better. Well, I did think them out, you see. I was thinking about them for months. It was just that in the moment I was overcome, and I am not so easily overcome. I am supposed to be rather polished with public speaking and so on, and it was very—I know you know this about me, Victoria, you understand, I am not—oh, Christ."

He dropped her hand, pulled her close, and kissed her.

She kissed him back and quickly drew away, touching her lips. "I didn't intend that."

"I did. That's precisely what I meant to say. Don't go."

She had only moved a few steps in the shifting sand when he caught her arm and pulled her close to the side of the house where the scent of cedar shingles overtook the smell of saltwater. "Do not run away again," he whispered. "Do not tell me that kiss was nothing to you. I should have done it before. I should have told you what I felt months before all that mess and not blurted it out like a fool."

"But you didn't. You didn't feel that way months before."

"Didn't I?"

Victoria could only breathe.

He kissed her again and again, opening her lips with his. The gentle brush of his hand along her neck held her against the wall and stilled the twitch in her feet.

"It has been torment not seeing you and believing I ruined my chance." His breath heated the space around them as he pressed his cheek to hers, whispering as though the ocean might overhear. "Have I ruined it?"

"I don't know. My life is taking a different course now. I will be in Durham so much for my training, and I—"

"I will come to you," he whispered. "If you want me. The course you set for yourself is part of what I admire about you. I wanted so much more of your spirit and your strength, to learn you and love you, and then I botched telling you. I know we only talked closely a few times before but Victoria, those times imprinted on me and I cannot shake them. I have missed you ever since. Tell me you've missed me."

"I've missed you." She stroked his hair back from his forehead and kissed him again. "I am mortified about how I responded, and I should not tell you this but I am still drawn to you in ways I shouldn't be."

"You should be drawn to me." He tipped her head up so

he could kiss her neck. "As I have been drawn to you for a long time. My darling, this is how it should be."

"This is madness."

She kissed him again and spread her hands over his head, his chest, his back, pulling him in with aching need every time he drew back for a breath. The unfamiliar hunger inflamed her, for where had such longing come from in a matter of minutes? Had every reserve and precaution dissolved into the sand with one touch of his lips? Her resolve hadn't bent—it simply shattered.

He kept her close, pinning her shoulders and then her hips to the wall with his weight.

"An honorable man should have proposed before kissing you like this," he murmured. "Perhaps I just wanted so much to kiss you last year I thought I should do things in order."

Her pulse hammered in her wrist as she stroked his face. "You are naturally very orderly. I always liked that about you. You know what you're doing."

"I do. And you disrupt the natural order of things."

She tried to slow her breath. "That doesn't sound like it should appeal to an orderly man."

"It's the only thing that appeals to this one."

The salt and cedar wrapped around them and he kissed her again.

Chapter Fifteen

The weekend in Amiens passed quietly, as it often did since the fighting moved toward Belgium, and reminded Victoria of shift work in peacetime. Home normally felt a million miles away instead of a thousand, but a day without surgeries—a day inspecting dressings and supply carts, wound checks and bedside care with patients and taking her lunch break on time—nudged memories to the surface and left her as restless as she was during her training program and the years after.

Matthew remembered that restlessness, she had no doubt, but he was not so insensitive as to bring it up when he held her in his arms. She gave up a half-dozen tears before regaining her composure the day of the tunnel emergency, and he wiped them from her cheeks without remarking on how much she used to love a hectic day at Raleigh Methodist. She stitched wounds and helped set bones on those hectic days, and left work ablaze with pride and energy because she did something that mattered.

Years ago, she and Matthew had dissected that feeling. He

claimed something similar happened when he had a particularly exuberant day in court and earned a ruling in his favor. They celebrated their triumphs with dinners out or evenings in at his parents' home or hers, sneaking kisses wherever and whenever they could, since they could never be truly alone. She melted at the touch of his lips.

But even in their celebrations back then, tension had gathered in her hands sometimes when they kissed. She would twitch her fingers and set them wildly roaming his body as though clutching him would keep her from falling into the gloomy realization that while Matthew's triumphs were about justice and good, hers could only come when someone was hurt.

On Monday, Victoria was summoned to the head nurse's office.

Philippa Perry was a Boer War veteran like Dr. Bowden. Eagle-eyed and battle-minded, she kept a map on her wall and moved red and black pins every week like a ritual to mark the shifting lines. Behind her back, it was suggested she read the Red Cross rule book on Sundays instead of the Bible.

"Victoria." Nurse Perry crossed her hands on the desk. "I think you know why I asked to speak with you today."

"Yes, ma'am."

She'd anticipated the reprimand. Her defense rested with Dr. Bowden and Dr. Wentworth, who would surely vouch for her overstepping her role during the emergency. No one was hurt. In fact, one man might have died if she didn't run the machine, and the Red Cross should not complain of that.

"I realize one person's circumstance is not the same as the next," Nurse Perry said, "and I value your experience and expertise. I try to do right by you girls and make sure that when discipline is needed, it is to help you learn and grow, not to shame you."

"Of course, ma'am." Victoria's eyes darted around the sparsely furnished room and landed on the map peppered with pinholes around Amiens.

"And to be clear, you answer to the Red Cross, not the Royal Army Medical Corps."

"Yes, ma'am. But if I may explain about what happened Friday, I was authorized to—"

"Nurse Harper, no one authorized you to practically crawl into bed with Corporal Berger."

She gasped. "I did no such thing."

"Then tell me what you did."

It was not the reproach she expected, and Victoria stumbled on her words. "I came here Friday to see him as a visitor, and I was pulled in to help with the tunnel emergency. I worked for more than four hours on my day off, without complaint and in my best shoes, which might be ruined. When I was done, I went back down to see Corporal Berger. I was exhausted. I may have rested against his shoulder for a bit, but I certainly did not crawl into his bed."

"Is there anything else?"

She lifted her chin. "He kissed me. Again, I was not in his bed."

"It is not like you to be so defiant."

"Could a local girl come kiss her sweetheart if he were a patient? I was not in uniform. When I went to help, I did not leave until the work was done and I was dismissed. Then I was a visitor again. I did not break any rules."

It wasn't a lie as long as they were talking about her behavior as a visitor, not as a surgical nurse. Her heart pounded and she drew in a slow breath, willing her body to relax before she snapped and said something regrettably rude. "I am very upset that someone has made it out to you that I was behaving inappropriately. Who said this?"

Nurse Perry ignored her question. "You have spent a lot of time with this young man since he arrived. Your affection for him is obvious. People notice."

"I don't shirk my duties for him, ma'am. I visit on my breaks or after work."

"Victoria, your work ethic has always been impeccable. You are a fine example to our younger girls. But because of your role as a mentor and friend, your deportment has more impact than what we write in any rule book. If Nurse Harper is acting coquettish with a patient, may I do the same? If Nurse Harper is cozying up to a soldier on her time off, is it all right for me?"

Victoria was silent.

"I would rather not lose any more of my trained nurses to marriages with convalescents they've known for two weeks." Nurse Perry stared out the window overlooking the street. "I know you would never display such poor judgment, but you must understand the greater impact you and the other senior nurses have. Soldiers cannot quit, but nurses can quit if they wish or take the more honorable route out of service and get married. We are low on soldiers, Nurse Harper. And we are low on nurses."

"I understand," she whispered, staring at her hands as she

willed herself not to pick at a dry cuticle. “But as to the matter of marrying Corporal Berger—”

“Has he asked you to marry him?”

Victoria dug her nails into her palms, furious at the slip. “Yes, he has. Three times.”

The older woman’s mouth fell open. “He’s been here a week.”

“His brother is married to my sister, and we’ve known one other for ten years. He asked me in 1909, 1911, and 1913. Until he arrived here, I hadn’t seen him since that last time.”

Nurse Perry’s tone softened. “It seems he’s overdue to ask again.”

“Things are quite different now.”

“You are obviously still devoted to one another.”

“I believe I have been strictly professional when I am on my shift. If you believe otherwise, please tell me in plain terms what I should do differently so there is no confusion.”

Nurse Perry sighed and fussed with her gray-streaked black bun as she looked away. “I did not know you had a background with this man and I made some assumptions I shouldn’t have. I apologize. But the fact remains, others will make the same assumptions based on your behavior.”

“If the concern lies with others’ opinions and not facts, perhaps I should post a note in the hall with the details of our romantic history in case anyone assumes I am flinging myself at him for a ticket home.”

“Nurse Harper. Victoria.”

Her fingers twitched with annoyance and she pushed her hands into her apron pockets. “Since I cannot address whoever is spreading misinformation about my conduct and ask why they are so bothered by it, please tell me plainly what you want me to change while Corporal Berger is our patient. I will follow the rules, Nurse Perry, but I must understand exactly what they are."

"It would be better if you contained your social visits to your non-working hours, out of uniform. And perhaps you should not be so outwardly affectionate."

"May I or may I not kiss him while I am off work and not in uniform?"

"Nurse Harper, we do not need to dissect every detail."

"It is a detail that apparently matters to others, and they have made it matter to you." She fought back another urge to spout a snotty defense of her behavior. "I understand and respect what you said about the younger girls seeing me as a role model. What is the rule?"

Nurse Perry stared longingly at her bookshelf as though the Red Cross manual might pop open to a page with clear guidance about off-hours displays of affection that were neither lewd nor strictly forbidden, only inconvenient.

"Use your good judgment," she said, not meeting Victoria's gaze. "I will discount this as a rumor."

"I will have my social visits out of uniform. It would be rude not to speak to him during my shifts, so I will stay at arm's length."

"That is acceptable."

Victoria rose. "Will there be anything else, ma'am? I am scheduled to start cases with the colonel shortly."

"If you will indulge me, why did you decline this man three times when you obviously still care for him? You are careful with yourself, Nurse Harper, and that is why I like the younger girls to look up to you. You are not free with your kisses, I think."

She shook her head. “If I had married him, I would have had to give up everything I worked for. He didn’t have to give up anything. My younger self couldn’t make much sense of that. I wanted to do the work I felt called to do, and he waited longer than most men would have, I think.” She glanced again at the map. “But in the end, the stalemate always breaks.”

“It was exceedingly awkward, girls.” Victoria shook out her hands like they were wet. “Do yourselves a favor and keep away from the patients, lest you have to justify yourselves to Nurse Perry.”

Nora scowled. “I cannot believe someone reported you. Who would do that?”

“I have no idea.”

“We’ll tell all the girls to keep an eye out in room five and see if your man has any female admirers who might want you out of the way. It might be anyone on the first floor of the other buildings, like that nosy Eugenie Baxter in the medical unit across the courtyard. You can see right across.”

“For heaven’s sake, Nora.”

“At least Nurse Perry was a little sympathetic at the end,” Ingrid chirped as she skipped over a hole on the cobbled sidewalk. “She left nursing to get married, and she came back.”

“Yes, but I call widowhood less-than-ideal circumstances,” Nora said. “What a wretched mess men make of us with their rules. Supposedly we will all go hysterical if our husbands are injured, and we will become simpering fools who can't care for patients. That is their logic."

"I've also heard it suggested men might sneak away for visits with their wives if they are close," Victoria said. "While that's not good judgment, it's hardly a reason to exclude so many willing workers."

"It's somewhat the same as us being forbidden to socialize with the Army officers, isn't it?" Ingrid asked. "They think it might compromise our ability to work together. How silly."

"I don't disagree with that rule," Victoria said. "Dr. Bowden is not so intent on segregating the enlisted men, but he holds his officers to a higher standard. It's fine to be friendly and a little informal because we all work so closely, but the moment a man in authority thinks of his colleague as a bit of skirt and not a professional, the working relationship is compromised."

Ingrid swung around a lamp post as they turned onto Rue de Renard. "Well, no rule can help how anyone thinks of someone."

"Men start the wars, yet they think we are the ones with poor judgment." Nora looked up at the crowded row of houses and colorful awnings, then shot a curious look at Ingrid. "You are not thinking of any particular gentleman, are you?"

"Goodness, no. I had a nice letter from George the other day, but I am not sure where things stand with him. There's no need to complicate things."

"That's wise," Victoria said. "I felt like a child being lectured at school. It was all I could do to keep from rolling my eyes and getting into real trouble. Then I had to walk down and tell poor Matthew I have to stand away from him just to talk on my lunch break."

"I'd have told her I'll follow the rules as written," Nora said.

"I did tell her that. The Red Cross holds that we should not be lewd or immodest even outside of work, but it was a kiss. One kiss."

"That old bat just wants to complain."

"Nora Scott, listen to yourself. And look at yourself. We just walked past Anne-Marie's and you didn't even look at the lemon trifle in the window. Are you sure you are not ill?"

"We can talk later." Nora glanced at Ingrid and back at her favorite bakery, now half a block behind them. "You know, Victoria, when someone you love loves you back and he has waited for you for a decade, why choose war? One day, you won't want surgery anymore either. You'll see. Kiss him all you like. Marry him."

"It's not that easy to just make a choice to upend your world."

"Coming here upended your world and you chose that lickety-split. You told me you signed up right away." Nora's chin trembled. "You don't have to stay here with old women henpecking you. Don't tell me you don't love him. Go home with him and be happy."

Victoria shot her a sideways glance and dodged a puddle in silence.

"I would rather not discuss it," she said finally.

"I have some good news," Ingrid said. "Maybe this will cheer you both. Do you remember Harry's joke that was not funny?"

"Of course."

"Well, today when we were hanging the laundry, he said he liked the joke but wanted to change it so it was better for our side. We came up with a new version. Would you like to hear it?"

"Yes, please," Victoria said. "We could use the amusement."

Ingrid patted her chest. "All right. I am a German worker going to Brussels. I am stopped at a checkpoint for my papers. The man asks 'Name?' and I say 'Ingrid Russell.' The man asks 'Occupation?' and I say 'Not this time. We learned our lesson.'"

Nora snorted a laugh and tried to hide her smile behind her hand. "Well done, Ingrid. Perhaps you should be a diplomat."

"I think Harry isn't so bad as I imagined. He reminds me a little of my sister's husband, sort of like a big brother to me. Very kind and a little silly."

"How old is he?"

"He's twenty-four," Victoria said, grateful for the turn in the conversation. "I always thought he looked younger, which is strange because of how this war has aged the rest of us."

"How does one emerge from a war so carefree?" Nora asked. "The trenches must be the darkest, bloodiest place on earth, and here he is prancing around the place, pleased as punch to hang laundry. It baffles me. I don't know how I would sleep if I'd seen what those men have seen."

"They do their best to keep each other's spirits up and chase away those thoughts," Victoria said. "You hear them singing and joking and cheering each other on with their games. The Canadians always have bawdy tunes that rival Dr.

Carraker's tavern songs. Everyone does what they can to forget."

"Perhaps Harry has to manage his own morale since he's kept away from everyone else," Ingrid said. "I'm sure it helps that we treat him kindly. I shall have to tell him he's been adopted."

"Please don't. He'll demand birthday presents and a seat at Sunday dinner." Victoria paused. "He is just being friendly and brotherly, isn't he? He's not flirting with you?"

She blushed deep red. "Oh no, nothing like that."

"*Das ist gut. Der Oberst* doctor would not approve."

Nora laughed again—a short bark of a laugh, a fake laugh to Victoria's ears. Her smile was just as false but desperate to believe in itself. "I am sorry for being a dark shadow, Victoria. Ingrid, your cheer brings me hope I desperately need. It's as good as any Canadian drinking song."

"It's hope we all need," Victoria said, trying to catch her eye, but Nora turned her face to the evening sky and didn't look down.

Chapter Sixteen

Dear Mother,

By the time you receive this, you will have heard from the Bergers about Matthew's injury. I visit him every day, and he is in excellent hands with Dr. Swann and Emily Dotson, who you may recall I told you is hiding the cat in the nurses' quarters. He is in good spirits and as pragmatic as ever, without an ounce of self-pity or complaint even when his life has been turned upside-down.

Seeing him again has sent my heart all topsy-turvy.

I haven't been so unsettled or felt so lost for years. We still care about one another a great deal, that much is plain, but the future is foggy for the same reasons it always was. The old hurts still hurt. Perhaps it is still hopeless and always will be. Heaven knows I thought that the first day or two he was here. Dearest Mother, you would not have been proud of my conduct—bickering with him about my girlish simpers, after an injury like that! But something is different in his eyes now, and I am not sure whether my unease is about him specifically or about all this confusion since his arrival that may have nothing to do with him at all.

Nothing at work today is any more difficult than it was last year, but the entire hospital feels uneven and strange. We had an emergency last week and I snapped into top form when Dr. B did all but give me command. I ran an anesthesia machine I was not trained to run, but I figured it out. A man would have died if I didn't. I made a real difference, and for the first time, it leaves me hollow. I cried in Matthew's arms when I told him. Where was my confidence? Where was my joyous boast about what a woman can do? When has a triumph like that ever laid me so low?

Darling Nora has had a rough go lately as well, so I am not alone. She once daydreamed about going to a women's medical college when the war is over. She doesn't speak of it at all now.

Since April, we've all had hopeful moments about the Americans coming and ending this pointless fight. Even so, the men are often bitter and feel abandoned by their own leaders and by Wilson waiting so long to join the war. It's been six months already and the American infantry won't be here for six more. Matthew says his unit was one of only a handful deployed early to Allied positions in need of certain specialists behind the lines.

The French troops, on the other hand, mobilized in a matter of weeks. Of course, this is their homeland, and in a way it is mine now as well. While they wait in the mud for relief, their war-weary men are now rising in pockets of mutiny. Mutiny, in civilized armies! I thought mutiny was for pirates, but this is how bad it's gotten, if you listen the whispers. The only ones in good cheer are the ones wounded badly enough to go home.

I wonder if my discontent has bubbled up lately because Matthew fills me with a homesickness I've kept at bay all these years. He is always in my thoughts now, a lovely, hazy nostalgia to block out the horror this world has become, or perhaps my own mutiny against reason and good sense. Perhaps all I want is to be home and safe and he reminds me of that, but I could not live with myself if I left when there is so much work to be done. This is my calling and my gift, just like Papa said. He would not want me to quit.

Matthew will be here for a few weeks, and I can only hope these feelings leave when he does. Our past is full of beautiful memories, but I cannot let that cloud my reason. I know this is not what you imagined when the Bergers told you I was nursing him back to health, but do remember I have no idea if he still sees a future for us, either. Perhaps he is also homesick and thinking of our life before, uninjured and uncomplicated, and his feelings for me are shadows, like mine must be for him.

Thank you always for your love and support for your unconventional daughter. I miss you dearly and look forward to your guidance in sorting out my thoughts. Even a thousand miles apart, I think there must be some motherly bond an ocean cannot sever, for you always see clearly the strain of my situation better than I do. Pray God to send me wisdom, preferably something clear and straightforward like a telegram from above, for what remains of my good sense takes up most of my head and I haven't much room left for divine translations.

Your loving and obedient daughter,

Rebekah Johnson

Victoria

Chapter Seventeen

Dr. Bowden settled a hand on the shoulder of a wide-eyed Scotsman shivering under a stack of blankets. "I hear you've got a wee problem, lieutenant, literally. I don't like to wait on kidney injuries."

"Sorry to push ahead, doc." The soldier's teeth chattered. "You got all them others to see."

Bowden gestured for Dr. Carraker to come forward. "It's all right. This fellow knows kidney injuries all too well."

"Personally and specifically," Carraker said. "I've only got one left, myself. Fell from a horse and took a hoof to the back. I pissed blood for three days before I let anyone have a look, and they missed the infection until the fever hit. The one was in such godawful shape they just took it right out. Did you know you could have just one kidney?"

"I didn't, sir."

"Well, you'll do just fine with only one if that's what it takes. How long have you had your fever?"

"I don't remember."

"He arrived with it yesterday afternoon," Frances said.

She handed him the clipboard from the end of the bed. "Thirty-eight degrees when he came in. Thirty-nine an hour ago."

"Let's roll him in right away, then."

Bowden snagged the clipboard from Carraker's hand. "A moment. Lieutenant Holter, you told the field hospital you were having trouble urinating a week ago."

"Yes, sir."

"Blood?"

"No, sir."

"When did you first notice the blood?"

The soldier pursed his lips. "Three days ago, sir. Haven't gone much, though."

"About right," Carraker said. "Let's have a look and make sure nothing's chewing up your renal artery, lieutenant."

Bowden pressed lightly on the patient's abdomen then held out his hand, opening and closing his fingers, waiting for something. The doctors stared blankly.

Victoria unwound the stethoscope from her neck and passed it forward. Bowden placed the bell on the upper part of the man's abdomen and lifted his right arm. When he looked up, she drew in a quick breath and he met her eyes for a blink.

"Thank you, Nurse Harper. Lieutenant Holter, when was the injury to your lower back that the field hospital said damaged your kidneys?"

"It was a while back, sir. They told me sometimes symptoms don't show for a few weeks."

"Indeed. Did you fall or hit something? Did something hit you?"

"I was near a blast that gashed up my leg, sir." He pointed

at his right calf, neatly bandaged. "It didn't throw me too far, though."

"Did you land on rocks or grass or in water?"

"I guess it was grass. Mud, really."

"Pain in your belly at all?"

Howard patted his stomach. "All the time, but not from that. The diet doesn't suit me lately, sir. Begging your pardon, ladies, it's not too pretty."

"Shits and farts," Bowden said.

"Ah, yes."

"Blood?"

He ducked under the blanket a bit more and shot a furtive glance at Nora and Frances. "Sometimes."

Bowden helped Holter sit up and he tapped several times on the middle of his back.

"Does that hurt?"

"No, sir."

"Don't be brave. You must tell me if this is even a little uncomfortable." He tapped again, higher and lower. "Here?"

"No, sir."

The younger doctors shifted behind one another so no one would be close enough for one of the colonel's interrogations, but Bowden looked only at the patient. He moved to the other side of the bed and instructed Holter to roll onto his left side. He listened in several places and tapped with two fingers in neat rows front and back, expressionless, then handed Carraker the stethoscope. Carraker's brows furrowed when he tapped and listened, and Victoria watched him grind his cheek between his teeth to keep quiet.

"Lieutenant Holter," Bowden said finally, "unless you misremember, nothing about that blast should have caused an injury to your kidneys. Kidney trauma is a sharp hit. Often a direct hit. If you'd landed on rocks, maybe, or something swung and hit your back."

"Or you took a hoof," Carraker volunteered.

"Or you took a hoof. It sounds like you got a good jolt, young man, and perhaps you have an infection of the urinary tract, but there is no sign of infection or trauma to the kidneys." He patted Holter's back and glanced at his men. "Percussion shows no indication of pyelonephritis or an abscess. The liver is perhaps a little inflamed. And so, why these symptoms?"

Dr. Wentworth spoke up. "Cancer of the—"

"Jesus Christ, don't scare the poor lad." Carraker smacked his arm. "You don't have cancer, lieutenant. Does anyone else have an idea what sends a man here with a fever, griping guts, and pissing blood?"

"Dysentery?" Jennings asked. "Some sort of lower gastric ulcer?"

"Close." Bowden turned to Victoria. "Nurse Harper? You're about to chew through your lip, so just say it."

The men fell quiet.

"It's an abdominal infection, sir. Another of your *Clostridium* pathogens."

He brightened. "Very good. Everyone, today's lesson is in not rushing to cut. The field hospital told us they suspected traumatic kidney damage and we were ready to open him up for a look. I thought it would be nice to show you all a renal artery repair, and Carraker was gunning to take out a kidney entirely so he'll have a spare in the cupboard. Our field hospitals do their damndest with very little in the way of diagnostics or time. We usually have the luxury of both. Diagnose, then treat. The incision is a choice. It is your choice, and you had better be able to justify it."

He patted the patient's shoulder. "Lieutenant Holter needs no incision today. He is dehydrated and feverish, two things we can manage promptly to reduce a great deal of his discomfort. Nurse Kendall, please start him on intravenous fluids and draw a metabolic panel. We will re-assess his symptoms in twelve hours."

Frances reached for a phlebotomy kit as Denys passed the coiled stethoscope back to Victoria. "How did you know that?" he whispered. "You couldn't hear what he was doing with the kidney and liver checks."

"No, but I heard him say 'horse shit' under his breath twice." Victoria shrugged. "Lucky guess."

Matthew stared, slack-jawed, as Victoria unpacked a basket on the courtyard bench after work. "Are you saying that lock-jaw, gas gangrene, and some sort of nasty infection of the bowels are all the result of fermented horse dung getting in everyone's wounds?"

"I am." Victoria set aside a tin of cheese and another of fruit and rustled in the layers of linen wrapping.

"But none of those things have anything to do with the others."

"They're three different pathogens causing three different things, but they're in the same family and so they function the same way." Her hand closed on the third tin. "They thrive without oxygen. Fresh air will kill them. Normally, they'd be underground in the excreted matter and wouldn't be a problem, but when you fight on farmlands..."

Matthew grimaced.

"That is why we are so particular about leaving wounds open," she said, not looking up as she popped the biscuit tin open to use its lid as a tray. "A nice, tight bandage is exactly what those nasty little germs want." She handed him the cheese and fruit. "But let us change the subject while we celebrate your victory."

"Cartwright let me win," Matthew said, his mouth already full of Camembert and apple slices. "He could have swung circles around me if he'd liked, but he wanted our story and he wasn't about to pester you for it."

"What did you tell him?"

"Only the important parts." He winked. "This is heaven, my darling. Thank you."

"I'll share your thanks with *Maman*. She prepared all of it, including a special treat for you."

"More than this?"

Victoria opened the third tin with a magician's flourish and handed him an éclair. "She saved everyone's sugar and butter this week and had enough to make one extra for you as thanks for livening up our dinner table conversations."

He held the pastry under his nose and inhaled before taking a bite. "Oh, I need a moment to savor this. It's heavenly. Thank your *Maman* for me. I haven't had such a treat in months. I don't even care what you've been telling your friends about me at the dinner table."

"Only the important parts."

He licked the filling off his fingers. "I feel like a traitor to home, but this is better than home."

"I've already decided Americans may prefer cheese, pastry, and wine in France and not be traitors, so you are excused."

"You were in England for a bit before coming here. So was I." His eyes sparkled. "I think we can safely prefer their tea."

"In Belgium we could prefer the chocolates."

Matthew grimaced. "I see no reason to go to Belgium."

Victoria popped a bite of apple into her mouth. "When we win it back, I mean."

"Indeed, but... you heard how it was up there, didn't you?"

She swallowed. The atrocities on Belgian civilians fed public sentiment against Germans around the world. No one knew just how much of the recruitment propaganda to stir patriotism was truth and how much was dramatized, but it was rooted in real suffering and violence, and that was bad enough.

"Of course I know," she said.

"And you're all right having a German soldier waltzing around the hospital like a free man?"

She bobbled the tin with the cheeses and barely steadied it. "Harry? It's not up to me where he waltzes, you know."

"He shouldn't be socializing with the nurses."

"Perhaps you should suggest to Dr. Bowden how he should run his hospital."

"Victoria, really."

She looked away. "Don't do this. It's not your place to decide who my colleagues and I socialize with. Or work with, in this case, because that's what you saw. He was working."

"Yes, I see him with Miss Russell every day and I can tell he's always delighted when you stop for a chat."

She shoved the cheese tin back into the basket. "Ingrid is

shy. Until she came here, she'd never been ten miles from home and all she knew were other people's opinions. It's good to meet people who are different from ourselves and learn to face our fears. She says he's friendly and kind."

He set down the éclair. "Victoria. The Germans shot a Red Cross nurse. They executed her. And now you're harboring one of them."

"Everyone here knows what happened to Edith Cavell. But do you know what happened next?"

He shook his head.

"The French army shot two German Red Cross nurses in retaliation. And do you know what happened after that?"

His lips whitened.

"The Kaiser told the Germans that if anyone else tried to even the score, they would answer directly to him." She scooted away from him. "Now tell me, who is the only person making any sense in this mess? I think it was the Kaiser. What does that make me? A traitor? Stupid?"

"You're neither of those things, darling." He picked up her hand.

"Harry is a human being. He is not an enemy state or a bloodthirsty government. He's just a man, and I trust the commanding officer's choice to keep him here."

Matthew swallowed thickly. "I suppose in the spirit of things I should trust his choice as well."

"I think if we must have one of the other side with us, it's nice that it's someone pleasant like Harry," she said. "His English is very good and he likes to tell jokes, and he wants to learn everything about America since it seems our joining the war has made a defector of him."

"What?"

"He said that when we entered the war, he knew it was over and the Germans were in the wrong."

"He knew they'd lose, you mean."

She twisted her lips. "He said the war was unjust and it was wrong of the Germans to invade sovereign territories."

"He only said that when he saw the United States Army mobilizing to plant a boot on his face."

"Matthew!"

"You are the last woman on earth I'd accuse of being naive, Victoria, but—"

"I've seen years more of this war than you have," she said, seething. "I have met hundreds of men from both sides who fought and died because some paranoid king's pride was offended. I've met men on our side who laughed about brutal killings, and men on their side who wept and begged God's forgiveness and mercy on their families. Shall I tell you about them?"

He opened his mouth, closed it, and sat back against the bench. "No," he said finally. "It appears that in our long absence from one another, I've forgotten how it feels to have anyone riddle my arguments with holes outside the courtroom."

Victoria steadied her breath. From the day she met him, Matthew was cool and collected with his words and never missed a stride in a debate. She'd watched him draw Cooper into an agitated fluster, talk circles around his brother, and even cause Maudie to throw up her hands and say 'fine, you win.' He was polished. Unruffled. His smug little smile when he won was the most delicious thing she'd ever seen.

The times she knocked him off-balance with an inconvenient fact or a clever retort filled her with pride and filled him with a passion that often overtook his reason. At the Truxtons' wedding, they had danced while he rambled the reasons to overturn North Carolina's new statewide prohibition on alcohol. Victoria said if the bill of repeal didn't include a provision for public health education on alcohol-related violence and disease, she'd campaign against it and the men could make do with their rotgut swamp whisky. Only seconds after she stunned him into silence, he had proposed.

A quiet settled on the courtyard and she put her hand back in his. "I think the armies would have you believe there is only right and wrong in this war. There's a great deal of both, and a great deal between. This is not just about Harry. Many people are fighting because they have no choice."

"I suppose at least I had a choice." He stared at his leg. "And of all people, I should be able to see a little nuance even if I cannot argue both sides of a thing."

"You're usually very good at that." Victoria watched his eyes, waiting for him to look up. "But I can see how in this case it feels different. I'm sorry."

"You examine me like a patient sometimes. Besides my leg."

"How do you mean?"

"I think you can check my pulse without touching me." He brushed a crumb of éclair from her cheek and lingered for a moment. "My arguments and emotions tick boxes on your checklist of symptoms and add up to some diagnosis you can see that often escapes me at first."

"It's always hardest to diagnose ourselves." She leaned into his hand on her cheek. "I'm sure you have pages of notes on my particular conditions and what they add up to. Please don't tell me your conclusions. I'm sure they're not especially flattering."

"Nonsense. You've grown up, Vi." He shifted his hand to her shoulder and his eyes darted around for curious watchers. "You're doing the work you longed to do, beautifully and brilliantly. Do you not see that?"

"I confess, since you arrived I feel as though I've slipped backward in time, desperate for my mother or Maudie or someone to tell me what to do. 'Brilliant' is hardly the word for it."

Matthew stiffened. "Have I upset you so much?"

"No. No, Matt, I don't think—certainly seeing you was quite a shock, but you have not upset me. There are so many little things adding up."

He peeled her trembling fingers one by one from the fruit tin and tucked it back into the basket with the others. "What is it?"

"Dr. Bowden wants to teach me properly how to run the Connell machine and the other anesthetometers. He thinks several nurses should be trained, just in case."

"Would you rather not?"

She shook her head. "I'll do it. It's my duty, and if he says we should be prepared, I will be prepared. But that is the sort of thing that would have brought me joy before, and now it doesn't. I should want it, and I don't, and I don't know why."

"You are weary of war, darling." He scooted closer and put an arm around her shoulders. "And you have every right to be. It is about more than anesthesia or operating on your former paramour's injury."

Former. She grimaced. Weary of the war, perhaps, but it was a war she chose years before her country tiptoed in.

What battles she fought and lives she saved had not yet added up to the satisfaction of having done enough.

'Enough' of what, she couldn't say. War or no war, there would always be patients. And seated next to her, pulling her close enough to breathe in the smell of his skin, Matthew was proof there was nowhere far enough to break the charge between them.

"War brought you to this place where your loving heart must build a fortress around itself because if you felt deeply for every man in your care, you'd break," he continued. "And do not think I mean you are weak for shielding yourself so. It is a matter of self-preservation, I believe. I am sure I do it, too."

She rested her head against his and closed her eyes. His words took root in the space of a breath. He meant keeping her heart at a distance from her work, not their love, but she might never be able to untangle the two again.

Chapter Eighteen

The squeak of Rosemarie's mail cart caught Victoria's attention as she placed a stack of surgical gowns, still hot from the laundry steamer, on a metal shelf outside the operating room. Rosemarie rarely ventured past the tiny office where the nurses had their mailboxes, and from the quiver in the girl's lip Victoria wondered if she was lost.

She poked a finger in her mouth and Victoria pulled her hand away.

"None of that," she said gently. "What is wrong? You look close to tears, dear."

Rosemarie's other hand trembled. She lifted it halfway to her mouth and then clamped it on the handle of the push-cart. "I cannot control my nerves today. You'll think I'm awfully silly, but sometimes the mail is more frightening than the ambulances."

"What do you mean?"

"Cables are always bad news. Especially overseas cables. Ada got one from Toronto when her mother died, remember?

And that orderly, Benji, got one when his brother went to prison."

"Who is getting overseas cables now?"

"Dr. Bowden. One yesterday, and several more today." She pointed at the envelopes from the transcriber's office in town, still neatly sealed with names typed on the front. Pink were from abroad, yellow from Europe and England, and the entire short stack was pink. "The last time he had so many, the fighting got closer and closer every day. Are they pushing us back again?"

"Oh, Rosemarie, it's not so bad. Listen to me. Dr. Bowden corresponds with a doctor in America who designed our new anesthesia machine. He reports about how we use it and our results, and he says they are anxious to provide the machine to the U.S. Army. Of course they must communicate quickly."

"Do you think that's what this is?"

"If he had a stack of yellow envelopes, I would be more concerned," Victoria said. "Those might be orders from London. A lot of news from close by comes by telephone, too, because it's much more private. I'm sure there is nothing to worry about with these."

Rosemarie's hand shook in hers and Victoria squeezed it. Again, her left hand rose toward her mouth and Victoria cleared her throat, stopping her before she got a finger in her teeth.

"I have something for you, dear." She pulled a tin of salve from her apron pocket and opened it.

"Whew!" Rosemarie fanned in front of her nose. "What is that?"

"It's eucalyptus and lavender, meant to be very calming. It clears your nose and lungs and helps you relax." She pressed it into her hand. "Put a little dab between your lip and your nose, or rub some on your chest at night. And if you accidentally get some on your fingernails, you'll find it tastes absolutely vile and you'll never want another nibble."

Rosemarie nodded. "You are so thoughtful, Victoria. Thank you for taking time to calm me. I know you're so busy. And I feel a little better already, but..."

"What is it?"

"One of the telegrams is for you."

Victoria's only overseas telegram had come when her father died a week after German U-boats sank the *RMS Lusitania*. Although his death was not unexpected after a long illness, Victoria's thrifty mother sprang for a lengthy cable to inform her of his passing and order her not to return home while civilian travel was unsafe.

Under Rosemarie's nervous gaze, the pink envelope crinkled as Victoria gripped it and willed her hands not to shake. Good news, like weddings and babies and parrots learning new words, always came by mail.

She stood straighter and pasted on a smile. "I'm sure all is well. Perhaps my sister is with child again. My mother might be too excited to wait and write a letter about that."

Rosemarie grinned, creasing her freckles as she poked a tentative finger in the salve. "Maybe the whole stack of telegrams is lovely. Maybe it's not such a bad day."

Victoria broke the seal on the envelope and shook out the slip of pink paper, still smelling of ink.

October 12, 1917
Mrs. Cooper Truxton

Rebekah Johnson

To Miss Victoria Harper

SAY YES.

Victoria read the paper again and counted the days. Maudie must have bolted to the telegraph office the minute she received the letter about Matthew.

"Is it good news?" Rosemarie asked.

"The mail is getting through quickly again," Victoria said. She folded the telegram into a tiny square and shoved it in her pocket. "Good news for the navy, at least."

She didn't know whether to laugh or cry. Maudie had been the only true advocate Victoria had in those hand-wringing years of wanting a life with two incompatible loves. Even Gerald and Ruby Harper began to despair of their daughter's indecision after two years of courtship with no ring to show for it. And now Maudie was taking sides.

Maudie and Cooper were Matthew's old friends and certainly biased in favor of a happy match, and Cooper had made plenty of pointed remarks over the years about how delightful it was to be married and welcome each other home at night instead of kissing goodbye.

If Victoria married, she might be allowed to do little more than change bandages and administer medications at any hospital in North Carolina, maybe in the South, if not in the entire country. They were men's rules, but neither Matthew as a lawyer nor Cooper as a legislator could change them for her with the wave of a hand.

Maudie understood women's unique struggles around ambitions and love, and kicked her husband under the table when his good-natured teasing verged on obnoxious. Her support during the years with Matthew, and later without him, had meant the world to her.

"I am desolate," Maudie said to Victoria the night before she left for England in late 1914. "Desolate to be losing you and yet so proud and excited for you, darling. Did your dreams ever carry you across an ocean to work?"

"Never," Victoria confessed. "Nor did they include operating on men blown to bits by artillery close by."

"Are you frightened?"

"Only that I will prove stupid and ill-prepared to learn what is needed of me," Victoria said.

"Impossible." Maudie squeezed her hand. "There is no one more capable than you. Britain needs men at the front, and more will be expected of women than ever before. This journey might be everything you ever wanted."

Victoria's gaze had flickered out the window of her parents' home, up the hill into the trees as if she could peer through foliage for a mile or two and see Matthew at his house, perhaps alone since all of their mutual friends were at her farewell party.

They hadn't spoken for more than a year. Perhaps he wasn't alone.

Another squeeze brought her attention back to Maudie, whose blue eyes read the sadness in Victoria's gaze.

"Things might be different here, too," Maudie said. "When you come home, I mean. Different for women. And if you can—"

"It will be a grand adventure," Victoria said. "I am ready."

With the telegram still in her pocket. Victoria escaped supper early and retreated to her bedroom. She opened her correspondence box and scanned pages and pages of letters saved from friends at the hospitals where she'd worked at home. At Raleigh Methodist, the hospital president and chief of surgery maintained vise-like grips on personnel decisions and neither were keen on a woman in the operating suite at all, let alone a married one. The hospital in Durham where she'd completed her advanced training was the most liberal in the state, and even there she was only allowed in operating rooms for "women's matters."

Nothing had changed.

She unfolded the telegram. *Say yes*, Maudie said, but say yes to what? Matthew hadn't asked her anything, and likely wouldn't. They'd been apart for years, separated by stubbornness and changed irrevocably by war. He liked order and predictability, and Victoria had always let him down. Even now, a betting man would look at his odds and predict a fourth rejection.

Dearest Maudie (and Cooper, because I know you are reading this),

I see my letters are getting through mighty quickly these days, a pleasant change from the start of the war when it took a full two weeks. Your telegram amused me, and alerted me immediately to the likelihood you sent Matthew a message with similar guidance.

We spend time together most evenings. I come home and change so I don't look like a misbehaving hussy (more on that another time!) and then we sit for an hour or two in the courtyard and he brags on his progress with the crutches. I can see in his eyes and the way he moves that he is still in pain, body and mind, but he insists it disappears when I am there.

How different things might have been if Matthew and I had been of like mind only a few months earlier, all those years ago. Our timing is still terrible, and look at us now. He will leave soon, probably in four or five weeks for a rehabilitation hospital, and I will stay here until someone runs out of soldiers, ammunition, or pride.

"Victoria, what is that?"

She looked up from the writing desk as Nora shut the door to their bedroom. "A letter home."

"No." Nora jerked her head at Victoria's bed while she unfastened the top buttons of her work dress. "That."

The telegram lay crumpled on the coverlet and Victoria's cheeks turned as pink as the paper. "It's only Maudie having a laugh."

"A transatlantic cable is an expensive laugh."

"No one back home has to pinch their pennies to buy sugar on the black market. They can spare a dollar for frivolities."

"But you are not laughing. Is it about Matthew? Surely she's not making light of what happened to him."

"Heavens, Maudie would never do that." She folded her unfinished letter and tucked it in a book. "I am certain she is devastated."

"Then what is it?"

Victoria looked at her bed, at the telegram a bright bloom amid the letters she'd strewn over the blanket. She started picking up the pages. "Do you believe in signs?"

"From God?"

"Or anywhere. Anyone."

Nora shook out her dress and reached for a hanger. "I don't know. Many times, I've thought a sign clearly meant a certain thing and I was entirely wrong. Perhaps what we call signs are merely the ways we justify our own foolish decisions."

"Oh."

"Is Maudie sending you messages from above?"

Victoria stacked the letters and the telegram in her correspondence box and shoved it under her bed. "Perhaps she is," she said, and flopped back onto her pillow. "So perhaps it is fortunate I have no foolish decision to make."

Chapter Nineteen

The next morning, Nora groaned when she read the nurses' schedule, hastily erased and re-scribbled in Nurse Perry's pinched handwriting.

"I knew it," she said, pointing to their names when Victoria approached. "Did you see that broken leg yesterday? Clean across near the knee and splintered about six inches higher. That poor man. It will be better than an amputation, though, if we can manage it."

The physical exertion of preparing femur cases in traction frames often left the surgical team sweaty and annoyed before the procedure even began. Some fracture sets were delicate work, and Victoria's slender fingers were well-suited to holding bones in place while Dr. Bowden drilled and placed steel plates. The thigh bone, however, could require the muscle of two or three men to manipulate into place while the nurses positioned the frame.

"Oh, look." The color drained from Nora's face. "You, me, Dr. Bowden, Dr. Hawkins, and—"

"The Duke of Hazelnut Porridge," Victoria finished. "Delightful."

"Hazelnut porridge sounds too nice," Nora said. "It sounds rather tasty. Think of something nastier."

Victoria chewed her lip. Since his confession the day of the tunnel emergency, she'd tried to be nicer, or at least not so sour, to Dr. Wentworth. Still, he did suggest to her face that Harry should be shot and a woman shouldn't meet the Swiss delegates.

"Lord Troutwhistle Bile of Henceforth Rotting."

Nora lifted her chin and patted her pale cheeks to bring them to a blush. "That's much better."

Four hours later, Nora found a sliver of sunlight and slumped against the wall in the hallway outside the operating rooms. "Dr. Bowden will never want me on a case again."

"Darling, it wasn't so bad."

"What nurse hands a surgeon a curved forceps when he asks for a straight one? You saw my hands shaking on the retractor. He had to ask Gi—Dr. Wentworth to take it."

"He wasn't angry. I think he looked downright sympathetic. He knows you haven't been feeling well." Victoria squeezed her friend's hand and thought of Dr. Wentworth's situation with his wife. "And don't let the Earl of Barleycorn Bamboo bother you. I think everyone's been a little grouchy lately. Let's get something to eat before the next case so you're not so wobbly."

"I want to go home."

"It's only a few more hours, but if you're feeling poorly—"

"I want to go home, Victoria. Home. I cannot do this anymore."

"All right," she said, hands on her hips. "This is about more than a difficult case and a head cold. Something else happened. I see it plain as day, so why won't you tell me?"

"You don't tell me everything," Nora countered, turning away. "That telegram. All these evenings with Matthew. Aside from the lecture you got from Nurse Perry, I don't know what's going on with you either. Why won't you share your happiness when the rest of us have so little?"

Victoria froze. "I wasn't trying to hide anything from you. I'll tell you all about it, if you like."

"It doesn't even matter. I am an utter wreck and a shell of myself and I want to go home. I want—Victoria, I want my mother. I cannot stay here any longer." Tears seeped from Nora's brown eyes and she swiped them away. "Look at me. One bad case brings me to tears. This is not who I am."

"It isn't just one bad case. You've had a difficult few weeks." Victoria searched for answers and shielded her friend from view when two other nurses walked by. "Let's ask Nurse Perry if you can have a short leave. I'm sure when she knows you're in such a state, she would prefer to grant a leave and keep from losing you entirely. Go see your family. Is everything all right with your family?"

Nora didn't answer.

"Will you go home now and rest? Can we talk about it tonight?"

"I can't leave my shift."

"Today you can. We're well-staffed. Bridget can cover in surgery and we'll bring in someone else to do dressing changes and all that. I'll take care of everything."

Victoria almost believed her own cheerful words and held her false smile in place, waiting.

"You always do," Nora said, looking up with pink-rimmed eyes. "How do you do it?"

"We all just do our best, darling. Some days, our best is a shining star. You know I've had my own days feeling like a grimy shadow."

"I feel like trench foot and slurry. That's it. I'm the Duchess of Trench Foot and Slurry."

Victoria curtsied. "To bed with you, Your Grace."

Victoria returned to the hospital in her favorite peach dress after dinner, dragging her feet in their freshly scrubbed boots through room five as she called out hellos to the other patients. "Hold me," she demanded when she dropped into the chair at Matthew's bedside. "It's been such a frustrating day."

He scooted up and embraced her. "You know, you needn't have a bad day to ask for my arms around you. I'm delighted to hold you whenever you're so inclined."

She breathed him in and rested her cheek on his shoulder, slowing her lungs and thoughts as her hat tumbled the floor unnoticed. His arms and the natural way she could nestle into them hadn't changed across time or ocean or injury. Alone in her bed at night, she twisted herself tight in her sheet to feel that cozy, protective closeness and told herself she just missed her mother. As her breathing steadied, the excuse collapsed into ash. It was the shape of his embrace imprinted on her, no one else's, and nothing before or since had ever felt so sweet.

He stroked her hair and she blinked quickly, catching a tear before it fell.

"I have you now. I'm here, Vi. It's all right."

"I have lived through bombings and artillery, and lately all these little personal things are shaking me up in a way I am not accustomed to." She sat up and looked at him. "I don't like this sense of... of not knowing what I am doing."

"I know that feeling well. Be fair to yourself, dearest. That emergency situation last week was enough to rattle anyone."

She forced a smile. "As though one's old sweetheart showing up out of the blue wasn't enough of a rattle."

"Old sweetheart?" He took her hand and the curl of his lips was nearly a taunt to kiss him. "I don't like that title. It sounds so... old. Give me a new one. Better than the ones you make up for his lordship the surgeon, please."

He flirted with the tone of his voice more than any wink or sly smile, and Victoria rose to the challenge. "Then I shall draw on the vast legal knowledge I've gathered from you over the years and appoint you the Duke of Bona Fides ad Absurdum."

"Now that is uniquely flattering. 'Good faith to the point of preposterousness.'"

She poked his nose. "It suits you."

"Preposterously so." Matthew grinned. "Shall I have it engraved on a nameplate for the office?"

"I think you get an ermine-trimmed cloak and a fine income with a dukedom. Some rambling old pile of an estate might be in there as well."

"I suppose I should also get a duchess."

She caught her breath and Matthew didn't give her time to respond. "Victoria, forgive me. That was in poor taste."

"No. No, it's not in poor taste." She twitched her head, shaking off the idea as though the pink telegram wasn't crinkling in her pocket as a reminder of what they must talk about. An excuse might hold for a minute to clear her head. "I am just distracted. Part of my frustration today is because something is wrong with Nora and she won't tell me what," she said. "She was supposed to rest this afternoon so we could talk tonight, but I went home after my shift and she was out. This is not like her."

"Would you like to sit outside for a bit? The fresh air might soothe you. I know a delightful bench. It's somewhat concealed by that large tree over there."

"I think there's rain coming in."

He eyed the sky beyond the gingham curtains and pulled her close to whisper. "Maybe just for a bit. There's something I'd like to talk to you about without Cartwright listening in."

Her pulse thrummed when his lips brushed her cheek.

Gray clouds rushed over the courtyard, but the buildings shielded them from the wind as they settled on the wrought-iron bench. Matthew swung himself onto the seat with ease and propped up his crutches with one hand.

"You're getting quite good at that." Victoria draped her wool coat over her shoulders, glad she'd chosen it over her prettier but less practical capelet made for warmer weather. "And there's something I'd like to talk to you about, too."

"Ladies first, then."

"Did you receive a telegram from home?"

He choked out a laugh. "Well, that was what I wished to talk about as well. Miss MacDougal brought mine this morning. We have such delightful friends. What did yours say?"

Heat rose in Victoria's cheeks. "It said 'Say yes.' What was yours?"

"Mine said 'Ask her, idiot.'" He pulled his black hair back from his face and then brought her fingers to his lips. "Our personal morale boosters. I know they mean well."

"Of course."

"Victoria, look at me."

His gray eyes were calm and warm, darkening with the gathering clouds in the slate-colored sky. She searched them, diving deep, and when he let go of her hand, she knew that whatever he was about to say might be the truth, but it wasn't the whole truth. His touch always gave him away.

"Darling, I cannot imagine a world in which I do not love you," he said. "It will be the end of days, I think. But despite our friends' well-meaning interference, I will not put you in the wretched position of having to decline me again."

She stopped breathing.

"I can handle a battered heart," he said, "but what I cannot do is selfishly ask you to give up your life for me, knowing full well that if you say yes, you will come to me with resentment. Seeing you here, I understand more than ever what your work means to you. I promise I won't let my desires overcome my respect for you and ruin whatever it is we're building here."

Her dry throat tightened. She forced air into her lungs so she could push out trembling words as the breeze picked up, whipping dried leaves around their feet. "What do you think we're building here?"

He cupped her chin in his hands and brought her lips to

his. "I don't know," he murmured before kissing her again. "Maybe it is the seed of something that will bloom again one day. This war cannot last forever."

The war was not kind to promises between lovers, but his lips were on hers and *one day* lingered between them with a sharp pang of regret.

She softened in his arms and leaned into his kiss, longing for the breathless desire that overtook them so many times before when he snuck her away from a crowd. These new kisses were tender, not passionate, with a sweetness that flowed through his fingertips as he stroked her neck. She responded with hands in his hair and over his back, drawing him closer in the privacy of the tree's shadow and the darkening sky.

"Matthew?"

"Yes?"

"I love—" A bright white light flashed close by and she sat bolt upright. "Did you see that?"

Chapter Twenty

Matthew grabbed her as he dove to the ground. Gravel tore into his left palm when he landed and rolled, collecting brush and dirt on their coats. His right hand tangled in her hair and he had barely enough time to yank her against his chest and protect her head from hitting the path when he tumbled.

She whispered his name and the word echoed.

He shifted and covered her with his body, propped on one forearm to keep his weight over her and still cupping her head in his hand. His fingers were wet in her hair.

"Shh, Vi. I'm here. I'll protect you."

"Matthew."

"I've got you, my love. Never forget that." His voice rose in a panic. "Never."

The explosion muffled his hearing like a blanket. His heart, and hers. His breath, and hers. Beyond that was the rush of ocean waves and rainwater drowning out artillery fire. The ground shook. Overhead, another rumble. Perspiration dotted his forehead.

He lifted his head and searched her brown eyes for fear and found a curious calm. The panic was his, only his. Then her eyes filled with tears and the peace melted away.

"It's all right, my darling. I've got you. You're hurt. Stop—Victoria, stop moving." He pushed down on her, digging his knees into the dirt and his hips against hers. A stab of pain seared his left side and shot up his spine as a high whine screeched in his ear. "You must stay here until it's quiet. Don't move."

"But dearest—"

He clenched his eyes shut. "You cannot run away!" he shouted. "It's not safe! You cannot!"

"I'm not running, Matt." She stroked his face until he opened his eyes.

Her breaths came quicker, pressing her up and against him so close her heart beat inside his chest with his own, shaking him. His teeth chattered. Another noise, too loud and too close, and a whiff of the dirt inches from his nose took him back to the sour mud that filled his mouth when he fell after the blast. He tightened his hold on her. He was losing his breath and losing her with it.

Again. He would ask her to marry him every day and live with every rejection if he could restore his hope that one day the answer would change, but that hope was further away than ever. He had always misjudged the time to ask if she was ready. Smothering her with his love until she couldn't breathe, she said. That was how she saw it. That was how he made her feel, and that was how he lost her. In the end, demanding everything left him with nothing.

Every stitch in his leg burned and shot daggers of pain up his knee and thigh as he tried to still her. The air was thick and clogged his throat, as warm as the blood on his fingers, still holding the back of her head.

"We're safe, Matthew." Victoria's voice trembled. "I promise."

"Not yet. Be still, darling. We cannot go yet."

She was happy and thriving in a world where he had no place. To ask her again would cost him the last threads of her faith, and he'd had enough loss for a lifetime.

The ground shook again with a low groan that chilled his neck with goosebumps. He squeezed his eyes shut, tensing his damp fingers in her hair while his other hand scrabbled in the broken twigs and mud for a grasp on anything to keep him from collapsing and crushing her.

She squirmed beneath him and winced. "If we could only just—"

"Don't move, Vi. Listen. There it is again."

Chapter Twenty-One

"We're safe, darling."

Matthew didn't reply. His chest heaved and in the dim light his gray eyes stared blankly into hers, flinty and unreadable.

The buttons on his coat dug into her stomach. She wriggled an arm free and reached up to stroke his cheek, cold despite the sweat on his brow. "Look at me. We're all right, dearest. It was thunder. Only thunder."

He squeezed his hand tighter in her hair. "I've got you, Vi."

"I know. I'm right here with you. We're safe."

"No. It's not over. You're bleeding."

"It's the rain. It's raining now."

"But I heard it." He shook his head. "I felt it."

"Lightning hit somewhere close by, and the thunderclap after was the loudest I've ever heard." She smiled. "I jumped so high. You scooped me right out of the air."

"I know that sound, though." His lips were pale as he fought for breath. "The shells."

"We're safe." She traced the curves of his jaw and the line of his nose with her finger. "Look at me, Matt. We're safe. There's no shelling."

His voice was weak. "But it's not raining."

"We're halfway under a bush and you slung my coat over our heads to cover us. I see it doubles as a fine tent."

His weight still pinned her to the ground and every time she writhed to escape a pebble digging into her back he pressed down harder—or she pressed upward and he pressed back, someone pressed into someone and stayed.

"Did I just throw you on the ground when I heard thunder?"

"Well, it was dreadfully loud and it did sound like an explosion." She moved her hand to his chest. "It's all right. I'm not hurt."

"But—oh, God. Look at us." He pushed the coat aside and the cool droplets hit his face when he tried to roll off her. Struggling to shift his unbalanced weight, he dug his teeth into his lip to stifle a shout when he jammed his leg into the gravel. "I've got you on your back in the middle of the courtyard, and—Christ, that hurts, dammit, I'm so sorry. Now you'll really be in—"

"*Sauhund!*" Harry's voice sliced through the rain as he slammed his boot into Matthew's shoulder. "Mad brute! American dog!"

"Stop it!" Victoria struggled to her feet and pushed him back. "Get away from him!"

"The man was on you, Nurse Harper. Are you hurt?"

"Am I hurt? I'm not the one you just shoved a boot into!" She dropped to her knees at Matthew's side. "Darling. I'm so sorry about Harry, I—"

"This is Harry?"

"Yes. And Harry, please. This is Matthew. I know him, and nothing was wrong here. It was a misunderstanding."

"How does a misunderstanding get him on top of you in the dirt?"

"Never you mind. I'm quite all right. Please go."

"No, you come along and we will tell *der Oberst* what this man has done."

Matthew forced a dry laugh. "The Kaiser's boy thinks it's his place to save you, sweetheart. That's a fine one to write home about."

"It is your place to have her on her back like that?" Harry demanded, swiping rain off his face. "I see the American dog cannot even wait for the bedroom. And out here where anyone can see, like an animal? Filthy."

"She'd have a knee in my balls if she was as disgusted as you are. Why don't you do as she asks and go on your way?"

Harry's fists twitched. "Sometimes ladies make excuses for bad men."

Victoria grabbed Matthew's hand.

Stonefaced, he looked at Harry towering over them and jammed his boot squarely into his shin so hard Harry yelped and hopped back. "Strike me again and see if you still wish to speak to the colonel," Matthew said. "Nurse Harper asked you to leave her alone, and you haven't. You delude yourself about what you mean to her, and Bowden might be interested to know that."

Harry bristled. "I will not leave her alone with you. She is my friend. I don't know what you mean of deluding."

"Matthew, darling, it's not like that."

"I know it's not to you, Vi, but I have it on good authority this scoundrel wishes his American tour to begin with a ring on your finger."

Victoria jerked her head between the two of them. "What on earth? Who said that? Harry, what is he talking about?"

He didn't speak.

"Answer me. Why would someone tell him this?"

"Why does anyone tell anyone anything?" He threw up his hands, scattering rain droplets. "Perhaps I am mis-translated. It happens to me a lot."

Matthew smirked. "I know well the desire to marry her. I have a measure of sympathy for you, Kraut, but please run along."

"You must not be worthy of her if she tells me only last week she does not have a special man."

"Why should she tell you anything? She asked you to leave and that hasn't stuck in your head so well. Go on now."

"I will go nowhere. I can keep her safe, and her friends." Harry scoffed, grinding his boots in the gravel. "Many men try to keep the Germans away from this place. I don't see another man who can do it sitting on his ass, as I do."

Victoria's mouth fell open. With a wicked smile, Matthew tapped his chin like he had all the time in the world to sit in the cold mist and slice Harry's pride to ribbons.

"Indeed, old boy, you are quite the prize. If we cannot be rid of you by asking politely, you may as well amuse us. Tell us more about how powerful you are. Or how powerful papa is."

"There is shame in a father protecting his son?"

"You play him false by accepting his protection if you've truly turned on Germany." Matthew's eyes flashed in the dim light. "If you're well enough, traitor, why don't you carry our flag instead of cowering under it? You can join up with our countrymen who inspired you to turn your coat."

Harry seethed. "Such high words from a man on the ground."

Victoria rose and slapped him. "That is enough. Leave right now, or I will drag you to the soldiers' quarters by your ears and let them deal with you without Dr. Bowden's kind supervision."

"Please, Nurse Harper, I must explain what he heard." Harry held his jaw, wincing.

"I don't care what he heard before, or who he heard it from. What he just heard directly to his face was you calling him a dog, refusing to leave us alone, and mocking him for an injury caused by your army. You, who half the people in this place would happily ship to prison or shoot in cold blood because of where you were born. How dare you?"

His lip quivered and his proud facade began to crumble. "It is expected of the Kaiser's boy, yes? The Kraut."

"I expected better of you."

His shoulders drooped. "I am sorry."

"I am not the one you kicked and insulted."

Harry swiped his damp hands over his coat and held one out to Matthew, glowering. "I am sorry, Mister...?"

"Corporal Berger." Matthew eyed him, brows lifted, but didn't reach out or move from his seat on the damp ground.

"*Oberleutnant* Kurz. Allow me."

"I am quite comfortable, thank you."

"It is raining and muddy and cold, Corporal. I see you mean Nurse Harper no harm, so I will help you up, yes?"

"No."

Victoria knelt at Matthew's side and whispered so her lips brushed his ear. "Let me help you to the bench, at least."

He took her chin in his hand and turned her to look at him. The rainfall dissipated but the sky above them still rumbled with rapidly shifting clouds. He didn't speak, but his eyes were still dark with fear beneath his sarcastic mask.

She sat on the muddy gravel next to him.

"Please go, Harry."

"I wish to explain."

"And so you shall, but not today. Thank you for trying to help when you thought I was in trouble. I am fine now. Please go."

Hollow-eyed, he retreated into the mist.

Clouds covered the moon and stars with a gray haze and left the air heavy with the scent of earth. When she tipped her face to the sky, the fog pressed down on her like a lid over the courtyard. The damp soaked her dress, darkening the peach fabric to a dingy rust. She wrapped her messy coat around herself and leaned against Matthew's arm in the shadows, banishing the thoughts of his panic while she waited for the sensation of his body on top of hers to pass. It lingered as she waited for him to speak.

"Are you chilled?" he asked after a long silence. His eyes were calm.

"A little."

He rolled onto his hip and shifted to hold the side of the bench. "I'm going to get up by myself, and then I'm going to help you up."

"All right."

His knuckles whitened as he gripped the wrought iron and he swallowed heavily, cording his neck with strain. "I'm off balance. No, don't touch me. Just tell me what I'm doing wrong."

"Get your right leg tucked under you first, not out to the side. Knee bent, ankle bent, foot flat."

He shifted his weight, grimacing as he leaned on his left hip. "I keep jabbing my bad leg and it hurts like hell because I hit my stitches on the ground, but then I do it again. My knee moves on its own, trying to do this like before. Is that normal?"

"It's entirely normal. Use your arms to take your weight off the left side while you move your right leg—just there."

"Better?"

"Yes. While you get your balance, follow your arms up. Pull up with your arms until your right leg is steady."

He breathed slowly, forcing incremental movements on every inhale and relaxing his tensed muscles on each exhale. When he reached a standing position, he didn't smile.

"Halfway done." He held out his left hand.

"Other hand."

She reached for him. "Hold onto the bench and let me pull you this way a little. Just plant your foot and bend your knee a bit."

He grinned. "And I don't let go of the bench, right?"

"Don't you dare."

She rose next to him. He took his crutches from where they leaned on the back of the bench and situated them under his arms. "Victory. Both arms around you again."

"Not so fast."

"Darling Vi. Aside from calling him a Kraut, I didn't actually insult him."

"You goaded him into a temper."

"You asked him to leave once and I followed it asking a half-dozen more times. The man stayed. I used what weapons I had on me."

She tapped his forehead. "The rapier thrust of your wit can lay a man low."

"I might have gone easier on him had I known he was unarmed."

"Matthew Berger, you are a pompous ass."

He smiled a little and turned his face to the sky. "Didn't you say I would always win the war of words? I'll admit, he had me there at the end, but it was a cheap shot."

Victoria slumped and Harry's words rang in her head. "I didn't expect him to say such a degrading thing."

"Sticks and stones and missing bones. I did goad him a little. Perhaps I had it coming."

"You certainly did not. You may call each other Krauts and dogs all you want, but for him to mock you for that injury is beyond the pale."

"Never mind that nonsense. Come here. Let me hold you properly without acting like a frightened child." He swallowed thickly. "I am so sorry. I don't know what came over me."

"Do not be sorry." She stroked his face, pressing the warmth of her palm into his cheek. "It happens to many soldiers. The doctors call it shell shock. Sounds can etch themselves in your memory and your body reacts without thinking."

"Will that always happen?"

She nestled into his embrace, steadying him as she stroked his neck. "I don't know."

"I felt entirely out of sorts," he said. "And Harry—shit. I've gotten you into a world of trouble, I'm sure." His breaths deepened. "It galled me more than it should have. My pride is a fickle thing lately. I know you call him your friend, but—"

"You're my friend too."

"A moment before the sky cracked open, you said you love me."

"Did I?"

"I'm certain you did."

Victoria looked up to see him fighting a smile. "Do you remember how you used to kiss me outside at the beach house where no one could see us?"

"I do."

"We could walk to the outside of the hospital and find a quiet place where they can't see us from the windows." She tapped his crutches. "If you can manage a short stroll."

"Just out there?" He pivoted on his good leg and swung up the gravel walk. "If there's a kiss from you at the end of that stroll, I'll make it."

She matched her steps to his, flushed with desire to feel his lips and arms on her again and tinged with embarrassment that such a chaotic few minutes set every nerve tingling to touch him. He held her to the ground in a state of panic, not passion, but the weight of Matthew's body on hers filled her with longing. Even after he arrived in Amiens, and even after he kissed her and pulled her close only days before, she hadn't allowed herself to indulge in the memories of the last time. Those final days at the beach years ago once felt like the beginning of something, but all that came of them was a long farewell.

The tender warmth of the memory fluttered in her chest.

She glanced sideways at his smug smile while he swung through the courtyard archway to the front of the hospital.

He stopped where the schoolhouse walk met the stairs to the sidewalk. "Where are we headed?"

She took his elbow and led him behind a brick half-wall to the shadows. With the sky still overcast from the brief rain, they stood mostly hidden between the building and a lilac bush. "Right here," she said, and nudged him against the wall. "Just like we used to."

He bent his head and kissed her and one crutch fell into the dirt. "It feels a little different to be in your position. I was always the one chasing you to steal kisses before."

"How do you like being chased?" she whispered as she leaned him back to the wall. With her hands on his chest, his heartbeat reverberated through her body. His breaths deepened and she pressed her lips to his. The fire they had that last night at the beach flickered in her chest in the glow of the Amiens street lamp, and it warmed her as the memories came.

"I love it," he murmured, and were his breath not so warm on her cheek, she would think the past was speaking. "I love you, Vi. I never stopped, and God help me, I never will."

Chapter Twenty-Two

Four Years Ago: 1913

"What's Nag's Head like in the fall?" Victoria asked as Matthew turned the car onto the eastbound road out of Raleigh. "Besides cold?"

He laughed. "I don't even know if it will be cold. We may take some of this warm weather with us. Either way, we'll be living a little rough. At the end of the summer we pack away the blankets and cushions and all that against moths and mice, so we'll have plenty to wrap up with if we're chilled. And that hamper in the back is full of food, so as long as you like apples and bread, we won't starve."

"Will the electricity be on?"

"I'm not sure."

"Won't any shops be open?"

"I don't know. This is the adult version of taking off into the woods with a knapsack and a packed lunch. Thank you for coming with me. This will be an adventure."

She scooted across the seat to hold his hand. "You and your brothers have never gone to the beach house out of season?"

"Never. I always wanted to."

"How fine it is we were both able to escape work for a few days and live out your dream."

"I have many dreams, you know." He squeezed her knee. "One of them is playing house with you all alone, like we're about to."

Victoria rested her head on the shoulder and let the car's rumble run through her bones. It would be a long drive out, a long drive back, and only two nights there. Never mind fixing her schedule to take several days off from the hospital in a row—escaping her parents' home for so long was the real trick. A white lie about work seminars and covering shifts for a friend had done it. Maudie would have been happy to lie for her and say they were taking the children to the mountains or joining the circus or taking flying lessons, but the moment Matthew said "just us," Victoria decided not to tell a soul. No nosy friends, however well-intentioned. No expectations, no itinerary, no world beyond the Cottage Row and a little piece of the Atlantic Ocean.

She stole a glance as he watched the road. The satisfied smile on his lips spread to hers. After the debacle of a proposal the night she finished her training program two years before, she thought she'd never see him again. The irony of celebrating her achievement and asking her to give it up the same night was lost on him until he presented the ring and she looked at him like he was crazy. But, just like the first time, he squeezed into her life again with apologies and hungry kisses and promises to learn from all the times he made assumptions. Since that day, all he ever asked in return was for her to kiss him back.

Victoria thought she could kiss him forever, and when he said he would stop asking her to give up her work for him, she finally believed it. What remained if she didn't though, was uncertain. Courtship either led to marriage or it didn't, and she and Matthew were a tired topic for even the most dedicated gossip-mongers.

I heard she declined him.

Then why is he with her tonight?

He's always with her. Look at him. He's mad about her.

A woman doesn't smile like that if she's not in love. Why did she say no?

I heard she's working in the city hospital.

He has a fine job now. She doesn't need to work like a factory girl.

It's that Maudie Truxton's influence, I'll wager. Lovely girl, but her talk about women's equality is awfully brash. That wild husband of hers should correct her.

At least they got married and had children. What about these two? They can't carry on like this forever.

The salt air on the Outer Banks was a gusty wind that whipped Victoria's skirts up to her knees as they unlocked the house. The driftwood stacked in the shuttered screen room made a crackling fire in minutes. Long-salted by the sea, the wood spouted green and purple flames and a particular tangy smoke that filled the chilly air with summer. Split logs went into the two-story Russian fireplace. Its thick stone walls would warm the central part of the large house and keep the coals red-hot all night.

"Bedding and towels are done," Matthew announced as he walked downstairs. "I do hope you like the smell of cedar. Apples and bread for dinner, or did I pack anything better?"

She handed him a mug of tea. "I saw what you packed, you sneak."

"How on earth did that chocolate cake slip in there?"

"And peach pie. You made a stop at Miss Cinnamon's."

"The peach pie is for breakfast. It's practically a strudel."

"You're practically a strudel."

"I adore you." He held his mug with both hands and breathed in the steam. "Who knew such well-bred young people as you and I could be so rebellious?"

She puckered her lips and blew him a kiss over the rim of her teacup. "Pie for breakfast, indeed. What scandal next? I fear my virtue is in jeopardy."

"Only if you want it to be."

"You're quite the adventurer now."

"My adventurous side often has pathetically poor timing." He winked. "I blurt out foolish sentiments at weddings. I stupidly insult the woman I love on a day celebrating her achievements."

"Matthew."

"But perhaps I have learned my lesson. The woman I love has been very understanding."

Wrapped in thick wool blankets, they ate bread and apples on the sofa in the living room and watched the driftwood blaze as the sun set. After talking for hours on the drive, they tendered the conversation to the crackling fire and the whistling wind between the houses.

Victoria rested in his arms. They had talked about work all day, his cases, her patients. Three nurses in the hospital had been let go since summer for getting married. What would she have to talk about without her work? Sewing circles? Children? He wanted a big family like he grew up in, and she had daydreamed of dark-haired babies with gray eyes. His many siblings had kept their mother busy—the kind of busy Victoria liked to be, nurturing and teaching. Of course, with a brood like that one, she'd likely be nursing sick children half the year as well, but that might not fill the space hospital nursing would leave behind.

"Matt?"

"Vi?"

"Would you excuse me for a minute? It's not terribly comfortable to cuddle up with you all buttoned and laced."

"I put your things in the first room on the right upstairs."

"I'll be right back, then."

When she slipped back down the stairs, she saw his jacket, tie, and waistcoat draped over a chair. "Matthew? Where are you?"

"In the kitchen," he called. "Blackberry wine, or shall we put some of Rigby's homemade brandy in the tea? His distilling efforts are somewhat less toxic these days."

"Wine, please."

He came back to the living room, smiling and with his

shirt unbuttoned at the top, and nearly dropped the glasses when he saw her.

"Do you like it?" She twirled like she was in a ball gown, and the decadent green silk tunic and harem pants floated as soft as rose petals over her skin. "Georgia said some French designer made something like this for a costume party, all done up with beads and spangles. She thought they would make pretty pajamas."

"She was right. And you are exquisite, my love." Firelight flickered across his face as he set the glasses aside and reached for her, warm hands through the thin silk over her back and waist. "Damn the wine. Let me drink you in."

"You're awfully thirsty," she said when he let her pull back from a kiss.

"Parched." His breathing sped up as he pulled her next to him on the deep couch. The red cloth cushions smelled of the cedar storage closet, a whiff of the woodsy fragrance of the shingled walls outside. "I could feast on you, Victoria. Come over here so I can watch the fire make gold flecks in your eyes while these emerald pajamas bring out the green."

"Your eyes are the stormy sea. All shades of gray. Deep and thoughtful, with so much beneath the surface."

"Unless my eyes and hands deceive me, there's not much beneath the surface of this green silk."

"It's not very accommodating to the superfluous undergarments I am expected to wear."

"How delightful we have no expectations here."

"None?" She plucked open two more buttons on his shirt and slid her hand over his chest.

"Desires and expectations are very different things. I expect little. But I think you know I desire very much."

She let out a short gasp when he slipped his hand under her tunic and spread his fingers wide on her bare back. His touch was a magnet that closed the space between them.

She kissed him again and again, relishing the pressure of his fingers and the way her wandering touches made his body tense in response.

"I will love you like this as long as I breathe." He squeezed her tight. "I cannot shake you, Victoria. If you break my heart again, I still cannot imagine admiring and wanting another woman as much as I do you."

The timid girl she once was still peeked out sometimes and wondered if he would love her so much when she didn't have her work for him to admire. Would he admire her for keeping house and raising children? Anyone could do that. Even Maudie only worked now when Cooper ran for re-election. Her life circled around their growing family.

Not every woman could earn a nursing certificate, and not every nurse could complete hospital training. Not every hospital-trained nurse was allowed in the operating room.

"And although your work often takes you away from me," he continued, "how lucky am I to be in such skilled hands? My every breath is in your care." He pressed her hand to his heart.

"Every breath?" she asked as he stroked her hair. "You are such a romantic."

"It's the truth."

"Sometimes I cannot breathe around your love."

He froze. "Am I suffocating you with affection?"

"No, I—well, I only meant that sometimes your love makes me want to stop breathing."

"That's not especially flattering, either."

She tried again. "I want so much to be still with you. Your love is vast and tidal, always moving but never changing. I often feel pulled in different directions, but right here, if I hold my breath, maybe time will stop for a moment." She moved on top of him and he sucked in a quick gasp. "I love you, Matthew."

The flames sparkled in his eyes and he brushed back her loose hair from his face. "I love you." He cleared his throat and pressed her tight against him. "But before I say anything else, please note that I made up two beds."

"I don't wish to presume on your space." She pushed back from his chest, smiling, as if she meant to get up.

He yanked her back against him and kissed her hard and deep, lips and tongues in a breathless tangle. "Please do. I prefer my space to be in your arms, in your bed, and everywhere I can reach you."

"My toes?" She wriggled her feet on his.

"Can't reach them from here."

"My ankles?"

"Not quite."

"My knees, then. Scandalous bits you can only see at the beach."

"Almost." He slid his hands over her backside, squeezing until she sighed. "There. That's as far as I can reach like this, darling."

"It must be some sort of crime for a man's hands to feel so lovely when doing things they really shouldn't." She brushed her fingers over his cheek. "Yours are felonious."

He reached for her hair and looped her long curls over his arms. "Shackle me," he whispered, "and I am at your command."

In a visceral way she didn't understand, her wanting churned in her belly with a warm ache as she touched him, kissed him, pulled him up from the couch and led him up the stairs to a little wood-paneled bedroom with lace curtains over a window darkened by latched hurricane shutters. Desire tingled in her fingertips as she unbuttoned his shirt, and it chased down her spine when her silk pajamas fluttered to the floor and she met him beneath the cool cotton sheets.

"My love, you are a vision." He kissed her bare shoulder, exploring her body with long, lazy strokes of his hand. "You color my days with happiness."

She caught her breath as his hand wandered lower and cupped her breast. "You are always the brightest part of mine."

"And you fill my nights with the most exquisite dreams."

His lips and teeth met her skin and she gasped. "But I think you are wide awake right now."

"You invited me to your bed. I'll be awake for hours. Days, if you wish."

She kissed him, pulling him close and cutting off his speech as she arched against him, flooding her senses with his skin, his scent, his arms. Her hands roved him hungrily, memorizing muscle and bone as she pressed her body to his, thighs and stomachs and chests smothered in kisses.

He broke from her kiss, breathless, and rolled on top of her. His lips were tender, his eyes questioning.

"Victoria, my love."

She froze. "Please don't say it."

He bent forward and kissed her forehead, rocking his hips against hers. "One day. I know it's not today."

The words unlocked her, and she sank into the bed beneath his weight, every muscle unwinding. “Yes. One day.”

She winced at the quick pain as he entered her. His eyes were stormy and ocean-deep and she couldn’t look away from the beautiful planes of his face, the strong angle of his jaw and stubborn chin and the sweet glimpse of his tongue between his teeth. Wind whistled around the house as he moved in her gently and whispered.

Words failed her. *I love you* was not enough. She opened her mouth to speak again and again, but there was only his breath, his kisses, murmured devotion and promises as they clung to one another, shifting together as the bed creaked. The wanting rose again to a fever pitch, curling her fingers and toes. Her body ached all over and her muscles burned, demanding him.

Matthew kicked off the blanket, sweaty and laughing. “And to think I worried we’d be cold.”

She grabbed his arms. “You cannot pull away from me like that. I forbid it.”

He kissed her. “I wasn’t pulling away from you.”

Victoria moved her hands over his shoulders, down his back, over his hips, clinging to him. He *was* slipping away, even as he held her in the warmest intimacy, the tide was taking him. She gripped him tighter, squeezing her fingers and scratching his skin.

He responded with a leisurely kiss and nuzzled her cheek. “I’m right here, Vi. Don’t worry. I’m right here.”

Three weeks later, Victoria shivered on the bench in front of the law office and wrapped her cloak tighter. Raleigh's crisp autumn was on the cusp of winter, and a chilly breeze emptied the branches of the city's majestic oak trees. She watched, toes tapping nervously, as a little tornado of dried leaves swirled on the sidewalk. Matthew would be in a client meeting for another thirty minutes, and she hated waiting in the dark-paneled lobby with the gossipy secretaries' eyes on her from across the room. The whispers were always the same.

She's just leading him on.

It's a shame he puts up with it. I know half a dozen girls who'd love to have him.

And you're one of them.

Well, just look at him. And she'll grow out of her looks at this rate, so we'll see what he thinks then.

A pair of dark shoes polished to a mirror shine stopped in front of her.

"Miss Harper, you are welcome to go inside."

"Mr. Shipley." She bobbed her head at the white-haired man, Matthew's boss, the senior partner. "Thank you. I've been inside all day and the fresh air is welcome."

"Ah, yes. How is work?"

"Busy, as usual," she said, and did not elaborate. She'd learned not to, in certain company. Very few people really cared what she was learning, and no matter how much her love for her work overflowed in her words, her excited babble often met with awkward silence.

"Indeed." He gestured at the door. "Your young man's last meeting was cut short. I'm sure he'll be pleased to see you."

"Thank you, sir."

He touched the brim of his hat and turned away.

The secretaries' eyes burned into her back as she walked past without greeting them or asking to be admitted, and Matthew's face lit up when she stepped into his office.

"Darling. What a delightful surprise." He greeted her with a peck on the lips, then paused when he drew back and looked into her eyes. "Or is it a surprise? Did I forget something?"

She took a deep breath. "No, it's just that it's been a few weeks since we got back, and I thought you should know I am regular as clockwork. I wanted to tell you as soon as I was sure. If you were worried about any untoward outcomes, you needn't be."

"I wondered, Vi, but I wasn't worried."

"Why not?" She fidgeted with her gloves. "We could have been more careful. I cannot believe I didn't insist."

He shrugged and scooped up the books scattered around his wide chestnut desk, tucking them into the crook of his arm. "I wasn't worried because I figured if something happened, we would manage."

"We would manage?"

"We love each other." He kissed her cheek over the armful of books and turned to the shelf. "We have the means to support a family. And we agreed it's going to happen one day, so if it happened sooner, no, I wouldn't be put out."

"Of course you wouldn't." She sighed. "You're not the one who would have to give everything up."

He dropped the books with a heavy thud on the desk.

"Matthew?"

Chest heaving, he stared at the thick leather cover of a study on North Carolina civil statutes. "I wonder if in some tiny, inadmissible way, you might have preferred a little mistake," he said slowly. "Perhaps that is why you didn't insist on certain precautions even when I offered."

She jerked her head up. "I beg your pardon?"

"We've gone on for years because you won't make a decision. If you were with child, you wouldn't give up your career. You'd have it taken away. You could live without second-guessing your choice because the choice wouldn't be on your shoulders anymore."

"It would be in my belly, a fine improvement. How dare you?"

"How dare *I*?" He leaned across the desk, his voice hoarse. "Indeed. How dare I hope that something will tip you off this tightrope you've strung for yourself? How dare I be a little impatient after four years of being thought weak for having the audacity to respect you? And how dare you pretend this mess is all the fault of other people's expectations?"

"You know perfectly well that I cannot—"

"You could be a midwife or do house calls with a regular doctor if you wanted to marry me, and I've waited years for you to reach this conclusion yourself. Married women work, just not in hospitals. What if you were with child and caught pneumonia or measles? Maudie balances her work and family, so why can we not do the same?"

"Maudie has her letter-writing campaigns to Congress

because she is good at that sort of thing and passionate about her causes," Victoria snapped. "I cannot make my own schedule like she can, but I am a good nurse and passionate about my work. I thought you admired and appreciated that."

"Darling, of course I do."

"Maudie and I are not the same. We never have been."

"Do not try and twist this," he said. "For the hundredth time, I am not trying to equate you. Every time you harp on how I used to feel for her, you only drive home how my admiration for independent women is the problem here."

He shoved a book into its place on the shelf so hard he rattled the volumes next to it. "I love your ambition and your mind and your fearless spirit, and yes, she has some measure of these things, too. But Victoria, I love you for yourself, and I didn't know desire before I knew you. Nor did I understand that these things I love about you are the very things that will tear us apart."

Victoria seethed. "I suppose you resent that Cooper got the wife whose ambitions align so neatly with his."

"Well, it would certainly be easier if your life's ambition was to be the world's fastest and most accurate typist," he snapped.

"Yes, and I'll come home pouting because you took on a case with a Mr. Quinn and the 'Q' is so far from my poor delicate pinky finger. Or perhaps I won't have time to pout. I'll be too busy seeing to your dinner."

"Christ, Victoria, I'll hire help if that's what you want. I can afford it."

"So can I."

"Delightful." He paced the worn carpet in long strides

and sharp pivots. "We will pay for someone to keep our house and cook our food if that's what makes you happy."

"It's not as simple as that, and you know it."

"What I know is that you promised me you'd find a way to make this work for us. I cannot ease that burden for you, because you're the one whose position must change. I cannot hire you at a hospital, and I cannot do a damn thing to make this right or fair. This was always your choice."

"I don't—"

"You don't know what you want." He dragged his hands through his hair and stopped pacing. "You love me, which I have never doubted, but you don't know what you want from me. I don't think you even know what you want from yourself."

She turned for the door and gripped the brass knob to steady herself. Matthew understood her and respected her. He preferred comfort over confrontation, and he always came around.

"We will talk about this later," she said. "Sometime."

"No, we will not."

"What?"

The ruddy flush that had gathered on his cheeks drained away and he walked toward her, pale-faced and calm.

"We took a stolen weekend where we played at being married and said one day we would make it real, but pinning down that 'one day' is still too much for you." His breath hitched as he pulled her back from the door. "And I don't think it's enough for me."

A chill shot through her body. "What do you mean?"

"Marry me, Victoria. Say you'll marry me, or leave."

Her throat closed as she met his red-rimmed eyes in stunned silence.

"If you walk away without answering, that's still a choice." His voice was raw and pained. "That means no, never. 'One day' is no longer an option."

She forced her numb lips to move as her eyes welled. "Matthew, we can talk tonight. Please don't do this."

"The conversation will be the same tonight as it has been every other night. It will be the same tomorrow and the next day and the next until I put a stop to it and demand an answer. So I'm demanding it now."

He released her and stepped away, leaving her path to his arms as clear as her path to the door.

"Say yes," he said, "or leave and let me have the last word on this matter. I cannot bear to hear you decline me again."

Chapter Twenty-Three

A gusting wind swept Amiens overnight and whipped the drying leaves from the trees in the hospital courtyard. It whistled along Rue de Renard as Nora tossed and turned and Victoria wrapped herself tight in her blanket in a restless sleep. The weather had calmed by morning, but her thoughts whirled like a hurricane through breakfast and her walk to work. The heat of Matthew's hands and lips outside the hospital the night before still warmed her skin, and color rose in her cheeks every time she indulged a thought of what it would be like to go to bed with him again—whether the dark curls on his chest felt the same, whether the smooth shift of the muscles in his arms would set her thirsting to kiss them.

Then, just as quickly, the storm winds changed and chilled her bones when she remembered walking away from his office, from their life together, from *him*, mute and dazed and dry-eyed. He slipped away because she didn't hold tight enough.

When she crossed the threshold of the courtyard, she cast

a wary eye up at the window to the administrative offices. Nurse Perry had likely left for the day when the confrontation with Harry occurred the night before, but if Harry had seen them on the ground, perhaps someone else had, too. Watching eyes and listening ears were everywhere. Explaining shell shock might work to defend Matthew's behavior, but she would still be reprimanded, perhaps forbidden to see him at all.

As for Harry, after what he said to Matthew, Victoria wasn't sure she cared anymore whether he stayed or went. Soldiers became infatuated with nurses and VAD girls all the time, mistaking their tenderness and care for love after months or even years away from such affection. Victoria thought she was careful to mind the men's hearts as well as their limbs. She and Harry enjoyed idle chatter and got along well, but she racked her brain for a time she might have given him the impression she thought of him as anything more than a friend, and found nothing—not that it mattered. A misunderstanding would be forgiven, but the insults were worth some ire. Matthew handled it with dignity, but she was still seething.

The operating room was her refuge. Nurse Perry wouldn't dare pull her from surgery for a dressing-down, and Victoria calmed her nerves for a lengthy case with Dr. Bowden and Dr. Hawkins repairing a bone splintered by a deep bayonet wound in a patient's shoulder.

"Look here," Bowden said, pointing at the shoulder with a probe. Beneath the swipes of orange iodine, telltale red streaks extending from the wound signaled gas gangrene. "Do you remember at the start of the war, we heard a rumor the Huns painted their bayonets with some concoction full of measles? Horse shit. They never needed to. Harp, how are we on blood pressure?"

"A little low."

"Level him out." He nodded to the Connell machine.

"What settings, sir?"

"What do you think?"

Hawkins narrowed his eyes and watched her inspect the valves and flowmeters he set to begin the case.

"I'd favor the oxygen about five percent," she said.

"Go ahead, please. Now Hawkins, let's have a look around."

Bowden lingered after the case when Victoria began sorting soiled instruments into trays. He checked the hallway and shut the door.

"A word, Harp."

Her stomach clenched. "Dr. Bowden, if this is about what happened last night with Matthew, I think you'll agree with me—"

"Something happened last night?"

"That isn't what you wanted to talk about?"

"It is now. Ladies first."

She untied her surgical mask and exhaled heavily. "I was going to tell you anyway, I promise. If Nurse Perry hears, she'll be furious."

"And?"

"When the storm came in, I think he had a bout of what you call shell shock."

"Go on."

"We were in the courtyard when a huge clap of thunder

startled us. He panicked and pulled me to the ground, and he got on top of me to protect me."

Bowden pressed his hand to his forehead. "You're all right? He's all right?"

"Yes. He was in a strange state for only a minute and I reassured him over and over that we were safe. He thought he heard bombs and shelling. As soon as he realized what happened, he was mortified and sat me up right away. I'm sure it looked awful, but he didn't hurt me and I wasn't in any danger."

"If it comes up, I'll talk to Nurse Perry. There's not a lot he can do to stop it. Good girl staying calm." His shoulders drooped in an undignified slouch as he closed his eyes. "Thunder sounds like shells and planes. Railroads, like artillery. Any two pieces of metal crashing together at speed. A whistle. Any man's scream. This goddamn war. It kills the people it doesn't kill."

The pale blue walls seemed to tighten around her, and she shivered. "Will this always happen to him?"

"This war has given us louder, more violent ways to attack the enemy than ever before." He scooted a handful of probes together, the steel handles clinking like chimes. "It's given us better medicine, so men who would have died in any other war go home to their families. We have yet to fully grasp what the memory of those weapons will do to the men who survived them. We can stitch them up and cure their ailments, but no surgery can excise what these men have seen." He squinted into the sunlight that crept past the window's edge and blazed a bright stripe through the room. "Last night. Did anyone see it happen?"

"Harry did."

"Oh, hell. Tell me that clumsy bastard didn't break his shoulder again trying to wrestle Berger off you."

Victoria sighed. "I almost wish he had. I told him I was all right and asked him to leave, but he didn't go and the men had words."

"I imagine they did. Go on."

"Harry insulted him. Matthew said he thought he was staying here not because he wished to be our ally but because he had romantic feelings for me." She watched his eyes. "Harry did not deny it."

Cursing, Bowden yanked his surgical cap off his head and pitched it into the linen hamper. His thinning gray hair stood up in unruly tufts as he composed himself. "If Cupid makes another flight over this hospital, I'll shoot the bastard down myself."

"Sir?"

He flipped a probe in his hand and pointed at her. "I am not worried about you. Berger's not one of mine, and he has no means to take advantage of you, not that I think he'd dare try. I'll deal with Harry, but there is something more unpleasant we must address with some haste."

"What is that?"

"It's about Nurse Scott."

Victoria's breath caught in her throat. "Yes?"

"I will offer her two options." He fidgeted with a square of cotton gauze. "Most people don't get a choice, but I have some sympathy for her situation, all things considered."

"Her situation?"

"She can return to England. That will be the Red Cross's position. If she wishes to stay, I can make that possible. Either way, I will deal with Wentworth for his part in this."

Victoria's cheeks went as cold as the steel knives in her hand. "Sir. She never told me."

"She never told me, either, but I told you not to discount what an old man can see right in front of his nose, didn't I?" He scooped up a row of clamps and dropped them into a sterilizing basin with a clatter.

"But are you sure it's him? I know Nora. She would not go with a married man."

Nora wouldn't go with any man. If she wouldn't give the time of day to the handsome young Dr. Lambert who was at least single and sweet, why would she engage in such a way with Dr. Wentworth, of all people?

"Think it through, Harp."

She snapped upright. "Oh. He and his wife do not have a good marriage. He suspects her of infidelity and may have told Nora he was separated or divorcing."

"And there we have it," he said. "Nurse Scott is no fool, but she is anxious to advance her skills in surgery and he's a silver-tongued lecher who happens to be good with a knife. I believe when Wentworth flattered her work she warmed to him because she felt appreciated." He snorted. "He probably told her his wife doesn't understand him like she does. Working with her makes his day brighter and motivates him and rot like that."

Wentworth had openly disdained women's work, and for such a man to thaw and treat one with respect could make a girl feel special. It happened to Victoria as well, on the day of the tunnel emergency, when he placed her on his level and said they were both professionals. How Nora would have loved to hear that.

Women at home don't understand what a war does to a man,

he said to her that day, complaining about his wife. Poor Gloria Wentworth might not understand, but her husband could have painted a pretty picture for Nora, telling her how smart and clever and sweet she was to understand him the way she did.

White-knuckled and silent, Victoria opened and closed a bladed forceps, twisting it in the light to see the glint on the sharpened edges and needle-fine point.

"Don't get any ideas." Bowden shoved a tray across the table. "Wentworth will choose tonight between a one-way ticket home to his wife in disgrace or a transfer to a field hospital up north. We'll see where he'd like to get his nethers tickled this time."

"Nora is strict with herself," Victoria said, struggling for words. "I don't know how this happened, but I'm sure she's very sorry, sir."

"How this all happened does not matter. Why it happened is always the same. A man with some authority uses a woman's hope for the future to get what he wants. Whether I call that conduct unbecoming of an officer or verminous turpitude, I will not have it in my ranks." He straightened his shoulders. "If Nurse Scott wishes to go home, she will have my support in getting what she needs from him. If she wishes to continue in her job after he leaves, I will relieve her of her burden."

Victoria grabbed an alcohol vial from her tray and waved it under her nose. A quick whiff steadied her while the emotion in Bowden's normal matter-of-fact tone drove home his pity.

"Easy there." He took her elbow. "I want you to tell her

and help her make her choice, if she needs help. I believe hearing it from me would frighten her."

She stood taller and composed herself. "I know she will appreciate your compassion."

"We'll do it tomorrow night, if she wants it done. I would like your assistance."

"I'll tell her this evening."

"You're a good friend and an excellent nurse, Harp." He flicked the vial in her hand. "A bit of a wobble here and there is human. We must remain human."

"Thank you, sir."

She stared at the instrument trays after he left the room. Picking through them, she separated the mass of steel into piles and counted everything three times. A pile of Ochsner forceps. A pile of Halsteds. Curved, straight, locking, unlocked, flat, rounded, sharp, blunt. Scissors, knives, probes, retractors, needles, empty beakers and ampoules amid black rubber tubing coiled around it all like snakes. She nudged the hanger for intravenous drips and rolled it a few feet away. The discarded cloth cover from the saline container waved from the hook like a white flag.

She slammed her foot into it and it crashed into the wall, teetering for a moment before it fell to the floor. The clatter rang around the blue walls of *l'école maternelle* and the painted alphabet mural that danced above the windows with its cheerful message.

Nous aimons apprendre!
We love to learn!

She picked up the pole, threw away the cover, and took the instruments away to be washed.

Chapter Twenty-Four

A chorus of men's voices raised in a peppy rendition of 'God Save the King' greeted Victoria when she entered room five, still dazed from her talk with Dr. Bowden. The sun had begun to set outside the blue gingham curtains, and Major Cartwright was up on his crutches and swinging jauntily from bed to bed to convince his countrymen to join in the singing.

"Come on then, Berger!" he shouted. "God bless a Yorkshireman, and God save the king!"

"Your king, my friend," Matthew said, eyes down as he wrote a letter. "But God save Wilson too, while we're at it. Pershing might be better, if we're doing any saving. Come to think of it, why do your people not ask God to save the field marshal?"

"Come on, mate. It's fine news. Don't you want to go home?" Cartwright looked up and spotted Victoria lingering in the doorway. "Ah. Bit different for you then, isn't it?"

"I can hear you, Major Cartwright." Victoria waved him

off. "Go rally the troops. Have fun." Still in her uniform, she leaned on the end of Matthew's bed.

He didn't look up.

"What is he talking about going home for?" she asked. "After a surgery like you both had, you should spend several weeks here."

"It's good news from the front lines, I suppose." Matthew tapped his pen on his letter. "Well, not good news exactly. The storms are gathering near Ypres again, they say, and whether that's good for us or bad—"

"Casualties, of course."

"Thousands of men to move out of the field," Matthew said. "Swann thinks they will need all the hospital beds from here to Rouen. I imagine they'll be shipping them out of the field hospitals and down here as fast as they get them in."

Victoria blanched. "Surely they're just sending Cartwright and his men back to the rehabilitation hospital in London. That's for the British. You'll have to wait here and see what the Americans want to do. Do you know where your unit is?"

"Maybe in the thick of it by now." Matthew gulped and his gaze flicked to the window as though he could see his friends up north—already two men down, maybe more. "But Swann said they're sending me with the British now and the U.S. Army can pick me up at its convenience. They are making plans for our transport in about ten days."

Her breath seized in her throat. She closed the curtain to the courtyard and moved a privacy frame between his bed and Cartwright's. Damn the rules and whatever Nurse Perry thought would be 'better.' It would be better if she didn't lose him only days after she got him back.

"You cannot go already," she declared.

"I don't have a choice, Vi."

"I'll swab some sick man from the medical ward and rub it in your nose. You can't travel when you're contagious. I helped Harry play sick. I can help you."

He stifled a hoarse laugh and didn't smile. "On the bright side, you said the hospitals in London are top-notch. Bowden's friends, right? The finest new prosthetics?"

She sat on the mattress and squeezed his hands. "Matthew, please."

"Please what? I have no choice in the matter. I don't like it, but I have no choice. It's a familiar situation to me."

He finally looked up and Victoria drew back at the sight of his red-rimmed eyes.

"What do you mean by that?" she asked.

"I think you and I are more alike in some ways than I thought. The army tells me where to go, and I go." His voice cracked. "The world always told you where you could work and not work, and I don't think I fully understood until now how much easier it is to resign yourself to taking orders than trying to upend it all and fail. It's rather appealing, really. When you can choose for yourself, whatever goes wrong is your fault."

"Matthew—"

"Today, I go where the army sends me. In days past, I painted myself as your patient, heartbroken suitor but in reality, I could have stood up at any time before that last day and said we must make a choice. I had a choice and avoided it, just as you did, because I couldn't bear to be the one at fault." His hand opened and closed as though he'd reach for her but held back, grasping instead at the thin cotton blanket. "A fine time to recognize one's own hypocrisy, isn't it? Had I a mirror, it would hurt to look in it right now."

She scooted closer and pressed a hand to his chest. "Dearest, you were never at fault. It was always my choice, just as you said, and all that's past. We don't need to unearth that pain. We have ten days together now."

"Ten days."

"That's ten days more than we ever dreamed we would have again." She stroked his cheek. "Perhaps I can take a leave and we can go someplace for a little while. You're obviously well enough to go to England, so why not? We could just find an inn in Amiens and get away from all these prying eyes and listening ears. We could be alone."

"I don't know if I could be the way I was the last time we were alone." He cleared his throat. "Forgive me. It is bold of me to assume you might want that, when we—well, when I—"

"Speaking as your nurse, there is nothing about your injury that should affect you in any intimate way. Speaking as the woman who loves you, that is not why I want to take you away from this place."

"And it is not the reason I want to be alone with you. But are we setting ourselves up for another heartbreak if we do this?"

The beach house with its shuttered windows, cool sheets, and fresh salt air was a thousand miles away, wrapped in memories, and it should stay there. He was in front of her, her Matthew, in a uniform he'd bled on, in a haze of antiseptic that stung her nose, and balanced on the edge of reason where he might give her another chance to break him.

Victoria cupped her hand gently over his like she held

their hearts between them and didn't give herself time to take it back.

"If we are on borrowed time," she said, "let us make the most of it. I'll buy a chocolate cake for dinner. A very tiny one, since it will be worth its weight in gold."

He gave her a wry smile. "Even if we do not have the same adventurous itinerary, perhaps we can also find a peach pie for breakfast. How do we arrange this?"

Her mind raced through her options. "Bowden can release you. I'll have to ask Nurse Perry for my leave. She might be delighted to have me away for a bit so I don't set a poor example for the younger girls."

"Indeed." He grinned. "As I recall, you're not supposed to be sitting so close to me in uniform. Shame on you, Nurse Harper."

"Well, this is for your morale, soldier." She kissed him. "And for mine. I am about to have a terrible evening and I won't be able to come back for our usual visit."

"What's happening this evening?"

She glanced at the men celebrating. "I'll tell you privately tomorrow if we can get outside."

"You're all right, though?"

"I'm all right. But Nora isn't, and I need to help her."

"I'll wait." He pulled her close for a kiss, a deeper one, lingering. "I'm quite good at waiting when I have your kisses to look forward to. I'll take that to tide me over."

Chapter Twenty-Five

Marie didn't wait until they were all seated for dinner before blurting out "Dear Diary, today I had to organize dead men's clothes. I washed my hands a hundred times after and I still feel so awful." She dropped her plate on the table and hung her head, muffling her voice. "And it was very strange, but I survived."

Frances reached for her hand. "That's one of those things you simply can't let yourself think about too much. Everywhere in the laundry service, you are faced with messes of unspeakable origin. It's a job that must be done, and we're glad you're here to do it."

"I'm not glad."

"Our patients are grateful for those uniforms."

"But everything on those shelves is from a man who died."

"Yes. That's true."

"And the men who use them don't have to be reminded of their own injuries every day," Bridget interjected. "Even if the trousers aren't quite the right shade or the fabric is a little different, they can feel a little more like they did before they came here. It's good for their morale."

Nora watched the exchange in silence, pushing food around her plate as Victoria eyed her shaking hands.

Ingrid looped her arm around Marie's shoulders. "There now. We are all here to help others even if our work must be distasteful, and that's just what you're doing. I don't like that closet, either."

"It is normal and natural to feel this strain," Bridget added. "Sometimes it will make you furious and sometimes it will be horribly sad. I threw a pair of bone forceps at the wall after a bad day. The sharp ones, and I stuck them right in there, too. When the schoolchildren come back, they will think we took enemy fire."

"I kicked an IV pole into the wall today," Victoria said. "It made a spectacular crash when it fell over. Sometimes the silence is just too loud."

Ingrid shook her head. "You are all so gloomy. Who has a more cheerful diary entry to lift Marie's spirits?"

"I'll share a funny one," Frances offered. "A laugh at my own expense, though. Do you know Dr. Forrester, who usually works with Dr. Swann? I hardly know the man at all. He was called up to work with Dr. Carraker today. I was setting up my trays for our case before anyone came in, and I was singing under my breath."

Bridget giggled. "Preparing for a case with Carraker? Oh, no. What were you singing? One of his Scottish favorites?"

"It was the one about the lady in the loch." Frances brushed her hair behind her ears and raised her forks like a torch. "And this man I do not know walked right in while I was singing 'and she's above while I'm below' and brandishing a handful of knives."

Victoria nearly spit a mouthful of soup and Bridget, wheezing with laughter, smacked her back to keep her from choking. "Oh, that is splendid. He's going to get in trouble one day for singing those songs around women."

"In trouble with whom? He'll just tell Nurse Perry none of her innocent girls would understand the innuendo because we are too pure, and she'll be far too embarrassed to suggest we aren't." Frances snorted a quick laugh. "We should all be able to handle men's humor by now."

"What aren't we supposed to understand?" Marie asked. "Above and below?"

Setting down her forks as daintily as scalpels, Frances cleared her throat. "In any case, since I am his senior assistant, any other woman in the room should complain to me first."

"What does the song mean, though?" Marie asked again.

Frances popped a slice of bread into her mouth so she couldn't answer. Nora stood and picked up her plate, still full, and walked to the kitchen.

Marie persisted as Bridget and Frances ate in silence, stifling their laughs with vegetable soup and baguettes. Blanche tutted her disapproval. Wide-eyed, Ingrid glanced among them and told her petulant friend that she didn't know what the song meant, either, and she didn't care.

After finally distracting Marie with the secret about the cat in the nurses' quarters and promising to take her to see it, Victoria escaped the table. She cornered Nora in their room and locked the door.

"We need to talk, darling. Here. Now." Victoria plopped onto the bed next to her. "We should have talked about this yesterday, or weeks ago. When you said you wanted to go home, you did not mention you might be sent home whether you wanted it or not."

Nora's chin trembled. "Who told you that?"

"Dr. Bowden figured it out. He told me. But Nora, why didn't you?"

Her tears spilled. "I wasn't so sure there was anything to tell until last week when I realized how long it had been since I bled. I haven't been regular because my nerves are so shaken and all my symptoms just come and go, but—oh no. How does he know?"

Victoria sat next to her on her bed and took her hand. "He says he's seen it many times and he has sympathy for your situation because of the other person involved."

"Oh, God."

"Nora. Darling."

"I know you hate him." Nora pulled away and wrapped her arms around herself, shivering as she wept. "Don't ask me why, please. I am such a fool."

"Whyever it was, you deserve so much better than what he can give you."

"He said his wife was unfaithful and she was leaving him," Nora said. "He said I understood him and she never had. He said that I brightened his days and he couldn't imagine working without me, and it all sounded so pretty to think of being home with a lovely husband and no more war, and I—I must have lost my mind, but I believed him."

Victoria stroked Nora's dark hair and caught a tear before it fell to the rose-patterned bedspread. "Affection addles the brain a little, and this war has made us all vulnerable in ways that make little sense. You're not a fool."

"But then he—when I told him what I suspected, he was very quiet but he said he would take care of me. Then he was so awful only a day later. We were only intimate twice, but he said it had been too long and if it was his I would have known sooner, so I must have gone with someone else."

Victoria covered her mouth and whispered between her fingers. "Oh, that rat bastard."

"He said he wouldn't pay me a maintenance to care for the child or anything, and that if I claimed he was the father he would call me a liar."

She put her arm around Nora's shaking shoulders. "Dr. Bowden will vouch for Dr. Wentworth's part in this. He's sending him away, either to Flanders or back to England, and he will write a letter that will help you win over the courts for maintenance payments. Nora, think about his influence. He served with Douglas Haig in India. His niece just married an earl. His word will support yours."

She shook her head, hiccuping as words tumbled out. "I cannot bring anyone into the world like this, unwanted and ashamed. Do you know how many fatherless children there are in England now? It doesn't matter if I get a maintenance payment. My parents will cast me out and I will lose everything I worked for. Why did I believe him?"

"It doesn't matter why."

"I have asked myself over and over, how did I delude myself into thinking I'd be a baroness?" Nora pressed her hands to her damp cheeks. "What have I done? His wife is probably lovely and faithful, poor thing. I would ruin her life, too, if I fought to make him to support me. Everyone would be better off if I flung myself from the ship home."

"No. No one is better off without you." Victoria shook her arm. "Don't talk like that. Darling, you made a mistake and believed a bad man, but that doesn't warrant anything so extreme or tragic. Dr. Bowden can help you if you want to stay here."

Nora turned to her slowly, lips slack with disbelief. "You cannot mean—he wouldn't."

"He is sorry one of his men took advantage of you and he says you should be able to choose your future. He will do the procedure tomorrow night if you wish." She wiped the tears from Nora's cheeks. "I will be with you if this is what you want. I will be right there, helping him."

"But if Nurse Perry finds out—if anyone finds out, I'll have to leave anyway. Maybe you will, too."

"What will be, will be," Victoria held her closer. "If you want the procedure, I will be there."

She slumped in her arms. "What kind of woman am I for wanting it? I'm a fool and a whore and a despicable sinner and—"

"You're a surgical nurse. Many more children might be fatherless if it weren't for you. You've helped many wives and mothers welcome good men home, and you still can."

She didn't respond.

"Nora, you have so many gifts and so much left to give. There's no wrong answer here, but there must be an answer."

Her breath was warm through Victoria's blouse as she sniffled and let her hair fall over her face, shielding her from view. Beyond the pink linen curtains, a car horn announced someone's impatience on a nearby street, and in the quiet that followed, the tension lifted from Nora's neck and shoulders, and her shaking stilled.

"There is no wrong answer," she whispered finally. "But there is no right answer. I have forced the situation on myself in my foolishness. I suppose I am lucky to have this devil's bargain at all."

Victoria waited.

"Giles can go to hell or to Flanders for all I care." Nora sat up. "Oh, his poor wife. Heaven forgive me, but there will be nothing but pain if I go back, for his family and mine, when he and I are the only ones who deserve it. Perhaps I could forgive myself one day by helping people here instead of hurting people at home." She brushed her hair off her damp cheeks. "I'll do it. I must. I cannot believe I really can. You and Dr. Bowden could both get in trouble."

"He could make up a dozen reasons that you need some sort of treatment and explain we did it at night for your privacy," Victoria said. "I'd like to see anyone in that compound tell a colonel he can't use his operating room as he wishes."

Nora rose and faced herself in the mirror. A cool breeze snuck in the window and brought color to her cheeks as she blotted her face with a handkerchief. "I suppose we must take his good advice and get on with it, then."

"Nora?"

"Yes?"

"The baroness of what, exactly?"

"Of nothing, it turns out. He's the youngest son of a baron, with two older brothers. He's just some useless little lordling."

"Yes, but lord of what?"

"*Clostridium* pathogens, I suppose. Battlefield horse shit."

Chapter Twenty-Six

The morning dawned crisp and clear with the type of brisk breeze that usually energized Victoria on her walk to work, but the tasks she would face that day had her dragging her feet down Rue de Renard and over the bridge. Ingrid tugged on her arm.

"Why are you so droopy today?" she asked. "You went to bed so early. How can you be tired on such a pretty day?"

"It's cold," Victoria said, tightening her coat around her.

"Yes, but the sun helps."

"If you're in a hurry, go on ahead. I don't mind. My shift doesn't start till nine. I'll dawdle."

"Are you going to see Matthew?"

"I will try."

"Well, I am going to have a good day." Ingrid bounced a little. "I am moving off laundry duty and to the canteen. Nurse Perry worried I am too slight to move the baskets of all the wet things. No more of that horrible soap that burns my hands."

"That will be a pleasant change."

"Harry has already complained he will miss our talks, but he'll be fine with Marie or Sophie as *Hauptmann*. He likes meeting people."

The courtyard confrontation had not been shared in the daily round of 'Dear Diary,' and the tangle of emotions it wrought might never be confessed. She tried to write it out for Maudie and couldn't make it make sense. Matthew's momentary breakdown still chilled her. He was coping with the amputation as well as could be expected, but the blast itself might shadow him for years.

She packed it away to focus on seeing Nurse Perry about her leave first. Then, it would be on to Harry about his explanation. The box in her mind with Nora's name on it would wait until the day's cases were through.

Victoria rapped on the open door of the head nurse's little office and stepped inside. "Nurse Perry? Are you here?"

"This way," came a voice from behind the door. She emerged with an armful of folders and dropped them on her desk. "More volunteers are on the way, thank goodness. We're clearing out soldiers in batches now and Dr. Swann hears from up north we should expect new ones by the dozen."

"Yes, that's what I wanted to speak with you about. I know it is short notice, but I wonder if you will consider my application for a short leave."

Nurse Perry's brows knitted. "Absolutely not. With all those patients coming in?"

"No, before that." She handed her a form. "Corporal Berger will be part of that batch of soldiers leaving, and I would like to spend some time with him before he goes. As you said before, it doesn't look professional to visit with him here. If Dr. Bowden will clear him for a few days out with a nurse by his side, I would like to visit with him a while longer. Since it is short notice, we thought he might take a room at an inn here in town. I could stay home, and I'll be available to work in an emergency."

Nurse Perry scanned the paper and didn't look up.

"It would be less disruptive than him coming and going from the hospital," Victoria said, trying not to trip over nervous words. "Many places have wheeled chairs and ramps to help all the convalescent soldiers in the city. We could try some nice restaurants and see the sights and—"

"And visit the *Hôtel de Ville*? It's a lovely historic building."

"I'm sorry?"

"You're not planning to marry him on this leave, are you? Since he's overdue to ask you again, that is. I wondered if a stop at City Hall was on your itinerary."

Victoria bristled. "Well, he hasn't asked me, and he's made it clear he's not going to. We are enjoying one another's company and if things tend toward marriage, I imagine that will be back home, when our situation is more secure."

"When does he go?"

"Nine days from now."

"And when did you last have a leave?" She squinted at the paper. "Oh my. It's been some time."

"I can't make it home like some of the other girls can. England is a short trip, Raleigh is not." Victoria made a small pout. "It's wartime and I will do my duty. Only it is so lucky I have this chance to see someone from home for the first time in nearly three years."

"Five days, then."

"Five?"

"Would you prefer only three, as you requested?"

"No, ma'am."

"Five days approved then. Let's have a look at your schedule now. We'll shuffle things around to see which five days." She paused. "And I will be very glad to have you rested, refreshed, and unmarried for this influx of wounded men when you return."

Victoria skipped down the stairs, counting them in fives. Five days with Matthew, abroad in Amiens playing tourist and maybe playing house again. Five glorious, free days without anyone watching or listening—or kicking and insulting.

"Harry?" She knocked on his door. "It's Nurse Harper. I'm here for my explanation. You have ten minutes."

He opened the door, disheveled blond hair sticking up and a red splotch from his pillow on half of one cheek. "I should have asked you to make an appointment. It is very early."

"This is the time I have. I will be on leave for a while and you wanted to speak to me." She sat in the little wooden chair by the door when he gestured her in. "Please explain what Corporal Berger was talking about in the courtyard."

"You have not asked him to explain?"

"I do not wish to upset him further, and since his information is second-hand, I thought I should ask you first."

"This is difficult. We are friends, Nurse Harper."

"I thought we were. What does this mean?"

He lifted a book from the stack by his bed and stared at its blue cloth cover for a moment before speaking. "It is obvious you do not think of me as I think of you."

"I never encouraged you."

"You did not need to. And maybe it is what you call a little smash—"

"A crush."

"As you say. But you are clever and funny and kind, and your beauty is that of dreams. Your hair is spun gold like Rapunzel and your eyes are milk chocolates. How do I not fall in love with you?"

"Pretty compliments are not love. A little crush is not love. It's an infatuation."

"Again, I am mis-translated." He shook his head in frustration. "I do not know what you call it in English to want to be with someone always. But you are the sun in this prison. You are the sky."

"You are not in prison," she said drily. "As I recall, you just sit on your ass here and think you're my hero."

He closed his eyes. "I was in a little temper, I know. I am foolish and had false hope. But if you had said before you had a special man or a lover, I would have kept my tongue."

"Held your tongue." She sighed. "You would have held your tongue. No one slashed it out, although I was rather inclined to when you insulted him."

"He insulted me. Kaiser's boy. Kraut. A traitor."

"You call yourself a traitor."

"I can call myself traitor, but he cannot. I am the one who is—is—" He snapped his fingers in a disjointed rhythm, looking for the word as he muttered. "*Drehen. Mantel*?" He stamped his foot. "*Scheiße*. I am the one who is traitoring, and it is not his affair."

"I told him I was not pleased with him for that, but for you to attack him for his injury when he was on the ground in front of you was unspeakably cruel." She waited until he looked at her. "I still cannot believe you said such a thing."

He turned away and bounced on his toes with nervous energy. "I know that was unkind."

"I'm glad you see that, at least."

"Do not pull me by my ears. You must help me apologize to him like I did Captain Russell. I will do his laundry and make up his bed and fetch and carry. It is hard for him to carry now, yes? I called him a dog, so I will be the dog."

"No."

He broke his stride. "You must. We will make peace and be friends and you will not be angry with me anymore."

"He doesn't want to see you or speak with you. That is his choice."

"But you helped me with Captain Russell."

"She was afraid of you because she was taught to be afraid of all Germans. I will not tell Matthew how he should feel about a personal insult."

"And now I must live with being dreadfully wrong. He will not hear me out, and I think you already decided you will not come visit me again." He threw up his hands. "So that is it."

Victoria didn't look away. "You can complain about how rude he is or how cold I am to spurn your affection, or you can learn a lesson. We must all live with our mistakes. I certainly live with mine."

He stared at the ceiling for a moment, then jumped to touch it. "You will be a good mother, Nurse Harper. You lecture with good sense and your children will never fool you playing sick."

"I can't believe you fooled the Swiss, to be honest."

"We had fun together that day, you and I."

"We did."

Harry jumped again and smacked the ceiling harder. "I would be a good father, you know." He looked at her. "Not like my own."

"You are young and you haven't seen but a handful of women in years," she said. "You should have your American adventure and meet someone to share it with. Someone who likes all your jokes. Someone who wants to discover baseball and cowboys and that whole huge country with you."

"You like my jokes."

"I don't care for baseball."

"Do you believe I am a coward? Afraid of your army, like your man says?"

Her stance softened and she unclenched her hands from knotting the fabric in her pockets. "Not long after you arrived here, you said you disagree with the war and you don't support Germany's government any longer. That's what I know and believe of your feelings. Frankly, I don't care why you changed your mind, as long as it's true."

"It is true."

"I'm glad to hear that."

"And if sitting on my ass in this hospital keeps you safe, then I will sit on it." He plopped back onto his bed and glared at the ceiling. "I will break my arm again if I must. You may tell your man the Kaiser's boy is very brave and devoted to you."

"Why did he think you had romantic feelings for me? Who did you tell?"

Harry's cheeks flushed in an instant. "I asked Captain Russell if she thought you would consider my proposal. She said I should not think of anything like that while the war goes on. Perhaps she told him about that."

Sweet Ingrid, doing her best to make Victoria happy, certainly ran with the news to Matthew so he could secure his position first—but in doing so only added to the pressure he already felt from Maudie and Cooper's telegram. Victoria didn't have the heart to be angry at her interference.

She slumped forward in her chair. What a mess it had all become in such a short while. Nora, Harry, and everything with Matthew—bickering the first day, dreading seeing him the next, and now unable to imagine a day without him.

His promise not to propose stung more than she expected, for she could not pin down in her own thoughts what on earth she wanted or would say if he did. Her thoughtless insistence on taking him away for a few days suddenly loomed over her head with the decision that must certainly follow: he would leave, she would stay, and what then?

"Nurse Harper, you look so sad," Harry said. "I am sorry I upset you and I will not complain. I hope you will think of me as good company again."

"I have a riddle for you."

His eyes brightened. "I'll have it."

"What is my first name?"

His lips twitched, frowned, and finally bent in a resigned smile. "I suppose my proposal would not have been so good after all."

Chapter Twenty-Seven

Room five was dimly lit and its usual chatter hushed, confined to four men seated around the card table inspecting their hands of poker. Several others gathered around. The lights on one side of the room had been extinguished, and when Victoria entered, Major Cartwright waved from the card game.

"Your fellow's having a rest." He jerked his head at the darkened side of the room. "Bad headache since lunchtime, and the stubborn arse won't take anything for it."

She nodded and ducked out of the room, returning moments later with a cold compress.

"Matthew?" She pulled up the chair to his side and patted his shoulder. When he didn't rouse, she pressed the compress to his forehead, and he put his hand over hers.

"Stay, my love."

"Does your head still hurt? I could get you medicine."

"Would you, please? I couldn't ask anyone else."

"Why not?"

He opened his eyes. "I can hardly ask Dr. Swann to send me out on the town still complaining of pain."

"And so you suffered." She clicked her tongue. "A headache is not the same as the kind of pain you'd feel if you had an infection or trouble healing."

"All the same, I wouldn't risk it."

She dug in her apron pocket and found a pouch of aspirin. He gulped down two without water and smiled. "I did ask him, by the way. He said he will approve it if Bowden will. Did you have any luck?"

"I asked Nurse Perry for three days."

"And?"

"And, since we will certainly be very busy after you leave, she gave me five."

He pulled her close for a kiss. "Dearest. Sorry. You're in your uniform. But not sorry, really." He kissed her again. "No one's looking. Five days?"

"Five whole days. We could go to Rouen or maybe even to Paris if you like, but I would love to show you my city."

"You must, darling. I would like to see my competition for your heart."

She drew his hand to her mouth and kissed his fingers. "Amiens has seen so many wounded soldiers that many places have ramps and help for men who can't get around on their own. There are lovely restaurants by the riverside and our cathedral is the finest one in France. We can see the floating gardens, though there's not much in bloom right now, and—Matthew, are you really unwell?"

He leaned back in his pillows and closed his eyes. "It sounds delightful."

"And we can have peach pie every morning, if you like."

"You can't stay with me this time. No decent place will let to an unmarried couple, will they?"

Victoria chewed her lip. "I'll find a way. There must be an accommodating innkeeper. You might need—"

"I will need. Not might. I will need assistance with damn near everything. I haven't even tried to go up and down stairs on my own. I cannot move around a room without crutches. I can't carry anything." He looked up and his forehead creased with worry. "Sweetheart, I am practical and even optimistic about these advances in prosthetics and therapies and all the grand things you tell me are to come. I swear, I am. But today, it hurts like the devil, a waking hell again, when I think of all I cannot do."

She fidgeted. "Things will get better in time."

"And we only have five days."

"I can help you with all those things," she stammered. "But please do not be ashamed of depending on me. You said your pride wouldn't be a problem."

"It is not my pride." He scrubbed his hand over his flushed face and pushed back his hair. "Forgive me. Tell me all the incredible things we'll see and the places we'll go. Fill my mind with dreams for tonight."

The sadness in his eyes was familiar and wrenched her heart. It was the look he wore when he struggled to put rational words to racing thoughts and shoved emotion aside. She recalled so many nights he seemed to bottle up some sort of declaration—of joy, of annoyance, of worry—and he held it all in with an off-hand remark, such as *let's not spoil the evening*, or *enough about that*. Or simply, *forgive me*.

"There is nothing to forgive, Matthew. I want to listen to

anything you have to say, even if it is hard to hear. As long as you wish to say it, I'm listening."

"Vi, I wasn't going to ask you this."

Her breath caught in her throat. "Ask me what?"

"We said not long after I got here that we wouldn't pursue certain uncomfortable topics that might leave us arguing again." He squeezed her hand. "But there is one question that has rolled around my head like a marble for nearly two weeks now, and just to silence it, I wonder if I ought to ask against my better judgment."

She waited.

"The morning after I arrived here, what did you mean when you said you loved me long before I loved you?"

Victoria's cheeks went cold. She'd blurted it out in a moment of pique and tried to hide it by playing up her annoyance at being compared to Maudie. That wretched, whining girl she'd once been had piped up at just the wrong moment, then tried to outrun it by leaving the room before he could demand an explanation or chase after her.

She stared at her hands. "I only meant that I was interested in you for some time before you expressed interest in me."

"But when? We never talked before we worked on Cooper's campaign together, and even then it was just friendly." He chuckled. "Well, friendly until the day you shouted in my face when you thought I was rude to Maudie. You seared that look into my heart. When you followed it up by talking the North Carolina Socialist Party into helping us on election day, I knew I would be smitten for life."

"Don't you remember me before that?" The words came out a pathetic squeak and Victoria straightened her back.

"Before Maudie and I were roommates, I mean. When we first met."

His brows knitted. "We first met at William and Edith's wedding, but that was only for a moment."

"We danced. Just once." She tugged her apron pocket until the seam loosened. "And I know I didn't make much of an impression on you. I was dreadfully shy. I was afraid to look interested or catch your attention even though I wanted it more than anything in the world. Maybe there was nothing remarkable about that dance to you, but I knew that night that there was no other man in the world I wanted to know like I wanted to know you."

"Oh, Victoria."

She stroked his dark hair. "I don't blame you for not remembering. I didn't have much to talk about back then besides what I was knitting and who was calling on whom. I didn't even tell you I was starting my nursing program because I was afraid you'd ask me questions and I'd trip on my tongue." Her voice fell to a whisper. "You talked about how excited you were to start law school and how much you missed playing football with Cooper. You told me about growing up with William and how you pushed him out of a tree and he never told on you. I probably said stupid things like 'how lovely' and 'that's delightful,' but in truth I was just mesmerized by how smart and confident you were."

"I remember myself then. I was arrogant."

"You were so sure of yourself and your path in life, and your humor came from a place of ease. You enthralled me. My sister was taller, prettier, and better at everything, and your brother was infatuated with her. Maudie said if I wanted anyone to be infatuated with me, I had to figure myself out and be true to what I wanted first, and then the right man would beg for my attention."

He nodded and his eyes told her to go on.

"Maudie knew I cared for you. She tried to put off your advances gently so you would still come around and perhaps notice me instead." Her voice broke and she crumpled her skirt in her hand so she wouldn't rip the pocket from her apron. "I didn't mean to make it sound like it's your fault for not noticing me at first. It's not. I wouldn't have noticed that girl, either."

"Victoria, sweetheart."

"You noticed me the day I shouted at you. I was as shocked as anyone that I found my voice to do that."

"And all those months, you were waiting for me and I didn't see you."

"It was just poor timing." She blew out a long breath. "If anything, I blame myself for not trying to be stronger sooner. Why was I such a dishrag to begin with? Perhaps it took this realization to push me the direction I needed to go."

"But if I had known—"

"I wanted to win your affection, but I also wanted to be like you. I love the way you love to study and find all those little tidbits that help you put together just the right brief or make just the right argument. I love watching your mind click them together like puzzle pieces. It makes you so delightful to talk to."

"I love watching you do that when you come home with some new paper or article to read. When you go to lectures and you're the only woman in the room, you come out bursting with energy." His voice went hoarse. "Vi, I am so sorry."

"My work has been our biggest obstacle, but it brings me so much joy and I have you to thank for that. You helped me find who I am. I didn't do it for you, but I did it partly because of you. Because of meeting you, if nothing else."

"Because of me ignoring you."

"That is not what I meant."

He tightened his fingers around hers. "I feel remarkably foolish."

"Is that what you take away from everything I just said?"

"It is my immediate impression, yes."

"Aren't you a little proud of what you've inspired in me?"

"I pushed you away." He tried to pull back his hand and she squeezed it tight. "And right now I feel guilty as hell for not knowing sooner who that quiet girl was at William's wedding. Perhaps I could have made you fall in love with me then, before you fell in love with your work."

"But this is what I mean," she said. "I wasn't the kind of girl you fell in love with back then. Would you have been so devoted all these years if all I did was prattle about luncheons and babies?"

"Yes."

"Matthew, darling, you just said I won your heart by shouting at you and carousing with socialists. I never did such things before."

He yanked his hand from her grip and smashed his palms to his temples. "I cannot think just now. My head is aching and swimming and I have never felt stupider in my life."

"But you didn't do anything wrong."

"Then why didn't you tell me all this years ago?" he demanded. "Why weren't you teasing me for being blind to how much you cared for me?"

Her cheeks burned. "Because it was embarrassing to be so forgettable. And look, you're embarrassed to have forgotten me. Why would I bring it up? You never, ever teased me about panicking and running away when you proposed."

"Perhaps because you discovered you liked being chased."

"That's not true."

"And if you ever married me, the chase would be over."

"Don't put words in my mouth," she snapped. "Don't give me motivations I didn't have. You always knew I loved being with you in every way I could be. Don't you dare undercut that."

"You said over and over that you'd come up with some way to make it work," he said. "I waited. I longed for you to find this impossible way around my guilt and your resentment. It was always 'one day' or 'not now,' but never 'no.' You couldn't have just said no."

"Was I wrong to try and fail instead of giving up right away?"

"I don't know."

"What are we trying right now? You said it was the seeds of something to come. Do you really believe that?"

"I don't know." He balled his hands into fists and slammed them into his pillows. "Goddamn it, Victoria, I don't know. What do you want from this?"

"You are not the only one whose head is swimming. Right now, all I want is to not assist in a heartbreaking surgery." She rose. "I want to not have to hold my dear friend's hand tonight and whisper pointless reassurances when she feels like she's on the edge of a cliff."

"What do you mean?"

"Baron von Bastard got Nora in a fix. He has been sent to

the front, and I have elected to do the unthinkable." She stepped back from the bed and smoothed her apron as she calmed her breath and her words. "After that is done, I have one more day of work, and then you and I will have five days alone and away from this. We will talk at length and give our future the consideration it deserves."

"We've had plenty of time to consider it."

"Matthew, we've had less than two weeks. Everything has changed since we considered it last, and I will not answer you tonight when I have to answer to God and my conscience for something else."

His gray eyes had mesmerized her during their first dance, and nearly ten years on he could still bring her to a blush with a sideways glance or a furrowing of his black brows shading the gray from silver into steel. Victoria could read raw emotion in his eyes like a thermometer.

She held his gaze.

"Your strength of spirit is a sight to behold, my darling." He swallowed thickly. "I am being unfair. I was an arrogant bastard back then, and I see I still am so deluded I can imagine myself a whole man again, chasing after you and kissing you until the last four years don't matter at all and the years before them are all we need to build on."

"You are a whole man."

"If I were a whole man, I wouldn't be here," he said drily. "And if I were a wiser man..."

She waited.

"Never mind." He held out his hand. She took it but didn't step closer when he tried to pull her to his side. "Victoria, please forgive me. I was overcome for a moment, and I am not so easily overcome. Let's talk of something more pleasant."

His eyes couldn't hide the strain of those simple words: *forgive me*. He bottled himself up for her comfort again, steadied himself so she wouldn't run, and deftly side-stepped the debris from their bursts of emotion. If she ran from his questions again, she might lose him forever.

She looked at the clock.

"Matthew, I—forgive me. This is a terrible time."

"You have to go." He closed his eyes.

"I have to go."

Chapter Twenty-Eight

At just past eleven that night, Victoria folded her surgical gown and covered the basin of used instruments before shoving it behind the line of trays she'd already prepared for the next day. She'd sneak it into the pile with the ones to be cleaned after the first case and no one would be the wiser. The soiled linens went into a bag under the table to would join the rest of the laundry in the morning.

"I'm ready to go home." Nora yawned and pulled a pillow to her chest. "I'm not dizzy or anything. Just tired."

Victoria glanced at the clock. The procedure had been a short one, but a puff of gas to help Nora relax required extra precautions. "Not for another twenty minutes. Then I'll check you one more time for any bleeding, and we'll go."

"Off your feet tomorrow," Dr. Bowden said. "I will say you showed symptoms of influenza today, and I know Nurse Harper will ensure we are well-staffed with nurses who are not contagious."

Nora's eyes welled. "Thank you, sir. For everything."

"Chin up, Nurse Scott. Gratitude does not require irrigation. Your future is yours again, and I know you will use it wisely."

"I will, sir. You have my word."

"And do I also have your word you will lie here quietly for twenty minutes until Nurse Harper returns to walk you home?"

"You do."

"Rest, then, and please excuse us." He folded his surgical gown and set it atop Victoria's. "Fancy a smoke, Harp?"

Little traffic passed the schoolyard at late hours. The night air was windless and cool beneath a flat black sky that bled into the shadowy bare trees lining the street. Amiens at night in the Rue de Trois-Cailloux, a few blocks past *Maman*'s house, was festive and bright at the cafés and restaurants. Even during the most dangerous spells, streetcars clanged with life, and soldiers on leave found their way out for food, wine, and other amusements. Paris was too far, home was impossible for many, but Amiens was enough to refresh them before they went back for another chance at dying.

In front of the schoolhouse-turned-hospital at eleven o'clock, the dusty, cobbled street was still.

Bowden rustled a tin of rationed cigarettes from his pocket and offered her one. "Haven't needed these much in recent months, have we? The damn box is dusty."

Victoria accepted the cigarette and turned it over and over in her hand as she considered the exhausted nights they used to spend blowing smoke at the sky after a bloodbath of a day. Their little hospital was more of a field unit than a base when the fighting moved down the Somme, and their days were spent saving what lives they could and stabilizing wounded men to ship to Rouen for recovery. Rotating twelve-hour shifts. Rationing anesthesia. There were no tidy flap amputations and delicate abdominal repairs during those days.

"It's a good night for it, Dr. B."

"Nights like this usually are. I know what you want to ask. Go on."

"How many times have you done this?"

He struck a match and lit her cigarette, then his own, and flicked the match into the gravel. "Three times in this war. Once in each of the others."

Victoria exhaled a small puff. "Has anyone said no?"

"Once here, once in South Africa."

"Do you think it was guilt, or because they thought they were in love and he'd come around?"

Bowden smiled and sat on the steps that led back to the courtyard. "Religious guilt, both times, and I did what I could to see they were taken care of. The other women all imagined for a moment that the man who walked away would come back and there would be some declaration of devotion. But when they were offered a chance to make a future that was not dependent on men who would abandon them, every one of them spoke like Nurse Scott, with repentance and promises to make the best of her second chance."

He sighed heavily. "These are men in my command. The type of man who will behave honorably if he gets a girl in trouble is usually not the type of man who gets a girl in trouble in the first place." He tapped a column of ash onto the step. "Hence, the offer."

"Mistakes happen between couples who love each other."

"And no offers are made in those cases." He tipped his head back and stared at the starless sky. "If it happened to you and Berger, I wouldn't offer. These other girls... well, I don't know what to do sometimes, short of hiring a nanny to whack my officers' arses if they crave a woman's touch so much. No, Harp. You and your fellow understand one another. If you say yes to him, you know what you're doing."

"You sound more sure of it than I feel."

"What's so unclear to you?"

She studied the overcast sky and blew a stream of smoke. It lingered in the still air. "Marriage was always our breaking point. I wasn't supposed to work, and I wanted to. I am not sure who I am without it."

"Would he have supported you working?"

"It wasn't his choice. It's a rule, just like it is for the Red Cross. I had hoped that women proving their usefulness in wartime would change men's views a little." She inspected the glowing end of her cigarette and frowned as she sat next to him. "I correspond with some friends at the hospital at home. Nothing has changed. The girls say even in London with half a million wounded men, married nurses can do little more than rock babies and wrap bandages. I don't know if I can go backward like that when I am capable of so much more."

She sighed and let her shoulders droop. "Even as a single woman, I have no idea whether I will be welcome in any operating room in America. What the war demanded of us may turn to dust in peacetime."

"I've served on three continents," he said, "and let me tell you: from the Boers to the Boxers to these bastards, men are always the same. They don't know what to make of a woman who can run a Connell machine and stitch a flap. These are good men, most of them. None will suggest you are stupid or weak. They won't get past wondering why you want or need to do it. In a profession where we all ought to stay abreast of the latest research, we throttle our progress because so many cannot grasp the ground-breaking notion that a woman is capable."

The spiderweb of cracks in her foundation had grown every day since Matthew arrived, each strand so intertwined with the others she could not untangle love from desire nor homesickness from hope. The ground beneath it was the war; the sky above it was a whisper of one word, her own battle since the night she saved Philippe Bouton's life.

Enough.

The whispering voice made little sense. She hadn't done enough. Idle hands, not nursing work, would give her hysterics. Enough? There wasn't enough of anything. Not enough milk or sugar, not enough soldiers or nurses, not enough hours at Matthew's side or days before he must leave and take the sunlight with him.

Victoria nudged a pile of ash into the gravel, still glowing, and tamped it out with her foot. "He understands and respects me enough to worry that I might resent him if I gave up my work to marry him. I fear that too, although he said outright that he won't ask me again."

"Ah, well, there's always Harry."

"Splendid."

He blew out a long breath and coughed when the smoke clouded around them. "You might be interested to know that at my rank and advanced age, I am inclined to set an example. I'll flaunt my pretty stripes and medals and collect my salutes before I tell them to go to hell if they don't approve of my surgical assistants. How would you like a proper teaching hospital in London?"

Victoria shook her head. "London is your home, sir. Not mine."

"You'll have many friends there when this is over. Even if we are all speaking German, God help us, England may have more to offer than midwifery and house calls on invalids." He nodded at the hospital door. "This all goes for Nurse Scott, too. Many of your fellow nurses—I'll welcome your applications."

"Married nurses?"

"That part might take some finagling."

"It's a flattering offer, but outside of the situation with Matthew, I promised my mother I would come home. Edith thinks she is lonelier than she lets on."

"Consider it, at least. Bring dear Mama along. She'll have a jolly time."

Another variable, another maybe, another risk in a foggy view forward. She forced a smile. "I'll consider it."

He stubbed out the end of his cigarette. Yellow light from the street lamps deepened the creases on his face and shaded his eyes with his brows. "Wherever you land, Harp, you'll stand among the pioneers of your sex. Women have been at the back of battlefields for centuries. In my experience, I have seen that men hold their usual places and women tend to find a place men didn't see for them. Men show up and do the jobs they've always done. Women will elbow their way in and prove their worth unasked. It's another of those things that has gotten better with every war. Another year of this horse shit and I expect to see ladies driving tanks."

"An impressive way to make a place for ourselves."

"London's a fine place."

"So is Raleigh. Dear little Raleigh, with nothing of note besides the people and places that mean home to me." She caught his sideways glance. "Go on. Ask me why I left."

"I know why you left. He's in room five and you love him so much you crossed an ocean to get over him."

"That's not exactly how it happened."

"Isn't it?" His chuckle echoed against the stone walls. "I suppose you expect me to believe you remembered your duty to king and country."

"We've had our own war since that king." Victoria fumbled with the end of her cigarette. "The war within left us with other enemies, and we've quite forgotten our little revolution."

"We've had a hundred wars since that king," he said. "Defending an empire is a tiresome thing, and I think that if this war doesn't end civilization, it will still be my final tour. I'll salute my last while I'm still sane enough to teach."

"Speaking of tours—"

"Granted. Swann told me you'd ask. Corporal Berger will be in excellent hands."

"Nurse Perry's condition of my leave was that I don't come back just to wave farewell."

"How sad that some women put other women in the very shackles they complain of." He stood and offered his hand.

"But you know how I feel about all that. London is a risk, but Raleigh is too, in its own way. Whatever path you choose, let me know if I can help you."

"I will, sir."

He glanced at the window to *l'école maternelle* where Nora rested. "Perhaps the choice will be easier when you realize you have more options than you thought."

Chapter Twenty-Nine

The next morning, sleep-deprived and anxious, Victoria breathed a sigh of relief when she entered an operating room appropriated from a class of seven year olds—a much-needed change of scenery after her uncomfortable late night. The room's walls were a pretty peach and decorated with a stenciled border of red grapes and green vines swirling around the chalkboards, fortunately without a cheery announcement that learning was meant to be fun.

"Delighted to have you in our room, Nurse Harper." Dr. Carraker welcomed Victoria with a surgical gown tossed her direction. "Bowden is a boor and a pig for playing favorites with the schedule all the time. How have you been? Your fellow's healing up all right, isn't he?"

At the head of the bed preparing the gas tanks, Dr. Denys shot him a quizzical look.

Frances waved from the other side of the room as Victoria hung her apron on a peg by the door. She was Carraker's favorite assistant, and he liked to tell her she was Victoria's superior in every way but he would never tell anyone else, lest Bowden steal her too.

"He is doing well, sir. I shuffled my schedule to make time for a short leave." She pulled the gown over her shoulders and tied it in the back. "I mean to show Corporal Berger a little bit of our dear city before he leaves, but I'm all yours for the day."

His eyes lit up. "I'm tickled. You must tell me everything Bowden is boring you with these days. The latest drivel on the effectiveness of Dakin's solution? We all know it works. How many milligrams of calcium will speed fracture healing? Drink some damn milk."

"He's teaching me to close an amputation flap."

Carraker stared for a moment, then chuckled. "Nurse Kendall, shall we sign you up for that? A nurse stitching up a flap. I suppose you've stitched up some cuts, but that's a little different."

Frances shuddered. "No, thank you."

Nicholas Carraker, the hospital's second-in-command, was a jovial lieutenant colonel from the Scottish borderlands, polished by the finest English schools and roughened at the edges by six years in India, two in South Africa, and a bone-deep annoyance at the imperial military. He was informal and improper, the polar opposite of their academic and duty-minded commandant, and was the one officer Bowden didn't trouble to rein in when he made a little noise.

"Fetch the patient, Denys," Carraker announced. "Private Wilton, room seven, brown hair, yellow blanket, probably reading Sherlock Holmes and sitting very still since he's got a wee bullet lodged in the back of his neck. I gave him some morphine. I think I gave him some morphine."

"No, I did, sir." Frances didn't look up from arranging scalpels in order by size, spacing them with precision. "Twenty minutes ago." She handed Victoria a stack of scissors and gestured to a draped tray.

Denys looked at them and back at Carraker. "The nurses usually bring the patient."

"The nurses are handling all the sharp things," Carraker said. "When you are handling sharp things, you will stay in the room and they will fetch and carry. Quite fair, isn't it?"

Denys ducked his head and left.

"We would have been happy to get him," Frances said. "Don't frighten that poor man."

"Poor man, indeed," Carraker said from the sink. "I'm annoyed with him and he should know it."

"That's not like you, sir."

"He earned me another rant from your matron about these insufferable boys in my charge making cow eyes at her darlings. Him, personally and specifically."

Victoria stiffened.

"You must be joking," Frances said, trying to stifle a laugh. "And you must tell me who."

"One of the new VAD girls, and he's not shy about looking, heaven help us. What is wrong with these children?"

"Is she looking back at him?"

"She ignores him, bless her. You ladies are a fine example to everyone the Red Cross sends. You can get your work done and have a laugh and keep your wits about you like adults." He eyed Frances. "I saw that little twitch, darling. You want to tell me how I'm being a poor example."

"Sir."

"Ah, come on, Nurse Kendall. Say it."

"It's only that if you don't want your men ogling the ladies they work with, you might consider dropping 'The Buxom Bess of Inverness' from your routine when you sing in surgery. Or at least the little winks that tend to accompany it."

He guffawed and nearly flung water over the instrument table. "Only one man in this place has the balls in his trousers and the stars on his coat to call me a fool to my face, but God, it is a delight to be put in my place by a woman. You are entirely correct. I adore you, Nurse Kendall, with the utmost professionalism, and I thank you for your candor."

She winked at him. "You're welcome, sir."

"Would you slap some wisdom into Dr. Denys while you're dispensing advice?"

"Everyone wants to find something beautiful in the midst of this mess," Victoria interjected. "Love can give a person a sense of being and belonging. Dr. Denys is new and I imagine he feels very alone. I hardly think your bawdy tunes pushed him over the edge."

"New or not, he is a commissioned officer and should behave like one. Your young man has made you a romantic, Nurse Harper." Carraker shook the water from his hands, reached to scratch his chin, then thought better of it and scraped it against his upper arm. "I've heard about that as well. You're not running off home with him, are you?"

"And leave poor Nurse Kendall to deal with the twittering lovebirds alone? I could never."

"I could manage, Nurse Harper." Frances grinned. "As we can see, the women in this hospital are not the ones causing trouble."

. . .

Victoria watched the clock as the case dragged on, handing and accepting instruments and hardly looking. Carraker whistled instead of singing as he addressed muscle and nerve and let Denys work on the shattered vertebra.

"Well, that looks awfully nice, Denys." He nodded his approval before they began to stitch. "Tidy work. Reconstruction suits you, doesn't it?"

"It does, sir."

"You're far better than some of the clods who have been at this for a decade. With Wentworth gone, we can use steady hands like yours. Goddamn fine job."

Denys smiled and Victoria thought his neck relaxed for the first time since she met him.

"Where did Dr. Wentworth go?" Frances asked.

"Passchendaele, and good luck to him." Carraker made a sloppy left-handed salute with a retractor and nearly threw it. "The man does decent work and he won't flinch under those conditions. Safer there for him, anyway."

"Safer?"

"The word from Bowden is that Nurse Perry received a detailed complaint about him personally and specifically, and it wasn't the first time. Whoosh, off he goes." He eyed Denys. "His Majesty's Army needs every man, and when we have a complaint from a lady, we will make sure good hands are put to better use."

"I'm going to dash home over lunch and check on Nora," Frances said after their second case. "I don't want her to be alone, and this is *Maman*'s usual day at the church. Her voice sounded awful this morning, poor dear."

"A sore throat usually heals quickly with peace and quiet," Victoria replied. Nora had no spotting or fever or any concerning symptoms after their long night. They decided a sore throat was more likely to give her a single day off than faking influenza and being stuck at home for at least three. "I left her with a mug of tea and a hot kettle."

"All the same, I'll check in. Come with me?"

"Come with me for a moment first. I'll run downstairs and tell Matthew I'll visit after work instead. He doesn't have lodging for tonight, so our break begins tomorrow morning."

Room five was half empty, and laughter rising from the courtyard drew their attention. Matthew was outside with Dr. Lambert and several other men at their exercises.

"I'll just come back when we're done for the day," she said, smiling as she watched him. A stack of his freshly laundered clothes perched on the edge of his bedside table atop a handful of crisp, white envelopes addressed to Raleigh, ready for Rosemarie to collect. Victoria scooped up the clothes and opened his haversack to put them out of the way. Two envelopes fell from the table into the bag, and when she retrieved them, she pulled out a third.

It didn't match the others. The envelope was unsealed, battered and dingy around the edges. Matthew's normally precise script was shaky on the front.

Miss Victoria Harper
Red Cross Hospital No. 43
Amiens, France

She slid the first page up to read the top. The letter was dated two days before he arrived.

> Victoria, my dearest, my only love,
>
> I hope this letter never finds you. If it does, someone found it and sent it on my behalf, and the only way that could be is if I am dead.

She covered her mouth with her hand and the words spun on the letter he said he wrote in the field hospital and never sent. *I wasn't in the best state and feared I wasn't going to make it,* he said when she asked if he'd already written home. *It was perhaps a little too honest.*

Four pages fanned out from the envelope and she crouched over the bag as her vision tunneled on his words. *My only love, I hope this letter never finds you.*

Chapter Thirty

The letter lay in Victoria's pocket like a weight all afternoon, so heavy it pulled down her shoulders and the corners of her mouth into a frown. Reason froze her hands every time she reached for it, tempted to peek. She forced smiles when needed and drooped again after. An hour-long lunch break wouldn't be enough to digest whatever was in those pages and leave her any peace to manage three cases that afternoon.

She owed Matthew a conversation to break the tension from the night before. They had plans to make. They had to secure lodging for their days off. They had to pack and plan for crutches and wheeled chairs and other transportation. And somehow, they had to talk about what would come next.

She could not have that conversation with the battered envelope whispering what-ifs. As soon as her shift ended, she bolted from the hospital and ran home, dodging puddles and jumping over mud from the morning's gray drizzle. She kept her hand shoved in her pocket, clenching the letter so no errant breeze could swirl her skirts and send it flying.

Sneaking through the front door, she dodged Nora at the piano. Strains of Debussy disguised her ragged breaths while she tiptoed past Ingrid and Marie in the dining room. She jumped the creaky step as nimble as a cat and locked her bedroom door behind her.

The paper was thin and scratched in a few places where Matthew's pen dug in and disrupted a word. His dusty fingerprints lined the edges.

> Victoria, my dearest, my only love,
>
> I hope this letter never finds you. If it does, someone found it and sent it on my behalf, and the only way that could be is if I am dead and free from any shame at unburdening myself today. A man should write home at a time like this, and that my heart turns only to you is no surprise. The life I built alone is fine and satisfying, but one place remains empty. It is yours alone, molded to your figure and melded against mine. There has been no other.
>
> Before I left, Trux and Maudie told me how to reach you if I found myself nearby. I told my field hospital I will wait for any ambulance going to Amiens. It may be another day or two, and they think I am mad. The pain in my leg is a shattering of the nerves I never imagined. They are skint with the morphine but I am due some more soon. It will be worth this agony to see you once more, to touch you and talk to you and feel your breath... even if it's from you sighing in frustration that I've once more weaseled my way back into your life. I am quite the expert at that.

Her breath hitched and a tear dropped on the inky scrawl

swiped between the lines. His handwriting was more steady in the lines that followed.

> Morphine addles my thoughts while numbing my leg to a loss that pales in comparison to the loss of your love and friendship. I long for your quiet comfort in this clamor and for your voice in every stillness. Thoughts of you bring the ocean waves to my ears when I can't bear the noise or the silence any longer. They tell me men survive this wound. If I do not, I'll watch driftwood fires at peace in your arms.
>
> I'd rather like to do that alive again, if it's not too much trouble. Darling, if it's not too much trouble, I'd like everything. One day.

His agitation showed in the wobbly ink. A thick line skidded off the paper from the tail of the 'y' and the letter resumed in calmer script a few inches down.

> I know you have made a life that suits you. I should do you a kindness and let you alone. Yet the ache that now consumes me brings me to wonder whether we might yet make sense of this senseless war. Nothing is assured anymore. Nothing is safe. But how funny it is that what kept us apart might now reunite us, and if we are together, it may not hurt so much to each lose a piece of ourselves.
>
> Forgive me. The audacity of imagining myself enough for you now when I never was before... I shall blame the morphine. The delusions come and go, but they are so pretty, hazy and golden and faded around the edges.

Her breaths shortened and she pressed her hand to her chest in a futile attempt to slow her hammering heart.

> I should destroy this letter now in case I succeed in my aim and see you once more. None of these bold words will leave my lips in the right order, I am certain. But if I am gone, I would like you to know I died loving you without an ounce of regret or bitterness. Until that day, my every breath remains in your care.
>
> I'll sleep now only to dream about this impossible way you always promised would one day break the barriers in our path. Everything else in the world has upended, so why not dream a little longer? Darling girl, if I wake, the answer is yes to whatever it is, whatever it takes. I love you, Victoria Harper, and however long or short my life is, I will love you until that final breath.

"Until I see you again, one way or another, Matthew." Tears streaked her cheeks and lined her lips as she read the final words, from a trickle to a torrent as her memories and regrets and dreams crashed over and over into the solid brick wall of things she could not do.

The choice that cost her his love years ago should have stayed an ocean away. It should be gone and buried. The specter of that choice haunted her again every time she was chastised for visiting him, every time she missed a special moment like helping him stand again. She would never stop paying for loving him and leaving him, but she still couldn't turn away. It wrenched her stomach until bile rose in her throat and for the first time in years, she felt on the verge of vomiting. She clamped her hand over her mouth as her shoulders tensed and hunched. No blood or bone was as nauseating as the idea of losing him again.

She pulled the little waste can from next to her bed and held it on her lap as she tried to slow her weeping, inhaling through her nose and exhaling though her mouth as the lemon-yellow walls of the room closed in around her. One breath. Two. Ten. Her shaking hands stilled.

One place remains empty.

I should do you a kindness and let you alone.

If we are together it may not hurt so much to each lose a piece of ourselves.

His jumbled thoughts tangled with hers. That dream he cherished was a promise she never fulfilled because she was too frightened to forge a trail where there was none. She had blamed society. Rules. Men who said no. Women who judged. The guilt he would bear if she gave up her work. The resentment that would always simmer if she quit. Sweaty hair stuck to her forehead and cheeks and she brushed it back with clammy hands. How had he loved her strength so much when she hid behind excuses and fear?

The audacity of imagining myself enough for you.

Piano music floated up the stairs. The choice was hers alone, as he always said. Setting the waste can aside, she walked to the little desk by the radiator and picked up a pen.

Ten minutes later, she tapped Nora on the shoulder with two envelopes and interrupted *Deux Arabesques*. "I didn't even hear you come in," Nora said. She pointed at her throat. "I am fully recovered from today's illness."

"And otherwise?"

"Aside from possible eternal damnation, I am healthy enough, strictly speaking." She mustered a wry smile. "And forever grateful."

Victoria turned the envelopes over in her hands and glanced around. She inclined her head to the sound of Marie and Ingrid chattering in the dining room and lowered her voice. "Risks are halved when you truly trust the people keeping the secret with you."

Nora's cheeks flushed. "You are the dearest of friends."

"As are you. The relief on your face makes the risk worth it."

"A piece of my soul must have broken off the day I began listening to Gi— to him. I believed every word he said because I allowed myself to believe him. I am no fool, and I will not forget there are two guilty parties here, however you balance who is most to blame." She pulled out the cross necklace tucked into the collar of her dress. "This second chance belongs to God, Dr. Bowden, and you. I will make you proud of me, Victoria, I swear it. I'll get into that medical college when the war is over. I'll help children. I'll help a hundred of those children who have no fathers. I'll help their mothers."

"I have no doubt you will."

She played a little trill of twinkling, bright notes. "What are those?"

Victoria looked down, still fidgeting with the envelopes. "A little errand."

"If you're going out, I'll come with you. Fresh air will feel good."

"It will be a long walk," Victoria said. "These must go to

the hospital, and then I have several places to visit in town. You should rest a while longer."

"Then you go to the hospital so I don't get in trouble for being up if Dr. Bowden sees me. Come back here, and we'll cut over the bridge. Can we get wherever we need to go on the streetcar?"

"I think so."

"Why do you look so sad, darling? These errands are for your little getaway, aren't they?"

"They are."

"Then what is the matter?"

She squeezed the envelopes tight. "I have a secret I need you to keep for me. I think I do, anyway. I dearly hope."

Chapter Thirty-One

The next morning, Victoria paced her bedroom as she braided her hair and waited for the other girls to leave for the hospital. After Nora departed with a wink and a reassuring smile, she pinned on her prettiest hat, a deep blue felt with black and white feathers that reminded her of Edgar. With shaking hands, she tucked Matthew's letter in the bodice of her lace dress, borrowed from Bridget since her peach one was still damp from scrubbing out the stains. Her heart beat against the pages.

The air was crisp on her walk, and she paused on the green bridge to take in the picturesque corner of Amiens as if seeing it for the first time. The hospital complex was a distant blur in her view, overshadowed by the cozy streets of homes and shops, buildings half-timbered in the Norman fashion of northern France. The Somme's canals lent a cool, brackish fragrance to the air that distracted from the soot and smoke and gasoline of the central city, and the cathedral's bells tolled nine o'clock.

Her gloves protected her from the rough edge of the

handrail on the green bridge where the paint had chipped away, and she picked out a tiny splinter from the seam to flick into the water. The water beneath her had flowed to Amiens from the river's origin in Aisne, through the blood-drenched battlefields. It would carry Matthew to the ocean in only a few days' time. She had waited long enough.

Room five was bustle and chaos. Since everyone's healing regimens would be disrupted on the journey back to London in a few days' time, Emily Dotson had assigned a volunteer to each patient to make him memorize a training regimen for his recovery. Private McKeever groused loudly about how his crutches weren't made for a large man, and was sharply admonished by a young volunteer half his size with pigtails poking out under her veil. Cartwright's volunteer had already deduced he could be flattered into compliance, and named him the calisthenics coordinator for the hospital barge that would take them back to England.

"Ho there, Nurse Harper!" He grinned when Victoria entered the room. "Have you come to take us all for an outing today?"

She waved the major off with a quick greeting, and Matthew, the lone quiet man in the middle of the tumult, looked up from his book and smiled as she pushed a wheeled chair to the side of his bed.

"I think you're just here for me, aren't you?"

"I'm all yours."

He reached for her hands. "You are radiant today, my darling."

"It's the dress." She swished the cream-colored lace skirt. "Perhaps a little out of season."

"The dress is lovely, but you are glowing." He pulled her closer. "Did you rest well? The only reason I slept at all last night was your sweet note about your errands for today. You'd have been right to let me stew in my stupidity a little while longer."

"Matthew, don't be ridiculous."

"I'm trying not to be now, but the last time we spoke, I was an ass. You are well, though? And Nora?"

Victoria's throat tightened and she did her best to sound normal. "We are both well. Thank you."

His eyes were bright and warm, so open and trusting her heart churned with sudden, unwanted memories of other times she'd seen that boyish happiness shattered by her rejection. A corner of the letter tucked against her breast tickled her through her chemise and she wriggled a little.

"Come here," he whispered, drawing her closer. He pressed his lips to her cheek. "Tell me what we're doing today. I've adopted your mindset of gratitude for this borrowed time of ours, and I dearly hope your errands yesterday included a pie. Your people feed us well enough here, but I—"

"I have it all worked out," she interjected, jerking away so she could scoot the wheeled chair closer. "I'll tell you someplace quieter."

She glanced around the crowded room just as Private McKeever mis-stepped with a crutch and landed his full weight on another man's toe.

"I can manage a short stroll with my pack on," Matthew said. "I practiced yesterday. We could get a taxi out front."

"No, I want to talk to you first, and I think you'll want to sit down."

The words sounded bleaker than she intended, and his ruddy cheeks paled. He set his jaw as he scooted off the bed into the chair. With his haversack and crutches on his lap, Victoria wheeled him past the flurry of activity in the ward but stopped short of leaving the building.

She pushed the chair into the equipment room and locked the door. Her words dried on her tongue, plans whisked from her brain, and all she could think to do was pull the envelope from the bodice of her dress.

Matthew's hands went limp and one crutch clattered to the floor.

"I found this when I put your clothes in your bag yesterday," she said. "It was unsealed."

His voice was hoarse. "Did you read it?"

"I did."

The other crutch fell as he tried to rise. "Vi, darling, I was —I was in so much pain and perhaps not thinking straight."

"I looked for you, Matt." She set his haversack on the floor and kicked the crutches away as she pulled a chair to his side.

"What?"

"Every day, I looked for you. Since Maudie told me early in the summer you'd be in France, I've checked every ambulance manifest." Her heart pounded heat through her body. "I asked my friends at all the other hospitals if they would look for you, too. We all look for each other's friends and loved ones, and I hoped I would never find you. If I didn't find you, I could believe you were safe. But when you weren't safe—"

"I looked for you." He slumped forward, hands in his hair. "Please don't be upset I didn't tell you. There you were in that crowded room and all sense left my head, as it tends to do when I am overcome with feelings for you. I told myself perhaps it was fate, even if I arranged it a little. Perhaps it was fate that I even had the option."

"I saw them bring you in," she said, fighting tears. "And I —I walked away to try and get on with my work. I told myself I would just see you later, for surely you were already in good hands. But I have never been so frightened, so close to you and still a thousand miles away. All the time you've been here, I haven't been able to make sense of that feeling." She looked down at the envelope. "Or perhaps I have not allowed myself to make sense of it, until something in this letter struck me."

"Oh God. What did I say?" He reached for the letter. "Give me that. Forgive me. I may have been a raving madman."

"You said you still wanted everything with me, and 'if we are together it may not hurt so much to each lose a piece of ourselves.'"

"Victoria, please." His eyes were panicked. "I know I have disrupted your entire life by coming here and I was far too forward the other night when we spoke. Whatever we are building, I am happy with. Whatever timeline we take. I won't ask you to fit your life into my schedule anymore."

"Then don't ask me again." She knelt in front of him and placed the letter in his hands. "Will you marry me?"

The chatter of room five faded into the walls as his mouth went slack. She kept her chin lifted, her hands on his, and willed him to speak. He moved his lips and no sound escaped.

"Matthew, you cannot feel guilty for asking me to give something up because you are not asking," she said quickly.

"I cannot resent you for asking because I am offering this of my own free will. You said you had a pretty dream for us, and I know how to make it come true. I didn't know before. I didn't see it. Yes, you disrupted my life, but it needed to be disrupted. What we want doesn't have to be a dream any longer, and you said that whatever it takes—"

"I said yes to whatever it takes." He cupped her face in his hands and kissed her, then bent his forehead to hers and whispered. "Yes, my love. I will go home a happy man with this promise. However long we must wait for you to join me, my answer is yes."

"Oh, we're not going to wait. We have five days."

He jerked back. "Do you mean to come with me? Victoria, please, if you must quit hospital work when we're home, see this through if you want to. I know you feel your duty is here. It can't be much longer."

"But you have waited long enough on my indecision," she said, "and so I will not leave a single doubt in your mind. Every woman who was dismissed for getting married told people she got married. I will not do that."

"It cannot be that simple, or other people would do it."

"Perhaps they do. How would we know?"

"Oh."

"Listen." She kissed him and lingered with her cheek pressed to his as she spoke. "We have five days to marry and have a little honeymoon. I will conduct all my affairs as Victoria Harper as long as I am here. There are a few little safeguards we can put in place, and the Red Cross need never know. And when you leave—" She kissed his cheek again. "You will take our marriage certificate just in case you cannot believe your wife is coming home to you."

His lips twitched, holding back laughter as Victoria tickled the back of his neck. "My wife will come home to me. I do like the sound of that." He kissed her again. "And when you do..."

"We'll be the subject of all the town gossip again."

"I meant, a little ruse might work well enough here, but you're really not going to work at home?" His brow furrowed. "Vi, are you truly at peace with that?"

"I am going to work," she said. "I just need to figure out how. I made a place for myself here, and I can do it at home, too. It looks on the surface like the war hasn't changed old-fashioned rules, but it's changed me. I know what I am capable of. If no one will hire Mrs. Matthew Berger, she will make her old wartime friends proud and elbow her way in where she belongs."

"Say that again."

"It was an expression Dr. Bowden used when—"

"Victoria."

"That's Mrs. Matthew Berger to you. Or I will be, in a few hours."

"I love that. I love you."

"I love you."

Their kiss was sweet and unhurried as he stroked her neck and her hair. His hands were warm and his grip was gentle, melting her into his arms until her breaths finally slowed and she snuggled against his shoulder.

"A few hours?" he asked.

"Eleven o'clock, if you're free."

"Are you sure it shouldn't be tomorrow? It's bad luck to see the bride before the ceremony."

"It would be worse luck for me to cancel all the plans I've

already made." She waved the letter. "I knew you'd say yes. I had it in writing."

"What are today's plans?"

"We can do as we please this morning as long as we are at the city hall by eleven. After that, we will go to my house for my bag, and we can check into a sweet little inn on Avenue Quatrième any time after three. I told the *madame* at the inn that I am an American woman here to collect my poor wounded husband and take him home. She didn't have a first floor room for us, but the stair is not steep and the washroom is sizable, so you can use your crutches if you don't want my company in there. We can stay four nights."

He picked up her left hand. "What about—"

"I bought wedding rings. We will look the part."

A laugh shook his chest. "I still have the engagement ring I offered you the second time. That was the only time I planned it properly and I still did it wrong."

The diamond solitaire with its band of emeralds had glittered in the moonlight when he knelt in her parents' back garden the night of his second proposal. After she declined him, she never imagined he'd saved it.

"Why on earth didn't you take it back?"

He shrugged. "Despite not liking my question, I noticed you liked the look of the ring. I thought it might be nice to have on hand for a better time to ask again. I didn't think to specify which of us would ask." He scooted her closer. "I'll send that ring over and you can wear it without any trouble, even if you can't wear a wedding band."

"If it's safe to send it, I suppose."

"I wouldn't mind if you wore it to show that bastard Harry what's what, anyway."

She pinched his nose. "I can't wear any jewelry at work."

"Perhaps you could leave it on one day by mistake."

"Matthew, really."

"I'll bake it into some cookies and send it over as soon as I get home. Hell, I'll have Cooper go over to the house and grab it and see what he and Maudie can cook it into right away. That'll be a hell of a reply to their telegram." He pressed his cheek to hers and his lips to her ear. "Wait. Are we telling everyone at home?"

"Let's scheme that part up together. I've done enough on my own." The words tasted sweet. "I've done enough without you."

"And so have I." He grazed his fingers over the cream-colored lace and slowly worked his way down over the curve of her breast. "My beautiful, brilliant bride. You have stirred my soul and delighted my eyes for so many years, and perhaps it's because I finally let them give me a little pain medicine an hour ago, but I'm not entirely sure how this just happened."

Chapter Thirty-Two

In the center of Amiens, the *Hôtel de Ville* surrounded three sides of a stone plaza with a Gothic facade that lent the city hall the air of a romantic castle. Ever since Blanche told her about the brief German occupation when all national symbols were forbidden, the sight of the French flag on the highest tower made Victoria stand a little straighter in honor of her adopted country. She hummed a few bars of the French national anthem under her breath as they approached.

Looking up at the cream-colored stone walls and statues on the parapets, Matthew squeezed her hand as they passed through the iron gates and into the courtyard. "This city hall is more of a palace. I wonder if we could hire someone to take our photo on the steps later. We look fine and fancy today."

Her dress fluttered under her cloak as Matthew maneuvered slowly up the stairs on his crutches. She craned her neck to check the clock tower. "Our photographer should be here shortly."

"A lifetime of your clever surprises awaits. God, I'm a lucky man."

"Victoria!" Nora's voice rang across the courtyard as she dashed for the steps, her work dress hitched up to her knees as she ran with a bulky canvas bag bumping against her hip. "Yes, I remembered the camera. Yes, I remembered the film."

Matthew turned to Victoria. "You said we're not supposed to tell anyone."

Nora whipped her treasured Kodak No. 1 Special out of the bag and pointed it at him. "Smile," she ordered.

"The clerk told me yesterday we need your military identification papers, my passport, and witnesses." Victoria pointed over his shoulder to a smartly clad man following them into the building. "Nora will keep our secrets, and so will our other witness."

Matthew snapped into a salute and his right crutch clattered to the ground. Dr. Bowden swatted his hand down.

"Yes, hurrah, God save the king, you're welcome." He retrieved the crutch, kissed Victoria's cheeks and brushed an imaginary speck off his polished belt. "I supposed this was a fine time to dust off the hardware."

Victoria and Nora stared. They had never seen the scholarly surgeon out of the regular khaki all the British men wore. Even meeting the Swiss diplomats, he wore a service coat. In full dress, his uniform sported the cherry red facing of the Royal Army Medical Corps and was emblazoned on the sleeves with the same crown insignia as the badge on his cap. The crisp coat was laden with lanyards, stripes, and a bevy of clinking medals from forty years as a former regimental surgeon and a Deputy Surgeon General—a rank they sometimes forgot he had.

He assessed Matthew from head to toe with a critical eye. "I hear you knew Harp's father before he died, Corporal Berger."

"Yes, sir."

"Did he approve of you?"

"He did, sir. I asked and was granted his permission to marry Victoria years ago, and I like to think that permission didn't have an expiration date."

"What about the parrot? He's rather attached to her, you see."

Matthew shot a confused look at Victoria, then back at the colonel. "I've not had the honor of meeting Edgar."

"Hm. I suppose we will have to chance his approval." Another critical look, fighting a smile. "Do you support her desire to remain here and remain as Miss Harper until the war is over?"

"Absolutely."

"Good. I would not like to lose her and I don't fancy calling her 'Berg.'" He cocked his head at Victoria, offered his arm, and smiled. "I'd like to escort you in, Harp, so let's get started because Nurse Scott and I have a case in an hour."

Nora's camera clicked as they whispered and walked down the hall.

The ceremony was little more than a stack of paperwork and a lecture from a yawning civil authority who looked askance at their American accents until Nora stepped in to translate with her near-flawless French. The civil ceremony, the man explained as he checked their identification, was the precursor to any religious ceremony they might wish to have, but it was the one that mattered. He noted that their signatures in the city's marriage register would make the union valid in France, and a certificate should meet the legal requirements to validate the marriage in the United States.

"We think so. But no one has come back and complained it did not," he said with a shrug. "And so, *bonne chance*."

"Can we have two copies, please?" Victoria asked. "*Deux certificats*?"

The official frowned. "We do not usually do that," he said in French, nodding for Nora to translate.

"We only need one. I'll take it home, like you said," Matthew whispered.

"Dr. Bowden suggested I should have a copy here, in case... just in case, really."

Solemn words about 'in case' stuck in her throat. With a little bad luck, the Germans could push back into Amiens in a matter of weeks, and she'd be a fool not to consider that some disaster might leave her in occupied territory. If she was discharged, the Red Cross might send her back to England under their neutral flag. She could be 'caught' if she chose to be.

"We don't need to talk about why." Matthew nodded. "I understand."

"There is a fee," the officiant said, barely stifling a yawn as he rummaged through a drawer. "For the extra *certificat*."

Bowden slid twenty francs across the desk and motioned for the officiant to hurry up. "Berger, by the way, if you need her in an emergency, address the cable to me if you like. My communications arrive with more haste than most things move in this town."

"I appreciate that, sir. Thank you."

The official pushed the heavy leather-bound register across his desk and Nora translated as he spoke. "Your signatures in this register confirm a marriage valid in France. Should you make permanent residence here, you will be entitled to the legal benefits of a married couple. The registration of your marriage in your home country is your responsibility. Miss, you will sign here with your maiden name and sir, you will sign here with your name. Write your home city and country here. Witnesses, you are here and here." He handed Victoria the pen.

Matthew pulled a pair of gold bands from his pocket. "Are rings part of this process today?"

"It is not required by *le république*, but they say God may be interested," the Frenchman said. "So perhaps you would like to exchange them now while I make you another *certificat*."

Victoria spun Matthew's ring around her thumb. "I remembered to buy them, but I'm afraid I have nothing prepared for this part. I thought there would be a ceremonial part to say."

He bent his head to touch hers, eyes closed, lips almost close enough for a kiss. "Victoria Ruby Harper, I am eternally devoted to you. Do you take me to be your husband, for better or worse, to love across oceans or on ocean shores, and to boost my morale for as long as we both shall live?"

"I do."

He slid the band on her finger and Nora sniffled.

Victoria's racing pulse slowed. "Matthew James Berger, I will put nothing ahead of our marriage. Do you take me to be your wife, for better or worse, to cherish at work and at home, and to bring me peach pie for breakfast for as long as we both shall live?"

"I do."

He clasped his hand around hers when she pushed the ring onto his finger, and without another word tipped her chin up and kissed her. Nora's camera clicked as the Frenchman pushed two certificates across his desk.

"I wish you both *félicitations,*" he said, already fiddling with a cigarette and matchbox, eyes on the door. "Excuse me now, please. You may take more photographs in the courtyard if you like. The gardens are not so fine this time of year, though." He shooed them out with both hands.

"We could go by the river," Nora said. "That little green bridge by the house is a pretty spot. As long as we're going to the trouble of taking photographs, we may as well use up the film."

Matthew kissed her cheek. "Thank you for doing this. If you can get them developed in time, I'll take them home so no evidence remains here."

"Aside from the register we just signed," Victoria pointed out.

"Oh."

"Is this pretty little bridge on the way back to the hospital?" Bowden asked.

"It is."

"Good. Warmest congratulations to you both, and so on." He shook his head as he always did when emotion tangled his tongue, and winked at Victoria instead. "But we must hurry. Nurse Scott, we have a case in forty minutes, and I have to take all this shit off before people start saluting."

Chapter Thirty-Three

"Americain!" Across the dining room of the tavern at the riverside, a dark-haired man in a blue coat waved broadly, then pointed at his neck to indicate the buttons on Matthew's collar and the distinctive olive green of his uniform among the French blue and British khaki around them. "*Bienvenue*, Yankee!"

Victoria yanked her hand from the table and tucked it under her skirt. They'd chosen the tavern for a quiet, casual meal, one where she hoped not to see anyone they knew because she wanted to wear her wedding ring. They'd been ensconced at their cozy corner table for two hours, grazing on fruit and cheese and sausages, comfortably warm from two bottles of wine. Matthew chuckled and eased her hand back onto the table, then shot a quick wave at the man in blue.

The men at his table laughed. "Welcome, American," the soldier said again in thickly accented English. "First of your kind I see. Have our brothers in arms arrived so soon?"

The drunken murmur from the table and the soldier's Gallic shrug left Victoria wondering whether his words were a true question or a jibe. Matthew addressed the interloper with a wry smile.

"I was one of the first in, and now I'll be one of the first out." He tapped his crutches propped next to him on the edge of the table. "I'm sorry I couldn't be more help."

"*Malchance*," said another soldier, staring into a glass. "Bad luck, American. Or perhaps it is *bonne chance*, to leave this pit so soon."

"You will miss our victory," said the first man, his words slurred by drink. "But here you are today, and so are we. Come, Yankee, and we'll share a bottle of wine." He hoisted a bottle of burgundy. "You and your beautiful companion must join us."

The men shuffled around their table to make room as Victoria helped Matthew up. "One quick drink with them, darling?" she whispered. "Very quick."

"Yes, but I'm starving."

"We've eaten so much already."

"I haven't eaten so well in months. It would be rude to refuse," he whispered back as he kissed her cheek. "And I would like to talk with them a bit."

She dropped his hand. "On our wedding night?"

Matthew made his way to the other table, pivoting and swinging on his crutches between diners. She followed in silence, teeth clamped on her tongue to disguise her annoyance as she pasted on a smile that faded when they sat. His hand trembled on her knee under the table.

"Here, here," said the soldier, gesturing to the server to bring more glasses. "Our brave fighting corps. This is Alain, Léonard, *et* Étienne. I am Guillaume, but you may call me *le taureau*." He bowed to Victoria. "*Madame* may call me *mon amour*, if she likes."

Madame. She rolled her hand side-to-side in the dim light and the little gold band glinted. It told everyone to call her his wife, *madame*.

"The Bull?" she asked. "You must have a heroic story to go with that name."

"He made a daring charge through the woods," Alain said, pouring the wine. "A bayonet under each arm. I was down, bleeding and out of ammunition—"

"Because the officers hoard everything from butter to bullets," Léonard announced.

Alain didn't falter. "Bleeding and helpless I was, and *le taureau* scoops up my gun and goes for the man who shot me, like a bull with horns out." He patted his shoulder. "A clean shot and I healed well. *Le taureau* left him not so lucky."

"*Le taureau* had a taste for blood that day, like never before." Guillaume downed his wine in two swallows. "Sometimes, I think that the French fighting men and the German fighting men should all go home and let the officers have at one another with sticks and rocks in the mud. Let them do as they order us to do, and die for it."

Étienne, who had so far not lifted his eyes from his glass, nodded for Alain to refill his wine. "Let's all go home. A furlough in *un verre du vin*."

"*Un verre? Trois bouteilles*." Alain added a fourth cork to the center of the table with the others and handed Victoria a glass. "It is a foul state of things in the ranks, *Madame*."

"It sounds as though things have been very bad for you," Victoria said after a cautious sip. "I hope you have some relief soon."

Matthew's hand jittered in hers under the table.

"It is hell, *Madame*, but I am sure you know that." He nodded to Matthew. "If you did not have a lovely wife at your side, I would offer you a stuffed boot and take you back north with us. If you can still fire a weapon, you have a place in the French army."

"You are so poorly equipped you wish the aid of a cripple?" Matthew asked.

"A cripple?" Alain pretended to look around the tavern. "I see only fighting men here. That's the ugly truth, isn't it? You and I, we have no choice but to fight forever now. The war could end tomorrow, and every man alive who fought in it will go on fighting until he dies."

"Enough." Léonard crossed his arms. "You sour the wine. Yankee, tell us about American baseball. The newspaper makes little sense of it. How are they stealing bags but leaving them in place?"

The wine was woodsy and rich and lent a pleasant blur to the conversation as Matthew explained base-running and the soldiers bobbled between English and French to tell their stories.

Victoria leaned on Matthew's shoulder and said little as he smiled and laughed and clutched her knee with a trembling hand under the table. Every time she stroked his thigh or snuggled a little closer, he pulled her hand away and clasped it tight, still shaking, until she stopped trying.

A plate of bread and soft cheeses appeared as the soldiers grew drunker. They exchanged addresses scribbled on register paper when the hour grew late.

Matthew was in fine spirits as they made their way back to Avenue Quatrième and the inn where they'd left their bags in the afternoon. Their room was up a single flight of stairs, which he managed despite the generous portion of wine. Victoria followed quietly and locked the door.

The porter had brought up their things, and her suitcase sat on a wooden luggage stand at the foot of the bed with Matthew's haversack propped next to it. The room was sparse but pretty, with gingham curtains and a dark-beamed ceiling over wide-paneled wood floors.

"The honeymoon suite." Matthew swung himself onto the bed, rattling the porcelain water pitcher on the table. "I've had quite enough stairs for one day." He reached for her hand and pulled her close to kiss her fingers. "Perhaps we won't need to leave at all for a while."

"Perhaps." Her voice wobbled and she swallowed a yawn.

"Victoria, are you all right?"

She walked to her suitcase and undid the clasps without looking back at him. "I'm a little tired," she said finally. "We stayed out longer than I expected."

"I'm sorry. I needed to—"

She whirled to face him. "You needed to spend several hours at a tavern drinking with strangers on our wedding night?"

"Yes."

"Why?"

His labored breath was the only sound in the small room, and his right foot tapped and twitched on the faded blue rug, pacing in place. One foot didn't take him anywhere and didn't let him grind through the gears of his thoughts.

"Courage, maybe? My words are failing me."

"What are you afraid of?" She sat next to him and reached for his shaking hand. His fingers danced over her palm and wrist and twisted her ring. "Matthew, tell me. You must tell me."

"I'm trying." His cheeks flushed. "Knowing I'll leave without you has made missing home a great deal harder. I married you today without my father or my brothers or my friends at my side, and—"

"Darling, I'm so sorry." Victoria's irritation shattered. "I pressed this on you. I should have asked before I made plans."

"No." He slid an arm around her waist and squeezed. "I would not wait another minute. I regret nothing about our wedding, I promise."

"Then what is it?"

"I felt deeper today that I am out of my place and out of my own skin sometimes. Those men felt like friends I haven't had for a while and might not have again until we are home."

"The men in the hospital aren't your friends? You get along well and have been through the same struggles."

He snapped his fingers. "That's precisely it. Tonight is the first time since this happened that I've been in the company of men who don't treat me like I'm broken. We are all broken men in that room, even to one another. Your doctors mend our flesh and bones, but they do not tend to the brokenness. They study us and they pity us."

She reached for his arm.

"Those men at the tavern treated me like any other fighting man," he said. "I was not a convalescent or a patient anymore. I was no one's noble war hero who needed his morale boosted."

She smiled. "Shall I cease my efforts?"

"Never. But Vi, none of those men pitied me or told me to cheer up. They were honest and unflinching."

"Why did you need that?"

He stared at the carpet, tapping his foot over the pattern of blue and red flowers. "It's a feeling I had back at the hospital. It lies on every man in that room with me, heavier than any weight we lost." He patted the wrapping on his knee. "The fear of disgust and rejection from the women we love is enough to strike any medals from our chests. This loss makes no one a hero. It unmans us."

Victoria faltered. "Of course it's a period of adjustment."

"At night, that room is a different place. Even Cartwright shuts up. You see, in the dark, the pain isn't about the injury. It's about uncertainty of what lies ahead and whether any of us will feel like men again." He slid his hand to her waist and toyed with the ivory Alençon lace. "It is as Alain said tonight: we will go on fighting forever. After everything you've seen, I know you're not disgusted, but this is part and parcel of the brokenness."

"Matthew, darling, if it helps, we needn't try anything tonight. Just let me rest in your arms. I don't need your left foot for that."

His voice grew husky as he slid his hands over her hips. "I am balanced on a knife's edge some nights in that room when I hear other men groan in frustration. They think of the women they love and their fear strangles them before they can finish. I wanted to talk with some people who did not hide their discontent in the dark or behind a happy chorus of marching songs. The man I was when I last made love to you needs to face the man I am now."

She stepped away from him and began to unbutton her dress.

"Sweetheart."

"I wasn't planning to sleep in this, so I'm putting on something more comfortable so I can lie down with you."

Matthew said nothing when she pulled the green silk pajamas from her suitcase and shook them out. She turned away and slipped the dress off her shoulders, untied her petticoat, and let her stockings fall to the floor. With a quick tug she unclasped her corset and shimmied out of her drawers before pulling up the green silk pants under her chemise. Still facing away, she lifted her chemise and put on the rosebud-dotted tunic. The only glimpse he had of her skin was the pale curve of her back and waist.

She stepped to the mirror with her hairbrush and undid her braid, shaking out long blonde waves. Without a look over her shoulder or a flirtatious wink, she brushed out the tangles as he watched. Her wedding ring gleamed in the lamplight when she turned to him.

"I remember those pajamas." His lips hardly moved.

"They always reminded me of you."

"They have a prominent place in my mind's picture album of you."

She grazed her fingers over his coat. "Can I help you get a little more comfortable? It will be so nice to lie down to talk to you. Far better than the courtyard bench or the little chair by your bed."

He nodded and she set her hands to the clasps on his collar and then the buttons down to his waist, the stiff wool tickling her fingers.

"Is that better, darling?"

"I'm still a little warm."

His heart pounded beneath her palm when she undid the buttons on his collared shirt and pulled it over his head, leaving only his undershirt.

"This has to go immediately." He yanked it off. "It's as clean as it will get, which after a summer here is still not clean enough. I'll burn these shirts when I get home, and—oh." He looked down at his bare chest and his labored breathing matched hers as she watched him. She didn't move to undo his breeches. His gaze followed her as she walked to the other side of the bed and slid under the blanket.

"Come here. Talk to me for a while."

The aged wooden bed squeaked a protest when he lay on his side to touch her, gliding his hand in a tentative stroke down her neck and arm.

"What should we talk about?" he asked.

She kept her eyes on his, reading the same vulnerable look as the day of his surgery when she whispered him to sleep. *It won't hurt this time, Matt. I'm right here.* He would never be just another man, but he was another soldier facing uncertainty and far from where he belonged.

What's your name? she asked her patients. *Where are you from? We'll fix you up and get you back there soon. Watch my eyes now. Take a deep breath.*

She nearly said it aloud: *It won't hurt this time.*

"Let's make a plan," she said instead. "How will we tell everyone at home, and when?"

"My parents are incurable gossips and your mother might accidentally tell the Red Cross on us." He twisted a lock of her hair between her fingers and brought it to his lips. "I am already strangely keen on keeping this only between us.

What do you think of this? I'll send your engagement ring and we can tell everyone we plan to celebrate our marriage when you come home, which is technically the truth, but not the whole truth."

"Lawyers are so sneaky. It's perfect."

"Your mother will have time to teach Edgar to say 'congratulations,' and I'll have time to win his approval."

The tension in his jaw relaxed, and his smile encouraged her to keep him talking.

"What will home look like for us in Raleigh?"

He kissed her fingers and thought aloud. "I suppose it can be whatever we like. I'll stay with my folks for a bit and let my mother get her fretting out of the way while I learn to get around on my own. Shipley told me I'm welcome back at the office when I return, so I'll get to work and we won't be destitute." He rolled onto his back and pulled her to his chest. "We can choose a place together," he said. "Or."

"Or?" His bare skin warmed her cheek and she pressed her palm over the tangled dark curls to feel his heart.

"Or I'll choose our new house and get it ready for you. I'll send you one picture in every letter. If you don't like my taste, you'll have to announce our marriage immediately, come back right away, and set me straight."

The idea set her giggling. "Well, I can't think of a single way you'd abuse that opportunity."

"Nonsense. As I recall, you like bright blue velvet, shiny red satin, and miles of gold fringe on everything. All the floors will be painted lime green and the ceilings will be purple, which I believe is your preference."

"Aside from the bright blue velvet, don't you dare."

"Gold fringe, though?" His eyes sparkled. "Give me something to do to keep from going stark mad at home without you." He draped her hair over his chest and tickled her nose with a few strands. "I'm always better off busy, just like you are. I don't want to fall back into spending nights at the office like I did for a few years because I had little to distract me."

"I trust you completely." She scooted up to kiss him. "Even with the fringe. I love your idea about the pictures. You are so thoughtful."

He toyed with the tie on her pants and brushed the silk cord over her stomach. "You brought these pajamas across an ocean thinking of me, didn't you?"

"Oh, you never crossed my mind. These are just quite practical and easy to wash."

"Hm." He slid his hand over the green silk and cupped her breast in one palm. "Beautifully practical."

Victoria tipped her head back and let him kiss her neck. If he wanted to wait, she would wait, but the hunger of beach house kisses and stolen embraces in stairwells and on dark porches tensed her body as he drew his hands over and under the silk. Her fingers twitched to pull him closer so she could wrap her arms and legs around him. The gold band on his left hand traced a warm line over her ribs and down her stomach.

He moved lower and paused, and the hitch in his breath betrayed his thoughts.

Victoria placed her hand over his. "Matthew, I have something to confess. You might think I am mad, but I must say it."

"Say what?"

She trailed her fingers over his face, onto his ears and into his hair. "That night in the courtyard when you jumped on top of me... I liked it."

He stiffened. "Don't flatter me, Vi. I was an utter wreck, afraid of thunder."

"I don't mean to flatter you," she said quickly. "Only to say that I was quite surprised to feel that desire for you at such a difficult moment, and I was a little ashamed of myself until I thought about it later."

"That was not desire," he said. "Pity, maybe. Surprise."

"Don't you still want me like you used to?"

"God, of course I do." He squeezed her. "How could I not, my love? But everything about me has changed."

"You mean your body has changed, but that does not matter. When my very reasonable and orderly lover gets unreasonable and disorderly is when I want him most," she whispered.

He was silent and gripped her tighter.

"That night, I would have gotten right up and shoved Harry back in the building myself, but my knees were shaking." She pressed her hand against his heart and his pulse raced through her. "That feeling of your body on mine inflamed this passion I have always had for you, and no time or injury has changed that. This body. The one you are in right now."

He twisted her hair in his hands and Victoria snuggled closer, pressing her thigh to his. "I wondered what was wrong with me for desiring you at a time like that. But I have always loved those moments when you show me a glimpse of your heart and mind and hold nothing back."

"When I bumble my careful words or panic at the sound of a storm."

"You could hardly get a sentence out the first time you kissed me. That was rather sweet."

"I remember." He found her lips for a quick kiss.

"Then you know I'm telling the truth." She whispered against his ear. "It's always been you, and only you. If you are truly uncomfortable, it's all right if it's not today."

He closed his eyes and touched her, spreading his hands wide to traverse the green silk over her back and breasts, warm palms on bare shoulders, slipping lower to follow the curves of her hips and thighs. She luxuriated under his touch, pressing into his hands as she moved hers through his thick hair and down his neck, over his back and arms as she leaned in to kiss him.

His mouth drew her in, hot and desirous. He picked up her left hand and kissed her ring, then guided her hand over his stomach to the buttons of his breeches. She worked them down over his hips and caught her breath when he rose to her touch and a little groan rumbled in his chest.

"Matthew," she whispered. "Are you sure—"

"Now. Today." He drew the silk pajama top over her head and sent it sailing off the bed, followed shortly by the matching pants. "I've waited years to make love to my wife," he said as he covered her stomach with kisses. "And it would be a shame to drown in this puddle of my pride and miss my first chance."

"That tickles," she complained between giggles. "Get back up here and let me touch you."

"You were always rather greedy to touch me in bed." He kissed his way up to her lips, warming her navel, ribs, and collarbone. "You held me so tight I had scratches from that weekend at the beach."

"Oh no."

The hunger in his kiss turned tender. "Oh, yes."

The ache of wanting bloomed inside her once more. His touch filled her body and spread frissons of pleasure to every limb. She traced the curves of his arms and chest, taut with muscle earned on the front, while he re-acquainted his lips with her breasts and his hands with the softness of her waist and the warmth between her thighs.

His movements were as natural as breathing when he shifted between her legs, and without pause or declaration he claimed her again with gentle strokes, slow and deep. With a quick gasp, she took him in and brushed her hand over his cheek with a feather-light touch.

"I didn't mind the scratches." He caught her fingers and brought them to his lips.

"Are you hinting at something?"

"Now that you mention it, Mrs. Berger."

She tightened her grip around him and drank in the pleasure on his face—his flushed, smiling cheeks and the thin creases by his eyes from all the years they shared and all the years she missed. The bed frame groaned, unnoticed, and the man above her was no longer a memory or a regret. Their intimacy was no longer locked in a shuttered beach house, out of season. The gray depths in his eyes were as steady and sure as the tides, and she was the moon.

After a moment, Matthew shifted his weight, unsteady, and bit his lip with grim determination as he pulled her over to lay facing him on her side. Tangling their limbs together, he moved inside her again and kissed her lips.

"Is that all right, my love?" he asked, a little breathless. "It was a bit difficult to balance how I—"

"It's lovely," she murmured, rocking against him. "It's perfect. You're not slipping away this time, Matt."

With a wicked smile, he drew back almost entirely. "Aren't I?"

"Never." She grazed her fingernails down his back and hips, setting him shivering with goosebumps as she pulled him back in and whispered. "Wherever you are and wherever I am, I will not let you slip away again."

Chapter Thirty-Four

Matthew yawned, stretching his arms until he hit the bedpost and rapped his knuckles on the carved wood. "Where do you think you're going, little wife?"

"I'm checking the time." Victoria wrapped a sheet around herself and nearly tripped on the pajamas on the floor when she checked the mantel clock. "I'm starving, and we missed breakfast. We may be in trouble with the innkeeper."

"To the bakery, then. Pie. Later." He yawned again. "What a fine bed this is, and finer company in it. Get back here."

"Little wife, am I? That's a bit demeaning."

"Your Grace, the Duchess of Bona Fides ad Absurdum."

She laid down again and propped herself on her elbow. "Preposterous devotion. I won't contest that."

He kissed her lips and smiled. "Did you propose to me less than twenty-four hours ago?"

"I did."

"Thank you for sparing me the trouble of doing it again."

"It was nothing. I had the day off anyway."

"Convenient for you. And convenient for me to have my own personal nurse here since my cheeks hurt from smiling."

She stroked his face. "Sore cheeks are not exactly my specialty."

"Darling, I'm never going near your medical specialty again."

"How are you feeling this morning?" She glanced at his leg, shrouded in sheets.

"My morale is stupendous and my back is killing me, and the one is definitely worth the other."

"I have morphine and a hypodermic kit if you're in much pain."

"Don't bother. I intend to be in far greater pain very shortly."

"I love you so much, Matthew."

"And I love you. Preposterously."

She snuggled close, cheek to his chest, and her heart sped up to match his. A gray morning peeked through the thin cotton curtains, overcast with heavy clouds. "It looks like rain, dearest. A good day for a museum. Amiens has some fine ones only a short taxi drive from here."

"It might be a good day to stay in," he said warily. "Am I going to panic every time I hear thunder?"

"I asked Dr. Bowden, and he thinks the panic only happens when it's a sound you weren't expecting. Since it's gloomy and gray today, let's talk about the weather every time we step outside. Then if thunder comes, you'll be expecting it."

"Well, I'm game." He moved the sheet and pulled at the bandage covering his left knee. "Dr. Swann said I need to change this today or tomorrow and let you have a look."

She hadn't seen the end of his leg since she wrapped it in the operating room. The replacement dressings were crisp and clean, with only a few tiny spots near the sutures. "You're a fast healer," she pronounced. "The scar tissue is forming as it should, and you are delightfully free of any venous congestion."

"In English, please. It is still quite uncomfortable at times, and other times it's almost numb for a moment."

She traced her finger over his suture line, not touching him. "All the blood vessels in the flap were attached to other vessels before the surgery. Now that we've folded them up to cushion the bone and nerves, they have to reconnect to other vessels and change the path of your blood. The pain is normal and will take a while to settle down. Your nerves must also heal, and that takes longer." She twisted the gauze and tucked in the end. "So there you are, husband. Well-tended and well-dressed."

"I'm not dressed yet." He nodded at the floor where his breeches lay in a rumpled pile from the night before. "And I don't have to be."

She feigned a pout. "But I want to take you around the city."

"And I don't want you to leave this bed."

She dropped a kiss on his stomach and smiled when it rumbled. "What if I leave to get us breakfast and come right back?"

"Hm?" His eyes were closed as he played with her loose hair. "Sorry. I don't hear so well when your mouth is down there. What were you saying about staying in bed with your husband all day?"

Victoria pressed her lips to his stomach and breathed him in again. "We must eat, sweetheart."

"I'll take another taste of what I enjoyed a moment ago," he said. "And if you're so hungry—"

A loud rap at the door jolted her upright. "*Monsieur*!" the innkeeper called. "*Madame* Berger. A message for you."

Victoria hopped up and struggled into her dressing gown. "*Oui*," she said, breathless as she opened the door. "*Quel message?*"

The innkeeper, a broad, bald man with a curled moustache, thrust several envelopes in her hand and made an attempt at English. "A nurse from the hospital that kept the *monsieur,* she brought these for him. Mail from America." He peered around Victoria's shoulder and bobbed his head at Matthew. "Can I bring you anything since we did not see you at breakfast? My wife works in a boulangerie two streets away and I can bring you something when I take her lunch."

"Is peach pie in season?" Victoria asked as she handed the letters to Matthew.

"Peach galettes, *madame*, or apple, for the autumn."

"Something with fruit would be delightful, *merci*."

"Something with wine would be delightful," Matthew said when the man left. Goggle-eyed, he stared at the letters. "One from my parents. One from William and Edith, addressed to me, and one from Cooper and Maudie, addressed to you." He squinted at the envelope. "It appears Nora scribbled out your name and wrote Mrs. Berger to not alarm the innkeepers. How thoughtful of her."

"Maudie and Cooper will have posted their letter the same day they sent their telegrams, and I'm sure your family wrote as soon as they heard your news. How sweet of Nora to bring them."

"Three envelopes of sobs and pity." He tossed them onto the bed. "I don't even want to look. Come lie with me again, Vi. We don't need to invite our families on our honeymoon." He pulled her back onto the pile of covers at his side.

"Don't you want to hear what they have to say?"

"Later." He kissed her ear and the warmth of his breath dizzied her. "Much, much later."

A light rain began before they emerged from an afternoon tour of the cathedral, and as Victoria helped Matthew out of the borrowed wheeled chair and back onto his crutches, she eyed the ominous gray sky. Darkening clouds to the east warned of a brewing storm, and despite Dr. Bowden's reassurance, she had no desire to learn more about shell shock if that rain came with thunder.

"Stay here," she said, tightening her coat around her shoulders. "I'll go down to the street and find a taxi. We'll go back to the inn for a rest and wait out the rain."

"It's a short walk. I'll be fine."

"Wet stones and crutches don't mix. When we get back to the hospital, ask Private McKeever how he knows that."

He squinted into the drizzle and the crowd of cars waiting for a streetcar that seemed stuck on its line. "By the time we find a taxi in this traffic, we could walk back." He bobbed his head toward a bright awning. "I believe you are concerned about the weather. May I offer you some refreshment, Mrs. Berger?"

"You can refresh Mrs. Berger anywhere you like." She rubbed the base of her left ring finger through the thin leather gloves that kept their secret.

The café was larger than it looked from its narrow street-facing facade. It stretched back the length of the building, dimly-lit but homey with a stone fireplace that crackled with fresh logs. A young woman came from the kitchen and smiled at the U.S. Army shield on Matthew's jaunty cap.

"Anywhere you like, *monsieur, madame.*" She gestured at the rough-hewn tables and benches. "Choose quickly. In any rain, we become busy. Coffee?"

"*Oui, merci.*"

They had no sooner settled at a small table near the fire when a crack of thunder drowned out the hostess's voice as she greeted another customer. Victoria leapt from her seat and scooted onto Matthew's bench. His face was pale but his eyes were calm when she pulled him close, arms around his shoulders.

"I'm all right," he murmured. He tipped her chin up to kiss her lips. "Thank you, my love."

She placed a hand over his and weighed down the shaking. "We're all right."

"We're all right."

A young man darted from the kitchen with a laden tray and panicked eyes glancing at the front of the café where a dozen damp patrons had just arrived and were shaking umbrellas. The door opened and three more came in.

"*Deux croque madame,*" he said, breathless as he shoved the plates in front of them. "*Et deux café au lait, et bien.*"

"We didn't order these," Victoria said, but the man disappeared into the kitchen without a backward glance.

"*Merci*," Matthew called in his direction, then looked at their plates. "What is this? Breakfast? It's three o'clock."

"There's lunch under that poached egg. *Croque monsieur* is a ham and cheese sandwich. Add the egg and you've got a *croque madame*. It's on every menu in the country." She rose to return to her side of the table and he caught her arm.

"Stay by me. We have a fine view of the door together this way, and we can make up translations for all the gossip from these busy people."

She unfurled her napkin as she scanned the tables, all full now, and caught sight of the waiter begging forgiveness from the couple whose sandwiches he misplaced.

"He's saying he's mortified," she whispered. One of the patrons tapped her watch and the other reached for his hat. "They are threatening to leave and write a letter to the owner of the café, because they have waited terribly long already and have somewhere to be. The waiter says he will have the cook make the sandwiches again, first in line."

Matthew jabbed a fork into her sandwich, popping the yolk of the poached egg, then quickly cut into his own and brought a bite to his mouth. "He can't take ours back now," he said when he swallowed. "Oh my God. This is not just a ham and cheese sandwich."

"That's Gruyère cheese and béchamel sauce."

"I'm a traitor for éclairs and now sandwiches." He took another bite. "Why the hell did Wilson wait so long to send us to save France?"

She snuggled into his shoulder, his wool uniform jacket warm on her cheek. "*Maman* taught all of us how to make them just right, you know."

"Darling wife." He speared a bite with his fork and held it

out to her. "Is it terribly offensive to ask a modern girl to make her husband sandwiches?"

"Deeply offensive."

"Forgive me in advance, darling." He nudged the bite against her lips. "Please."

The salty ham collided with the rich sauce and the tang of the cheese in one bite and she pressed her fingers to her buttery lips as she savored it. "Heaven, isn't it?"

"This is," she said. "Right here, with you."

The firelight gleamed on her ring and brought a smile. She had loathed gloves since Matthew put the ring on her finger, and loathed even more the idea of putting it away in her room when she returned home.

Someone called her name.

Victoria jolted upright and her eyes darted around the room, panicked at the sound of another American voice.

"Yoo-hoo!" the voice called again, and a young woman in a Red Cross uniform waved her arms. "Victoria!"

"Oh no." She tucked her hands under the table and yanked at her ring. "Matthew, help me."

"What?"

"I have butter on my fingers and now I can't get my ring off. Can you?"

She pasted on a smile and nodded at the woman making her way through the crush of damp patrons at the front of the café. Matthew contorted in his seat to reach her elbow. "I've got it," he said, closing his fingers around the band, still buttery from her last attempt. "Hold still."

His fingers slipped and the ring didn't pass her knuckle.

"Can you call it an engagement ring?" he whispered, trying to grasp the thin gold band. "Tell her I'm a pauper and this is the best I could do. You can have an engagement ring, can't you?"

Victoria kept her chin up and her smile on as Matthew gripped her elbow with one hand and wrapped a napkin over her fingers. He yanked at her wedding band one more time until it came free with a *pop!* and he nearly tumbled over trying to keep it in his hand.

"Hi there," the woman said, breathless as she appeared at the end of their table. "What a gully-washer out there, huh? Can I sit with you all until it lets up? I was on my way home."

Victoria steadied herself, rubbing her sore finger under the table. "Of course, Helen, please join us. How lovely to see you."

She and Helen had trained in London together before coming to France and had many mutual friends among the nurses who transferred in and out of Amiens. Victoria wasn't anxious to share a minute of Matthew's time, but with her ring safely tucked in his pocket and the deluge swamping the streets, she counted herself lucky her husband was upright and not shouting about German bombers over the thunder.

"Matthew, this is my friend, Miss Helen Phillips. She's from Tennessee and works at another Red Cross hospital here in town. And Helen, this is Corporal Matthew—"

Helen clapped her hands. "Corporal Matthew Berger, as I live and breathe! Oh honey, you found him!"

Matthew's mouth went slack as Helen scooted onto the other bench. "You found me, did you?"

"I told you I asked a few friends to look out for you. Helen was one of them." Her cheeks warmed. "We all look out for each other's friends and family if anyone asks."

"And did she ever." Helen reached over the table and

patted Matthew's hand. "Look, everybody's watching for their folks and everybody's got a list a mile long, except this lady."

"Helen, everyone with a list a mile long has had an army in the war for years. Everyone's families and sweethearts are on one front or another, except ours."

"Yes, but even I have a few people. Four, including that gorgeous man from Sussex who we met during training. Alistair. He writes me every week. And your list?"

Victoria flushed so red she could see the tip of her nose pinken when she crossed her eyes. "Just the one. But no one else I knew had—"

Matthew leaned back against the booth and crossed his arms, smug and satisfied. "Just the one?"

"Look at her blushing." Helen laughed. "Always so calm and collected, so when she told me the one-that-got-away was on his way over, I was fit to be tied, and—oh."

She looked at his left hand.

"I guess you already got tied down beforehand."

The heat that scalded Victoria's cheeks seconds before drained away in a blink. She could see rumors tingling on Helen's pouted lips—rumors that would swirl around the nurses' quarters for hospital No. 7 as soon as she left the café. *Poor Victoria. Her sweetheart married someone at home while she was off to war and looking for him. Poor, poor, Victoria.* But everyone at No. 43 knew Matthew was not married and was head-over-heels for 'poor' Victoria, who they all envied rather than pitied—and when the two accounts collided, at the center of it all would be the gold band on her husband's finger.

She cleared her throat. Fidgeted. Drummed her fingernails on the table. "Well, I can explain," she said finally, when Matthew pointed at his ring.

"Do you mean this?" he asked. "I forgot I had it on. Sorry, darling. I didn't mean to make you look like you were trawling the town with a married man."

Victoria's eyes popped open when he pulled her close and kissed her cheek.

Helen glanced between them, brows furrowed as she re-pinned her veil. "You forgot you had your wedding ring on?"

"Not mine." He wrangled it off and cupped it in his palm, tapping it absentmindedly without looking up. "I lost a friend out there, and I thought I should take this back home for him. You know how easy it is to lose things when hospitals are given charge of your belongings—"

Victoria poked him.

"—so I thought it better to just wear it. A wedding ring is a precious promise, and I know just how valuable this is." He dropped it in his coat pocket and Victoria smiled at the tiny *ping* when it landed on her ring.

"How awful." Helen's eyes welled. "But I mean, how lovely of you. You're as fine a man as she said you were, Matthew Berger."

"Tell me more of what she said about me." His eyes shone. "Details, please."

"How's work?" Victoria interjected, anxious to change the subject. "Are you still rooming with Ada and Gwennie? How are they? What do you hear from home?"

Helen ignored her. "So if he's not attached at home, are you two...?"

"Helen, really." Her cheeks flushed pink and then scarlet

when she noticed Matthew doing a very poor job at hiding a smile.

"Oh, you worked it out!" Helen clapped again. "I bet everyone in old forty-three is just steamed about losing you. I'll have to get Bridget for the gossip, because I know you won't tell. Are you all packed?"

"No. We've decided to celebrate our marriage at home when this is all over." Victoria nodded at Matthew's crutches propped on the chair. "Matthew will be at the convalescent hospital in London for some time and I said I was here for the duration, so I will stay for the duration."

He picked up her left hand and kissed her fourth finger, still pink from fighting with the slippery gold band. "What do you think, Miss Phillips? Is it valid if I send her an engagement ring by mail and don't put it on her myself?"

"Oh, yes." Helen squeezed her arm. "What a modern romance. The woman is at work while the man is at home, and yet it all makes perfect sense."

"It would be a waste to keep such a delightful princess locked in a castle," Matthew said. "She can handle a scalpel, so why not a sword?"

"That's the spirit. I say, three cheers for love in the midst of war. It's a shame the Red Cross is so fussy about marriage." Helen signaled to the panicked waiter and held up one finger to order a coffee. "When did we last talk? Have any of the other girls succumbed recently?"

"Jane Major is Jane Thornton now. She's nursing her wounded husband back to health in London," Victoria said. "Annabelle Darrow is now Annabelle Sharp and she is bored to tears, sitting on her bottom in Essex with her new mother-in-law while her husband is hunting U-boats."

Helen grimaced. "Poor Annabelle. And what a waste of her skills. Why did she marry her fellow if she couldn't be with him now anyway?"

"Perhaps she wanted him to know she was truly his and would not change her mind," Victoria said. "Maybe she let him slip through her fingers in the past and wants to hold him tight however she can now."

Matthew clasped her hand. "Maybe she wanted to make a home for him to come home to, and cherish some hopes that are more 'when' than 'if,' with as much certainty as any of us are allowed."

"Oh, the two of you. Just the look of you has me all misty." Helen leaned forward on her elbows and sighed, then slapped the table and sat upright. "Do you know what I would do? If Alistair was wounded and asked me to marry him right now, I mean?"

"What?"

"I'd marry him and send him on home without telling anyone." She lifted her chin like she'd just talked the Kaiser into a treaty herself. "Wouldn't that be clever?"

Matthew stammered. "Why—ah, why would you do that? Quite risky."

"Who's going to tell on me? We have work to do, and no one wants to send a nurse home. As long as I don't tell anyone outright that I'm married, what reason would they have to send me away?"

"Well, when you put it that way—"

"Plausible deniability." Victoria nudged his ribs and smiled. "I believe that's all it takes to win a case sometimes, isn't it? If you can make the case that you probably didn't know something, you can't be held liable for the outcome of that something."

Helen smiled. "Look at that. I have a legal defense. Now I just need the handsome convalescent to try it on." She glanced at Matthew's crutches. "But I don't mean I wish something would—I meant, I should know better than to joke of such things and it's quite awful, what happened to you. I'm sorry if I offended you."

He snuck an arm around Victoria's waist and squeezed her hip below the level of the table, unseen. "No offense is taken, Miss Phillips. I am grateful to be alive, and blessed beyond measure that everything I need to enjoy this life is still attached."

Chapter Thirty-Five

For three more days, the letters from North Carolina sat unopened as the newlyweds dodged more rain and took in the sights of Amiens that hadn't been damaged or closed when the town was occupied in 1914. They picnicked on a boat through the city's famous floating gardens, *Les Hortillonnages*, and their guide smiled indulgently when they ignored his narration in favor of kisses. Another long dinner at the tavern by the river led to a late night with their new friends in the French army. Victoria joined in their marching songs with gusto, then demurred when they asked how she already knew them.

"Shouldn't we open these?" she asked, holding up the letters on their final evening at the inn.

Matthew eyed the half-bottle of wine on their bedside table with a wicked smile. "Those letters will be nothing but pity and panic," he said, waving the letter from his parents aside. "This is our honeymoon. It's our last night together."

"Don't say that."

He swigged the wine. "This is our last night together for a long time."

"If you get sentimental with me now, I'll cry and ruin it," she said. "Let's open Maudie and Cooper's letter since they think they're so smart with their telegrams. They will be concerned for you, but they are obviously not gloomy or moping. We'll come up with something clever to send back and keep them guessing."

"Mmhm." He nuzzled into her neck and made short work of the buttons. "What?"

"Or we could tell them, if you think Cooper won't accidentally announce to all and sundry that he was right all along. You can tell them when you get home. I'll leave it up to you."

He pushed her dress off her shoulders, down her arms and over her hips, and the touch of his mouth on her breasts was warm and inviting. "Did you say something, little wife?" He slid his hands over her stays and loosened the busks.

"Well. Nothing of importance."

The last embers in the fireplace went cold overnight, and Victoria drew a blanket closer to her shoulders and snuggled into her husband's arms. The rich aroma of eggs and coffee from the dining room below didn't even tempt her to poke a toe out from under the covers.

Behind the thin curtains, daylight began its slow ascent, and she was almost asleep again when Matthew twisted a lock of her hair around his finger and kissed it.

"Why did you finally decide to marry me?" he asked.

"Because I love you and was long overdue in showing you how much I wish to spend my life with you."

He propped himself on his elbow and looked at her. "Why were you suddenly so confident about changing course in your work? Not that it must change," he added quickly, "but you said you don't know what it will be. You never wanted such uncertainty before."

"I don't especially want it now." She wriggled against him when he pulled her closer. "But I always tried to separate my emotions from my work before. I thought that made me stronger. Then by some terrible luck, you showed up at my hospital."

"I promise, I just wanted to see why you liked surgery so much."

"I thought a great deal about separating my emotions from my work when Dr. Bowden offered me a place at his hospital in London after the war."

"London?"

"He says he's going to make it different there for women. Maybe for married women, even. A teaching hospital with women in the operating rooms. It's everything I wanted."

Matthew didn't move.

"I considered it. And I turned him down."

His breaths grew ragged. "Did you really want to turn him down?"

"He said the offer will always stand, but I will not take him up on it."

"Victoria, perhaps we should discuss—"

"I cannot keep pretending like a little girl that the world will change for me if I wish on a star or say a prayer," she said. "Even if you wished to move to London, and even if he could hire me in surgery, that work might not accommodate us having a family like we wanted. And we'd be so far from ours. The things that have made me happiest are always at odds with one another. I think I will never be fully happy if I must give either up entirely, so I must find a way to balance a bit of both."

"Don't you think you'll regret that?"

"I regret missing your first steps on crutches because of a lousy father with a fat neck. I regret missing my sister's babies being born because I had to work. I have missed so much."

He smiled and she kissed his lips. "When I look back at my choices, I see I always counted on my work to define me," she said. "But I stifled other dreams that were just as real and important. I always wanted to marry you and have a family with you, but I thought I would lose myself if I gave up what I worked for. A few weeks ago, you became part of my work and those discordant halves of my life collided in a way I could no longer ignore."

"I would like to reiterate that I did not injure myself." He caressed her cheek and tangled his fingers in her hair. "But I am grateful every day that I could make my way back to you."

"I have not done enough nursing," she said, "but perhaps I have limited myself to this kind of nursing long enough. I know I have missed enough time with you already, and you have waited long enough for me to prove the one thing I know to be absolute truth: I am more intent on keeping you than I am afraid of losing anything else."

He drew her close and kissed her, brushing her long hair back when it fell against him. The warm rush of his mouth and the heat of his body melded them together.

"I love you, Victoria. More than any limb, more than life itself. This was a small sacrifice for all I have gained."

"I love you." She pressed his hand to her stomach. "And if these few nights change our path, I will come home to you right away with no regrets."

His lips were tender and lingered on hers, a tang of salt between them from sweating moments before. "And so we have it all planned." He kissed her nose. "You know how fond I am of having everything in order."

"I've always liked that about you."

"Would you like a dog or a cat to keep Edgar company? I'm eager to get started on this little family."

"And I am eager to get started on those letters." She sat up and clutched the blanket to her chest. "You may let yours sit until kingdom come, if you wish, but the one from Maudie and Cooper is addressed to Victoria Harper and Mrs. Matthew Berger."

"Alas, out-maneuvered again." He gave her a little push and she dove for her dressing gown.

Dearest Victoria,

I hope you and Matthew enjoyed our telegrams. I can see him rolling his eyes and hear that exasperated groan of his an ocean away, and I dearly hope they brought him a little smile. Leaving out how glad he must be to see you (and you him, I think), how awful. How absolutely, indescribably awful it is. I fell to my knees when I read your letter and could hardly stand until Cooper helped me up, after which he read it and also nearly keeled over.

It inspired us to advise you both, with the wisdom of almost ten years wed, that you should consider

The ink flew off the edge of the page and the handwriting resumed a few inches lower, stark and angular, not like Maudie's elegant script.

> He still loves you, Victoria. Don't let that old grouch tell you otherwise. Ask him if he went to your place on purpose. He knew right where you were. The man is my dear friend, but I imagine that if you did anything less than fall to your knees and propose, he grumbled while he flirted with you and swung between desperate longing and pretending he was quite all right on his own. He's still codswallop at explaining his feelings, but perhaps he'll do better with the object of his affections on the receiving end instead of me.

Victoria pressed her fingers to her mouth to hold back a laugh. "*Das Fingerspitzengefühl,*" she whispered. "How timely."

"What?" Matthew sat up, propping himself on the pillows.

"Cooper had a vision of the future."

"Oh no."

"He'll be insufferable for years."

The letter resumed in Maudie's handwriting.

> I wonder whether this terrible war can bless us with the change we women need to break barriers and find balance between the work of our brains and the dreams of our hearts. We can work as well as any man, and we have proven it. Your English friends will go home to a country that lets them vote now, and how I wish I could say the same for this so-called land of the free. Yet it is home to the bravest woman I know, and that alone is enough to keep me fighting

for our suffrage while you fight for liberty on the one hand, and who knows? Perhaps something else on the other.

Ever so fondly,

Maudie Truxton

A short newspaper clipping fell from the envelope and Victoria's mouth dropped open when she read the announcement from Raleigh Methodist Hospital. "Matthew. Dr. Felton is retiring from the hospital presidency. Retiring altogether, it seems."

"You're joking."

"Look. It's in *The News and Observer*. Maudie sent it."

Chuckling, he flopped back on the pillows. "Good riddance to that antiquarian. I still have half a dozen briefs outlined for ways to sue him."

"You certainly do not."

Matthew shrugged. "He was clearly negligent, and you won't convince me otherwise. The old bastard put orderlies in operating rooms to help out when he had an experienced nurse available, just because that nurse was a woman. Never mind that it's not strictly illegal, his patients should be furious. He's truly leaving?"

A wide smile spread across her face. "He is, indeed. Farewell to old men and old ideas, perhaps. This is a splendid sign." She handed Matthew the letter from his parents. "Now, with a bright spot on our horizon, let's do one of the others. If you feel awful after reading it, at least I'll be here to comfort you."

He turned the envelope over and over in his hands, bending the corners forward and back like he had on the letter he wrote her from the field hospital. Victoria watched in silence as he dragged his finger under the seal halfway, then stopped.

"This will be nothing but fuss about everything you blessedly do not fuss about. Cartwright is forty-five years old and said his mother screamed over seven pages at him when she got his news, on and on about how she told him not to join up. My mother will be weeping that I'm a cripple and she'll imagine me bed-ridden for the rest of my life."

"Well, we'll show her how wrong she is." She cleared her throat. "I'll vouch for your endurance."

He sat up and kissed her nose. "These last few days have numbed me to this injury, and I'd like to hold onto that feeling as long as possible."

"I understand. But let me look at it and see if there's anything pressing. You can read the rest another time."

He handed her the stuffed envelope and she opened the seal. She counted nine pages folded inside, covered front and back with script, and her eyes went wide deciphering four different types of handwriting scribbled throughout.

"Who's still at home with your parents?" she asked.

"Anthony and Lily. This is his last year at A&M and she's gadding about the social circuit and volunteering at church. Did they write as well? Please God, let that not all be my mother's mourning."

Victoria scanned the lines, flipping past paragraphs of Mrs. Berger's desolate lines and Mr. Berger's attempts at patriotism. "Fuss, fuss, fuss," she murmured. "Oh, here's something. Lily signed up with the Red Cross and asks you to pray for her. I suppose she'll go to the center in Charlotte. That's awfully good of her to..."

"To what?"

"When she wrote this, she said she planned to go the next day to Norfolk and would offer to come over here with a Voluntary Aid Detachment." She squinted at the date. "Nine days ago."

He pushed up from the bed to stand and Victoria jumped to catch him as he fought for balance. Taking the crutch she offered, he shoved it under his left arm. "How can my parents allow that? Lily can't tell a bandage from a bayonet."

"She's twenty-four years old. They don't have to allow anything, but your mother does not sound pleased. And it seems Anthony has some news, too."

He swallowed thickly and sat back down. "He's been drafted."

"No. He signed up." She flipped the page. "And he will murder every German on sight with no remorse. Revenge. A boy's braggadocio."

Matthew stared at his left leg for a moment and then dragged the blanket over it. "Every German," he said flatly. "Well, don't invite him for a visit."

"What?"

"I'm glad you are staying here because you want to. I'm glad that if you must stay, Harry stays too."

A satisfied warmth engulfed her heart, and she let the silence hold his words. She set the letter aside and climbed back onto the bed with him. "The rest of it is fussing," she said, and kissed his bare shoulder. "Now, let me hold you a little while."

She curled against him on her side, his back to her chest, her arms crossed over him. Words rose and fell in her throat and refused to spring free even when the tension in his neck softened and his breaths grew deep. Every minute of their short honeymoon had been packed with a day's worth of emotion, stacking all the years they missed into a whirlwind of wine, laughter, and tangled sheets. The enormity of her husband's strength in the face of such terror and loss awed her, but she was unsurprised by it. A man who loved the way he loved wouldn't let anything break him.

"I love you," she whispered. "I will protect us and I will guard us fiercely. Anyone or anything that tries to come between us will find no space there." She pressed her hand to his chest. "Not work. Not war. Not even the ocean."

He pulled her palm to his cheek, sliding it over the sandpaper rasp of three days too busy eating, drinking, and making love to shave. Drawing her fingers to his mouth, he kissed them one by one. "So many fortunate men have touched these beautiful, talented hands." He rolled over to face her. "But these lips, if you are so inclined..."

Chapter Thirty-Six

Victoria was determined to keep a good mood when she returned to Rue de Renard after delivering Matthew to the hospital. It would do neither of them any good to mourn their separation before it happened. The morning had been fraught with emotion and tender kisses between smiles and laughter and making love. They had stayed in bed until the innkeeper knocked and reminded them to leave. A quick stop at the house so he could meet her dear *Maman* soothed the ache in her heart from not telling her own mother the news.

Another evening in her beloved green pajamas would keep him close and warm her with the imprint of his hands, and she hummed as she unpacked her things and shuffled through the hastily-developed photographs Nora had left on her bed.

Ingrid burst into the house and collided with the umbrella stand, sending its contents clattering through the hall before the front door closed. "Victoria!" she gasped, nearly out of breath as Frances and Nora ran to her. "Where is she? She's back, isn't she?"

"She just returned from taking Matthew back to the hospital. Oh heavens, you're bleeding." Frances pulled on her blouse, stained red and torn open over a scrape that covered her left elbow. "Sit and let me take care of you."

"No. I need—where is Victoria?"

Bridget poked her head into the front hall and her eyes went wide. "Ingrid, darling. You're red as a poppy. Are you all right?"

Ingrid pressed on her chest as she struggled to breathe. Drawn by the clatter, Blanche came from the kitchen to usher them all into the sitting room. Ingrid's eyes darted frantically among them. "I just need Victoria," she said finally. "I'm quite fine. All of you, go on."

"Did you fall?" Frances asked as Blanche pressed a cold cloth to Ingrid's bleeding elbow. She inspected her muddy skirt. "Are you hurt anywhere else?"

She shook her head. "No. I just need to speak with Victoria."

Victoria twirled into the living room. "I'm here," she sang. "Dear diary. Today I—oh my goodness, today I saw my friend Ingrid looking like she just escaped the trenches." She rushed to her side. "What happened?"

Ingrid's lips trembled. "It's Nurse Perry. I saw her at church this evening and I heard her talking."

"About what?" Nora shot Victoria a panicked glance.

"She was talking to another woman about the Americans coming, and the woman said the Americans were already here, and she had one of the wounded soldiers to stay at her inn."

"That's not so bad," Bridget said. "Matthew was on a leave and it's not Nurse Perry's business where he stayed. Maybe it wasn't even him. There are four other hospitals in town, and who knows if someone else from his unit was wounded."

"No. No. The woman said it was an American soldier named Berger and his American wife."

Nora's mouth fell open and Victoria froze.

"Of course she would assume they were married," Frances chimed in. "It's the polite thing to assume, really, if a woman is staying overnight with a man. And of course Victoria had to be there to help him. You didn't have to panic, darling. At the very worst, she'll get a little conduct lecture."

Ingrid shook her head, cheeks still flushed bright red. "No. When she said that, Nurse Perry asked her specifically if they were married and the woman said they wore rings and he called her his wife." She met Victoria's eyes. "And then the woman winked and said the soldier seemed to be healing well."

Victoria gulped. They hadn't exactly been loud, but they hadn't been especially quiet, and she had spotted the saucy wink from the innkeeper when they paid their bill. Every eye in the room turned to her bare left hand.

"She said she would have to send you home if it was true. Did you marry him?" Ingrid asked hoarsely. "Are you leaving?"

Her lips went numb.

"Is who leaving?" Marie chirped from the hall. "And goodness, who tipped over the umbrella stand?" She pulled her apron over her head. "I'm on laundry shifts with Harry now, and I have to tell you girls the funniest thing that—" She stopped in the entrance to the sitting room. "Oh. Is someone really leaving?"

Victoria's chest rose and fell with deep, draining breaths as she scanned the room and grasped Nora's hand in silence. They were the oldest and had been there the longest, the so-called good examples for all the women of the Red Cross, whose rules they'd so flagrantly broken.

"I married him."

Blanche put her hand to her heart and Ingrid squeaked in protest. "But you—"

"I am not leaving until the war is over, and none of you will tell a soul." Victoria turned over and put her feet on the back of the sofa, letting her head dangle just above the floor. "Nurse Perry needs to fix her ears if she heard otherwise. Legally, my name is still Victoria Harper. We're not even telling our families, let alone the Red Cross."

Nora flipped over too and tucked up her dress. "If a woman will do her duty and stay in a war zone while her husband goes safely home, I say let her. Who disagrees?"

"Did you know about this?" Bridget demanded.

"I was their witness and I took photographs." Nora stuck out her tongue. "And I'd do it for any of you."

Victoria grappled for Ingrid's hand and settled for a handful of her dusty skirt. "Thank you for worrying for me, dear. I'm sorry you're hurt. What happened?"

"I was running around the corner on Rue de la Dauphine and I tried to squeeze by a woman with a cart and—no, just a moment. You tell us what happened."

Frances giggled. "Dear diary, today I got married to a dreamy man who loves me. It was not strange at all. It was delightful."

"Dreamy?" Victoria craned her neck and smiled.

"Those eyes, darling. And lashes to make a woman jealous. Tell us how he proposed."

"Well, the first time—"

"Not that time," they chorused.

"The second time?"

"The one after your hospital training course? No." Frances shook her head. "That was so thoughtless of him. I really didn't care for him after you told us that."

"The third time, then?"

Bridget frowned. "All you said about that one is that it was awful."

"That's all, then." Victoria folded her hands across her stomach and smiled.

"But how did he ask you this time?" Bridget leaned forward. "You must tell us the whole secret if we're going to keep it for you."

Her ring was put away in her bedroom, and she rubbed her fingers over her left hand where she had worn it for only a few days. "He didn't ask me. I asked him."

Marie collapsed on the divan. "Can you really do that?"

"Can't a woman do anything a man can do? I can, and I'm happy I did."

"But—but I told you we would be your bridesmaids."

"Marie," Nora said flatly. "It was a secret, so there were no bridesmaids or bouquets or dances. I was wearing my work uniform."

"Nurse Perry will call you in first thing tomorrow," Ingrid said. "You know she will. She will tell Dr. Bowden and won't let you hide in the operating rooms if you try to avoid her. What if she forbids you to see Matthew again? What if she—

well, what if she believes that innkeeper? It's the truth. What if she believes the truth?" Her voice rose with every question until she was nearly shrieking. "What will you do?"

"I'll lie. So will my husband. And so will you if anyone asks."

"Won't you?" Nora challenged.

"I will." Bridget's blonde hair swished over her cheeks with her emphatic nod. "These rules are antique and wrong." Blanche nodded agreement.

Frances raised her hand. "I'm with you. We are lucky to have you, Victoria, and so are our doctors and patients. If you say you didn't marry him, and if Matthew says you didn't marry him, is there any way she could prove you did?"

Victoria raised one finger. "The register we signed is kept at the city hall. But if she goes looking for it, I think that means she wants me out and there's nothing I can do about it." Still upside down, she looked up and met Ingrid's red-rimmed eyes. "But think about it. Why would she want me out? I decided it was worth the risk."

Ingrid's lip quivered and she flipped over next to her. She twisted her neck until it cracked and tucked her braids behind her head. "I'll lie if anyone asks. I'll go to the grave with it. You cannot go," she whispered.

"I don't intend to, darling. While this wretched war continues, I will remain here. I need this work. It fills something inside me and this is why I do it. Whether and how I will do it in the future is not certain, but it's another risk I will take. Matthew understands."

Dr. Bowden understood as well, but he was the ace she didn't want to play. The storm would blow over when the new patients from the field hospital arrived and everyone had a hundred other things on their minds. Matthew would be gone and a piece of her heart would go with him, but when he was far away, suspicious people might forget, and letters would still come for Miss Victoria Harper.

"You are so brave, Victoria," Ingrid said. "I don't know if I could do it. I want to do so many things you do, but it's frightening."

"When the time comes to make hard choices, you'll surprise yourself. You'll trust yourself," she said, thinking of skittish Dr. Denys who was so talented but so nervous. "Never be afraid to come to your friends for reassurance."

Nora cleared her throat. "Never try to do the scary things alone."

"Hospital training programs are not easy," Victoria continued. "And of course you must get your certificate first. But you will learn to be brave, Ingrid. Look at how brave you were already. You left a safe home to come here and place yourself closer to danger to serve your country. Marie did, too. And when more of these hard times come, you'll be brave again."

Marie forced a smile. "It's not so scary with friends."

Ingrid squirmed and stammered on the red brocade sofa. "But I never—oh, look at me." Her voice broke into nervous laughter. "I'm crying upside down now and I have tears on my forehead and in my eyebrows and I don't know what to do."

Nora rolled over and turned upright and Victoria followed. They pulled Ingrid up and her flushed face faded to blotchy, tear-stained streaks.

"How does your neck feel?" Victoria asked.

Ingrid twitched her head and her mouth popped open. “Oh my. Something just gave way in my ears. I can hear better. Is that what happens when those bones move in your ears? Goodness, this feels strange.”

Nora grinned. “But you survived.”

Chapter Thirty-Seven

The cheerful mural in *l'école maternelle* had greeted Victoria on every shift for two and a half years. *Nous aimons apprendre* was an echo of small voices from an innocent past that might not be restored even when the Red Cross and the army left and the French schoolchildren returned.

The little blue classroom bore the scars of battle. The school was requisitioned because it was built in 1912 and had running water. With no care given to appearances, army plumbers had hacked through the walls to put sinks in every classroom-turned-operating-room and patient ward, patched with sloppy plaster as an afterthought. Across from the sink, a V-shaped incision marked the spot Bridget's bone forceps bit into the wall on a bad day.

After scrubbing her hands, Victoria opened her sterile trays and counted instruments in silence to prepare for the morning's cases. Her visit with Nurse Perry would be brief, one way or the other.

To wait and let poisonous rumors and whispers fester would not help her cause. Nurse Perry might ask the innkeeper for more details. She might take a complaint to the Red Cross without even speaking to her. If Nurse Perry approached her, Victoria might be caught off guard, and the matron would have the upper hand.

Women had to elbow their way into respect and recognition, and the battle lines were erased and re-drawn over and over. Progress flickered, flared, and stalled. If she set herself up to attack instead of defend, to surprise her adversary and push her way through like the Germans did through Belgium, her battleground would be the little office with its Red Cross rule books and pin-prickled maps.

Victoria climbed the steps of the administrative building to the second floor where a row of child-sized wooden classroom chairs lined the wall. She squeezed into one and waited.

The Germans hadn't been pushed back inside their old borders yet, but they would be. She was sure of it. One day she might have to play by the old rules again too, but in this battle, she would stand her ground.

Philippa Perry's sensible black boots beat a steady cadence on the tile to announce her approach, until she stumbled on a step and nearly dropped an armful of personnel files when Victoria rose from her seat in the hall.

"Good morning, Nurse Perry." Victoria's smile was wide and bright. "Goodness, your arms must be aching. Let me help you with that."

Nurse Perry shifted the stack of files to Victoria's arms and opened the office door without looking at her. "Thank you, Nurse Harper. What brings you here so early?"

"We have busy schedule today, but I didn't want to chance missing you. I wished to thank you again for those extra days on my leave. We had a splendid time." She scanned the files quickly and didn't spot her name. "And Corporal Berger is in tip-top health, so Dr. Bowden will be pleased as well."

Victoria kept smiling and Nurse Perry eyed her warily. "How funny you should bring that up."

"I showed him all around. We tried to go to the Picardy museum, but I didn't know they'd closed it. The taxi driver recommended the Amiens circus, and that was delightful. Did you know they are going to make a museum out of Mr. Jules Verne's home? Oh, and we took the guided tour at the cathedral, naturally, and you won't believe what happened next."

Nurse Perry sighed. "Is this your idea of softening the blow?

"Pardon?" Victoria asked, tilting her head.

"You married him and you are leaving."

"What? Of course not."

"But then what will I not believe happened next?"

Victoria laughed. "We saw my friend Helen Phillips at a café. Do you remember her? I haven't seen her in ages. She's still at number seven and sends her best."

"Oh."

"And the next day, we went to the floating gardens. Have you ever taken one of the boat tours? The guide was so amusing, and even in this weather, the greenery was splendid."

"But as I understand it—"

"We bought a little painting from a street artist to commemorate it. The man's right arm was badly maimed, but he is fortunately left-handed."

"And you're quite sure Corporal Berger didn't ask you to marry him?"

She cocked her head again. "Well, he did. I told you he did."

"You just told me he didn't."

"I meant, I told you he did three times."

"Nurse Harper, why did you want to see me, exactly?"

"I only wanted to thank you for the extra two days and let you know I am rested and refreshed for our new patients, just as you said." She paused. "Have I done something wrong?"

Victoria kept her face neutral and waited. If it all went wrong, and it still might, going home with her husband was hardly a punishment. She might not win exactly what she wanted, but she couldn't lose.

"Where did you lodge during your leave?" Nurse Perry asked finally.

"The Red Cross has no rules about where I lay my head when I am on my leave, Nurse Perry. I checked, of course."

She sighed. "Were you with Corporal Berger?"

"Matthew had a room at an inn on Avenue Quatrième."

"Did you stay there with him?"

"He cannot get around well on his own yet, and he needed my help."

Nurse Perry pressed her hands flat to the desk and leaned forward. "I know the woman who runs the inn," she said stiffly.

Victoria bobbed her head like an agreeable puppet and smiled again. "I recall she was very nice."

"She says you registered as man and wife."

"We thought we should, for propriety, since he needed my help to get around the room."

"And you wore rings."

She giggled. "Well, it would have reflected poorly on the inn to let a room to an unmarried couple, so of course we had to look the part. But luckily, the Red Cross doesn't think to forbid any silly play-acting with one's old sweetheart. It seems even the governing committee understands there are some things not worth regulating."

"She also says you—you *behaved* like man and wife."

"We what?" Victoria's brow creased. "I don't understand."

"You and Corporal Berger."

"Yes?"

"She says you behaved like man and wife."

"Yes, just as I said. We wore rings."

"Nurse Harper." The older woman's cheeks flushed and her frown deepened. "You know what I mean."

"Having never been married, I am a little unsure about what your friend said or meant. But perhaps the words are different in French." Victoria tapped her chin. "Of course, we mis-translate poor Harry all the time."

Nurse Perry rose and stalked to the door before slamming it with a quick thrust of her arm. "Did you marry him?"

"Who, Harry?"

"Victoria, did you marry Corporal Berger?"

She abandoned the innocent facade and pursed her lips. "If you do not value my service to this organization and our patients, you need no reason to send me home. I do not need to break any rules for you to transfer me out or recommend my expulsion. Do you want me to leave?"

The question hung in the air, sharp as a pin from the map.

"Of course I don't." Nurse Perry's tense stance softened. "It would be a great shame to lose you."

"Then why are you trying to make me say something that will force me out?"

Nurse Perry stood at the map of France and did not answer. A long stretch of the paper a few centimeters from Amiens had thinned and torn, and she poked a finger at a black pin—Germany—near Ypres.

"If you would like me to stay," Victoria continued, "I will remain for the duration of the war. Matthew and I will celebrate our marriage at home with our families when it is over."

"You do not plan to go home with him now?"

Victoria shrugged as though the question was not one on which her entire life hinged. "I made a commitment to serve here. When the war is over, I will go home."

"And so my friend at the inn was merely taken in by what you call play-acting."

"It would seem so."

"But if you are with child—"

"I haven't broken my hands or sustained a brain injury. I know of no reason I cannot do my work today as well as I could do it last week. If that changes, I will address it with you promptly."

Nurse Perry turned to the window that overlooked the

courtyard and peered above the building opposite them, northward, toward the fighting. She dragged her hand over her jaw, skin slack and softened by age. "Promptly," she echoed.

"Are these files for the new VAD girls?" Victoria ran her thumb over the stacked papers, ruffling the edges.

"They are."

"May I help you with them in any way?"

Nurse Perry turned back to the table and tapped the files but did not look up. "Please collaborate with Eugenia Baxter in the medical ward and select twelve of our auxiliary girls to assist with bedside duties. We will fill in their spaces with the trainees."

"I will meet with her today and we will have a list for you tomorrow."

"Thank you."

"You can count on me," she said. "Always."

"That wasn't so difficult." Victoria held her hand to her forehead, feigning a swoon into Matthew's arms on the courtyard bench. "I claimed I was not your wife, but said I pretended to be your wife, all while actually being the thing I pretended I was pretending to be. Goodness, why did none of us see this solution before? Lie a little to bend a dusty old rule and carry on working."

"Because other women want to go home with their men," Nora said, reaching around Victoria to poke Matthew's shoulder. "You have the unique and enviable situation of a man who supports the work you wish to do."

"Even if she won't be joining you in London after the war." Matthew poked Nora back.

"She's mine for now, Berger."

"Legally, she's mine forever."

Victoria put her arms around them and leaned back, face turned up to the afternoon sun. "I love you both dearly. And I love this beautiful day on this beautiful bench in this beautiful little patch of sunlight."

Nora smiled. "Did you catch a whiff of the ether?"

"Let me savor my little victory before we go have to amputate something after lunch."

"What are you up to?"

"Four hundred and fifty-six without a moment's faintness." She turned her cheek to Matthew's shoulder and his wool overcoat warmed and tickled her skin when she snuggled close. "This does not include the many other things that have dizzied me lately, but I do count amputation revisions, so you are among my triumphs."

"I do not mind being one of such an impressive number, since I am the only one to get your kisses and not just your hands." Matthew leaned his head against hers but stiffened when footsteps approached. Victoria opened her eyes, blurred with rainbows from the bright sun, and the tall figure in front of them was a dark silhouette.

"Corporal Berger."

She jumped up. "Harry, this is not the time."

"It is the time," he said. "Your man is leaving soon. Did you tell him what I said?"

"About breaking your own arm to keep her safe?" Matthew asked. "Yes, she told me."

Harry stood straighter, almost at attention. "I am sorry for how I offended you, Corporal. Nurse Harper loves you, and so I know you must be a good man. I should take your words to heart about traitoring."

"What is he talking about?" Nora whispered. Victoria sat back down and shushed her.

Matthew waved Harry off. "Don't think of it. I shot off and lost my temper a bit, too. I shouldn't have said that."

"You are shot?"

Matthew held up his hands like guns. "Shooting a pistol, like an outburst. Bang, and you say something stupid."

"This is something your army says?"

"Maybe it's an American expression. I've seen it in Westerns and cowboy stories in a few magazines. The six-shooters and all that."

"Shot off, then," Harry said, tapping his temple as if to inscribe the phrase in his mind. "As you say."

"I hope no circumstance arises for you to break your arm, *Oberleutnant* Kurz. On Victoria's behalf or otherwise."

"Thank you." Harry put out a hand and Matthew shook it. "You know, I have a joke about cowboys."

"Do you now?" He leaned back on the bench. "I'd like to hear it."

Harry's eyes lit up and he patted his chest. "I am a German man visiting the American West, and I buy a horse in town. I go to have a drink and return to find my horse is stolen. So I say very loudly to all the cowboys, 'whatever man stole my horse will bring her back, or I will do what I did in France!'"

Victoria glanced at Matthew as he watched with lifted brows.

"So I have one more drink," Harry continued, "and I go

back outside, and my horse is returned. A man from the bar says, 'Listen, Kraut. Nobody wants your trouble again. Go on your way.' Then he leans close and asks me, 'But what did you do to the man who took your horse in France?'"

He paused.

"Come on," Nora demanded. "What did you do?"

Harry grinned. "I surrendered."

Chapter Thirty-Eight

At the edge of the river's main thoroughfare, Matthew gazed over the water and the sunlight reflected in its chilly waves. "From reading about the war in the newspapers, I expected the Somme to be red with blood," he said. "It's strange to find it so peaceful, weaving its little canals through your city and knowing you cross it every day like thousands of others, just going about your affairs. In America, that water is a battlefield and little else."

The waves lapped gently against the docks, barely audible above the mechanical din of the boats and trucks.

"Perhaps America doesn't remember what it's like to fight for its land," he continued. "Men like Alain and Guillaume are tin soldiers in a toy box at home. Their homes are threatened. Their families, their flag. I cannot fathom an invasion of America."

Victoria nestled into his arms and ignored Cartwright's wolf-whistle from the dockside. "Being here does shift one's perspective. I am glad you understand why I must stay. You have every reason to argue it is my womanly duty to be at your side in a time of such adjustment."

"I know better than to argue such a thing with you, my love. I will have plenty of help at home. The help you can give belongs here."

"I am glad I came, and glad I am staying."

He patted his left thigh. "And I am glad I came as well. It breaks my heart to leave you, but our marriage is a balm on every wound I acquired here. I have those lovely photos to remind me of my wife, and what pain I still have will fade."

"Shh."

"No one can hear us."

Twenty meters away, the patient transport barge waited for the convalescents to board for the journey upriver to Saint-Valéry on the Atlantic Ocean, and onward to the English Channel and London. Major Cartwright swung along the dock's edge on his crutches, hat perched precariously on the side of his head, leading a chorus of 'God Save the King.'

"God save the field marshal!" Matthew shouted over the singing. "America has no king!"

"What's that, Berger?" Private McKeever called.

Matthew waved. "See? And if they could hear us, none of these fellows would mind. I daresay they'll raise a drink with me when I tell them I was able to successfully—"

"Matthew James Berger, you will not."

"But it's for their morale." He nuzzled against her hair. "Mrs. Berger, indulge a man with a moment of glory before you send him back where the only Mrs. Berger is his weeping mother."

"I love you so much." She allowed herself one sniffle and

sat straighter, then pressed her hands into his. He brought her fingers to his mouth for a kiss.

"You are courting disaster, my dearest," he murmured. "You had better take that ring off when you take these gloves off."

"I needed it today. Where is yours?"

He tapped his chest, making a small clink of the ring against his identification tags. "I'll bake your other ring into a cookie and send it as soon as I can."

"It's probably safe to mail without baking."

"But chocolate is a rare treat here. I'll tell Cooper and Maudie to send you something to share."

"Maudie can't bake. She's liberated."

"Cooper makes incredible chocolate and hazelnut cookies."

Her mouth fell open. "You're joking. Who lets him around an oven?"

"Maudie does, of course." He poked her nose. "If you won't be old-fashioned about what women can do, you can't confine men that way, either. Maudie runs his campaigns and he bakes cookies."

The wind ruffled his hair and Victoria tucked a few strands back under his cap, fighting tears she blamed on the breeze and dry air. The automobile clatter blended with the boats' horns and the lapping waves in pleasant blur as Matthew leaned forward and kissed her.

"Every breath," he whispered, cupping her cheeks in his hands. "That has never changed and never will. I love you so."

"And I love you."

"Harp."

Matthew's hand shot up in an automatic salute and Dr. Bowden swatted it back down. "You need to break that habit, Berger. With me, anyway. Might want to keep it up otherwise until you get home."

"Yes, sir."

"Have you come to see him off, sir, or am I tardy?" Victoria asked. "Frances was going to cover for me this morning."

"So she did. And Carraker covered for me, so I'm sure the place is alive with song." Bowden gave a wry smile and clapped Matthew on the shoulder. "Your wife is in good hands, Berger, and I'll ship her home myself if the situation is dire. Do you have arrangements to get home from London?"

"I haven't heard," Matthew said. "Dr. Swann is tossing me in with the rest and we'll see how long it takes them to notice I'm in a different uniform."

"I'm sure you would rather be at home than in a strange city. I'll write to some people about it and see what we can do."

"Thank you sir. I appreciate that."

"Recent circumstances have certainly eased this part of your recovery," Bowden said, smiling as he inclined his head at Victoria, "and I do not mean to discourage you, but there is a long road ahead as far as returning to a normal life. If you are at all interested, I have some friends working on new prosthetic limbs. They will be looking for men to test them before long. I can put you in touch."

"That's generous of you, sir. Thank you. I'd be thrilled to give it a go."

"Thank you," Victoria echoed.

"That is all I came to say." He rose and jabbed a finger in

Matthew's face. "Don't get up and don't salute." He held out his hand.

Matthew shook it. "If there was ever a reason to feel good about leaving one's wife in a war zone, it's knowing she's in your company, sir."

Bowden nodded. "Harp."

"Yes, sir?"

"One o'clock."

"I'll be there."

He raised his collar against the chilly breeze off the water and disappeared from the dockside.

"Did you expect him to come down here?" Matthew asked.

"Not at all. It was very kind of him."

"Of course. But do you know what he meant about saluting him?"

"Sometimes it annoys him when he's just going about his day or trying to have a regular conversation. Every man in the hospital is supposed to salute him."

"No." Matthew shook his head. "He told me I needed to break the habit with him. When am I ever going to see him again? Does he think we're moving to London?"

"He couldn't possibly. I was very clear about that."

"Isn't it strange to you?"

"It sounds like it's awfully strange to you."

He shivered. "It's a feeling. Not a bad one. There's... something."

A horn sounded from the patient transport barge and the men on the dock proceeded, with the help of orderlies, wheeled chairs, and crutches, to the gangway. Matthew kissed her one more time, a tender touch of the lips, not so weighty that it could feel like a last kiss or the last word on any matter.

"Vi?" he whispered, halfway turned to board.

"Yes?"

"Gold fringe on the entire house. Purple ceilings."

"A blue velvet chaise for my overdue swoons."

He pressed his cheek to hers and whispered. "Come back and stop me. Come home soon."

Chapter Thirty-Nine

Interlude
1918, Amiens, France

Before American troops joined the Allied forces on the Western front, Germany's spring offensive pushed rapidly south through France in March and April 1918. Amiens was subjected to extensive shelling, but many of its significant sites, including the Cathédrale Notre-Dame d'Amiens, sustained minimal damage. Outflanked, the Germans struggled to advance on the ground. They battered Amiens from a distance, stalled at nearby Villers-Bretonneux by the British and Canadian armies who quashed their aim of taking the city.

Wearing a French army coat taken from the supply room and stripped of its insignia, Harry Kurz paced in the courtyard every day, his blue eyes skyward and grim, as the German bombers overhead noted the Red Cross flags and passed them by.

The Battle of Amiens began August 8, 1918, and marked

the first phase of the Allied Forces' Hundred Days Offensive. Shrouded by fog in a surprise morning attack, hundreds of thousands of British, French, and Canadian soldiers caught the German officers at their breakfast. They breached the enemy lines and advanced eleven kilometers on the first day.

A flood of wounded men from both sides of the conflict filled the local hospitals, and No. 43 served as a clearing station for around-the-clock surgeries and evacuating stable patients as soon as possible. At least once a week, Rosemarie delivered letters with photographs of Matthew's progress on a yellow house in Raleigh with gingerbread trim and a gabled roof. Dr. Bowden dismissed Victoria from her shift on one occasion to respond with an urgent telegram.

August 13, 1918
Miss Victoria Harper

To Matthew J. Berger, Esq.

DO NOT BUY THAT WALLPAPER.

After their victory at Amiens, the Allies waged an autumn campaign to liberate parts of northern Europe that had been under German control since 1914. The Armistice was signed on November 11, 1918, ending the fighting on the Western front and effectively bringing an end to the Great War.

November 12, 1918
Matthew J. Berger, Esq.

To Miss Victoria Harper c/o Col. Malcolm Bowden

WEAR YOUR RING. SEE IF FIRED.

After the Armistice, the Red Cross launched a months-long effort to help thousands of sick and injured soldiers prepare for safe transport before closing their hospitals. Giles Wentworth arrived in Amiens by ambulance after being shot twice in the groin under mysterious circumstances three days after the ceasefire. Suspicious of the nature of the injury, Dickie Lampett kindly dropped the disgraced surgeon off at Red Cross Hospital No. 7 instead of with his former colleagues at No. 43.

November 15, 1918
Mrs. Matthew J. Berger

To Matthew J. Berger, Esq.

ALAS NOT FIRED. NURSE P KNEW.

Epilogue

July 1919, North Carolina

Matthew stood at the edge of the new gravel driveway that connected the old carriage house with the beach house looming over them, freckled with fresh cedar shingles among weathered gray ones. He poked the crushed stone with his left foot—the latest copper-aluminum alloy, a test piece from a manufacturer in Scotland—and smiled a little as he shifted his weight.

"That'll do," he said to the late afternoon clouds, then cast his eyes down to the sandy expanse between the house and the ocean.

"Are you ready?" Victoria asked, balancing two hatboxes and a valise as she came to his side of the car.

"This is as fine as any sidewalk," he said, tapping the gravel. "Give me those. You shouldn't be lifting anything."

She clutched the hatboxes tighter. "You made me promise

I wouldn't treat you like you were helpless. You're supposed to do the same."

"My darling, I shouldn't have to explain to you that growing a child and missing a limb are very different physical limitations." He sighed. "Perhaps it is true. Women do lose their smarts when they marry."

"Your wit is priceless. Take these, if you're fine and steady." She shoved the hatboxes into his hands and nudged the valise into his grip. "I'll carry the trunk."

"Victoria!"

"I'll send one of your brothers to get everything." She placed the boxes on the car's long hood and stepped into her husband's embrace. "Everyone is anxious to spoil us a bit, and I propose we let them."

He nuzzled his cheek against hers and kissed her tenderly. "Do I not spoil you enough, Mrs. Berger? A cook to tend to our meals when you are in the clinic late? A housekeeper to keep all the gold fringe sparkling?"

Victoria took his elbow. "I am spoiled rotten by the most perfect of husbands who knows exactly how to spoil me."

He steadied himself on the gravel and found his stride as they walked toward the house. The limp and drag in his step might never leave him, but the improvement over his first false limb of wood and steel shocked him every time he put the new one on. A gift from one of Dr. Bowden's many friends, the prosthesis was a skeletal, almost mechanical-looking thing, and came with a large journal of questions and charts for Matthew to log his experiences wearing it for various activities, lengths of time, and on different surfaces.

He had tested gravel and was used to it. His first steps on sand, he saved for Victoria.

She was still in Amiens in the summer of 1918, and although he went to the shore with his family in July as usual, he gallantly refused every offer of help to walk from the steps to the ocean. He read on the porch swing and wrote endless letters and waved to his nieces and nephews picnicking on the beach, but he waited.

When Victoria arrived home in February 1919, they announced their year-old marriage and sent Maudie into a swoon, Cooper into a blustery storm of "I knew it!" and Matthew's mother into a delighted tizzy. Ruby Harper, holding her youngest daughter close, said she had her suspicions as soon as she saw how happy Matthew looked on returning home.

"Are you ready?" Victoria asked him at the base of the stairs. She nodded once to the house and once toward the ocean. "We could do it now, before anyone knows we've arrived."

Wordless, he passed his hand over her stomach.

"The baby is the size of a bean, and I am plenty strong enough to help you if you wobble," she said, pulling his hand away. "And if it gets to be too much, I'll just let you fall. It's only sand."

The salt air was tangier and the late afternoon sky a more vibrant blue with Victoria at his side, and the waves that eavesdropped on their first kiss greeted them again with a white-capped reach toward where they stood at the end of the drive by the porch steps. High tide would bring it within thirty yards of the house, but even at a distance, it beckoned him.

He kissed her and took a step off the gravel without thinking, unwisely leading with his left foot. He grasped for Victoria's arm when his knee buckled and he fell sideways, and she pushed him off just in time to avoid tumbling over on top of him.

"It's only sand," he said, after spitting out a mouthful.

She crouched next to him and took his hands. "And I'm so glad I was here for it."

Steady practice over the course of a week emboldened Matthew's steps. He filled the research journal with copious notes on the use of the device on wet sand, dry sand, even knee-deep in the ocean with the water rushing in and pulling back. His brother William supported him on one side for that test and Cooper Truxton, freshly arrived from Washington, D.C. with his wife and children, held onto the other.

"I cannot believe a Berger is as good with secrets as you have turned out to be," Cooper said as Matthew leaned on his arm. "I had my suspicions about your marriage, of course—"

William snorted. "You pompous ass. If you had suggested they were already married, it's only because there are only so many ways to string together the words that fall out of your endlessly yammering mouth."

"What I was trying to to say," Cooper said, rolling his eyes, "is that Maudie would have been knitting up a storm if you had told us you were expecting, and she's furious you didn't tell her before we arrived."

"Perhaps if you two hadn't moved hundreds of miles away, you would have known sooner," Matthew said, casting a glance over his shoulder at Victoria and Maudie on the porch.

"We have work to do in Washington," Cooper huffed. "I'm raising hell for veterans' benefits, and you're welcome."

"Well, you're still not the last to know about the baby. Vi hasn't told anyone abroad yet, either. I imagine I'll have to cover my ears with all the squealing that will greet us at every stop."

"When do you sail?"

"Early August, and do not lecture either of us on the timing." Matthew lowered his voice. "She'll be in the most capable hands in the world if she has even the slightest pain. Her mother and aunt will travel with us and do their own visiting. We'll see Vi's nursing friends and Dr. Bowden in London and pass a week or two in France with Ingrid and their *Maman*. Harry, too, if he's still around. He's been dawdling."

William narrowed his eyes. "Why do you continue to correspond with that Hun?"

"Harry's an all right fellow," Matthew said. "Call him what you will, I think his loyalties are clear. I send him magazines now and again since he likes cowboy stories. He's a funny sort." He wriggled his toes in the water and smiled. "On that note, would you like to hear a joke?"

"I could have been knitting for ages if you'd told me," Maudie groaned as she flopped onto the wicker chaise, its floral cushions stiff with salt and age. "You have no idea how long it takes to make a proper layette, but I've gotten quite good. I should have it done by the time your baby is about three years old and will have no use for it."

"By then I might have another one," Victoria said from the porch swing. "I wonder if I will ever shed this feeling of needing to make up for lost time with Matthew. I wanted two different lives for years, and now I want everything at once. Perhaps I could have twins or triplets and speed things along a bit."

"How will this all work with even one baby? There are only so many hours in the day, darling. If you are going to keep the clinic—"

"I am absolutely keeping it. I've only just begun." She pushed off the wall to set the swing moving, creaking every time it swayed. "People seem to think a man can just buckle into a new leg and be off for a walk. I had a patient come in with a stump so painful and deformed from a field amputation he cannot wear the false limb the army gave him. There are hundreds like him stuck between doctors who think their work is done and families who don't know how to help."

"Those poor men," Maudie said. "I go through a stack of pennies every time I go for a walk and hand them to the veterans begging in sight of the Capitol. I think there are more every day. How fortunate that Matthew had you and your friends to fix him up with their studies and new techniques."

"We had time the field hospitals did not have," Victoria said. "But revision surgeries could help any man, even years later. I've offered my expertise to one of the physicians who takes my referrals."

"You're joking." Maudie sat up. "You must be joking. I thought you only did rehabilitation. This doctor would let you in the operating room?"

"We shall see in good time," Victoria said, smiling as she

rested her hand on her stomach. "I am most satisfied with my work when I make a real difference, and a baby or two or ten might re-route my course a little, but I can still use my experience to help these men. A letter of introduction from one of the world's foremost experts in orthopedics doesn't hurt my cause."

"Your dear Dr. Bowden is still looking after you," Maudie said. "How I wish I could join you this summer and meet him. But with the suffrage amendment passed, we must do all the ratification rallies. We're taking Emmeline and Calvin along so I'll have to keep them up on their schoolwork, and—yes, the clinic." She pointed at her. "Do not think you have distracted me."

"I will work as long as I feel healthy," Victoria said, brushing her fingers over her stomach. "My second-in-command is a Red Cross nurse, too, and our trusty manual says a Red Cross nurse is diligent and clever." She watched her husband laughing, nearly knee-deep in the surf, his black hair a tousled mop in the wind. "Matthew and our family will come first, but I don't think they will ever be my only loves."

"I know you won't like to be idle during your recovery from the baby," Maudie said, brightening. "You must join our letter-writing campaign. I am infuriated at everyone on Capitol Hill for refusing to release promised money for our veterans, and I need angry letters. You should set all your patients writing to their congressmen immediately, and you can write a million letters even with a new baby at home."

"My daughter is the last person I expect to see idle in any state," Ruby Harper said as she walked up the porch steps with a suitcase and a birdcage draped in a large, raw edged scrap of seersucker.

"Mother!" Victoria jumped up and wrapped her in a quick hug. "We didn't expect you until tomorrow."

Her graying blonde hair brushed Victoria's cheeks as she kissed them. "Young Anthony told me he was driving up today and gallantly offered me a ride. I couldn't wait to see my baby and her baby any longer."

"Oh, I see you did tell someone early," Maudie said, feigning a pout. "Does that wretched bird already know as well?"

"Victoria," Edgar squawked from the covered cage. "Hello, Victoria."

Ruby set down her suitcase and blew Maudie a kiss. "Dear girl. I knew before Matthew did. Mothers can always tell. Edith is expecting again, but she doesn't know it yet."

"You are impossible, Mother." Victoria rose. "And yet I don't doubt you for a moment. I'll go see that your room is made up so you can settle in. That long drive is so tiring."

Ruby waved her away. "Nonsense. I know how to make a bed. Call your dear husband up here, though. I stopped by your house to bring your mail, and I see I must feast on humble pie. That plum-colored ceiling he had painted in your sitting room looks quite nice with the woodwork after all."

"Victoria," Edgar agreed.

They shuffled through their accumulated mail on the red couch in the living room and sorted it into piles. Matthew stacked the latest *Saturday Evening Post*, *Life,* and a pulp fiction quarterly together and pushed them aside. "I'll send those on to Harry via Ingrid, I suppose. If he's already left France, perhaps she and *Maman* will enjoy them."

"I wonder why he's lingering," Victoria said as he handed her a letter from Dr. Bowden. "He was in such a hurry to travel here."

"The place might have grown on him." He snuggled her close. "Some loves you simply cannot shake."

"Or he found himself another crush to moon after. Heaven help us if that is the case."

"Then I shall write to him with all my good advice." Matthew kissed her cheek. "I have expertise in the art of waiting on a woman. Now, what does the good doctor have to say?"

> My dear Harp,
>
> I write today to complain of Nurse Scott's behavior once more.

Victoria giggled. "Ah, this will be about her acceptance to the women's medical college. I knew this would happen. That is what happens when you lift people up. They may lift themselves onward without you."

> I am thoroughly irritated to be losing my best assistant not only in the operating theatre but also in the classroom. Please write to her immediately and convey my displeasure, for thus far all I have managed to say aloud is the inconvenient truth about how proud I am and so on and so forth. *Nous aimons apprendre* is ever our battle cry.
>
> I hope the new prosthesis is serving Matthew well. The Scots have given it to two dozen men with similar circum-

> stances and eagerly await his assessment. It has the potential to ease the difficulties your many patients with the guillotine amputations now face. I would say God damn the Germans, but I had a letter from Harry the other day and so I am feeling rather neutral once more. I will not give away the punchline of his latest stupid joke in case he sends it to you, but at least it's a good one.
>
> After all these years, it should not surprise you to hear that I often found myself in your late father's place when I did not intend to be. Perhaps some of that was our luck, landing where we did in the same place at the same time—such a difficult time for you to be away from home. Perhaps some of it is an old man seeing a woman young enough to be the daughter he never had, looking for someone to believe in her like her father did.

Victoria pressed her hand to her mouth as she kept reading Dr. Bowden's precise, tight script.

> And so, since I had the honor of walking you down the proverbial aisle to your husband, I think it only fitting that I claim some manner of grandparenting with this child of yours.

"What?" She jumped from the couch and nearly lost her footing. "How does he know about the baby? I didn't tell him. I haven't told a soul over there. Did you?"

Matthew held up his hands. "Not a word. What did he say?"

She showed him the letter and his mouth fell open.

"How does who know what, dearest?" Ruby asked,

looking up from situating Edgar by the window in the adjacent dining room. She walked toward them and squinted at the letter in Victoria's hand. "Oh, is that the one from Malcolm?"

She turned slowly. "Malcolm?"

"Well, that's his name." Ruby took the vacated seat on the couch. "What does he know that he shouldn't?"

"I never told him I was expecting, and he's talking about acting as a grandparent."

Ruby covered her mouth with her hands. "Oh, dear. I thought you told him. Really, I did. I mentioned it in my last letter, and I—oh, darling. I'm sorry to spoil the surprise."

Victoria's breath hitched. "Leave the surprise aside a moment. What do you mean, your last letter? You have written to Dr. Bowden regularly?"

"Of course."

"Of course? Since when?"

"He wrote me the kindest letter after your father passed away, sweetheart." Ruby's smile softened. "He offered his condolences, of course, and apologized that you couldn't be with me. But he wrote at length about you and how you passed your days, and I think he knew how much it would mean to me to hear that you were well and had someone looking after you so far away."

Victoria stared at her mother, dumbfounded. "I had no idea he wrote to you even once."

"I had to write back, of course, and thank him. And he wrote again as well, naturally, to tell me no thanks were necessary, and since then we just... wrote."

"For almost four years now?"

Ruby shrugged and pointed at the birdcage as Edgar

hopped onto a wooden swing. "He does tell such interesting stories, and Edgar only knows eleven words."

"Interesting stories?" Victoria dropped the last pages of her letter and sank into the chair at Matthew's side. She gripped his hand until her knuckles went white and he had to pry her fingers loose. "Mother. He talks about cartilage degradation and fecal-borne diseases."

"Indeed. Did you know you can put color on bacteria under a microscope to know how to treat them?"

"Yes. I knew that ten years ago."

"And he told me all about the kind of procedure Matthew had and how you learned to use a needle driver."

Victoria rubbed her eyes. "I'm sorry, but this does not make sense to me yet. Why didn't either of you tell me?"

"Grown-ups' business, dearest," Ruby said. "Perhaps a tiny sense you might feel unnerved by it while you worked with him. He is a splendid correspondent, and I always felt that in some way your father blessed that adventure of yours by leaving you in good hands."

"He left me in the best hands, Mother. Yours."

"Yes, but I was here and you were there. It eased my heart to know that if my daughter must be in a war zone, she's under the watchful eye of a good-looking man who can order people to shoot things."

"Medical officers cannot order—he's a what?"

"A good man who can—"

"You just called Dr. Bowden a good-looking man." Victoria crossed her arms. "Mother. The only way this bewilders me further is if you confess to writing *love* letters to him."

Matthew nearly choked on a laugh.

"Well, it's not as though we were swapping pictures for lockets," Ruby huffed. "But he was in several of those photographs you sent of your friends and coworkers every Christmas. I may have sent him a photograph of you and Edith and I once, but only because he always enjoyed stories about you and Edie when you were young. And you must admit, he was very well turned-out for your wedding pictures."

Victoria's brows shot up. "Did he tell you when we married?"

"No. He kept your secret, darling. He cabled me the day Matthew arrived to see whether he should encourage your friendship or keep you busy elsewhere. Naturally, I suggested he let you choose your course." Ruby laughed. "And then I thought of a hundred other things to tell him about the two of you. I think I sent four telegrams in one day because it all seemed so very urgent. You'll understand when it's your own child, darling. Malcolm was most amused."

"Malcolm." Victoria sighed. "I cannot even think of him with a first name. It's disrespectful. He's a brigadier now, you know. Oh."

"Yes, dear, I know."

"Well, I think it's a fine development." Matthew winked at his mother-in-law before pulling his wife into his lap. "If you recall, my love, he had an inkling a year and a half ago that I might one day need to break the habit of saluting him. I wonder what was on his mind."

Victoria buried her face in his neck. "This is entirely too strange," she mumbled. "What next? Grandparenting, really? Grandfather Malcolm? I ought to lie down."

"You kept your marriage quiet, and that was a far greater

secret. This is only a correspondence," Ruby said. "And I am far too young to wrap myself in widows' weeds and stay home the rest of my life."

"Malcolm," Edgar squawked.

Victoria stared at the bird. "Only a correspondence." She stretched across the couch and poked her mother's shoulder. "Were you planning this all along when you asked to join us for the London leg of our trip? Since you wished to 'visit with friends,' as you put it?"

"Well, Malcolm tried to talk you into going to London once before," Ruby said.

"Yes, but that was for work."

"You said you'd come home to me after the war, and what did he tell you then?"

"He told me to bring you along," Victoria said, her words muffled as she pressed her face against her husband's neck again, breathing in the salt mist that had settled on his skin. "You two are as sneaky as any spies, aren't you?"

"Let them have their little victory, darling." Matthew cupped her cheek in his hand and pulled her up to face him. "Only good can come of this. We ought to be delighted."

His mischievous smile calmed her and she pressed her lips to his. "I suppose you're right," she said. "After all, the last time two separate parts of my world collided, what seemed at first like a catastrophe was really a second chance at something very important."

"A second chance?" Matthew stifled a laugh.

"Very well." Victoria kissed him again. "A fourth chance."

Next in the Series

Dance Around the Rules

Frances Kendall has always had a close friendship with Dr. Nick Carraker, but her post-war plans don't include following an army surgeon around the British Empire—as if Dr. Bowden's rules against the romance weren't enough to dissuade her. By summer 1918, Amiens is under attack and Nick's qualms about pursuing his long-buried desires are fading fast, but the work of wooing Frances proves to be a delicate operation.

The Series

The Truxtons

How to Measure a Man

A Race With a Rogue

La Croix-Rouge

Don't Ask Me Again

Dance Around the Rules

Reader reviews help authors gain exposure in search rankings in a saturated market. Your reviews on Amazon, Kobo, Goodreads, and any platform of your choice are always appreciated.

Afterword

Confessions of Artistic License

Few American troops were in Europe in fall 1917, but since I wanted Matthew and Victoria to have a semi-lengthy separation before she came home, I needed him there before the big deployment in spring 1918. Some National Guard and reservists did go over in 1917, so Matthew went, too.

Matthew's recovery is somewhat accelerated, but not impossible if he had a best-case scenario with no infection or retraction—so let's say he didn't.

The Red Cross and the British army maintained more than one hundred hospitals during the Great War, but didn't use the number 43. Base hospitals moved in and out of Amiens during the war; I elected to create No. 43 and make it stay there for simplicity's sake. The hospital's hierarchy and roles are an amalgam of arrangements between the army and the Red Cross.

There probably weren't any trenches or tunnels close enough to Amiens for Dickie to have heard any explosion from the cathedral, but I needed a good, dramatic mess. The explosive-laden battlefields near the Somme were close-ish.

I have no idea whether Harry's situation as a patient-prisoner-turncoat lodged at the hospital is remotely plausible, but he is a treasure and will be back in the next book.

Actually True (Nous Aimes Apprendre)

Clostridium pathogens, the evacuation chain, requisitioned schoolhouses, French army mutinies, shell shock, Edith Cavell, the sandbagging of the Amiens Cathedral, "shot off" and "crush" as period-appropriate slang—all true.

Descriptions of below-the-knee amputation revision and recovery are based on documentation from the American Expeditionary Forces in WWI, via the U.S. Army Medical Department's Center for History and Heritage. Surgical instrumentation and equipment are referenced from the 1917 Haslam catalog and the Wood Library Museum of Anesthesiology.

Acknowledgments

To my colleagues from the hospital a lifetime ago: the incredible nurses including (but not limited to) Colleen Becker, Jim Thomas, and Beth Govero, and Dr. David Jaques, who once compared our post-operative infection rates with his in field hospitals—my years with you are all over this book, and I am forever grateful.

Danielle and Jess and all the early readers, thank you for tolerating my drafts and challenging me to make this the story it deserves to be.

Brent, your diligent hen-pecking at history and the resulting grumpy *poilus* (and proper ordnance) are an absolute gift. Mac, thanks for helping me rename pretty much everyone (and "Wrong army, but..."). Jesse, thanks for sharing the journey and listening to the highs and lows.

To the ladies of the Brunch Club, thanks for keeping my spirits high and my feet on the ground.

www.ingramcontent.com/pod-product-compliance
Lightning Source LLC
LaVergne TN
LVHW041309150826
845673LV00008B/2813
* 9 7 9 8 9 8 8 0 9 4 1 6 6 *